M000034646

One of the more suspenseful and fully engrossing books I've read in a long time, DEADLY FOCUS grabs you in the first chapter and never lets go...

—Sonja Massie (G. A. McKevett)

A "Thinking Person's" Mystery/Thriller

This well-crafted, deeply absorbing mystery/suspense/thriller takes the reader from the tight camaraderie of an LA television news room staff to the terrifying violence-controlled drug cartel kingdoms of the Mexican jungle.

—Carolyn Olson Adams, Amazon Reviewer

Mystery readers will fall in love with Lucy Vega in this debut novel and devour this edge of your chair mystery. The pacing is breathless, but don't turn the pages too fast, so you can enjoy all aspects of this well-built mystery. Sue Hinkin has found her purpose in this well written, engaging and clever novel. Already looking forward to the next one!

—Susan Myhre Hayes

Lucy and her wild, page-turning exploits in a remote Mexican jungle will definitely satisfy those looking for a story chock-full of adventure and chicanery with a tough, tenacious, and tender heroine at its heart.

—Colorado Book Review

# Praise for *Low Country Blood*

Hinkin, a former TV news photographer, skillfully portrays irredeemable characters as well as likable but flawed ones in this first installment of the Vega and Middleton Mystery series... an exciting opener that delivers murder, drugs, and romance.

—Kirkus Review

This story is a thrilling adventure from the first page to the last. The reader is engaged in a fast-paced, scary plot. Yet, the author has skillfully developed the story line, providing balance throughout the book.

— Deborah Lloyd for Readers' Favorite

Author Sue Hinkin hits the ground running in her second novel, Low Country Blood. From the initial murder, to an Afghani heroin cartel, to a kidnapping by one of the cartel henchmen who turns out to be a sadistic killer with history in Savannah, Hinkin keeps the story moving with intense action and gripping plot twists.

—Colorado Book Review

# The Burn Patient

A Vega & Middleton Novel

Sue Hinkin

Literary Wanderlust | Denver, Colorado

*The Burn Patient* is a work of fiction. Names, characters, places and incidents are either the product of the author's imagination or are used fictitiously, and any resemblance to actual persons, living or dead, business establishments, events or locales is entirely coincidental.

Copyright 2020 by Sue Hinkin

Published in the United States by Literary Wanderlust LLC, Denver, Colorado. www.LiteraryWanderlust.com

ISBN print: 978-1-942856-45-0
ISBN digital: 978-1-942856-52-8

Cover design: Ruth M'Gonigle

Printed in the United States of America

# 1

Sister Catherine Lucia Ruiz was a healer. As the only *curandera* in a remote corner of the central Mexican highlands of Guerrero, it was a challenging place for a woman of integrity and faith to ply her trade. She chose not to question but to trust in Him. All were God's children and deserving of compassion. And every day there was an opportunity to bring a sinner back to the Father. She trusted that the Lord had placed her in the center of the world's black tar heroin production region for this reason.

Tall and slim, she was strong and sinewy with thick silver hair woven into a braid that hung down her back. Sister's hands were as elegant as a ballerina's despite being well used, and her face held a mature beauty that had only been enhanced by age and experience. Such finely chiseled features and intelligent brown eyes would turn heads even now as she closed in on eighty.

She stirred a fragrant eucalyptus-tinged brew on her wood stove, then removed the pot from the fire and placed it next to her pump sink to cool. As she did often, Catherine Lucia leaned back against the counter and smiled. She never tired of admiring her home and medical clinic. Indeed, it was a dream come true. In exchange for her services, men from the village and surrounding area had helped her build this *clínica* many years ago. The thick, white-washed stucco walls kept her cool in the summer and warm in the winter. Floor-to-ceiling built-in shelving overflowed with periodicals and books on science, medicine, herbology, religion, and fiction. A much-read Dorothy Sayers novel lay open on the kitchen table next to an empty coffee mug.

Sister Catherine Lucia also had a small outbuilding where she boarded her horse and kept goats and chickens. Completely self-sufficient, she had a well for water, a forest of wood for her stove, and a propane generator fueling the small refrigerator that preserved her medicinal preparations. She spent much of her time on the big porch that overlooked her garden. In the rafters above hung drying flowers and herbs that were the source of many remedies. Big clay pots of aloe vera sat on either side of the steps. A privy was hidden behind century plants that sprouted ten-foot-tall stalks blazing like pale yellow torches in the January sun. The chickens liked to roost beneath the plant's spiny fronds, safe from predators.

Tired from overseeing three challenging childbirths in less than a week, she pushed strands of lanky hair from her face. And then there was the chance discovery that Lucy Vega, a newswoman from Los Angeles working on a documentary team in a nearby village, was likely her niece. Sister's heart reached out to Lucy, but she'd made a decision many decades ago to be a ghost. She'd carved out a life that was peaceful at times, frenetic at others, but always rewarding. Catherine Lucia couldn't deny she was shaken by the appearance of Lucy. Or was the Lord opening a door on another path?

Her head began to ache. She must get back to work. There,

she was confident and at peace.

Sister was grinding dried herbs with a mortar and pestle when she heard approaching footsteps crunch through the leaves and gravel on the path to her house. The hens clucked and the horse nickered at the sound. Two gray tabby cats, curled on the rug near her feet, raised their heads and swiveled their ears like tiny satellite dishes.

She stepped down from the porch and wiped her hands with a linen towel as four officers from the *Policía de Agricultura de Guerrera Alta*, known as PAGA, carried a man on a canvas stretcher up the steep trail. Her home-clinic was over two miles from anything that could be called a road.

Now it appeared that Luis Alvarez and his drug cartel had another disaster for her to heal. Why couldn't they transport their casualties to the hospital in Tingo Tia? She would refuse no one, but these men were clearly not doing God's work. She would always, however, try to bring them to the Lord while they were in her purview. Crossing herself, Sister Catherine Lucia closed her eyes for a moment and prayed for God's support and blessing upon her efforts.

"*Buenos días*, Captain Alonzo. What challenge do you bring me today?" Sister stuffed the cloth she was holding into one of the big pockets in her apron. The men hauled the stretcher up the steps.

"Good day to you, Sister," Alonzo said, panting. He was in his mid-twenties and serious-looking, with a wispy goatee. "We have a burn victim. Male, mid-thirties, healthy, until this happened." The men bent down like pallbearers and placed the stretcher on the porch.

One of Alonzo's team pulled out a cigarette. Sister shot him an intimidating look of disapproval. She would not have nicotine smoke contaminating her herbs. He returned it to his pocket and mumbled an apology.

Alonzo glared at the soldier then turned his attention back to the nun. "I thought you should also be aware, Sister, that General Luis Alvarez is dead — happened yesterday. I understand you've known him for many years."

She felt her tired eyes widen. "What happened?"

"He was shot by an escaping prisoner. A woman."

Catherine Lucia feigned dismay but felt a flush of gratitude as Alonzo filled her in on the shocking, but welcome news. Could one of his drug-addicted child brides have wielded the weapon of his destruction? The big, brash bully of a man had been so drunk with power he'd refused to believe in his own mortality. Always a monster, as a child he'd pulled the wings off butterflies and set dogs on fire. He had created Dante's vision of Hell here in the Sierra Madre del Sur.

Catherine Lucia crossed herself then approached the patient. She lifted the blanket that covered his body and gasped.

"A car explosion," Alonzo said.

The man was literally melted from the waist up with third-degree burns, maybe even fourth on his shoulder. The skin and musculature there appeared to have been eaten through to the bone. At least he was unconscious. Small mercies.

"Mother of God," Sister said. "I don't have the facilities or expertise to treat this kind of injury. Transport him to one of the regional medical centers. His chances at survival with my meager resources here are slim."

"He won't survive a trip to Guadalajara or Mexico City," Alonzo said. "See what you can do. Try to stabilize him. We'll return at the end of the week. If he makes it that long, the plane will be back and we'll fly him out of here. Otherwise, we'll bury him. *Por favor*, do whatever you can, Sister."

The *curandera* nodded. "All right, bring him inside. Put him on the bed closest to the window where the light is good. But first, let me get one of my burn sheets for the mattress. I soak them in pure aloe vera and then treat them with a waxy substance that won't easily stick to the wounds."

The men picked up the stretcher and maneuvered it inside.

Sister went to the sink, vigorously scrubbed her hands, and then dried them with a fresh towel. Hurriedly, she prepped the bed, then helped the men move the patient onto the thin mattress.

Their duties complete, the men filed out of the clinic — all except Alonzo. He remained to assist and followed Sister's directions.

Catherine Lucia inspected the injuries and then covered the burn victim with one of her special sheets. She glanced out the window and saw the men gathered for a smoke at the top of the path, far from her porch. Sister shook her head. At least her rules were respected. Local lore had it that God was definitely on her side.

"First of all, we must keep him hydrated. I have bags of saline over in that cabinet. Captain Alonzo, please bring one over and hang it on that wall peg for me."

Alonzo hung the saline bag on the peg. Sister inserted a needle into the patient's scalded, densely tattooed arm. As usual, she hit the vein on her first try. Alonzo smiled and gave her a nod.

Sister smiled back. "*Señor* Alonzo, you are a bright man. It is not too late for you to leave this village and study science at the university. You're young; you don't have to live like this. You could be a fine healer." She glanced up at him.

"Thank you, Sister, but it's too late for me." The man's

affect turned flat and disinterested.

She gave him a hard stare. He looked away.

"I have made too many bad decisions. I am in it to the end —I'll probably be on the next stretcher."

"What a waste." Sister shrugged her shoulders. They'd had this conversation many times before. "All right, Alonzo, I doubt if he'll last the night but I'll see what God, and I as His instrument, can do. What is the man's name?"

"We call him the Snake." He glanced down at the serpent image on the man's skin. As it crawled closer to his shoulder and neck, the tattoo melted into a formless, purple stain.

"You don't know his Christian name? I won't call anyone 'Snake.'"

"His name is Mercer, Sister. He's an American."

"I see." A sense of foreboding thrummed somewhere deep in her brain.

"We must leave now." Alonzo glanced at his wristwatch and turned away. "*Adios. Gracias.*" The screen door banged shut behind him.

"God bless you, Alonzo," Sister called after him.

As the PAGA group retreated down the hillside, Sister Catherine Lucia worked on the dying man. She thoroughly cleaned his wounds and then sprayed his burns with a mixture of water, aloe, zinc salts, and tea tree oil, which had both antiseptic and anti-fungal properties. His eyes focused with a glassy, tortured stare as she covered him again with one of her infused burn sheets. The gash that used to be his mouth attempted to form words, but nothing came out. His body spasmed in a weak seizure.

Sister Catherine Lucia pressed her palm against her aching forehead, deeply saddened as she looked at the ruined, fevered man. She began mixing an elixir for pain control that would keep him in a state of semi-awareness. There was a legitimate medical use for opioids, and this was it. She prayed it would give him some relief from his agony.

Next, a poultice to ease the swelling would be applied. The ensuing hours would be critical, but regardless of her best efforts, she figured his chances were next to nothing. Sister made the sign of the cross over his forehead.

# 2

Lucy Ruiz, in her mid-thirties with dark wavy hair and brilliant blue eyes, entered the glass high-rise housing the CNN West Coast Bureau on Sunset Boulevard. She'd been a TV news photographer with KLAK-TV down the street for a number of years, but this was her first visit to the CNN offices. Security was ultra-strict. A bald, bull-necked official was such a stickler he even commandeered the miniature orange tree she'd brought to celebrate her friend Beatrice Middleton's new job. Bull-neck actually sent it through the x-ray machine.

"Really?" Lucy frowned. "Take it easy with the plant. I spent fifty bucks on that thing. It's not a two-dollar cactus from Safeway."

The guard handed the orange tree back to Lucy as if it was a puppy that had peed on him. He then directed her to a reception desk across the marble-floored lobby.

A spaghetti-thin woman wearing a snug white blouse tucked into a short, black pencil skirt presented Lucy a form to fill out for a visitor's pass. Eventually, the paperwork was greenlit and Lucy was handed a lanyard with a laminated guest card dangling from it. Okay, so I'm a mere peon visitor.

Lucy slipped it over her head.

"Ms. Middleton's office is on the tenth floor," pencil skirt said. "Take the elevators to the left." There was a quick flash of blindingly white teeth and then she was on to the next guest.

Lucy rode up in a car packed with grungy photographers and several gel-coiffed men in hip, pricey suits so body-hugging they could barely bend their arms. Three women who could be identical triplets despite different ethnicities were poured into tight sheath dresses — one green, one red, and a blue. The photogs and the gel-headed men all appreciatively watched the women step out of the elevator at the floor labeled Local News.

Their little flirtation, contrasted with the rawness of Lucy's recent assignment in central Mexico, made being back in Los Angeles almost surreal. People dead, colleagues shot, including Bea, her closest friend. A vivid reel of graphic images ripped through her brain. She gasped, and with difficulty, repressed the visions. A pang of claustrophobia seized her as the elevator stopped again and additional passengers pressed in.

She was here to celebrate her friend's new job, a new start, a new and happy chapter. Let it go, let the bad stuff go. Lucy took a deep breath and mentally limped back into the present.

The tenth floor bustled with activity. Big-screen newsfeeds were mounted on every available wall making the newsroom feel like a sports bar on an NFL Sunday. A bullpen of noisy cubicles was surrounded by small offices. Lucy immediately caught sight of Bea standing in a doorway with her arms around her daughter, Alyssa. Almost thirteen years old with a face that even the most jaded casting director would find stunning, she wore skinny jeans, a bright yellow sweater, and a purple backpack as big as she was.

"Aly." Lucy fought her way through the crowded cube-town toward her peeps, while protecting the orange tree. "Bea."

Bea welcomed Lucy and the tree into a group hug.

"I wasn't expecting you. What a nice surprise." Bea said, smiling happily.

"I'm on my way to see the lawyer in a few minutes about my uncle's estate," Lucy said. "Hardly a half-mile from here. I couldn't wait to see your new digs."

"May I assume this is for me?" Bea pulled the tree from Lucy's grip. "Oranges, how sweet. All I need is vodka."

"Mom!" Alyssa rolled her eyes.

"Please step into my office." Bea gestured broadly like a game show host about to offer a contestant a new car. "Not the corner overlooking the Pacific I had at KLAK for all of two weeks, but I can see the Hollywood sign, on a good day."

"Very nice — at least it's not a cube." Lucy admired the view as Bea plunked the miniature orange tree onto the black Formica of her desk.

Lucy ran her fingers over a slightly bent leaf. "They actually forced this guy through the x-ray machine on the conveyor."

"Poor little planty." Alyssa giggled. "I hope you know leaving it with my mom is more dangerous than any conveyor belt."

"You're probably right, Aly-kins. What do you think of your momma's new job?"

Alyssa looked at her mom and nodded her head. "It's cool. I'm proud of her."

Bea's eyes moistened. She glanced out toward the iconic hills, nicotine brown in the afternoon smog.

"How are things going?" Lucy asked Aly. The girl had recently moved in with her father, his new wife, and their baby girl. Bea's second ex-husband, Eli Strauss was a TV news producer and a conservative Jew. As it turns out, way too conservative for African-American Baptist-raised Bea. "Now that you're living with your pops, I'm totally out of the loop."

Alyssa stood up straighter and adjusted her backpack. "Well, I love having a baby sister. She's the cutest and everybody adores her. I miss my big bro a teeny tiny bit." She looked wistfully at Bea, and then shut it down. Her face transformed from sad to resigned. "My stepmom, Deborah, insists that I call her 'mother.' Seems really random but Dad thinks it's a big deal so I'm going along with it. I call her Deborah to my friends, but I have only one mother, and it's my mom."

She blew a kiss to Bea. Bea pretended to catch it. Lucy could feel it ripping out her heart.

"And the new school's okay?" Lucy hoped this would be a more neutral subject. She should have known that everything was a minefield. "Westwood Jewish Day School, right?"

"Uh-huh. It's good. I already knew some of the kids from sports and dance classes. I'm gonna have a *bat mitzvah* in June, so I'm learning a lot of Hebrew and stuff. Dad's really happy about that. Deborah wants me to drop dance team so I can study more."

"She wants you to stop dance? You didn't tell me that." Bea was incredulous. "You love dance, and you're so talented."

Alyssa shrugged. "I'm going to start volunteering at Cedars-Sinai Burn Center where she's on staff, starting next week. It'll look good on my college applications. Deborah keeps reminding me that I can't do it all. She says, and I quote, 'Studying Torah and helping the sick is better than leaping around on a dance floor.'"

"College applications? You're years from that." Bea's dark

brown eyes sparkled with anger. "Doesn't that woman believe in childhood? Or the arts?" she huffed. "I'm going to have to talk with her, again." Bea looked ready to explode. Lucy noted that she'd straightened out about a half-dozen paperclips as they spoke, fashioning them into little weapons.

Alyssa's cell phone chimed. She took a quick glance at the text message. "Whoops. Deborah's down in the car waiting for me. Off to my Burn Center Junior Volunteer orientation." She hugged both women tightly. "Love you guys."

"Love you more," Bea called after her daughter. Then she shut the door, broke down and cried.

# 3

Life can change on a dime. And when death spins the coin, there is often no heads or tails, only the final drop into some dark, irretrievable crevasse. No one was more aware of this uneasy truth than Lucy Vega.

Mere months ago, she'd get up most mornings and head out to her job as a TV news photographer in LA, enjoy her friends, hit the beach for a run with the dog, and teach an after-school TV production class at Santa Monica High School. Weekends were often spent at her uncle's ranch in the hills above Malibu.

But Henry Vega, more a father than an uncle, had raised her from early childhood when her own parents and little brother had been killed in a car accident. Now, Henry was dead, too. Murdered. Everything turned on that fact. Sadness came in great waves in these days after his death, pushing her over, swallowing her up and spitting her out.

Lucy was so distracted by these thoughts she lost track of where she was driving and almost missed her destination — an error that would have thrown her into a frustrating maze of one-way streets, no-turn intersections, and road construction.

At the last second, she wrenched the wheel and pulled into a faded pink concrete parking structure off Santa Monica Boulevard in Beverly Hills.

As she drove in, a machine offered up a time-stamped ticket which she grabbed and stuck in her purse. The parking gate opened into a dim garage with grimy, twenty-five-dollar-an-hour spaces. She hoped the lawyer's office validated parking.

Lucy squeezed her twelve-year-old Jeep between a freshly scrubbed Benz and a Lexus minivan. Maybe she should have run the old heap through the auto wash to be presentable in this part of town. Lucy checked her watch. Right on time for her meeting with her uncle's long-time lawyer, Alan Katz. She had no idea what was in her uncle's will, but Katz said she'd inherited enough to call herself a wealthy woman. Maybe she was rich enough to buy a shiny new ride for herself. The thought depressed her. Nothing, however new or shiny, could replace her uncle.

Crawling out of her car was painful. Her left knee was still swollen and stiff thanks to an injury she'd recently suffered while being chased out of Mexico with a drug cartel in homicidal pursuit. Recovery hadn't been as fast and easy as the laparoscopic surgeon had promised.

Lucy closed the Jeep door and leaned against the back fender as memories resurfaced. Her skin turned clammy and heart attack sensations began to tighten, vice-like, in her chest. Images of her time in Guerrero splattered like blood across her vision. The cartel had almost killed her. She tried to calm her breathing and dug into her purse for the brown plastic bottle of anti-anxiety meds. She tapped a couple of small white pills into her palm and swallowed them dry.

Her footsteps reverberated on concrete as she crossed

the garage over to the bridge that took her into the white stucco Mediterranean-style building housing Katz, Klein, and Klugman LLC, Attorneys at Law. Although they had many high-profile clients, their second-floor headquarters were modest and hadn't been updated since Katz's wife passed, many years ago. Klein and Klugman were his two fifty-something daughters who seemed to share their dad's lack of interest in decorating.

Lucy had only been to the office a few times with her uncle, but she was welcomed like an old friend by Alan Katz himself. Short and round with a monk-like white tonsure surrounding his bald dome; he was fumbling with the Keurig machine when she arrived. He couldn't get the little cup of ground coffee to set just right with his arthritic hands but he had no trouble offering up a big hug to Lucy.

"Sweetheart." His accent was still Jersey after a lifetime in LA, "I'm so sorry about Henry." He wiped moisture from his bleary old eyes.

Lucy helped him make a cup of coffee for each of them, then they retreated to his book-lined sanctuary. They sat next to each other at a big mahogany table, its surface etched by years of use. Katz pulled a sheaf of papers from a manila folder and spread them out.

"So, my dear," he began, "First of all, how are you?"

"As well as can be expected, I guess." She reached for the box of Kleenex on the table, in case.

He nodded. "And the knee?"

"Healing a little slower than I'd hoped. But it's on the mend."

He heaved a sigh. "All right, then. Might as well get this over with. I'll send you duplicate copies of all this, and you can call me with any questions, but I wanted to go over the big pieces with you in person. It's all pretty straightforward."

Katz put on a pair of dented, metal-rimmed trifocals and rustled through pages highlighted with neon green sticky notes.

"Before we get into details, can you give me a thumbnail?" Lucy asked, already feeling overwhelmed.

"Certainly, my dear. I was about to do that." The phone on his desk rang but he ignored it. "Your uncle was generous to his favorite charities — gave them each enough to make a significant impact in their work. As you can see, the bequests range from fifty-thousand to five hundred thousand dollars."

Katz pushed a list toward Lucy and she reviewed the organizations. She knew he was rich, but not that rich. She was gladdened to see that education, the arts, minority business development, and community healthcare were at the top of the register. She felt a swell of pride at the scope of his work in Los Angeles. What a loss.

"He left the Malibu ranch and its one-hundred-and-fifty adjacent acres all to you with an endowment for upkeep." The old lawyer presented Lucy with additional documents. "We can discuss how you want to handle the disposition of his business involvements at another time. I'm sure this first pass is more than enough today."

Lucy nodded, grateful for his patience. The pain in her knee intensified.

"Henry left the rest of his money, 2.5 million dollars, to his sister, Catherine Lucia, in Guerrero, Mexico."

"His sister?" A stab of confusion rocked her brain. "No, that can't be right. His siblings are dead, Mr. Katz. — all of them have been gone for decades. You must mean that there's a non-profit in Mexico and he's bequeathed a gift in her name."

Katz shook his head and placed a papery hand over

Lucy's. "Your uncle has been sending money to his sister, Catherine Lucia Maria de la Vega, to fund her rural medical clinic, for quite some time. She's alive, Lucy, and is a Catholic nun. Hasn't been receiving a lot, but twenty thousand a year goes a long way in that part of the world." The lawyer pulled out a faded receipt and studied it for a second. "This year she purchased a used ultrasound machine."

Lucy felt stunned, like a bolt of electricity had tasered her synapses. Her thoughts slowed to a crawl toward the old woman in Pitacallpa, the rural village that had been the cover for an international heroin ring. "This can't be true. My uncle always said his brothers and sisters were gone."

Katz pushed up his glasses. "I'm sure this is shocking news. Henry confided in me about his sister only because I interfaced with the accountants who handled the disposition of funds each year."

Lucy gulped hard and recalled her time with the *curandera*. There had been an intense *déjà vu* quality and an easy connection between Lucy and the nun. The feelings now took on an entirely new dimension. There was something about the woman's hands, the way she gestured when speaking, that reminded Lucy of her mother.

"Oh, my God. I think I met her in Mexico a month ago. In fact, I'm sure I met her. She ministered to one of our documentary staff members who'd been bitten by rattlesnakes." Lucy rubbed at her tight neck muscles and closed her eyes. "I have an aunt. I've met her, talked to her. She held my hand."

Katz gave a little shrug and sighed. "A shame neither of you knew the connection at that point, but Henry said she insisted on anonymity. Kismet that you two happened upon each other."

"Fate, indeed, or perhaps divine providence of some kind." Lucy put her elbows on the table and held her head in her hands. The room spun with the news that she had a living aunt. "What do you know about her? Why did my uncle keep the relationship a secret?" Lucy asked.

Before he spoke again, Katz took a long swallow of coffee and finished it off with a chaser of bottled mineral water.

"Here's what I know," he said. "The twins, your Aunt Catherine Lucia and your uncle Timóteo, were the eldest siblings, with Henry in the middle and your mother the youngest. Your grandpa was a Mexican diplomat and your grandmother was a talented equestrienne and artist, a painter."

Lucy nodded — she knew about her grandparents, although they had passed away before she was born. Now she was eager to hear more.

"Henry was always a businessman, but Timóteo went into the priesthood and Catherine Lucia chose nursing school and then became a nun shortly after receiving her certification. The twins craved the religious life and were both assigned to the same small community in southern Mexico which was a hotbed of revolution at the time. Two years into their service, Timóteo was murdered by insurgents. Catherine Lucia and the two other sisters she worked with were severely abused."

"How horrifying." Lucy's voice broke with tears.

A week later, your Aunt Catherine Lucia, she went by her second name, Lucia, to family, was the only survivor among those at the convent and monastery. Your family reported that she went mad — disappeared into the jungle without a trace. Sometimes I think that's what killed both your grandparents."

Lucy pressed her fingers hard against her eyes. She wanted to pluck the nightmarish scenes she was imagining out of her head.

Katz was silent for a moment. "Are you sure you want to hear all this right now, my dear?" he asked.

"Yes, of course." Lucy reached for her coffee, finished the last cold dregs and grimaced.

Katz patted her hand again and then continued. "Your uncle took numerous trips to Mexico looking for his sister. He finally found her in a ramshackle hut in the mountains of Guerrero, ministering to the local indigenous people with prayers and herbs. She made your uncle swear he would tell no one he'd found her, or she would disappear again."

"Why would she do that?" Lucy shuddered, overwhelmed and devastated by what her aunt had endured. "Why would she want to abandon her family and remain a secret to us?"

"Your uncle called it survivor's shame. She believed that she didn't deserve to live through this brutal insurgent attack when the others didn't survive — her sister nuns, and particularly, her own twin brother. Short of killing herself, which is a mortal sin in Catholicism, she wanted to disappear, symbolically end her existence. So, she did."

Lucy drew a sharp breath. "How awful." Then realization struck her. "We're the last of our Vega line. She's the only family I have, and she's — what — almost eighty, at least? I have to see her again."

"Your uncle said she was becoming more open to the world the last time they'd met. He left her contact information for you, knew you'd want it."

Katz smiled and passed her an envelope. Lucy accepted it. Her hands trembled. Would this be a blessed new chapter in her life or a Pandora's box?

# 4

Sister Catherine Lucia sat on a wooden chair next to the burn patient, reading her Bible aloud. She'd selected passages on forgiveness from the Gospel of Mark — forgive, if ye have committed wrongs against any: that your Father in heaven may forgive you as well.

The pages were well-worn and she found the words healing to her battered soul. She hoped they could provide the same solace for *Señor* Mercer. His wounds suggested he might have much to forgive and be forgiven.

A week had passed. Still in critical condition and hooked up to oxygen and an IV drip cocktail of painkillers and antibiotics, Mercer had a long way to go before he was out of the woods. One foot still hovered over the grave, but he was still alive. Clearly, the young man was a fighter. Arrangements had been made by PAGA officials to send him to the Cedars-Sinai Burn Center in Los Angeles, which was his hometown. The hospital had hyperbaric chambers and modern modes of treatment that Sister knew would be required to heal him fully.

He had been more lucid the last several days and his

eyes constantly followed her movements. He was stubborn, no doubt of that — and watchful. He'd managed to shake off the aloe-soaked gauze pads no matter how many times she'd replaced them. His lids were non-functional so his eyes had to be kept moist to prevent blindness. She kept telling him that, but he was hyper-vigilant, constantly scanning his surroundings.

"What is it you want to say?" Sister asked him. "I know you can speak because you talk in your sleep. You say my name, Lucia."

Mercer's ruined mouth curved up as he laughed. He then wrenched into a coughing fit. His damaged lungs could kill him if he contracted pneumonia. Sister patted his hand, the one with three fingers, barely singed and still functional, as compared to the other that was a fused mass of dying flesh.

Sister Catherine Lucia glanced at the clock on the wall above her medicine cabinet. "The men should be here soon to get you on your way to Los Angeles," she said. "I am so proud of you. You've done well, *Señor* Mercer, endured the pain of treatment without a protest. God willing, you'll continue to heal in *el Norte*." Gently, she pressed a small wooden crucifix, warmed from her touch, into the rawness of his hand. He dropped the gift onto the floor. The sound of the crucifix landing was quiet yet sharp like a distant gunshot, a reminder of violence on the mountain.

A cold current of air raked up her spine and Catherine Lucia was seized by a dark hallucination. She shuddered and grabbed the back of the chair to steady herself. The man was beginning to heal on the outside, but his soul smoldered — not with passion for Christ, but with something foul and sulfurous. She could almost smell it.

The cats yowled and skittered out through a flap in the

screened front door. Sister slowly bent down to retrieve the crucifix then placed it on a table next to the containers of poultice and herbal ointments she'd spent hours producing to ease the patient's misery on his flight. She tried to shift her thoughts to the bright days awaiting him in Southern California, but the sun turned black and the landscape was enveloped in deep shadows.

She shook off the disconcerting images and focused on her work, her healing. When she administered the final bolus of painkiller Mercer would need for the trip, he began to settle down and so did she. Sister placed the damp, pale-green aloe pads back over his eyes.

The familiar sounds of crunching gravel and voices drew near. The hens clucked from beneath the century plants. In minutes, a group of four PAGA officers, the same men who'd brought the patient a week ago, collected on her porch. She watched them from behind the window screen. Muddy boots, rumpled camouflage clothing and the musky scent of poor male hygiene filled the air, but not a cigarette was in sight.

She glanced up at the rafters, hung with rows of drying herbs, and smiled. "Thank you, gentlemen, for your thoughtful consideration."

She opened the door to Alonzo who presented her with a large bouquet of fragrant eucalyptus leaves which she happily accepted. The others tromped in after him. She gave each young man, really just boys, an appreciative hug then helped them wrap Mercer in her special sheets. They carefully transferred him from the bed onto a canvas stretcher. This was clearly a painful process for the burn victim — she could see his teeth clench through an open gape of skin that was once a lip.

Sister Catherine Lucia slipped the small, wooden crucifix

beneath Mercer's pillow. She whispered into his ruined ear. "May this bring you blessings for your continued recovery and protect you from evil on your journey."

He whispered back, his voice like sandpaper on rough wood. "I'd thank you, Sister, but I'm afraid that gesture is a big mistake." Foamy saliva leaked from the sides of his mouth. "Evil is my only comfort now, so get that fucking thing away from me."

Breath caught in her throat, the air sucked from her lungs. She drew the gift away and put it in her pocket. It felt hot to the touch, like a relic from Hell. What hath God or the devil wrought?

Sister Catherine Lucia said a prayer and crossed herself as the men carried the stretcher from the porch and disappeared down the path toward the road.

# 5

Alyssa sat in the front seat of the Prius with her stepmother, Deborah. Aly chatted on her cell with a friend about a Friday night school dance. After disconnecting, she pulled out her tablet in its hot-pink cover.

"Can we do the interview now, Deborah? I mean, Mother?" Alyssa flinched — she kept making that mistake and was pretty sure it wasn't an accident. How could she be such a brat? She couldn't blame the woman for wanting to shape her into a perfect Westside daughter.

Still, since she was stuck, she'd try to do her best to be agreeable. So, Mother, it was. At least to Deborah's face.

Aly tapped on her tablet. "That career interview for my class with somebody who has an interesting job is due tomorrow. You said I could interview you. Is that still okay?"

"Of course. Most people think I do have an interesting profession," Deborah said, always so sure of herself and her value. "And it's certainly rewarding. Go ahead and ask away — we might as well take advantage of the slow traffic."

"Great, thanks."

"So, I assume you have a rubric of some kind?"

Rubric? No way was she going to admit she had no idea what that was. "I have a questionnaire. The teacher wants us all to use the same one. So, first on the list — what is your job title and what do you actually do?" Alyssa sat ready to enter the information.

Deborah drew herself up a bit in her seat and patted her perfect brunette bob. She glanced at herself in the rearview mirror as if to make sure her makeup was perfect. Like she was getting ready for a TV interview. "As you know, my title is Director of Psychiatry at the Carole and Morton Hoffman Burn Center at Cedars."

Alyssa felt her stomach begin to ache. Deborah constantly made a big deal about her job. She thought she knew everything about everybody because she was supposedly a mind expert. She waited for Deborah's brag-a-thon to start.

"I specialize in patients who have become severely disabled — paraplegics, quadriplegics, burn victims and such. Usually a result of vehicular and workplace accidents."

"Do you treat war veterans blown up by IEDs and that kind of stuff?"

"The people with military-related injuries usually go to the VA."

"Oh, okay," Alyssa said, a little disappointed. She'd hoped to meet some soldiers like the sniper guy she'd read about. She tapped fast on her touch screen. She didn't know why this simple little discussion with Deborah was making her so irritated. "Why did you choose this profession? That's question two — five in all."

Deborah hesitated for a moment. She punched a few buttons on the car radio and changed the channel from a rock station to NPR. "My younger brother, Adam, was in a motorcycle crash in high school and broke his neck. His injury devastated the whole family. I wanted to go into this type of medicine to help others in a similar situation."

Alyssa felt her eyes widened. "I didn't know you had a brother. How come I never met him?" What else didn't she know about this woman who was in charge of her life?

"He passed shortly after the accident. Fifteen years ago. His death was a blessing," she said matter-of-factly. "He would have wanted to die."

"I'm so sorry." Alyssa was taken aback by the cold tone of Deborah's voice. Maybe she was still mad or sad about her brother and it came out like she didn't care.

Alyssa thought about her own brother, Dexter. He was a pain sometimes, but it would kill her to lose him. She didn't like imagining stuff like that.

Deborah jerked a shoulder as if impatient to continue. "Next question."

"Okay, number three. We're practically halfway done — easy peasy."

"Good, 'cause we're almost at Cedars." Deborah honked her horn at the driver of a beat-up Toyota who'd poked along and made her miss the turn arrow.

Alyssa realized that her stepmother too often leaned on the horn and banged the steering wheel. Something was bugging Doctor Shrink, that's for sure. Okay, girl, focus on your interview, she told herself. Get this sucker done before Deborah changes her mind and gets too busy to finish up. "Next question — how did you prepare for this career?"

Deborah touched her bob again. "Straight A's in school like I expect from you."

Alyssa gulped. Where was her water bottle?

"Then a Bachelor's in Biology at Berkeley, med school at Columbia, and residency at Johns Hopkins. I'm board-certified in psychiatry and critical care medicine. Then, of course, I'm always studying and attending conferences. I'm a sought-after presenter. I have some DVDs I can lend you."

"Wow — this'll impress my class." Deborah was the queen of perfection and her stepdaughter would never measure up. Aly didn't want to be a doctor. Working with sick people — yuck. She continued to type Deborah's responses into her iPad. "Only two more questions to go." Sweet.

Deborah turned into the Cedars-Sinai complex and parked in her assigned spot right outside the entrance to the boxy, yellow-brick Hoffman Burn Center.

The brass entry sign in front caught Alyssa's eye and triggered a thought. "Are the Hoffmans any relation to you, to us?" she asked.

"They're your grandparents, step-grandparents. I can't believe you didn't know that. Didn't your father tell you?"

To Alyssa, Deborah seemed angrier by the minute.

"Uh, no. Sorry...Mother." Aly chewed at a fingernail. She felt nervous when Deborah was unhappy with her, which was often. "I didn't know they were the Carole and Morton Hoffman of the Burn Center." She took a deep breath. She'd met Nana Carole and Zayde Morty several times since her baby sister was born, but they didn't seem to have much interest in Aly. Their world revolved around the pink-cheeked infant who was already pegged for greatness.

"Ready for the last two questions?" Aly asked, not moving to get out of the car.

"Not now, Alyssa. Let's go." Deborah glanced at her platinum Breitling watch. "We'll finish on the way home." She jumped out of the Prius and was halfway up the steps before Alyssa could put the iPad away and drag her pack out of the back seat.

"Hurry up, Aly, I want you to be the first one at orientation so you'll have time to chat with the coordinators."

Alyssa started up the steps after her. She'd much rather be leaping around the floor, as Deborah called it, at her hip hop class than here. She stopped for a second as an ambulance pulled up to unload a patient, then danced toward the entrance after her stepmother. A little wiggle of the hips, a toss of the hair.

"Go, girl," a paramedic exiting his rig called out to her.

Deborah stopped in her tracks. "My God, Alyssa," she said, face pinched. "Behave yourself." She yanked open the entry door and Alyssa marched obediently inside.

# 6

Lucy had barely pulled her Jeep into the barn at the Malibu ranch when Elsa Nordstrom, her seventy-eight-year-old housekeeper, and quasi-grandma met her as she opened the car door. The comforting aromas of alfalfa and animals wafted in the air. Now, this ranch was hers to treasure and care for, her sanctuary, her safe, wonderful place. Home.

"What's up, Elsa? Everything okay?" Lucy asked.

Before Elsa could respond, Maddie, Lucy's aged golden retriever mix and Bugle the beagle, trotted up and jumped into the Jeep with kisses and breathless yelps of greeting. Howard the gray tabby cat lurked near a pile of hay bales, eyes narrow. In a flash, Bugle hopped across Lucy's lap, stumbled over the gear shift, and planted himself on the passenger seat, head out the window. He wanted a ride to the beach and then to the frozen yogurt place. She'd been cultivating some bad habits among her furry children.

Lucy gave him a good ear scratch then put Bugle back on the ground. She ignored the dog's sad puppy-eyes routine.

"You had a visitor," Elsa said. Her gray brows drew together in a frown.

"You look concerned. Who was it?" Lucy shooed the dogs away so she could finally get out of the car.

"The guy was big, dark clothes, a heavy accent — maybe Eastern European. Said he was a friend of Henry's and wanted to know if you lived here now."

"Eastern European?" Lucy stood and began walking arm-in-arm with Elsa back to the ranch house. She didn't like the sound of this visitor. "What did you tell him?"

"I said you lived down by the beach. I was vague." Elsa paused. "He scared me."

"Were you here alone?" Lucy turned and glanced up at her old apartment above the barn. "Was Michael home?"

"No, he's at the editing studio in Santa Monica. I was all by myself. Maddie didn't like that man either, and she likes everybody."

Lucy didn't want to appear upset and further alarm Elsa so she followed the old woman and the pups into the house. Hanging her purse and sweater on a coat hook in the foyer, Lucy kicked off her shoes and toed them over to the edge of the woven Tabriz rug that covered well-worn Mexican pavers.

"Cup of coffee, honey?" Elsa called from the kitchen.

Lucy joined her and slumped onto a wrought iron bar stool at the center island. Big wooden beams spanned the white stucco ceiling. Mexican plates from the village of Dolores Hidalgo hung on the wall along with blue porcelain ones from Norway. Somehow, they looked charming together. "How about some of that stress-buster tea? I don't think I could handle any more caffeine right now."

"We're out of stress-buster but I have some other good blends. The Ceylon tea Bea brought us from the Savannah Tea Room is yummy."

"Sounds perfect. Emperor's Bride?"

"Yes, indeed. And we're almost out. I'll have to order more." Elsa put a dented copper teapot on the stove, turned up the flame, and sat down next to Lucy while they waited for the water to boil and the whistle to blow. She opened a blue-and-white ceramic cookie jar and pushed it Lucy's way. The scent of freshly baked ginger snaps was delicious. They both dug in. Neither was shy about homemade cookies.

Howard leaped onto the soapstone counter and settled down nearby but out of reach.

"That guy, the creepy visitor, may never come back, but still, do you think we should get a security system?" Elsa asked, forehead wrinkled with worry.

Lucy nodded. "We had one put in once, didn't we?"

"We did," Elsa said, "but it hasn't worked for a decade. The wiring's still in place though."

Lucy pulled out her cellphone and began to scroll. "There's this product I heard about where you can monitor security on your phone from wherever you are in the world."

"I like the sound of that," Elsa said, brightening. She was not an oldster afraid of technology.

"I'll find the website and you can pick out the system that looks like it'll work best for us." Lucy could see the old woman's body tension begin to unwind. Elsa had been with Uncle Henry for at least thirty years. It was easy to forget that she wasn't a high energy middle-aged woman anymore. Blue veins road-mapped her hands and she napped as often as the cat.

The tea kettle began to sound. Elsa rose, turned off the stove and prepared their beverages. The soothing fragrance of the tea as it steeped, mixed with the scent of ginger cookies, was wonderful.

Elsa dug into the cookie jar and pulled out a second ginger

snap. Lucy did the same. "These were Henry's favorites." She wiped a tear from her eye with a paper napkin and then poured them both a cup of tea.

"Delicious," Lucy said, savoring a hot sip. "To Uncle Henry."

They tapped cups then sat quietly in comfortable silence enjoying the bracing hot liquid, crispy confections, and warm memories. Lucy's eyes closed with pleasure. Teatime with Elsa at the kitchen table had always been one of life's simple and profound pleasures.

As they relaxed, another idea to help Elsa feel safer and more comfortable in their home materialized in Lucy's brain. "I heard your nephew and his wife might be coming to UCLA for grad school," Lucy said. She grabbed yet another ginger snap. "Maybe they'd like to stay in the guest house. We could fix it up and they could give you some nice company and help around the place for free rent."

Elsa's eyes lit up and then she grinned. "That would be amazing. I'll talk with them."

They tapped their mugs to celebrate the idea.

In the meantime," Lucy said, still highly concerned about the unknown visitor, "tell me everything about that Eastern European guy you can possibly recall."

Lucy forwarded the security system site to Elsa's laptop then punched up the Notes page on her iPhone and began to take down Elsa's information.

# 7

Lucy nestled into a dark-blue cushioned Papasan chair on the balcony of the studio apartment above the barn. Her bare feet were propped atop the wooden railing. This loft and its lovely deck had been hers before she moved into the ranch house and turned the apartment over to Burleson. They needed to be together but also needed their own space until they figured out what they wanted from each other, and if they were capable of giving it.

She watched his truck make its way up the half-mile gravel road to the ranch house. Little plumes of dust puffed from behind the rear wheels while a red-tailed hawk rode a thermal high above, eyes likely searching for unwary prey. As the sun began its slow burn toward the ocean, cool, airy fingers crept into the canyons replacing the heat of the day, still warm as a puppy's tummy against Lucy's skin. It was hard to believe that a few miles down the highway millions of souls filled the landscape. Here, high in the Santa Monica Mountains with the Pacific in the distance was solitude and peace.

The truck door slammed shut in the barn below and boots clomp-clomped up the outside stairs. Then, a tall, slim man in his late forties with tousled blond hair and a golden-gray bristly beard, crossed the deck and dropped his belongings onto a weathered Adirondack chair. Lucy's pulse quickened.

He glanced at the open French doors to his bedroom. "Funny, I was sure I locked up when I left his morning."

Lucy stretched, the hint of a smile on her lips. "Sorry to bust in on your private space, sir, but this balcony calls to me, especially at this time of day." She slowly closed her eyes. The scent of night-blooming jasmine flirted in the breeze like a playful lover.

"No problem, ma'am. The woman who lets me stay here is gone for a few hours. So maybe you and I, uh, can, get to know each other a little before she comes back." Michael Burleson leaned against the railing and tilted his head expectantly. "She has me on a tight leash. Exhausting being her boy-toy."

Lucy sighed. "Ah, poor baby. Let me comfort you."

He tried to keep a straight face, but a teasing grin took over. "What did you say your name was, beautiful?"

"Beautiful works fine." Lucy looked up at Michael and extended her hand. His eyes were a translucent blue like sea glass. He sat on the edge of her chair, pulled her close, and tangled his fingers in hers. The insane week they'd had in Mexico changed them from adversaries to lovers. He'd saved her life. She'd saved his. Lucy wanted what they had at this moment to last forever.

She melted against him, savoring the warm solidness of his body. A momentary feeling of safety, of happiness, enfolded her like a tender swell of the ocean.

"Scary, isn't it," Lucy murmured, "this feeling of well-being?"

Michael gazed out across the golden chaparral and snuggled closer. "Not if you stay in the moment, the here and now. That's all anybody has, eh? And right now, the here and now's magnificent." He kissed her gently on the lips.

Lucy gathered a handful of his T-shirt and pulled him tight. A little shiver rippled her chest like a leaf caught in a quick breeze.

He tucked her head beneath his chin and smoothed the wavy dark hair exploding from her ponytail.

"Beautiful, Lucy — I'm sensing something unsettling. Does this have anything to do with the reading of your uncle's will?"

Lucy leaned back and took in the vista as gauzy clouds began to catch the last light.

Michael kissed her again and then rose and shifted to the chair next to hers. They continued to hold hands.

"It does," she said, "and when did you get so smart?"

"Since I started hanging with you." He gave his beard a contemplative stroke.

Lucy laughed. "You're full of it. Anyhow, the will included a big surprise. Remember the woman, the *curandera* who helped save Gregorio from the snakebites in Guererro? Long gray hair, pretty?"

"Of course, — Sister Catherine Lucia. She had a presence that was hard to miss. What about her?"

"She's my aunt."

"What?" Michael's forehead wrinkled. "Your aunt?"

Lucy shook her head, still not quite believing. "She's Uncle Henry's older sister. Had a twin brother, Timóteo, then came Henry and my mom."

"Family secrets. Whoa."

"Yeah. Pretty unbelievable, right? I'd been told she died twenty years ago. But my uncle has been funding her little medical clinic in Mexico for years. Left her quite a hefty endowment to continue her work."

"Wow, that's cool. But how about you? Did he take care of you?"

"He took care of me better than I could have imagined. This ranch is mine now. I'm truly blessed."

"I'm relieved to hear that" He squeezed her hand. "But what was all the mystery about regarding the nun, your aunt?"

"It's a painful story. Her twin brother — a priest — was murdered, along with her sister nuns and most of the villagers they served. After years of searching, Uncle Henry found her, but she insisted he keep her location a secret. The lawyer called it survivor's guilt. She didn't think she deserved to have lived, so she turned herself into, almost a ghost."

"How horrible." Michael gazed again into the distance; his face grim. Dusk was fast enveloping the landscape.

"I've got to find out more; I'm really fascinated. I felt this strange connection with her from the beginning. Unc's lawyer gave me her contact information. She has a post office box in Tingo Tia she supposedly visits every month or so. The Vega line still lives."

"That's sure good to hear." Michael squeezed her hand.

"I have so many questions I want to ask. I wonder if she'd ever venture out from Guerrero. Probably not." Lucy sighed; a sense of loss tightened in her chest. "She's been living in those highlands by herself for a long, long time."

"Would be cool to have her visit and to get to know her, show her where her brother lived, where you live. There's no way we could go back down there. We'd be targets, dead in a day."

Lucy nodded and blew out a long breath. "Would also be amazing to have her look at the documentary as it evolves. I have a feeling she could add a lot of perspective."

"Speaking of our project — mind taking a quick look at what I edited today?" He reached for his laptop.

"God, yes, definitely." Lucy grabbed at the distraction. "Have to feed the dogs first, though. Five minutes late and they whine like they're starving to death. Elsa's feeding the other critters." Lucy rose from her chair and cast one last glance toward the ocean. Was this land and fortune all really hers? How would she be the best steward of the resources? She felt dizzy. Too much to contemplate for now. "Let's bring the laptop over to the kitchen and we can watch at the table."

As Lucy and Michael crossed the yard to the ranch house, Maddie, Bugle, and Howard were lined up at the door ready for dinner. After their food was served and gobbled, the furry friends disappeared and the humans settled in to watch the dailies. Months ago, in Guerrero, she'd recorded the images over the span of a week tracking the men who killed her uncle and controlled the black tar heroin pipeline into Southern California.

Lucy winced as pictures of her nemesis and former colleague, Gary Mercer, came into sharp focus. He strutted around the plane supervising workers who loaded black tar bricks into his Cessna. She'd shot this footage a mere hour before being abducted by the traffickers.

As Lucy and Michael watched the piece, Elsa came into the kitchen and washed her hands. She lifted the top off a big pot of hot, fragrant chili. Cornbread muffins cooled on the counter. She sniffed and smiled. "Another half hour and we'll be ready to eat."

"Smells amazing," Michael said.

Lucy felt nauseous.

Elsa stepped over to the table and stood behind them, watching. Then she gasped.

Lucy looked up, concerned. "What is it?"

Elsa pointed to the screen and tapped on a figure. "I recognize that man."

"These are Mexican drug dealers, Elsa. The chances of —"

"Lucy, that guy was here, at our front door. He's the one who asked for you — the guy with the Eastern European accent."

Lucy gulped. "Oh, my God. Are you sure it's him?"

"Positive," Elsa said, her face pale. "When did you say that alarm system was being installed?"

Lucy looked at Michael and quickly updated him on recent events. Was the cartel still after them? Were Russians now involved? If that was the case, it would take a hell of a lot more than an alarm system to keep them safe.

—

The gentle draft moving across his skin felt as sharp as razor blades. Gary Mercer winced as the EMT prepared his gurney to leave the ambulance. A half-hour previously his private jet landed at Santa Monica Airport where the medical transport had been waiting. The earthy smell of the Mexican highlands was replaced by jet fuel and the faint salty tang of the Pacific. There wasn't much of his nose left, but what was there still worked despite the oxygen tubes pushed into the holes that were his nostrils.

Mercer was suddenly overwhelmed by a scent-memory of smoke and scorched flesh from the Land Rover explosion. And Lucy Vega made it happen when she emptied a round of hot ordnance into the leaking gas tank. He gritted his teeth and envisioned her burning slowly, painfully roasting like a pig on a spit.

He shuddered. This was not how he'd imagined his return home. LA used to provide reunions filled with drugs, booze, and partners willing to perform any amusement to gain his attention. This trip, however, had been hellish and now he was being moved into the Burn Center at Cedars-Sinai. Hyperbaric treatments, surgeries, and pain, on top of more pain, awaited him in this shop of horrors. Lucy Vega still had her pretty face, for now.

His gurney was pulled from the truck and bumped down onto the ground. He gritted his teeth. As he was rolled across the walkway to the emergency entrance by an energetic med-tech, a leading man type probably waiting for his big break, Mercer tried to get his bearings. He'd been born here at Cedars. Life had been full of promise once, now he was back as a ravaged monster, a role he'd somehow been preparing for all his life — since the day he crushed his mother's skull. All the King's horses and all the King's men couldn't put mother together again. Then he killed the King, too.

As Mercer was wheeled up the ramp, an officious-looking woman in an expensive suit ascended the steps to the main door, walking like she owned the place. She was followed by a stunning teen-aged girl who danced in her wake like a bright shimmer on water. When the woman disappeared inside, the tech called out to the girl like the tacky asshole he was.

She turned, smiling, in her own little world of unheard music, then sobered and followed the woman into the center. For an instant Mercer envisioned himself as that famous phantom of the opera, molding a pretty young beauty to his bidding. Although his physical self was wasted, he was not done with this life, not by far. He still had money, power, and enough rage to cause havoc. The Phantom was a Boy Scout compared to what he had planned.

Mercer would accomplish what Luis Alvarez never quite had the self-control and discipline to do. That is—command one of the world's largest economic drivers — black tar heroin production and distribution. General Alvarez had been too distracted by the mindless, meaningless perks of authority and by petty, regional pissing contests to take the business into the stratosphere where it belonged. With Alvarez gone, the Russians were chomping at the bit for their piece of the action, the Afghanis as well. Mercer'd fight to keep his hold on the business. Alvarez's people would be loyal to him now or face the dire consequences.

The door to the emergency entrance wheezed open like a gasp from a tuberculosis patient. Life was now a global game. He would play with relentless brutality until he controlled every last pawn.

# 8

Bea sat across from her son Dexter at the kitchen island, downing her second cup of morning coffee. Warm light filtered through the fronds of a date palm that grew near the large, multi-paned window overlooking the lush backyard. Although modest by Santa Monica standards, Bea couldn't imagine wanting anything more. It had been a happy home, a good place to raise kids, entertain friends, and escape from the stress of big-city existence. Somehow, however, life in this house was changing.

Dex slid onto a stool and poured himself a glass of orange juice. At almost seventeen, he was six-four and still growing. A new fade haircut with shaved fenders and a bowl-like thatch of springy hair about three inches high on top added to his height. Soon, he'd pass his dad's six-foot-nine height even without the extended 'do. Wispy whiskers darkened his face. The cheeky roundness of childhood was transforming toward more chiseled lines in his face and jaw, right before his mama's eyes.

Ever since returning from Savannah, where he had been kidnapped and terrorized, nothing had been the same. Innocence had been lost, obliterated, and her once endearing, puppyish son now carried the weight of the world on his broadening shoulders. Bea choked down her tears. Dex couldn't tolerate her sadness. It was another stressor he didn't want to deal with.

His thumbs flew across iPhone keys.

"Texting Cornelia?" Bea asked. Two years younger than Dexter, the girl had shared the awful experience in Savannah with him. They were bound by horror and, Bea guessed, first love. "Tell her, hey."

He didn't respond — just finished up his message then pushed his phone into the pocket of his hoodie. He reached for a bagel, slathered it with cream cheese then piled on lox and tomato.

"I invited her out here for spring break, but her mom and dad said no."

Bea hid her relief. She'd given him permission to ask Cornelia only because she knew her parents would never allow it. "She's young and her folks are protective right now, as they should be."

Dexter laughed without humor. "I'd say it's way too late to try and protect her. She says they barely let her leave the house." He looked ready to cry. "Sucks."

Bea sensed that he felt disconnected from everything and everyone, even those closest to him. She guessed it scared him to death. This was not unusual post-trauma but it was still hell. He was seeing a therapist weekly to help get a handle on his life, but he was looking for a magic bullet — something to make it all like it was before. It was never going to happen. Bea's heart constricted in pain.

"Tough times, sweetheart," she said. The words had a hollow clank.

He nodded and bit into the bagel. Cheese smudged the tip of his nose. He wiped it off with the back of his hand and licked his lips.

And there was yet another touchy subject that had to be dealt with — college. Bea's stomach clenched, but she had to put the questions out there. Now was as good or as bad a time as any. "I see you didn't sign up for the college visitation trip in June. The deadline is this week. And you have b-ball recruiters lining up and you won't talk with them. It's driving your dad a little crazy. What are your thoughts, honey?"

"I'm not playing basketball in college. I told him that fifty times. In fact, I'm switching to lacrosse for my senior year. I signed up for a summer high school league."

"What? Really?" Bea tried with minimal success to keep the shock she felt out of her voice. Dexter was on the All-State varsity basketball first team this season and his grades were great, too. A full ride to the school of his choice was likely a slam dunk.

"Really. I'm sick to death of everybody asking me what school I'm committing to or when I'm going pro, and if I think I can out-shoot the old man. Jesus, leave me alone. I am not my father."

The fury in his voice stunned Bea. She pushed her coffee away.

Dexter's eyes darted to the kitchen clock. He clearly wanted to cut this conversation short. "I'm also thinking about taking a gap year," he said, voice low.

Bea took a deep breath and nodded. Feign calmness, be cool, she told herself as she began to sweat. "I hear more and more kids are doing that. I guess it gives you some time to think, figure out who you are and what you want."

Dexter nodded and met his mom's gaze for the first time

in several days. "Thanks for not freaking out."

But I am freaking out, my sweet baby boy. "Sure. We'll talk more about it later."

"Rio thought it was a good idea," Dexter said. He finished the last of the juice then moved off the stool to put his plate and glass in the sink.

Rio was Bea's brother Luther's best friend from childhood, and one of the dearest people in her life. A professor at Emory University, he was an expert on PTSD. Dexter and Rio seemed to have bonded after the fiasco in Savannah. She was both pleased he'd confided in Rio and hurt that her son had consulted him first.

A car horn sounded from the curb in front of the house.

"Sean's here. See ya later, Mom." Dexter grabbed his backpack, planted a quick kiss on his mother's cheek, then stopped and turned back toward her.

His eyes were hard. "You shouldn't have let Alyssa go live with her father and that woman."

Bea's heart pounded. She'd been so ambivalent about the decision and it still frightened her. "But honey, she should have the right to live with her father if she wants to."

He shook his head. "You should have said no." Before she could further respond, Dexter fled out the front door.

Bea struggled against being overwhelmed with the upheaval in her life as a parent, but she was losing the battle. What the hell was she doing? Was she doing any of it right?

While she cleaned up the breakfast detritus, confused and distressed, her cell phone chirped. She rinsed out her coffee cup while checking the text message. A quad-homicide in Westwood. A Ukrainian hit suspected.

She grabbed her purse and sunglasses, on her way. Sometimes she felt more confident dealing with bloody murder than with her own children.

—

It took Bea forty-five minutes through snarled traffic to drive the few miles between Santa Monica and Westwood, home of UCLA. A strange mix of glassed-in, high-rise canyons along Wilshire Boulevard and quaint Mediterranean-style Westwood Village, this was not the usual place for multiple homicides. Bea pulled her silver Beemer into a public parking garage several blocks from the scene which was behind a meatball restaurant on Gayley.

The day was already warm and the smell of the dumpsters and dead bodies was beyond nauseating — and promised to worsen. One of the rookie cops, her round Asian face pale as skim milk, shuffled through the gathered group offering a container of Vicks VapoRub. Applied beneath the nostrils, it helped ease the stench. Bea waved her on.

Coagulated blood, lots of it, pooled in the potholes and cracks in the alley. A big rat skittered from behind a pile of cardboard boxes labeled as frozen french fries. A tang of bitter coffee rose in Bea's throat and she felt a little woozy. Probably should have swallowed her pride and nabbed some Vicks.

The four victims were covered with plastic tarps. Medical examiner's staff, police, and a dense cloud of flies swarmed among reporters doing televised stand-ups. Satellite trucks clogged the streets beyond the crime scene. The owner of the meatball restaurant brought sandwiches for the first responders and reporters. Bea couldn't imagine biting into something fleshy, dripping with red sauce right now.

She spotted West Bureau homicide detective, Marlene Simon. Marlene and Bea's paths had crossed often enough over the years that they had struck up a friendship. Bea trusted her and the feeling was mutual. Marlene was chatting up one of the assistant coroners, a skinny guy in his early forties with a head of thick, curly gray hair. Bea walked up to join them. Between enthusiastic bites of his meatball sandwich, he grumbled vociferously about the Office of the Medical Examiner's chronic under-funding, under-staffing, and inability to do the job professionally.

"We'll tackle that topic another day," the detective said. "You know we agree with you. But answer Bea's questions right now. She's on deadline and I gotta boogie on back to the cop shop — stat."

Marlene was fiftyish with straight black, shoulder-length hair and fair skin. Her brown eyes swept the scene from behind clear plastic glasses with lenses the size of headlights. She wore a camel-colored suit and no-nonsense brown flats, expensive ones. Her vibe was smart, intense, and a little crazy — one foot in Diagon Alley and the other on Westwood Boulevard. Her slightly eccentric demeanor was often her ace in the hole with perps who didn't take her seriously and then spilled their guts to Mama Marlene.

Drinks Friday at The Lobster?" she whispered as she passed Bea. Bring Lucy — I think this here shit might tie into that Mexico thing you two were involved in. Happy hour starts at four-thirty."

Bea nodded and gave the detective a quick hug. "See you then."

She turned to the over-worked coroner, his mouth smeared with red sauce, and began her questions. Marlene disappeared from the hideous scene of dead bodies, police, reporters, and rotting garbage.

# 9

Alyssa wheeled the squeaky cart down the hall at the Hoffman Burn Center. She'd been on the job for two weeks. Thanks to Deborah, she'd scored a special release from middle school so she could work from noon until five on Thursday afternoons. Most volunteers were fourteen or older, but Deb had finagled that, too. Alyssa was barely thirteen but Deborah valued doing everything "early." Alyssa knew she should be grateful for the opportunity, but instead, she felt nervous and a little freaked-out compared to the older students who seemed so cool and mature. She tugged at her blue "volunteer" polo shirt with a new plastic name tag pinned on it. Gently, she knocked on the patient's door.

She hadn't met Mr. Garrett Mark the previous week when he'd been in hyperbaric treatment.

"Hello, Mr. Mark." She forced a cheerful voice. "I'm Alyssa and I have some audiobooks you might be interested in and the latest magazines, too." She pushed the cart into the room on its wobbly, complaining wheels.

He turned his ruined face her way and smiled if it could be called a smile. All that remained was a gaping grimace where his lips once were. Nausea rose in Alyssa's throat. The patient's lidless eyes were hard as stone and his skin hung on his skull like melted candle wax.

She knew she was not supposed to react negatively to any patient's appearance, but his face seriously creeped her out. Alyssa was fast realizing that she didn't want to work with burn victims — bad dreams were beginning to haunt her sleep. Deborah would be so disappointed if she knew what a wimp-ass her stepdaughter was.

Alyssa cleared her throat. "We have the latest Michael Connolly novel, or maybe poetry by Maya Angelou? Or Sunset magazine, or Popular Mechanics? Anything sound interesting? We can order whatever you want. Takes, like, three days from the library." She was talking way too fast and knew it but couldn't slow down.

He didn't respond, just stared at her. The skin around his eyes was smeared with a creamy goo of some kind, like Vaseline. As much as she tried, Alyssa couldn't contain a shudder. She turned the cart, eager to flee. "I can come back another time if you aren't up to reading or listening to anything right now."

"Sorry," he blurted. "Alyssa, is it?"

She nodded.

"Where my manners? Don't think we've met before."

His voice was all mumbly and raspy, like that guy in the old Godfather film, Marlon somebody. Her brother, Dexter, knew all about vintage movies.

"I'm new. Only been volunteering for two weeks." Alyssa said. She picked at her name tag.

He responded but his words were lost on her.

Alyssa flushed with embarrassment, "I'm sorry, could you repeat that? Couldn't quite understand." His words sounded like they came from a mouth stuffed with mashed potatoes. She moved a little closer.

He spoke again, struggling to enunciate. "Been here, ah, two weeks, too."

The effort seemed to drain him.

"Uh, nice to meet you." How long had Deborah signed her on to do this volunteer gig? A year? Her stomach clenched — she didn't think she could last. Then the guilt swept in. It was a privilege to help people in need, but maybe there were other ways for her to help.

She had to stop worrying and pull it together. "Now about these audiobooks..."

Mr. Mark paused, looked at her closely, then spoke again. "Saw you dancing? Front steps?" He broke into a moment of coughing before continuing. "Ambo driver. He hit on you."

At first confused, Alyssa didn't know what he was talking about, then she remembered. And smiled. "Oh, yeah. I love dance. My mom, that is—my real mom—put me in ballet before I was three. I slept in those pink ballet slippers, wouldn't take them off. But," she sighed, "I'm cutting down on my classes so I can, you know, do more meaningful stuff." She heard the sarcastic tone in her voice and guilt came again like a cold poke in the ribs.

His mouth gaped open, breath labored, then he formed words. "More meaningful? To you or her?"

She flinched at the question. "To me, I guess. Deb, I mean my stepmother, she's head of psychiatry here, wants to make sure I become a good person, compassionate."

"Stepmother, Deborah Hoffman." Mr. Mark studied her; his horrible head tilted. He seemed to be thinking about something, hard. Each breath he took was a deep, awful gasp like he was strangling.

"Dr. Deborah Hoffman Strauss," Alyssa corrected. "She likes to use her full title."

"Ah, of course." He paused, then he spoke again, voice low. She had to step even closer to hear.

"Dance, more than fun. Doesn't understand. I feel your, uh, passion. Dance is, uh, art. Life." Coughing rattled his lungs.

He looked like he was going to pass out. A tearful lump began to tighten in Alyssa's throat. She felt vulnerable and wanted to run yet needed to stay.

"I'm sorry," he said. "What you're doing here is —" he coughed again, more violently, "—very important. You are a compassionate person." He was silent for a few moments then smiled that torn, lipless smile. He seemed to have caught his breath. "Wanna see what I, uh, looked like?"

Not really. "Okay."

He nodded toward the bedside table. "A picture. Open the drawer." He held up his bandaged hands and gestured toward the table again.

Alyssa released her grip on the cart handle and moved slowly toward Mr. Mark.

"Don't be afraid," he panted. "See my real face, in my heart. You'll be," he wheezed, "more comfortable."

She rubbed her wet palms against her jeans, opened the drawer and picked up a three-by-five color photo. Her eyes narrowed, flitted his way then back to the picture. "This is you?"

He nodded.

She studied the photo. "You look like Wolverine," she said. "I mean, Hugh Jackman, the actor. He's kinda scary." What was she saying? She'd probably hurt his feelings. "I mean you were, uh, pretty hot."

To change the subject before she made an even bigger fool of herself, she pointed to the image. Mr. Mark stood in front of a small airplane. It was parked on the tarmac in a jungle somewhere. "Cool plane. It yours?"

"Yep. Can't wait to get back in the air."

Somehow, seeing him prior to the burns made Alyssa more uncomfortable, rather than less. He had a creepy vibe even before his accident. She replaced the photo, shut the drawer, then immediately returned to the small comfort of the book trolley. She clung to the handle like a life preserver.

"I'm sorry for what happened to you," she said.

"Thank you. Enjoy your beautiful face, Alyssa. You never know the future."

A little chill tingled down her spine. "I'd better get going. Got a patient in the next room waiting for Fifty Shades of Gray. See you next week."

She made it into the hallway before wiping off the perspiration beaded on her forehead.

—

Lucy and Bea settled into the patio chairs at The Lobster, a seafood eatery that overlooked the bay at the historic Santa Monica Pier. A few blocks away from where Ocean Avenue met the California Incline, cars zoomed down the bluff onto Pacific Coast Highway, which wound like a dark necklace along the sensuous curve of beach toward distant Point Dume.

"So, how goes your first week on the new job?" Lucy asked after ordering their drinks and enough appetizers to make a meal. Music from the Ferris wheel, peals of laughter and squawking seagulls filled the brisk air.

"Been pretty damn intense, girlfriend. By the way, that orange tree you brought me is still alive on my desk," Bea said, an exaggerated look of pride on her pretty face.

Lucy chuckled. "Good for you. Maybe that thumb of yours is turning green after all."

With perfect timing, the waiter returned with a cold, dripping pitcher of strawberry margaritas. Lucy happily poured their drinks. Luscious chunks of freshly mixed berries bobbed in the frothy, pink liquid. She almost swooned.

They clinked glasses, then raised them again in salute as Detective Marlene Simon shuffled up to their outdoor table. Marlene lugged a purse the size of a steamer trunk.

"Just what I hoped you'd have waiting for me, darlings." Marlene plunked down across from Lucy. The fourth chair at the table was immediately filled by her purse/suitcase/portable office. "I need this view. Too much nasty shit going down in town today."

"Couldn't agree more. It was a great idea to meet for happy hour — it's been far too long." Bea poured Marlene a glass and they toasted again, sighing with satisfaction at the delicious summery drink. The pungent Pacific breeze rustled the table cloth, and appetizers arrived at the hand of the handsome server. Probably had his theatrical headshots tucked in that black apron. Lucy smiled. It was one of those short-lived great LA moments. Good food, a fabulous view, the company of friends.

Then talk turned to murder.

# 10

Lucy lowered the cocktail-sauced shrimp she was about to pop into her mouth. The sign and smell of the dead Ukrainians murdered in the Westwood alley wafted into her consciousness. She pushed back the images and turned toward Marlene, who was munching away. "You think this is a turf war, with Alvarez's death leaving a vacuum?"

"That's what we're speculating at this point," Marlene said. She replaced her oversized reading goggles with equally large sunglasses. "I'm working with Lieutenant Pete Anthony from the major narcotics division. You guys know him, right?"

"He was at the scene of my uncle's murder in Malibu," Lucy said, "with McNeill the Federal counterterrorism agent, and Sheriff Mortenson from County."

It was bad enough that she had to drive past the wrecked expanse of guardrail on Kanan Road every day. When would they repair the gaping reminder of her uncle's tragic death? Even then, she'd probably always see it ripped open like a wound refusing to heal.

Marlene continued. "The minute Luis Alvarez went kaput, the shit hit the fan. The Ukrainians came out of the woodwork, and it's been one helluva nasty week."

"I'll drink to that," Bea said and did.

Marlene licked her lips and reached for the crab rolls.

"Ukrainians, huh?" Lucy picked at a plate of prawns, feeling uneasy. "A man with an Eastern European accent came by the ranch looking for me last week. Elsa thought he might be Russian. When Michael and I were screening the dailies from our documentary on black tar heroin traffic outta central Mexico, she recognized him on the vid. Said he was the guy asking about me."

"That's disturbing," Marlene said. "Maybe we should get a patrol car on your place."

Lucy didn't think she'd ever feel fully safe again no matter what precautions were taken. "We put in a top-line security system yesterday, and it's my guess that having a black-and-white sitting at the end of the driveway would make Elsa even more fearful than she already is."

Marlene nodded. "Probably don't have the resources to do it for long anyway."

"When I first saw this guy Elsa ID'd," Lucy said, "he was helping load bricks into Mercer's plane at this off-the-grid airstrip in Mexico, supposedly for a California delivery. He seemed like he could be a supervisor directing the workers."

"Mind looking at some photos?" Marlene asked. "Maybe your visitor is one of the dead Ukrainians we found yesterday. Got their mugshots right here." She rooted through her huge bag, found a manila envelope, and pushed it toward Lucy. "They're not from the murder scene, so you can still enjoy your yummies."

Lucy nodded; not sure she was right. Stomach acid was beginning to burn in her chest. Where were her Tums?

Bea leaned over her plate of crab cakes; voice subdued.

"Could be that the guy creeping around the ranch still works for Alvarez's people — whoever they are now. Even if he's Russian — I mean he was with Gary Mercer in Mexico, right? So why switch allegiances?"

"On the other hand, why not go with your Ukrainian homeboys and bring your knowledge of the competitor along with you?" Lucy looked over at Marlene.

The detective took a long swig of her margarita. "Word on the street is that Carlos Alvarez, Luis's nasty baby brother, remains involved."

"Calling the shots from the federal prison up in Lompoc?" Lucy asked.

Marlene nodded. "Very possibly. We also think there's still an American with a heavy hand in it. Lucy, you and Burleson said you saw this Gary Mercer die, but his body was never reported found. I was hoping you two could fill me in on Alvarez and what went down in Guerrero this past January. I read the official reports but thought it would be better to talk to you in person."

Lucy almost choked on a strawberry chunk. He was dead. Mercer was dead. There were plenty of other Americans who could be entangled with the Alvarez cartel. "We saw him go up in flames when his Jeep exploded. He couldn't have survived."

"Even if he did survive," Bea added, "he'd be hours from any emergency care. All they have down there is a bare-bones clinic with one over-worked doctor, a few staff members, and a backwoods local healer, a *curandera*. Right, Lucy?"

Lucy nodded. She hadn't yet told Bea that the *curandera* was her aunt.

"The Feds talked to the medical team at that Guerrero clinic and they hadn't seen any burn victims come in." Marlene dipped a juicy morsel of flaky white lobster into a ramekin of drawn butter then gobbled it down. Still chewing, she said, "The local healer, obviously, wouldn't have the skill or resources to take on something that critical so we never followed through on that."

Lucy poured herself another margarita but her stomach was feeling sicker by the minute. She eyed the envelope, then slowly opened it, and pulled out the photos. She frowned and rubbed her neck. After carefully studying the faces, she shook her head. "I don't recognize any of these dudes."

"Maybe you could show me the dailies you mentioned so we have another face to watch out for?" Pushing up her drooping sunglasses, Marlene turned expectantly toward Lucy.

"Absolutely. We're leasing an editing suite over at Media House on Ocean Park near Twenty-third by the Santa Monica Airport. Can you two make it over tomorrow? We'll be there all day. Then we can frame-grab and email you any helpful images. I really want to know who this asshole scaring Elsa is."

Marlene wiped her buttery fingers on a napkin. "Good, I'll be there late morning, will text you when I'm on my way. Might bring Pete Anthony along. It'll be fun to see Michael Burleson again. I've known him for years — had a short stint at CNN before I came to LA." She gazed out toward the pier where lights were beginning to come on. Pink-and-orange reflections from the Ferris wheel spun slowly on the restaurant's floor-to-ceiling windows. Organ music from the merry-go-round floated from the beach.

Lucy couldn't resist digging further into Marlene's mention of Burleson. Bea looked at Lucy and winked.

"Okay, spill, Mar," Lucy said. "Fill me in on what a terrible person Burleson is and why I shouldn't have anything to do with him."

Marlene smiled and shrugged. "Quite the opposite, actually. When he's clean and sober, he's one of the smartest, nicest men in the business, with those damn blue eyes a woman could drown in. Not that we ever had that kind of relationship."

Lucy breathed a sigh of relief. She shouldn't care about his storied past, but she couldn't help it. It was like a splinter — not life-threatening, but definitely irritating.

"What's Pete Anthony like to work with?" Bea asked.

Marlene chuckled. "If you can get his attention away from shiny things that reflect his pretty face for a few minutes, he's smart and thinks outside the box. Very tenacious. Other than that, he's a pain in the ass and needs to be regularly kicked in that same location."

"Sounds delightful," Bea said. "When I meet him, I'll be sure to wear my stilettos."

# 11

After leaving Bea to her Uber and Marlene to a group of long-time friends from the Santa Monica PD, Lucy walked the four blocks to her condo. Pedestrians filled the sidewalks and drivers vied for parking spaces, all heading for a bit of Friday night relief at the bars and restaurants along the beach and Main Street.

The knee she'd injured in Mexico was still unwilling to stop inflicting pain with each step. It would be a while before she'd be fully kicking butt along with Bea. And there'd never be stilettos involved. She glanced down at her hot-pink Birkenstocks and the still-purple scar slicing the side of her leg.

Lucy's thoughts turned to her Aunt Lucia. What health or medical crisis was she monitoring tonight in her remote farms and villages? Childbirth? Fevers? Bullet wounds? Was she safe from the narcos? Lucy wanted to reach out to her and not waste any more time. Now that they both knew about each other, Alan Katz reminded her that it was up to Catherine Lucia and Lucy to take the next steps.

Burleson's words rose in Lucy's consciousness.

She's been living down there for decades, she could probably help us identify a lot of these faces.

Lucy unlocked her front door and headed for the kitchen where her laptop sat on the island next to an empty coffee cup and a vase of wilting tulips. The pups were with Elsa at the ranch and she missed them.

She slid onto a bar stool, fired up the PC and began to type a real letter. It had been too long since the last time she'd authored anything more than a typical email or text message. This important missive was going snail mail to Aunt Lucia's PO Box in Tingo Tia, Mexico.

Lucy stared at the blank screen. Nothing happened — no inspiration, no greeting card sentiments, or pithy insights — no words at all. She managed to avoid the task for almost a whole hour by checking email, Facebook, Instagram, Twitter, her favorite blogs, and shopping sites. After changing into cozy sweats, brewing some tea, and unloading the dishwasher, she couldn't procrastinate any longer.

She planted herself in front of the keyboard. The words finally began to form into coherent sentences and heartfelt thoughts. Lucy expressed her excitement at the newly discovered relationship, summarized her life in a page, and pasted photos of herself, Henry, Elsa, and the animals along the edge of the letter.

Lastly and hesitantly, she filled her Aunt in on the Alvarez cartel investigation, including the death of Gary Mercer, Uncle Henry's murderer. Should she even involve her at all? Could it bring harm to her in any way? Lucy closed her eyes for a moment and rubbed her skull, seeking a clear answer. There wouldn't be one.

If Aunt Lucia did help identify the thugs, it could save lives. Lucy printed out the pages including photos of the men at the airstrip and enclosed them in an envelope along with a little prayer.

In the morning, she'd drop the letter at the post office. After that, all she could do was wait and hope for a response.

—

Media House, a square, utilitarian box of a building without any identifying signage, stood in a business park several blocks from the Santa Monica Airport. Lucy enjoyed the campus-like feel of the area, which was populated by electronic gaming companies, small production start-ups, and an art and culinary school. Plus, hipster shops and restaurants were within an easy walk.

She and Michael had been at work for several hours when Marlene Simon showed up with Pete Anthony. Bea arrived minutes later and joined them all in the screening room. Ten cushy leather recliners, a counter full of goodies, and a giant projection screen waited for them to settle in.

Lucy had met Anthony before but had never worked with him. He was a tall, fit, dark-complexioned guy in his early forties. He had the kind of interesting, sometimes-handsome face that could anchor a "Stay Thirsty My Friends" beer ad. Word was that his favorite topics were himself, the Dodgers, and cooking. He stood a head taller than anyone in the room.

Marlene made the introductions.

Lucy was all too well aware Bea could spot a fellow Southerner as easily as a hawk spots a mouse with a limp from a half-mile up. Especially a tall dark and handsome one with a hint of insolence in his smile. Uh-oh.

Despite Bea's earlier kickass attitude toward Anthony, Lucy saw her slide into the back row next to the detective. In no time, the two seemed to be debating whether her hometown of Savannah or Anthony's New Orleans, had the better barbeque.

Lucy ventured a quick glance her friend's way and rolled her eyes. Then Michael called the group to attention.

"Thanks for coming, everybody," he said. "I know you're all busy so we'll get right to it. I hope this clip yields useful information. At least you'll see faces to put on your radar. Best case scenario, you'll notice someone you can ID. A long-shot, I know, but stranger things've happened, right?"

He pushed his hands into the front pockets of his faded jeans. "Any questions at this point?"

"Can we get hardcopy images of these guys?" Marlene asked.

Michael nodded. "We sent you all confidential headshots we've pulled from the digital feed. Anything else?"

The room went dead quiet as the lights dimmed.

Lucy's chest tightened. She braced herself for what would be a nasty walk down a nightmarish memory lane.

"Okay, without further ado, here we go." Michael sat next to Lucy in the front row and hit Play on a remote.

They all watched the seven-minute clip twice. When the lights came up, Lucy was curled up into herself, trying to hide her panicky breathing. Michael gave her shoulder a reassuring squeeze then stood to face the audience.

"Anything?" he asked. "Any familiar faces?"

Pete Anthony tapped away on his iPad, raised his hand quickly, then went back to typing for a moment.

"I think I got an ID," he finally said. All in the room turned his way. "I forwarded the photos you emailed us to a friend at HQ to run through facial recognition. We got a fast hit. I thought I recognized the big, tall dude, but the beard's new." He rubbed at his own chin stubble. "Looks like an ISIS mercenary now, but he's the grandson of one of the Medellin cartel founders in Columbia. He's a Stanford Business School grad. Go figure. Was supposedly being groomed to be one of Alvarez's top guns. Name's Valencia, Estevan Valencia. Word is he's their accountant. Follow the money trail, we should find him."

"I recognize him, too," Marlene said, "now that I can visualize him without the whiskers." She adjusted her glasses. "He's actually been on our radar for a while but dropped off the grid about a year ago."

Lucy rose in her seat and turned to face the group. She squeezed her ice-cold hands tightly into fists. "If this Valencia's any good at his job, that money trail's gonna be undecipherable, but Bea and I have a friend at a gaming company down the street who lives for undecipherables. Maybe he can help us. What do you think, Beebs?"

"Bijan? Oh, yeah. Brilliant idea. Let's go visit him right now. He likes surprises." She grabbed her purse and left Anthony behind with a look of hotness interruptus on his pretty face. "We'll get back with y'all later."

Lucy hopped to her feet, released her hands, and rubbed them together. When it came to the news, Bea moved faster than a hound on a blood scent.

"Wait," Marlene said as the two were almost out the door. "We have an LAPD unit who does this stuff. We should turn it over to them."

Lucy rolled her eyes. "This is the guy your cops call when they get anything complicated. Later, people."

They hustled out of the screening room.

# 12

Swathed in white like a mummified Lawrence of Arabia, Mercer sat up tall in his hospital bed. Surrounding him were three of his half-dozen trusted advisors. The business was volatile right now with challengers circling like sharks sniffing for blood in the water. His power group ensured that the Alvarez cartel remained not only in control of the black tar trade but also of an expanding criminal empire. They could show no weakness.

With Luis Alvarez's death and his own hospitalization, the competitors were already battling to fill the power vacuum. Mercer was well aware it was time to reconfirm his leadership, particularly to those who had the ability to spread doubt. Despite his damaged exterior, he knew that he was the one, the only one, who had the brains, drive, and steel to make the cartel the world-class success they all wanted.

He studied each face at his bedside and could feel their struggles to remain implacable under his scrutiny. Alvarez's former personal assistant, Brody Blackwell, was a legitimate big-time dancer/choreographer and head man with their porn ventures. His perfect body, copper dreads, and magnificent tattoos radiated a sexual magnetism that was often useful. A world-class pimp at heart, he was also a loose cannon.

"Brody," Mercer said, his tone grim, "I understand you've been recruiting white-silk girls again, baby *putas*, for select clientele." He struggled to enunciate. "What did I say about that when we last spoke?"

Brody tossed his dreads and tried to look innocent. It failed. He twitched in his seat. "Okay, you said to stay out of it. But I'm telling you, Gary, it's a goldmine. And procurement and disposal of the little bitches is a slam dunk. Hang out at the bus station for fifteen minutes, or at a runaway shelter..." He shrugged.

Mercer's felt his face crumple into a canvas of angry scar tissue. He lightly touched his cheek with his three-fingered hand. He saw Brody's eyes narrow as if anticipating danger.

"Luis Alvarez's proclivities for pre-pubescent girls, who he eventually got hooked on heroin and then discarded, was a major reason the man remained unfocused and ultimately failed at his business." Mercer's voice was like a rasp. "I'll tell you only one more time, Brody, it's not in our business plan. Too fucking dangerous. The authorities will look the other way until children are involved. If you can't accept my directive on this issue, I'm afraid working together will be impossible. No one is indispensable. Do you understand what I'm telling you?"

Brody stiffened and nodded. He picked at one of his dreads that was beaded with a silver bullet. Of his advisors, Brody was the wild child. Highly effective and creative, until he fucked up, then it could be epic.

With his hollow, lidless eyes, Mercer glanced again at Brody, then at Altamont, their enforcer. Would he have to use Alta's disciplinary skills against one of their own at some point?

Brilliantly resourceful, Altamont was a bowling ball of hard muscle whose ambitions rose only to creating Hell on Earth for the cartel's chosen victims. His tools of the trade were an ice pick and his teeth.

When he wasn't starring in a pornie, his common-law wife, Toulusa, liked to sit in a darkened room alone and sew soft, wet things together. Altamont managed to procure her an array of roadkill for his projects. Her stitches were perfect — she was making her lover a coat.

"I'm leaving the Burn Center next week, precisely eight days from today," Mercer announced. He adjusted the oxygen tube in his melted nostril holes. "I've engaged my own medical staff who'll finish my reconstruction and then stay with me at the penthouse until they're no longer necessary. Time to get back to work. Nice job on the Ukrainians, by the way, Altamont. Splattered across the alley behind a meatball restaurant." A scratchy laugh erupted from Mercer's throat. "Nice messaging. I have one more big surprise for the bastards but we'll discuss that later."

Altamont blinked acknowledgment.

"And of course, I hope all will find my appearance less unsettling soon. I've looked at hundreds of faces and think I've picked a lovely option. Toulusa has been my consultant. Altamont will harvest the subject." He dipped his head in a slight bow toward the enigmatic duo. "With support from an exclusive private surgery center in Santa Barbara and a world-renowned facial surgeon I've flown in from France, I'm ready to shed this burned man persona and take on something new." Saliva dripped from the edges of his mouth as he tried to smile.

He was pleased that Toulusa, seemed to find the fact that

Mercer was deciding which face to transplant onto his ruined visage, quite fascinating. Together they discussed the pros and cons of each subject as if they were casting a movie. Mercer put up with this spook of a woman because he was becoming rather attracted to her. He considered himself bisexual, but it had been a long time since his appetites included vaginas. More pragmatically, however, she was the only one who could control Altamont when he was in a frenzy with a need to inflict pain.

An alarm sounded on Mercer's iPad. He glanced at the screen then back at his team.

"Thank you for coming today, my friends. We shall soon meet again at the penthouse to review our progress." He waved them out of the room. They wished him well and filed into the hall as the volunteer girl, Alyssa, attempted to wheel her squeaky audiobooks cart through the door. Mercer saw her eyes widen with confusion as to the edgy-looking crew brushed by.

Mercer saw Brody visually feel her up with a wicked wink. A little gulp escaped her throat. She seemed ready to turn and bolt in the opposite direction.

"Alyssa, please come in," he said before she could flee. "So nice to see you. What have you brought me today?"

She turned her attention from his visitors, who quickly disappeared down the hall, back to her cart of goodies. She hesitated for an instant. "Hello, Mr. Mark," she said, a bit less stiffly than at their initial encounter the previous week. "I brought an audiobook about airplanes," she said. "It has fighters from World War II. You showed me that picture of you with your plane and I thought you might like this stuff."

"How thoughtful," he said, finding himself again entranced by her uncommon beauty. Had he wanted a woman's face, he would have chosen hers. But her doctor mommy would cause a major shit storm if baby girl disappeared. Not a time to risk distraction, he reminded himself. He had too many important plates spinning to risk one falling.

Mercer accepted the tape recorder and she showed him which buttons to push. The hand with three fingers was reasonably functional. "I'll listen to it tonight after dinner," he said, enjoying how she lit up with satisfaction at his interest. The girl wanted to please. How endearingly vulnerable and stupidly dangerous.

"Your voice is getting better," she said.

He nodded and dabbed at his mouth with a tissue. "Do you live nearby or is it a long commute to get here?"

"Nearby, Westwood area." A caution light flickered — never tell a stranger where you live. "You?"

"Westwood, too, near Century City in a big high-rise with a great view and a pool in every unit. We're neighbors. By the way, Alyssa, I mentioned you to my friend who's a dancer — he choreographed the Emmys last year. See the photo on top there. He's the guy with the dreadlocks who just left."

Alyssa plucked up the photo, took a long look then placed it back on the small pile of images. "He's cool-looking." She chewed at her sweet, full, bottom lip.

"He goes by a stage name, Michael O'Brody. He said he'd like to see what you've got. Why don't you check him out on YouTube? Has a music video coming up with a hot new artist from Australia and he's auditioning young, female dancers. You have any tape you can give me to pass on?"

"I can email you something," she said.

"Great." Mercer smiled and repeated his email address. Alyssa's eyes went glassy, likely with images of starring in a music video growing in her imagination. Then the joy drained from her face.

"My stepmother'd never let me do it. I'm sure she'd say I'm way too young."

"Really? Huh." He shrugged. "What would your real...I mean your birth-mother say? Is she as strict? Or not in your life?"

"Totally in my life," Alyssa said with a little blaze in her voice.

"I'm sorry, I don't mean to pry," Mercer said.

"Oh, it's okay." Alyssa let out a slow breath. "She's really strict, but in a different way. She might let me try it. She's in show business, well kinda — she's a TV reporter. But she gets it. She's more of an artist type."

"What's your mom's name?" Mercer asked, his curiosity rising. "Maybe I've heard of her."

"Beatrice Middleton. Goes by Jackson on-air because that was her married name when she started in LA. She was at KLAK but now she's at CNN. It's a better job. Maybe you've seen her on the news?"

Mercer barely controlled a fit of coughing. His brain seemed to shut down for an instant, then exploded like the Jeep fire that ruined his face and body. He sucked hard on his oxygen.

His head hummed as if it had been invaded by a colony of killer bees that were eating through his flesh. "Yes, I've seen her. She's good." Bees, Bea, Beatrice Middleton — buzz-fucking beautiful. This is her fucking kid. Fuck me.

"Are you okay, Mr. Mark?" Little Middleton's big hazel-colored eyes widened with concern.

"Yes, yes, just tired. Too much activity today. Forgive me." He could barely hear her above the noise in his skull.

"Cool, no worries. I'll go now. See you soon, Mr. Mark.

And I'll be sure to get you my audition tape."

"I'll look forward to that. Thanks again for the airplane book, Alyssa," he said, his voice a shaky whisper. His shoulders quivered with repressed glee.

# 13

An Iranian immigrant and former refugee in Finland, now a U.S. citizen, Bijan Rachmaji was the lead digital engineer at WarChallengeWorld. The game company cranked out digital fare featuring guerilla combat in all of its bloody brutality. A sweet, quiet guy who raised parakeets for fun, Bijan was thrilled to see Bea and Lucy traipse through the door holding a pizza box. He knew it had to be his favorite— Thai chicken barbeque.

"Ladies, ladies — welcome, welcome. What have I done to deserve such a mahvelous and unexpected visit?"

Lucy found a spot for the pizza atop a pile of magazines on the edge of his action-figure-packed desk. Then she gave Bijan a huge, happy hug. Slightly overweight with curly brown hair, he always had the faint scent of having slept in his clothes.

He hugged Bea with the same enthusiasm.

"Sorry to barge in on you," Lucy said, but we have a thing we need to talk with you about. Time is of the essence."

"A thing. Nice. Lay it on me, girlies."

"It's following some money, big honey," Bea said, grinning.

"Could be some contract cash in it for you," Lucy added.

"I can always use some extra *dinero*. I so enjoyed tracking your bad guys last time. Finding the hidden treasure, it's one of the ultimate games, right?" His eyes danced like fireflies at the prospect of the challenge.

"I swear to God you should come work for us as a forensic accountant," Bea said.

"Then I can't blow up digital shit all the time. I'll keep my day job, thanks." He smiled and opened the pizza box. "Dig in, ladies," he said.

"All for you, my dear," Lucy said.

"Nuh-uh, I'll take a piece." Bea passed Bijan a napkin then helped herself.

"My kind of woman." He winked at Bea before taking a large chomp from a slice. He moaned in pizza ecstasy while he chewed. "Can you fill me in on the particulars? I'm off work tomorrow so maybe I can get started right away."

"That would be awesome," Lucy said. Then she gave him the scoop on Estevan Valencia.

—

Bea walked into the house and kicked off her way-too-high-heeled shoes while still holding her jacket, purse, and a large pizza. Was she actually getting sick of clacking around in those uncomfortable, expensive, tree-top-tall pumps she'd always loved? She chuckled to herself. It was a slippery slope. It would start with going to flats, and the next thing you know, she'd stop shaving her legs and start wearing Teva sandals. Bea wiggled her toes.

Her stomach growled. The teaser slice of pizza she'd nabbed from Bijan whetted her appetite for more. She was too tired to cook and Dexter would soon be home from basketball practice, ravenous, as usual. She put the box on the kitchen island, dropped her purse on a bar stool, then returned to the front hall to hang up her coat. She tripped over Dexter's new neon-orange trainers that lay askew next to the closet door. Her boy liked shoes as much as she did — what was that old adage about the apple not falling far from the tree?

Bea went to the refrigerator, pulled out a pitcher of sweet tea and poured herself a glass. She savored the quiet moment, yet deeply felt the absence of her children and the crazy but wonderful energy they brought to the household. She was surprised when Dexter walked into the kitchen, chatting on his cell phone like he'd been hanging out at home all day. A niggle of concern began to ping on her motherly radar. "No b-ball tonight?"

He shook his head, placed two pieces of pizza on the counter for Bea then headed up the stairs to his room with the box in hand, still talking on his phone.

"Nice to see you, too," she called to Dexter. "And thanks for the two measly slices."

Before she could follow up with words like rude and surly, Bea's cellphone rang. She glanced at the caller ID and smiled. Alyssa.

"Baby girl! I miss you so much. How're you doing, darlin'?"

"Hi, Mom. You won't guess what happened today."

"Do tell. An 'A' on a math test?"

"Get real, Ma," Alyssa said. "I might have a chance to be in a music video. This guy who's in the Burn Center, a patient, knows this choreographer named Michael O'Brody who did the Emmys last year. He wants to see my demo tape. I texted you his link on YouTube. He's amazing."

Bea gulped. "Well, that's pretty, uh, cool. A music video."

It was one thing to have her daughter perform at a recital or a dance competition, but a music video was something else. So many were over-the-top sexy and objectified women as solely tits and ass. Images of young dancers and singers twerking their little butts off made her mildly nauseous. Why couldn't Alyssa be interested in joining a classical ballet company or a folk dancing troupe?

"Mr. Mark, he's the patient, I sent him a clip from my spring performance and he loved it. Forwarded it to O'Brody and he wants me to audition." Alyssa continued, gushing with enthusiasm. "Michael O'Brody wants me to audition! Like next Wednesday, over in North Hollywood."

"This is all happening pretty fast, Alyssa. What do you really know about this dancer guy?"

"Mr. Mark, he's really nice. I bring him audiobooks and we "schmooze," as Daddy would put it. Mr. Mark says O'Brody's one of the best, and it could be a big break for me. Can you believe it, Mom?"

Bea walked into the living room and collapsed onto the couch. She couldn't help feel her daughter's excitement and didn't want to quash it, but she was mostly terrified. Terrified as hell. Her baby girl was growing way up too fast. "Have you talked to your dad and Deborah about this?"

There was a pause. "Yes."

"And?"

"They're not too enthused. They don't get dance. Daddy kinda does, but Deborah, no way. She's against it. And he won't go up against her."

"I see," Bea said. "You're barely thirteen. I can't say they're wrong."

There was a sniffle. "Mom, please, you or Dex can even come with me. This is like a dream come true."

A nightmare you mean. Bea sighed. "Tell me more about these people."

"Mr. Mark, he's brave, has lots of pain. He's burned so bad

you wouldn't believe. Looks like a zombie. Oops, I'm sorry, he's not a zombie at all."

"I get the picture, Alyssa, and I respect your attempt to be sensitive."

"Anyhow, he was burned in South America or someplace like that, a couple of months ago. He showed me a picture of what he used to look like. He was really cute. He's old, but not too old, like in his mid-thirties, Lucy's age. Has an airplane, too. He's seen you on TV, by the way, Mom. Thinks you're really good. Will you help me, please, Mom? Talk to Daddy and Deborah?"

"Listen, honey, I promise you nothing, but is Deborah home?"

"Yeah, she just finished feeding the baby," Alyssa said.

Bea could hear the cautious excitement in her daughter's voice.

"Could I speak with her?"

"Uh-huh, I'll get her. Try to convince her, Mom. I have to do this or I'll die."

"Calm down, drama queen. I know it's hard to keep things in perspective, but this will not be your only opportunity."

"You don't know that!"

"Alyssa, get me Deborah, please, daughter."

Bea took a couple of deep breaths to help stem the spike in her blood pressure as she waited for Deborah to get to the phone. They exchanged expected pleasantries, discussed the situation, and finally came away with a compromise. They'd both meet with Garrett Mark the following day and get the scoop on O'Brody and the video. If they decided to let Alyssa attend the audition, Bea would definitely go along to check out the situation. If things weren't copasetic, Alyssa would be banished to pink tights and toe shoes.

# 14

In the wee hours of the morning, as Bea lay in bed obsessing about her children, a call came in. She didn't recognize the number, so she let it ring through, put a pillow over her head, and tried to force herself to sleep.

It didn't work.

In lieu of screaming in frustration and waking up the neighborhood, she sighed and picked up her cell phone. Bea squinted and held it close to her nose — she still refused to admit that she could use some reading glasses. The screen indicated that there was a voice message.

Pushing the hair out of her eyes, she listened — it was Marlene Simon.

"Sorry to disturb you, Beatrice, but Pete and I are in Long Beach — huge warehouse fire. Started in a neighborhood restaurant that's a known hangout for the Ukrainian mob. Thought you and Lucy might want to come down. Could be a story here. I'm texting you our location."

The Ukrainian mob. Again.

Bea sat up, threw off her covers, and dialed Lucy. She turned on the lamp next to her bed and commenced rounding up some clothes.

Lucy picked up on the third ring. Her voice was groggy. "This better be good, Beebs."

"Hey, girl, I need a stringer, a freelance camera, immediately. You're it. I'm not officially on the job today, so grab your gear and meet me in Long Beach ASAP. I'll text you the address."

There was a pause, then Lucy said, "I need more incentive than a simple job offer to extricate myself from my lover's arms. You know what time it is? He's so warm," she cooed, sounding like she was snuggling further into that embrace instead of disengaging.

"How about the Ukrainian mob's headquarters burning down? And warehouses all around it about to go up in flames? That do it for incentive? Marlene called and gave me a heads-up."

There was a short pause, then, "On my way." Lucy disconnected.

—

Dawn broke over the city as Bea sped down the 405. The hazy weather effect over the ocean known as "June Gloom" had settled in early this year, but she could still see black smoke on the misty horizon. Local news and police helicopters were beginning to collect like gnats overhead. Morning traffic was building, the lanes started to fill up and slow down.

Bea turned on the radio but nothing came through pertaining to the fire. It wouldn't be long before reports would be hitting the metro area news. On her way, she'd called in to CNN and they'd given her the okay to officially be on the clock. She didn't mention that she'd hired Lucy. HR would go crazy with unfilled-out forms and liability terrors. But, hey, a girl's gotta do what a girl's gotta do, right?

Twenty minutes and a large cup of gas station coffee later, she pulled into a parking space eight blocks from the corner where she was to meet up with Marlene. Bea crawled out of the car and took a breath of ugly, burned air. A familiar voice called from behind her.

"Bea, wait for me." Lucy panted as she approached, camera and pack clutched in her hands. "Let's go."

Lucy didn't stop as she passed, so Bea sprinted to catch up. She'd actually gone with jeans and Nikes today and was able to enjoy the feel of running. As a former USC basketball player, Bea could still move.

Marlene and Pete Anthony were camped next to the fire chief's mobile command unit when Bea and Lucy rushed up. A two-alarm? Three-alarm? More? Bea quickly counted seven engines, four ladder trucks, and several rescue vehicles, with additional personnel still rolling in. She noted this info on her iPad as Lucy recorded the visuals. Firefighters were everywhere, with cops and news reporters second and third in population. Huge hoses spewed water, drenching the adjoining rooftops.

"There's an illegal fireworks warehouse five-buildings downwind," Marlene said. Her long black trench coat had her looking like Keanu Reeves in a film noir version of The Matrix.

"Oh, my God," Bea said. "Explosives. Anybody know how much stuff they have stored?"

"Huh-uh, not yet. The owner can't be reached," Anthony piped in. "Asshole probably left the goddamn country already." His voice was low and sarcastic. He touched Bea's shoulder then moved off toward a group of law enforcement folks striding quickly his way.

Lucy waggled her eyebrows at Bea, who tried to ignore her.

Marlene startled as a new source of fire erupted with a whoosh atop a neighboring building. "LAFD's gonna clear us all out of here if they can't slow this monster real fast."

"See you later then," Lucy said. "I'm gonna get some shots before they start shutting things down."

"Be careful, Lucy," Bea yelled as her friend dashed toward the action.

Anthony was soon a quarter-block away, gesticulating up a storm. He appeared to be giving directives to a half-dozen beat cops and a tall, dark-haired woman in her early thirties. She wore a navy-blue Port of Long Beach Sheriff windbreaker. Bea saw Pete give Lucy a quick raise of the chin as she passed by, then immediately returned to his conversation. The guy was intense.

"Let's go talk to the fire chief," Bea said to Marlene.

The detective nodded agreement. "A whole passel of arson investigators has been running around. A half-hour ago the chief said they didn't have anything. Maybe they do now." A blast of wind from the ocean blew her long, dark coat into the air like bat wings. The fire crackled and greedily breathed in the oxygen.

The two women headed for the command unit.

—

Lucy pulled a lanyard with her KLAK-TV press credentials from her pocket and hung it around her neck, hoping nobody would notice the expired date on the ID. She was a familiar face to many of the cops and firefighters, so odds were good they'd leave her alone. Until, of course, she wandered into places off-limits to the press, which was where she did her best work.

After setup shots of the fighters on the job, stretching their lines, super-soaking the neighborhood, and risking their lives as routinely as many went for a morning run, Lucy found her way back behind the restaurant. Acrid smoke burned her eyes, and gray-black ash snowed down onto her camera and her hair. The bitterness stung her lips. She pulled on a Dodgers cap she'd stuffed into her equipment vest.

Behind this eatery, which the Ukrainians supposedly used as a central gathering place, the smoking ruins of a blown-up panel van lay wasted. Its nose had crashed through the restaurant's kitchen door. Half the vehicle was inside the structure, and what was left of the rear end stuck out into the alley between two mangled dumpsters. The smell of gasoline and burned rubber was dizzying. Lucy recorded the images and immediately emailed them to Bea.

"Back away from there," a man yelled, clearly pissed. "Back away, you idiot, now. This is a crime scene. You'll compromise evidence. Damn media. Get the hell outta here." He ran in front of her, hands out like he was trying to stop traffic. The guy wore an LAFD sweatshirt and a battered white hardhat. He was short, slim, and wiry, with a mouth as big as he was.

Lucy scowled. "I'm just doing my job, so lose the attitude."

He mumbled into his radio and three young cops magically appeared with yellow plastic crime scene tape they began to string around the perimeter. The LAFD guy looked smug. "Please leave now, ma'am, this area's off-limits," he said with a bit more cordiality since his minions were around to witness any bad behavior. Lucy nodded to one of the guys she'd known from when he was a rookie in West Hollywood.

"You think this van slammed into the restaurant and exploded?" Lucy asked the LAFD hardhat guy. "We talking arson?"

"When we collect all the evidence, we'll let the media

know." He turned and walked toward the blasted-out van.

Lucy snuck close-ups of the vehicle then took off in the opposite direction, winding her way through back alleys until she arrived at the fireworks factory. The faint but deadly smell of gunpowder and sulfur enhanced the stench of the fire as it ate its rabid way toward the warehouse's lethal contents. She certainly didn't plan to stay long. The wind was picking up from the bay, and bright sparks danced overhead like dervishes.

As Lucy circled the old, brick warehouse, a dark-skinned police officer in her mid-twenties, rounded the corner toward her with several colleagues following in her wake. Their eyes glanced nervously at the sky.

"You need to clear out of here, miss," she said as they passed by. "They're gonna drop that pink fire-retardant glop on this place any sec."

"Isn't that stuff for brushfires?" Lucy asked. The whomp-whomp of rotors seemed to be getting closer. Then the whine of a fixed-wing aircraft droned overhead.

"I think they're desperate," one of the other young officers shouted back.

Lucy hesitated.

The woman cop frowned at her. "Come on ma'am. News crew or not, you got to get out of here." She signaled for Lucy to follow. "Let's go, right now."

As Lucy was about to trail the police and seek safety from the retardant, a dark sedan with deeply tinted glass windows turned into the alley, trolling slowly in her direction. The vibes were strange — something felt off. What was a blacked-out late-model Audi doing cruising the area during a major fire?

Lucy's phone chimed. She dipped into her pocket and saw a text from Bea. "Get the hell out. Fire's ready to jump again.

We're all being pushed back."

The Audi eased to a crawl. A feral fight-or-flight instinct rose fast under Lucy's skin. She took a sideways glance at the driver as he pulled by. Through the smoky glass, she caught sight of the shadowy face.

The recognition was like a taser strike. Lucy slumped against the side of the warehouse, stunned. Thomas Rubio, real name Jorge Cardenas, had posed as a news photographer at KLAK. Under Mercer's orders, he'd tried to kill her. A few days after the attempt, he was spotted at the scene of a huge apartment complex blaze where an important witness and her family had lived. She'd also seen him in Mexico. Shit.

Maybe Cardenas, the fire-starter, was back in action. Was he working under the surviving auspices of the Alvarez gang? Fire seemed to be his *modus operandi*. It wasn't enough to kill the four Ukrainian mobsters — burning out their main gathering place offered a great exclamation point at the end of the bloody sentence. Or more likely, the final fuck you.

As the car pulled past, she tried to catch the license plate number. It was mud-spattered and unreadable. She took a quick photo — maybe the lab could decipher something. Then, the Audi slowed to a stop. The driver's window began to roll down and eyes flashed in the side mirror. What the hell? Had he recognized her? Lucy clutched her camera tight and fled in the opposite direction.

Just off the alley behind the warehouse, she'd noted a narrow passageway that cut between the buildings. Wide enough only for garbage cans and pedestrians, Lucy turned and ran for all she was worth toward the flashing lights where the walkway spilled out onto the main drag. Before she could reach the end, the trucks and radio cars had pulled back and flame retardant rained from the sky like an explosion of pink bubble gum.

Lucy pressed herself into a doorway and shielded her camera as the nasty slurry fell around her. It dripped down the walls of the warehouse and adjoining buildings like icing on a birthday cake. The noxious odor — eau de new car, times ten — made Lucy nauseous. The fumes were probably already planting cancer cells in her lungs. She drew up the neck of her T-shirt to cover her nose, but it did little good.

Lucy took off down the street, sidestepping puddles of Pepto-Bismol goop. The morning sky, now dusk-dark and ominous, felt as if a tornado was about to hit. There was a strange stillness in the atmosphere, despite all the activity.

Lucy picked up her pace.

When she finally caught up with Bea, her friend's face brightened with relief. "Oh, thank God."

"Bea." Lucy gasped for air. She put her camera and gear down on the sidewalk and pressed the aching stitch in her side. "I saw Rubio, I mean, Cardenas."

She tried to slow her breathing. "In a car behind the fireworks warehouse. It was him. Jesus. Another fire. One of those freaks who gets off on watching his sicko handiwork."

"Slow down, girl." Bea handed Lucy a bottle of water. She rinsed her mouth out and spit in the gutter then drained the rest immediately.

Lucy continued. "Jorge Cardenas, Alvarez and Mercer's henchman, may have started this whole thing. You know who I'm talking about — Tom Rubio, the guy who posed as our photog?"

"Yes, of course. Y'all think I'd ever forget that piece of shit?" Bea rubbed the shoulder where she'd once been shot. Cardenas had been partially responsible.

Marlene jogged up to the two women, her face smeared

with ash. "*Oy vey!* Come on, sisters, the fire chief is gonna talk to us. Word is we've got arson, a hundred percent."

"I got great images of a bombed-out van. Crashed into the back of the restaurant. It plowed right into the kitchen."

"That's where they suspect it started," Marlene said.

"And I'm damn sure I know who started it," Lucy added, still breathing hard.

Then a massive explosion rocked the ground on which they stood. Lucy's knees buckled. She clutched Bea's arm and they both went down. Windows erupted above and piercing glass hail showered the sidewalk, biting their skin like wasps.

# 15

Gary Mercer lay on the table in the OR at a private Santa Barbara plastic-surgery clinic and smiled at the ceiling. Having just enjoyed Daybreak News 9 which featured exploding fireworks, screaming ambulances, and harried firefighters — he decided to give Cardenas a big bonus for the extravaganza. The Ukrainians, what was left of them, had gotten the message. Their early morning phone call of contrition had made that clear.

He reached out and touched the donor on the gurney next to his. The man's skin was still warm. Mercer wondered if Brody would be able to identify his brother's face, or if it would be unrecognizable when stretched across Mercer's own, less defined, bone structure. He'd warned Brody only last week that there would be no more procuring of underage girls. Then, two more baby *putas* in bloody white silk panties were discovered near the Hollywood reservoir, molested and dead.

To Mercer's deep chagrin, the cops were all over it. If Brody didn't shape up in the wake of his brother's disappearance and quasi-reappearance, it would be the dancer's own mug that would be repurposed next time.

Mercer smiled. Toulusa would have a new pocket for her coat, and it would look a lot like a well-known Hollywood choreographer.

A blue-flocked group of surgeons and specialists fluttered around the operating room, readying for the hours-long surgery. A round-faced nurse behind a surgical mask turned on the sedative drip to begin the process. Mercer's last coherent thought was a question — could Brody Blackwell be trusted to do his bidding with young Alyssa? Brody would have to understand that this was not a nod to additional child procurement, but a final masterful conclusion. Mercer would think hard on this as he recovered with his lovely new face.

—

Car alarms still blared and Lucy's ears continued to ring as she, Bea, Marlene, and dozens of others milled around the paramedic's trucks where blast victims were being treated for bruises and cuts. Glass shards embedded in their skin were tweezed out and bandages applied. The direst cases had been triaged off to local hospitals. Over fifty had been wounded in the explosion.

Pete had been in the fire chief's van when the boom happened and had escaped injury. He hustled up to the women with a bag of burritos and sodas he'd scored from one of the food trucks that'd arrived on scene. Despite some minor trauma, all were still standing and ravenous. They dug in appreciatively.

Lucy had agreed to follow the detectives back to the station to officially ID Cardenas. She'd passed on a photo of him from KLAK to get them started on facial recognition. He'd called himself Thomas Rubio, then Cardenas, but who knew who he really was?

Bea would return to the office and file her story. Lucy had recorded a brief standup of Bea interviewing the fire chief and the detectives as they summarized the disaster. She forwarded her best cover shots over to CNN.

Pete walked Bea to her car, which was only a few blocks away. The two crunched awkwardly through mounds of glass and other fallen detritus. Lucy watched them turn the corner and disappear.

"What's that about?" she asked Marlene as she munched on a second burrito.

"Won't turn out well, never does with him," Marlene said. "I warned her, but what's life without a few lovely lapses in judgment, right?"

Lucy smiled. "I'm living with one now. Man, when something like that's good, it's spectacular." She knew she was smitten with Michael Burleson, but part of her was still waiting for the other shoe to drop and crush her heart. She rubbed at her chest.

—

Bea filed the warehouse fire story — it was a doozy, maybe even a prize-winner. Lucy's images were amazing but HR was still in a huff over the lack of official freelance paperwork.

Bea was coming down fast from an adrenaline high. Her cell phone chirped. If it was anything critical, they'd leave a message. She checked her watch as she trudged toward her car. It was just after noon. How could that be true? Dirty and wounded, she was exhausted and ready to head back to bed. The little cuts on her skin burned and itched. Minute glass shards sparkled on her black and gray Nikes. This was supposed to have been a long-needed day off.

With the press of a fob, the Beemer's locks thunked open. Checking her watch again, Bea groaned. A calendar event blinked. She was due to meet Deborah at the Burn Center at 1:30. They had an appointment to talk with her patient about the music video Alyssa was so hot on. At her daughter's insistence, Bea had gone online and checked out O'Brody. He seemed like a legitimately successful dancer and choreographer. His moves on YouTube were, in fact, pretty damn amazing. But who was this burn patient dude and how did he figure in? As usual, Deborah had been vague and hurried on the phone. You'd think the fate of the world relied on her every breath.

Bea was about to slide into the driver's seat when she hesitated. The car had been thoroughly cleaned by an expensive detailer in West LA. She knew she looked like she'd been swabbing down a truck garage and smelled like burning plastic. It was making her dizzy. She didn't want to contaminate the clean car. Too soon it would again smell of unwashed teen boys, harsh coffee, and bacon, egg, and cheese biscuits.

In the trunk, Bea opened her earthquake emergency box. Along with the water, first aid kit and energy bars were an old pair of grayish Chuck Taylors and a terry cloth beach cover-up. It looked like a washrag but smelled benign. She grabbed the clothes and ducked between her open front door and the large SUV next to it. She stripped off the ash-covered shirt she'd pulled out of the laundry before dawn and slid the cover-up over her head. It was as soft as an old bedspread. She dropped the rest of her clothes and shoes into a Von's supermarket eco-bag and slipped on ancient blue flip-flops. The image of her foot was embedded deeply in the rubber.

The sound of strong, slow clapping emanated from nearby. Bea looked up. A middle-aged construction worker and his teen-aged sidekick sat low in a banged-up Chevy truck a few spaces down. The older guy let loose a wolf howl. She gave him a mock bow and went about her business. Muttered asshole under her breath.

In the newly detailed silver surface of her Beemer, Bea saw her reflection. The hair was wild. She kind of liked it. Too many years of being perfectly coiffed were getting tedious. Maybe she'd let it go natural. She'd been considering it. Recent travel home to Savannah and the down-to-earth, life-or-death nature of her time there had taken an emotional toll. Fewer things really mattered now. Life clutter was beginning to fall away. Part of her wanted to hang on, another part knew she'd already slipped too far.

Bea sighed deeply. There was no stopping change. After chomping a big bite out of a long-expired energy bar, she tossed the bag of nasty clothing in the trunk and finally crawled into the front seat. The worker pulled his truck out past her and flashed a grin. The teenager scrunched way down in his seat.

This was not a day she could manage much reaction. Weary to the bone, Bea took another long breath and realized she couldn't meet Deborah to talk with her burn patient today. There was no way she could make it home, shower, and arrive at Cedars-Sinai in time. They'd have to reschedule. A pang of guilt piled on top of exhaustion.

Bea punched her car ignition button and the Bluetooth went live. She dialed Deborah. Surprisingly, the busy, busy woman picked up.

"Hi, Bea. I was about to call you to cancel for this afternoon."

Bea smiled in relief. She didn't have to be the one to bail. Small mercies.

Deborah continued. "I went down to Mr. Mark's room

and he's left the Burn Center, checked out this morning. I can hardly believe it — the fellow's scheduled for another surgery on Friday."

"I wonder why he split? Sounds foolhardy."

"Definitely. I spoke with our director and he said a whole medical team showed up and hauled him away. Very unusual. I hope he'll be all right."

Bea slowly pulled forward out of her parking space. "So, what's this guy's story? He a dancer, too?"

"Our records on him are kind of sketchy. He's a businessman, lives somewhere over near Westwood. Was flown up around a month ago on a private plane from Mexico where he was supposedly vacationing. Burned horribly in a car explosion. Given the level of damage to his body, we were surprised he was still alive."

"He shared some of that with Alyssa," Bea said. An uneasy feeling began to skitter beneath the surface of her skin. She had to control her paranoia — Mercer was dead and gone.

"Quite honestly," Deborah said, "he seemed a little too interested in our daughter."

Bea winced. She hated to admit it, but whenever Deborah referred to Alyssa as our daughter, it pissed the hell out of her. She's my daughter, she wanted to yell. The pain of not having Alyssa in her life day-to-day was terrible and she resented her ex-husband and this abrasive new wife for taking her away.

"Mr. Mark's unusual disappearance seals the deal for me," Deborah said. "I don't think we should allow Alyssa to participate in this video. Something doesn't seem quite right."

It galled Bea to completely agree. "She'll have other opportunities when she's little older and more mature. She won't buy that reasoning, but I'll call after y'all have finished dinner — tell her our decision. Sound okay?"

Deborah switched into her irritating lecture voice. "Yes, fine. I think it'll be better coming from you. I have enough drama with baby Arielle to deal with, let alone a young teen. She's not going to give up on this easily."

Bea struggled to remain composed. "By the way," she said, switching her focus to the burn patient again. Something about an LA businessman flown up from Mexico after a car explosion was ringing alarms. "This Mark guy..."

"Yes, Garrett Mark."

Bea could feel her hands beginning to grasp the steering wheel like she was strangling something. Someone. Garrett Mark. Gary Mercer. Impossible. "For Alyssa's sake, Deborah, it might be good to know more about him, in case he tries to contact her. Not that he's likely to bother with a twelve-and-a-half-year-old kid, but do a little checking on him, would you?"

Deborah acquiesced. "Okay, I'll see what I can find."

Bea disconnected. She realized she'd stopped dead in the middle of the boulevard. Horns honked. She pulled forward and proceeded toward La Brea where she'd turn downhill toward Santa Monica and the ocean. Although probably counter-intuitive, she preferred surface streets when she was ruminating.

Was she being crazy, thinking that a burn patient at Cedars could be somebody they were certain was dead? She was most likely freaking herself out for no reason. She contemplated running her thoughts past Lucy, but it would be cruel to put her grieving friend through unnecessary anxiety. It was all probably bullshit anyway. She mentally kicked herself for being so, what? Obsessed? So silly. Right?

Bea glanced at her phone and realized there was still a voice message waiting from an earlier call. She pressed Play.

"Mrs. Jackson, uh, Ms. Middleton, this is Coach Hewitt

calling. Give me a ring back at your convenience. Our basketball post-season strength and endurance training has been going on for a week and I haven't seen hide nor hair of Dexter. I've got his first-team prep All-State trophy here, too. He's not answering my emails and I'm getting concerned. Thank you, ma'am. Hope to talk with you soon."

Bea's head began to hum — a migraine singing at the door. What the hell was going on with her child that he hadn't even talked with his coach of the last three years, a man who had been a major mentor, to discuss his plans to switch sports? Dexter was playing way too fast and loose with his future and with his friends. Her vision began to pixelate and she groped in her purse for her meds.

# 16

In a small conference room outside the Homicide Division bullpen, Marlene Simon huddled around a table with Pete Anthony and a pile of photographs. The air smelled a mix of Irish Spring soap and burned coffee. She noted that Anthony's dark springy hair was wet from a shower. He wore a fresh form-fitting navy-blue LAPD golf shirt and blue jeans, pressed with a crease. Marlene, definitely feeling like she'd slept in her clothes for a week, was still dressed in her post-fire black slacks and a once-crisp white blouse, now peppered with ash and streaked with grime. She remained intent on the pile of screengrabs before her, tapping a ballpoint pen on the top photo.

Pete gently removed the glasses from her nose, held them up to the light and shook his head.

"Stop, now I'm blind," she said, frowning.

"I hate dirty glasses. I hate looking at people wearing dirty glasses. How can you see through these things?" He plucked a tissue from a box on the table, carefully cleaned the lenses, and then handed them back to her. "And stop tapping that damn pen."

She accepted the specs with a roll of her eyes then slipped them back on. "Jeeze, Louise. The guy in the picture with the beard is actually a golden retriever. I feel like I've had cataracts removed." She smiled. "You're way weird about glasses, Peter Pan, but thanks."

Anthony chuckled and tossed the tissue, hitting a corner bin like a Nerf Ball pro. "So, we've got ID on a couple of these assholes." He took the pile of photos from the session with Lucy and Burleson and arranged them in a razor-straight line across the table.

Marlene let him indulge in this compulsive behavior. It sometimes drove her nuts, but she appreciated his organizational skills. "We've got Jorge Cardenas whom Lucy thinks is the fire-starter," she pointed her finger at his thin, pale face. "And this is Estevan Valencia, the Stanford MBA accountant. Gary Mercer's dead, and who are the rest of these goons? Local help? Or real players?"

"We got nothing through facial recognition," Anthony said. "Too bad it's not as effective as on TV." He snorted his disdain. "Ten seconds and you've got a name, address, and jock size."

"Arson investigators have anything?" Marlene edged a photo out of sync then guiltily realigned it, a little smirk on her lips.

"Only that the van was a point of origin like Lucy thought. Said they used C-4 plastic explosives to detonate and gasoline as a further accelerant. Pretty standard terrorist shit. We've got to track down this Cardenas asshole. He's not just a fire pro, he's gets off on it. Why else would he be cruising behind a warehouse that's ready to blow unless he's getting one hell of a hard-on?"

"We need ears on the street," Marlene said. "An arsonist

this sophisticated is going to be tough to catch. The main way guys like him are usually nailed, if ever, is because they can't keep their big mouths shut."

Anthony nodded. "No shit, *grande* egos." He did a quick iPhone check then placed it on the table next to his notebook. "We have informants close to anyone in the Alvarez cartel?"

"We've never been able to manage that," Marlene said. She ran her hand through her hair and her fingers came back streaked with soot.

"Maybe Bea Middleton has ideas about somebody to approach," Anthony said, eyeing his partner's hand with disgust.

"Yeah, yeah, a little soot. I'm about to go home and take a shower, so zip that pie hole," she said. "And, yes, maybe Bea or Lucy might have some ideas. They've been all over these bastards. Of course, I'm sure you'll make a date to have dinner with Bea to discuss the situation."

Pete Anthony gave a fleeting, secretive smile.

Marlene laughed out loud. "You're not too sure about how your mesmerizing presence is going to work on her, are you, hot stuff? Not your usual cop groupie. Hell, she's been married to an NBA star and an Emmy award-winning news producer."

Anthony's face fell. Marlene actually felt bad for an instant — she'd never seen him doubt his appeal to the opposite sex before. She felt she had to throw him a minor lifeline. "But, big boy, you do have your charms."

"You think she'd, uh, go out with me?" he asked. He'd never ever asked her opinion on anything in his personal life before.

"Never knew you to not give it a try, even when the red and blue lights are flashing a big, fat DISASTER AHEAD sign," she said, then smiled again. "Plus, she told me she makes really bad choices when it comes to men, so I'd say you have a good chance of at least scoring a business lunch."

Anthony's eyes narrowed, and he rose from the table.

—

"Lucy-loo," Bijan called into the voice mail. "Call me, Lucia. Got some dirt on this accountant dude, Valencia." The sound of Black Sabbath screamed in the background. The guy prided himself on being a '70s throwback. He even had an old poster of Farrah Fawcett in her nipple-defining orange swimsuit on his wall.

Lucy smiled and pressed Call Back. He picked up immediately.

"Hey, Bijan, what've you got for us?" Lucy felt a mix of excitement and dread.

"I gotta tell ya, your man, Valencia, is a busy fuckin' bee." The music was turned down a few decibels. "Cha-ching to the max — laundering more cash than God. Billions, with a B. Shell companies, legit companies, off-shore and international accounts, probably has shit stuffed under his mother's mattress, too. He's definitely your money guy."

Not millions, billions. Lucy was staggered by the sheer volume — organized crime was one of the biggest economies in the world. Her stomach roiled. It hit her how dangerous poking around in hidden corners and turning over big dark rocks of the cartel cash machine could be.

"How do you find all this info, Bijan?"

"Game boy by day, flying-fingered forensic accounting phenom by night."

"I'm serious." This was not a video game to Lucy, but it was a game nevertheless, a lethal one.

"So am I, *chica*."

Lucy paused. "I'm worried we've asked you to take way

too big a risk. Bea and I both — well, actually, me, particularly — have a teeny-weeny tendency to step off the edge before looking down and noticing the alligators."

Bijan chuckled. "I can see your little baby brow furrowing right now. I'm cool with this, Lucy or I wouldn't have signed on. You're not the only one who hires me to do this shit, but you are the hottest. My brother works white-collar crimes for the CIA, treasury division. He tosses me a few access crumbs now and again, not that I couldn't hack in without them."

"That's criminal, Bijan."

"Criminal to some, Robin Hood to others," he said. The sound of Bijan digging into something crunchy halted the conversation for a moment. He loved Doritos. "I also developed a follow-the-money simulation game for the Feds called SUDS — the Sourcing Unreported Dinero System. It's pretty cool. They love it. Now go share this scrap of intel with your minions but leave my name out, of course." Another crunchy chomp. "Call me if you need details. We'll meet. This phone we're talking on is a burner, but nevertheless, I don't want to say more. It pays to be paranoid."

"Yeah, for sure." Lucy was glad to confirm that Valencia was big-time, bigger than they even thought — but knew she was walking a shaky tightrope with this information. A wrong move and it could let them fall, hard. "Thank you so much for doing this, honeybun. Your check'll be in the mail any day now."

"A couple more of those barbeque chicken Thai pizzas would do the trick," he said. "As long as you and Bea are the delivery team."

"Count on it," Lucy said. "See you soon, with food. And again, thank you."

Ozzy Osbourne's raspy, dirge-like voice grated and the

sound of Black Sabbath rose again to gut-pounding levels. Bijan wailed along off-key.

—

Dexter sat at a corner table in the Starbucks near Alyssa's school at the edge of Westwood, checking messages on his phone, or at least pretending to. He was having a hard time concentrating lately, even on the mundane crap.

Nearby, several students poured over laptops. A gray-haired couple with a Yorkie waited for their beverages. The steamer hissed and the smell of fresh brew permeated everything. He thought about the coffeehouse in Savannah last summer, of friends from the high school art program, about the beautiful Chinese girl with the long black hair, and endless pieces of Lowcountry peach pie with whipped cream. He tried not to think of the other stuff, the bad stuff he still dragged around like a heavy, rollerless suitcase of horrors. Therapy was helping, but he wanted to reset his life backward a year and start over. That wasn't going to happen.

He missed his sister. As annoying as she could be, Alyssa still had the sparkle of innocence and a sassy, unconditional love for her big brother. More and more often, he needed to feel that lightness to keep from going somewhere too dark to see. It had been a while since they'd hung out together, just the two of them without the parents lurking nearby, fishing for gossip and ready to offer unwanted guidance.

Dexter looked up as Alyssa walked through the door. Dark hair with springy nickel-sized curls, big green eyes compliments of Strauss family DNA, and fine features. He was shocked at how beautiful she'd become. Today, he saw his baby sister through a new lens, and the view was unsettling. She was growing up fast.

As usual, Aly was oblivious to the effect she created. It

wouldn't be long before she would wield the power it gave her. Until then, she was a butterfly still struggling out of the cocoon. She jogged toward Dexter's table and dropped her backpack on the floor. She wore bright pink Reeboks, black leggings, and a gray-and-orange Shalom Dance Team T-shirt. They embraced in a quick hug.

Dexter pushed a cup toward her. "Skinny caramel latte with soy," he announced.

"Perfecto." She slid into the seat across from him, picked up her coffee, took a sniff then downed a swig. "Yum, thanks. So, what's goin' on, big bro?" she asked. "Mom said you quit b-ball. Are you insane? You're so talented — I can already see one of those big gold championship rings on your finger."

Dexter sighed and glanced at the ceiling. "I do not need to hear somebody else ragging on me about basketball. Just because I'm good at it, and my old man was in the NBA, doesn't mean I have to make it my life. There are other sports."

"Okay then, take up frisbee golf for all I care." She gave a huff and a finger waggle.

He chuckled. "So whad'up, my baby sister? How're the grades?"

"Honor roll." She smiled and sat up straight and proud.

"Excellent." Dexter raised his coffee cup to her. "Any hot boyfriends?"

She took another sip of latte and settled back into her chair. "Not really. I liked Adam Davis for a few months, but I think he was into me because I'm black and he always wants to seem like he's all edgy and cool. His dad's a TV executive for some lame detective show." She sighed and glanced out the window. "Did you know that I'm the only girl of color in my school?"

"Shit, that's heavy. SaMoHi has a decent mix of kids. It's

all fine, the variety is cool."

"But my identity is more Jewish than racial. I can pass for either, though. It's kinda weird, not sure how I feel about any of it. Deborah wants me in this competitive Jewish high school next year. I'd continue my Hebrew studies, take lots of AP classes, and get into an Ivy if I want to. I'm pretty sure I can get the grades."

"You want an Ivy?"

She sighed. "I don't really even know what that means, other than some kind of academic hot shitness."

"If Mom heard what's coming out of that punk mouth of yours lately, she'd ground your ass for a month."

They both laughed. Alyssa dramatically pulled at her hair then raised her arms, shaking her fingers in jazz hands. "Maybe I want a public school like SaMoHi, or a performing arts school. Deb and Daddy would have a coronary either way. Mom would be cool with it. But hey, here's some awesome news." She leaned in and whispered. "I've been invited to audition next week for a music video. The choreographer did the Emmys last year. I'll send you the YouTube links." She shook her shoulders to an unseen tune.

Dexter smiled. "Wow, totally sick." They bumped knuckles. "But I overheard Deborah telling Mom that she thinks the dude's a little sketchy. They decided not to let you do it."

Alyssa's dewy soft features hardened, and her eyes narrowed to vivid green slits. "The guy who hooked me up with the choreographer's a burn victim. He's really sweet. Left the center before his final surgeries, so Deb's pissed at him. I mean, why shouldn't he split if he wants to? But, no, she acts like he committed a crime. Now she's convinced he's a flake."

"More power to him, I guess," Dexter said. "Sounds like

you're going to this audition no matter what the fam says."

"Mom and Deb want to keep me in pink tutus forever." Alyssa studied her bitten nails. They sported the remnants of glittery orange polish. "And don't act like Mom and your dad aren't freaking over you quitting basketball."

"You got that right. He promised me a new car of my choice if I stay in."

"Whoa, nice bribe. You're not gonna take him up on it?"

"Truth — I don't know what I'm doing. Savannah really fucked me up. I think I'm gonna go down to Atlanta and stay with this awesome friend of Mom and Uncle Luther's over spring break. Rio Deakins — he's a professor at Emory. Played Division I football, was in Special Forces, is a Ph.D. — and rides a Harley. Seems to get what I'm going through. We've been in touch."

"Sounds like an amazing dude. Mom should marry him." Alyssa finished her latte, checked her phone, then settled her eyes on Dexter. "But seriously, big bro, you're right. I'm going to the audition no matter what. And if you blab, I'll tell Mom about your fake ID."

Dexter laughed. "It got confiscated by a douche-bag bouncer last time I used it. Didn't believe I was a twenty-year-old white dude from Montana."

"You are such a dork." Alyssa rolled her eyes again. It seemed to be her go-to expression.

"Listen, Al," Dexter said, "I won't snitch, but how 'bout I drive you to this thing?"

Her face lit up. "That would be amazing. Actually, I'm a little nervous about going by myself. The dancer, the choreography guy, Brody, he's, like, almost thirty. Old — but still scary hot. I think I might have told to him I was, uh, sixteen." She examined the floor.

"What?" Dexter groaned and shook his head. "Dude, you're twelve." God, he suddenly felt parental and protective of the clueless adolescent across the table from him.

"I'm thirteen."

"Not 'til next month. And, duh, you're still jail bait for years."

"Am not." She huffed, sat tall and raised her head with a failed attempt to look down on him. She couldn't look tough if her life depended on it.

"Chill, tiny dancer," Dexter said. "I got at least two feet vertical on your butt."

"Well, seems like I'm not the only one in the family lying about my age."

"Alyssa, listen up," Dexter said, leaning toward her. "Never, I mean n-e-v-e-r, take off alone without telling anybody. It's a whole lot riskier than a fake ID. This world is a pretty fucked up place." He could hear his own voice deepen with concern. Must've been how Uncle Luther and Rio felt about watching out for Mom when she was a dumb-ass kid. "I'm always there for you, feel me? You know some of what went down in Savannah when I thought I could totally take care of myself. Crazy shit only happened to other people, or on TV. Don't make the same mistake, hear?" His heart raced.

Alyssa was like his friend Sean's toddler brother — all action and adventure with no idea that a fall down the stairs could kill him. "Hear me, girl?"

"Yeah, okay. I hear." Alyssa sat back and looked carefully at her brother. "Thanks." She bent down to hoist her backpack from the floor. "Gotta run. Dance team in ten."

"Okay, little sis. Keep the twerking G-rated."

She laughed, gave him a quick hug, and skipped out the door.

Dexter finished his drink. Rising from the table, he pressed his fist against his breastbone. A knot of anxiety began to twist and tighten in his chest. The door to the street seemed to be receding like it could disappear in the distance and he wouldn't be able to reach it. Dexter picked up his pace. As he stepped from the dim coffeehouse, the dazzling brightness of the day was disorienting. Where was he? The tangy, slightly sulfurous scent of pluff mud and southern swamp grass wafted into his consciousness. And blood, lots of it, coppery-smelling blood. Everywhere. Everywhere he turned.

Part of his brain knew what was going on, but another part was out of control, careening back toward the bad place.

An old white panel van slowly passed by and turned on Glendon.

Adrenaline rushed through his veins like water from a broken dam, consuming everything. His therapist had talked about triggers. The van was a trigger, but it was real, and it was coming for him. Wasn't it?

He fled to a storefront and hugged the portico wall trying to become invisible, but the assholes had spotted him and were coming, fast. He heard Cornelia scream, felt her hand, firm and insistent on his arm.

"Are you okay, mister? You on something?" A short, Hispanic woman with dyed red hair clutched Dexter's arm. It wasn't Cornelia. Cornelia was a hallucination; this woman was real. Heaven on Earth Day Spa was embroidered on her aqua apron. She called over her shoulder to a young man dressed in black who stood inside the door to the salon. "Brandon, should we call the cops or something?"

Dexter struggled back to the surface. "I'm okay, I have these, uh, these spells." He wanted her to somehow understand. "No cops. Sorry, so sorry." He pulled away and bolted down the sidewalk.

Where was he going? Where was his car? Sweat dripped down his face. He shivered in the heat. The panel van now came at him from an alley, cut him off and pulled past. The driver was a smoky dark mist. Dexter could see Cornelia's panicked face through the back window. The van accelerated, heading toward Wilshire. He ran after it, begging it to stop.

—

Lucy sat at the kitchen counter and fired up her laptop. She'd shared Bijan's info with Marlene Simon and in turn, Marlene updated her on what the detectives had discovered. It wasn't much. The probe into the leadership of the Alvarez cartel had stalled as tons of new product was hitting the streets. People were dying in its wake.

Then, Lucy's email alert pinged.

Her long-lost aunt, Sister Catherine Lucia, was reaching out to her online. Lucy flushed with excitement. The old gal was more tech-savvy than she'd given the woman credit for.

Lucy brought up the message and pressed her hand to the screen with an unconscious gesture of connection.

Then she began to read.

*Dearest, Lucia —*

*The local hermanos rigged a satellite dish that is procured from a small company in Oaxaca, so la gente llana, us common folks out in the county, can get service. My laptop arrived from Amazon. Is amazing. I am setting up a blog on indigenous medicine. My English not too bad, but I am writing this with a translation program. Praise the Lord, His milagros are muy bueno and astounding. This is a good word."*

Then came the photos from the airfield. The tone of the missive changed from joy to all-business.

Lucy held her breath, then the air gushed out. Sister had identified twelve of the sixteen faces. Excellent news. She'd forward the IDs to Marlene and Pete immediately.

And next came the kicker.

"By what remained of the tattoos on his arms," she wrote, "I recognized the pilot in your picture. He is a fellow I treated for bad burns from a vehicle explosion. With God's blessing, I stabilized him (I think that is the word) so he could be flyed to a special treatment center in Los Angeles, near where you must live. I wonder if he survived the trip? He was a strange man, full of hate. His name was Mercer."

# 17

The news landed like a sucker punch to the head. A crash through a plate-glass window. Bright shards of light glimmered and exploded in Lucy's brain. Mercer was alive and in Los Angeles? Her nemesis nursed from near-death by her own aunt? He had to be the patient Deborah had mentioned, the one who'd come in from a supposed vacation in Mexico several weeks ago. And he had taken an interest in Alyssa.

She grabbed her phone and pressed Bea's number on the list of favorites. No response.

She texted — SOS call me ASAP — and paced back and forth across the kitchen. Was it really him? And could he possibly know that Aly was Bea's daughter?

A shiver shook her body like a seizure. What had Deborah said the guy's name was? Garrett something. Mark Garrett? No, Garrett Mark. Oh, shit. Garrett Mark — Gary Mercer — could a fake name be any more transparent?

Bea returned the call in minutes. "That SOS scared me, Luce. Everything okay?"

It took Lucy a second to find her voice, then she blurted in a torrent: "I heard from my aunt in Pitacallpa. She took care of Mercer after the Jeep explosion. Saved his life. He's here in LA. I think, I mean I'm sure, he was the burn patient who was trying to connect Alyssa with the choreographer. Maybe he knows she's yours."

Lucy felt Bea's stunned silence.

"Sweet, Jesus," Bea whispered. "You trust your aunt's ID?"

"I do. She identified Mercer from one of the screengrabs I sent her."

Tears filled Bea's words. "Oh my God, I almost let my daughter get involved in this music video he's promoting. Even if Mercer doesn't know whose kid she is now, he would've eventually found out. Ahhh! My head's exploding. I'll call you right back, I have to make sure Alyssa's okay and give Deb and Eli a heads-up." The line disconnected.

Lucy stopped pacing and sat back down at the kitchen counter. Sister Catherine Lucia's email shown brightly on the laptop screen. She stared at the image of Mercer in front of the Cessna directing drug traffic. Then she switched to a kitten video on Facebook. Even the furry babies couldn't provide any relief from the terror that twisted her gut. Mercer would torture and kill them, too, if he had the chance.

Ten minutes later, Bea was back.

"Okay, the kid's where she's supposed to be, thank the Lord. Her dad and Deb'll be on her with eagle-eyes." Bea let out a shaky breath. "Blows my mind even to hear Mercer's name, let alone think about what he's capable of," she said.

"He hated us before he was burned. I can't imagine what he's feeling now."

"No shit—and heaven knows he'd use my baby to get back at me, at us." Bea gulped hard then blew her nose. "Thank heavens I pulled the plug on that audition. Have you given

Pete and Marlene the news yet?"

"I forwarded them the email after I received it."

"So, Mercer left the Burn Center. Where could he have gone?" Bea asked. "He's still in dire need of specialized care. We've gotta find out where he'd go to get it — somewhere private with top-flight resources."

"Makes sense. My guess is that he'd stay close to LA. Maybe Orange County or Santa Barbara. Or as near as Beverly Hills."

Lucy heard a beep over the phone.

"Pete Anthony's trying to get me," Bea said. "Probably about this. I'll call you back. And Lucy?"

"Yes, Bea," she said, hands shaking as they hovered over the keyboard.

"We're gonna get him this time and drop his sorry ass for good."

—

At a café, off Highland near CNN headquarters, Bea and Pete Anthony sat quietly together sipping iced coffee drinks. As he glanced up at a large, Eiffel Tower-shaped clock on the wall, his eyebrows scrunched together and his fingers drummed on the shiny oak tabletop. Neither needed that extra shot of espresso they'd ordered. Already stressed, Bea's heart rate took a leap as the caffeine hit. She pushed the rest of her drink away. Pete did the same.

"Marlene should be here any minute. Let's hold everything until she arrives, so you don't have to explain twice. Sound good?" he asked.

Bea nodded. She looked out onto the street and her eyes filled with tears. She wiped them away with the back of her hand.

"You okay?" Pete asked in his husky voice. His fingers

stopped drumming.

"Fuck, no." Bea took a deep breath and let it out slowly. She didn't know Pete well but knew she needed to talk or she'd break into full-blown hysteria. She sensed an underlying kindness in the detective despite his rough exterior.

"I'm really shaken up about how close my baby girl came to walking, or in this case, dancing, into the mouth of the dragon. And it would have been my fault. I would've let her go to that audition. Deborah, her stepmother, was totally against it from the start." She gulped hard. "I'm too permissive. And my son was almost killed by a psychopath last summer in Savannah. What is wrong with me? Why can't I protect my children?" Tears continued to roll slowly and wouldn't stop. She wiped her face. Traces of supposedly waterproof mascara streaked her fingers. Lovely. "You have kids?" she asked.

Pete nodded. "A fifteen-year-old daughter, Gianna, named after my Italian mama, and a nine-year-old boy, little Pete."

Bea nodded. "Are you a good father?"

Anthony paused for a moment. "I've been told a few times that I'm a shitty husband, but the sources were unreliable. I think I'm a really good dad, though. My kids talk to me and we meet for dinner every week." His fingers started drumming on the table again. "I'm a good date, too, by the way."

Bea choked, unsure whether she was about to laugh or cry even more. "You asking me out, Pete? While I'm sitting here weeping and miserable, questioning my fitness to be a parent?"

"Uh-huh, sorry." Pete shrugged, his smile flickered apologetically. "Social correctness, or whatever the hell you call it, has, uh, never been one of my strong suits."

"That's for damn sure," Marlene said as she appeared behind him. She gave Bea a hug, perched her rolling briefcase against a neighboring table, and sat down next to the detective. "If he asked you out," she said, nodding at Anthony, "*oy vey*, don't do it. 'Nuff said."

Bea laughed out loud and dried her eyes, feeling momentarily thrust out of self-pity.

"Shall we get to work here, kiddies? Or do I have to endure an episode of The Dating Game?"

Pete pulled out his iPad and sneered at his partner. "Just trying to lighten things up a little."

Bea was actually relieved to launch into an update on all they'd found out about Gary Mercer since Lucy and Burleson had last seen him on fire by the edge of the road in Mexico.

Marlene had run the images that Sister Catherine Lucia had provided through the recognition system. Besides the known participants, the program came up with hits on several So Cal gangbangers who seemed to be moving between Guerrero and LA.

"That's a huge lead Lucy's auntie handed us," Pete said. "Will help confirm which gangs the Alvarez assholes are in cahoots with. Excellent work. I'm gonna send this Sister Catherine Lucia an LAPD baseball cap for her help."

"That thoughtful gesture would probably get her killed," Marlene said, face grim.

Anthony chuckled. "True dat. How about a Disneyland T-shirt?"

The two detective's phones beeped simultaneously. He checked the text, then looked at Marlene. She was cleaning her glasses. "Time to ride, partner. Gotta get back to HQ. Chief wants to know what we got on this."

"Okay, *Kemosabe*." She rose and grabbed the handle of her mobile office and pushed the clean glasses up on her nose. "Bea, we'll be in touch soon. Thanks to you and Lucy for keeping us in the loop. You women are awesome."

Bea nodded and slowly rose to follow them out the door.

Pete hung back and put an arm around her. "We're gonna get these motherfuckers. And, Bea, I'll bet you're one helluva momma bear."

She hugged him back, afraid to admit how good it felt to be, even momentarily, in the strong, warm arms of a man who was a good father. Maybe she'd check out the good date bit, too.

Then, Bea's phone rang. She was going to let it go to voicemail but had a feeling she'd better check. No, let it go. Your kids are fine, you're worked up and paranoid right now. It was a number she didn't recognize anyway.

She bid Pete and Marlene goodbye at her car. With three minutes left on the meter and a meter man heading her way with hands flexing, eager to write that fifty-dollar ticket, she jumped into the front seat and fired up the engine.

The phone rang again, same number. She hit Decline, but in seconds, it rang yet again. The meter-reader passed by and waggled his finger as her meter expired. Bea gave him the evil-eye and pulled out onto Hollywood Boulevard behind a tour bus. She decided to take the persistent call and answered on her Bluetooth.

"Mom!" Dexter's voice was thick and teary. "Mom, I'm in County Jail. Please, come get me."

Little explosions popped behind Bea's eyeballs and she almost drove up over the curb and onto the sidewalk. "What in the world, what happened? Are you okay? Dexter, Are you okay?" Her throat constricted and she could hardly breathe. Had he been profiled? Had he been beaten? Worst-case scenarios ran through her head. Stop the hysterics, she told herself. At least he's alive.

"Dexter, answer me."

"Yes, yes, I'm okay. But I think I'm having, uh, some kind of, I dunno, a breakdown. They think I was stoned, but you know I don't do that shit. Come and get me, please."

"You're at men's central, downtown?" Oh, Lord, no.

"Yeah," he said, voice almost drowned out by raucous background noise.

"Let me grab a detective friend of mine and I'll be there as fast as I can. Dexter, I love you." Jesus, God, protect my boy.

—

Gary Mercer winced at his reflection in the stainless-steel oxygen tank next to the gurney. Like a mummy on a late-night horror show, his face was swathed in white bandages. Toulusa sat at his side holding his mangled, three-fingered hand. Her thumb massaged the dense scar tissue. Mercer's breath was labored, always would be. To his ears, he sounded as if he was breathing underwater with a scuba regulator.

He looked at Toulusa through the eye holes in the bandaging. Her face was serene and vaguely angelic. How was it this woman never seemed to be repulsed by ugliness? That common human trait was missing. She was, in fact, compulsively drawn to grisly visions, like a dog to a bloody bone.

A nurse, tanned, fit, in his mid-forties with a man-bun top-knot, entered the room wearing lilac-colored scrubs as if arriving on stage for a performance. "Are we ready to remove these bandages, Mr. Mark?" He placed a tray of treatments on the side table and swiveled it over the bed. "New day, new face, new opportunities. *Carpe diem*, as they say. All will be well because Dr. Dieter is the best of the best."

Mercer found the man's big smile and enthusiastic presentation highly irritating. If he'd had a gun, he would've used it on Richard Dillard, N.P.

Fortunately, he had a gentle way with the unwrapping. As each layer was slowly and meticulously removed, Mercer struggled with what he was going to see. An ill-fitting mask pulled tight over his knife-sharp bone structure? Joan Rivers in drag? Or a putty-faced mannequin? Would scars rip across this once-handsome face like a coyote caught in barbed wire? His heart pounded.

Another layer of bandaging dropped into the biohazard bag on the nurse's cart. Toulusa's darkly accented eyes widened at the reveal, but she said nothing. The last wrappings were tugged from his skin and discarded. It was done. The gently circulating air-conditioning in the room stung Mercer's sensitive, newly transplanted dermis. Dillard carefully coated his face in a thick, yellowish cream which provided some relief, however slight.

The chief of the surgical team that had spent almost thirty hours attaching the new face soon appeared at Mercer's bedside. Dr. Karl Dieter bent low over his patient. Breath minty with mouth wash, he paused for a moment, then his fingers brushed weightlessly against the sutures like butterfly wings. At first, the doctor showed no reaction to his handiwork. Mercer watched cold blue eyes assess the results of the procedure. Dieter was slim and ascetic, Mercer flashed on a photo of a Nazi physician he'd once seen, inspecting the second head he'd tried to attach to the unfortunate medical sacrifice. Experimental surgery or the ovens. Dr. Mengele or Dr. Frankenstein?

"Congratulations, Mr. Mark," he finally said. "The incisions are healing beautifully and the blood flow to the facial tissue seems excellent. You'll need several more surgeries, as you know, but this first is the most critical, and I'd say we did an A-plus job."

"Time to take a look-see, Mr. Mark," the nurse chirped. "I know this can be difficult, but I think you'll be happy with the early results. Once the swelling goes down, you'll be even more pleased."

Mercer winced as Nurse Dillard held up a mirror so the patient could take the initial glance at his new persona. Mercer coughed out a sigh of relief. Goosebumps rose on his arms. He might actually have a chance of looking, not normal, but less horrible than he'd thought. It could actually be an interesting look. The eyes were particularly promising, especially the nice, arching brows.

"The stitching is exquisite," Toulusa said. She gazed at the wounds with admiration.

Mercer noted the doctor's quick look of apprehension as the man took in the exotic, patchwork-wearing gypsy who sat at his burn patient's side.

"She's beautiful but strange and slightly frightening—like I am now. Wouldn't you agree?" Mercer asked the surgeon.

The doctor smiled. "Keep resting and continue to take good care. Listen to what Nurse Dillard tells you to do, he's a savant in the field of surgical recovery. I'll see you soon, Mr. Mark, and Miss..."

"Toulusa. Call me Toulusa." Her voice was light and melodious as wind chimes.

Quickly, the surgeon disappeared out the door.

Toulusa had that effect on people — they were fascinated, but wisely terrified. Mercer chuckled tightly through his new lips. He'd look forward to the fillers. Was Botox still the weapon of choice? He'd go for a look short of Kylie Jenner's plush pout.

Nurse Dillard gathered his chart, medical paraphernalia,

and followed the surgeon out the door. Then he paused and stuck his head coyly around the door jamb. "Fifteen more minutes, *Mam'selle* Toulusa, and then we must let the patient rest."

"Of course," she said with a wink.

As soon as Dillard was gone, Mercer asked, "How does Altamont feel about your spending so much time with me? He's my Hand of the King, as it were, and I don't want him resentful."

She smiled her enigmatic smile. "Altamont? He doesn't feel. We both just like a mutual good fuck."

"Ah. I can certainly appreciate that. He did well with Brody's younger brother. I quite like his face."

"You'll grow into it nicely. And I see something else growing." She eyed the tent-pole of his crotch. "We now have thirteen minutes left," Toulusa said, checking her watch. Shall I shut the door?"

"Yes, please." Mercer hoped the pain in his face would be eased momentarily with the application of other equally intense ministrations.

Mercer followed the movement of Toulusa's long, swishy skirt as she closed the door and dimmed the light. "May I put Phantom of the Opera on iTunes?" she asked.

"A fine idea," Mercer said. "I've always been a fan — even more so now."

She leaned against the wall and pulled up her skirt. "Surprise, darling."

Delighted, Mercer laughed out loud. "Come here my dearest girlie-boy and make the Phantom sing."

# 18

Bea loved her cozy house but since Alyssa had moved out and Dexter, though physically present, lived in a confusing and unknown sphere that Bea struggled to fully grasp, things had changed. Her sense of aloneness and loss was now a constant wound. She was grateful to have Lucy next to her on the old leather sofa, scuffed from wear over the years to the texture of suede. This was a woman who knew her well — knew her mom, her kids, her exes, and had no agenda other than to care about all of them.

A group of candles on the fireplace mantel flickered in the breeze, and sand-colored linen curtains gently billowed along the French doors to the backyard. Dark green leaves of a ficus tree rustled as soft, sweet breaths of ocean air transformed the heat of the day.

Lucy poured the last dregs of a Dreaming Tree pinot noir into their wine glasses.

Bea smiled. The two friends were still damp from an hour immersed in the hot tub, soaking away the pain. This was Southern California after all — pools and hot tubs were as abundant as aspiring screenwriters and sunscreen. Each wrapped in a colorful beach towel, they smelled of chlorine. Bea's hair was curly and wild; Lucy's lank and straight as she pushed it out of her face.

"Thank you for lining up the lawyer for Dex," Bea said and drained the glass. "Probably have to take a second mortgage on the house to pay for the bailout but who the hell cares. All worth it to keep my son safe."

"Alan Katz does wills and probates," Lucy said, "but he knows everybody. This Mitchell McWhorter guy he referred you to is supposed to be really, really good. He's already all over it. Even Detective Anthony approves of the dude, and Mar says Pete doesn't approve of anybody. It's all gonna work out, Beebs."

Bea was feeling spacey, bordering on drunk, but what the hell. She'd often acknowledged that neither she nor Lucy could hold their booze. The two did much better with chocolate than alcohol. They could eat anybody to the curb with that sugary, dark magic.

"He kinda asked me out." Bea ran her finger over the lip of the wine glass, then plunked it down on the coffee table atop a magazine with a picture of a pretty front porch from a less complicated era.

"Mitchell McWhorter?" Lucy snickered. "You're kidding me."

"Not the lawyer. Jeez, Pete Anthony."

Lucy kicked her legs up onto the ottoman. "So, you gonna go out with him?" She readjusted the beach towel around her shoulders.

"Maybe. I mean, yes. Why not? Hell, I'm looking to have some fun, not get married, heaven forbif, I mean, uh, forbid," she said.

"Yeah, why the hell not? Go for it. He has quite the rep,

but it seems like he's been decent to you."

"More than decent — he helped get my kid outta the slammer. Kept me from strangling that county deputy who implied Dexter was an addict and it was all my fault." A thin cry of anguish escaped her throat. "'Nother bottle?"

"No, darling, we've both had plenty." Lucy took the glasses into the kitchen and returned with Mason jar mugs of sweet tea and a plate of Lorna Doone cookies.

Bea took a sip and began to cry again. "Reminds me of home. Those mugs used to belong to my gram." She reached for a tissue and blew her nose. "I'd like to talk to Mama about all this, but with Daddy passed on and her still recovering from a heart attack, she's too fragile. I'm in over my head, Luce. Dex says he doesn't want to finish the semester. Can you imagine — dropping out of high school?"

"Oh, man. No. What would he do instead?"

Bea shrugged. "Definitely needs structure right now. Not sure a part-time job at the mall would be enough."

She downed a Lorna Doone then gulped more tea between sniffles. "His therapist suggested I send him to a PTSD treatment center in New Mexico. But he'd be around tons of people who've had terrible things happen to them. He'd hear all their horrific stories. That could make his issues even worse. It's called secondary traumatization, or something like that. I don't know what to do."

"What does his dad say about all this?"

Bea paused and sighed. She glanced over at the pile of Dexter's belongings that he'd dropped at the foot of the stairs before heading up to his bedroom where he'd immediately conked out after they'd finally gotten him home from jail. The stuff seemed shed from another life. "Kevin thinks the fix is a two-thousand-dollar-a-week golf camp in Scottsdale. Throw money and sports into the mix and all bad things disappear, right?"

"O — kay. Parenting's never been his best game." Lucy chewed at her lip then spoke. "Dexter mentioned this guy he met in Savannah a couple of times. Seemed to really admire him. A friend of yours from childhood, can't recall his name. Like, uh, River?"

"Rio Deakins." Bea slowly massaged the back of her neck. "Sometimes I think that man's the love of my life, but that's never going to happen — he's happily married. Anyhow, he's an expert in PTSD and war veterans. I know Dex and Rio email; they seemed to have had this instant connection."

"Call him in the morning, Bea. Call Rio and see what he thinks."

"Yeah, he's a man I trust with my life — and my son's."

"Then, you'll have done everything you can do for now." Lucy studied her friend. "You gonna be all right? Or do you want me to stay with you?"

"Hey, I'm fine. I think I'm finally ready to keel over." She snuggled into the couch cushions, her eyes closing. "Thanks, Lucy. Love you, girl. Tomorrow's another day to try and get it right."

—

Bea was relieved that Dexter had decided to go to school. It was the last day before spring break, and a big chemistry test he didn't want to have to make up, loomed largely. He clung to normalcy like a passenger holding onto the edge of a sinking boat. She was doing the same but sensed her grip slipping.

Dexter opened the refrigerator, foraging for snacks.

"I talked to Rio this morning, honey bun," Bea said, turning toward her son and keeping her voice upbeat. "He and Lindsay can't wait to get their hands on you and show you the sites in Hotlanta. You're booked on Southwest day after tomorrow. Leaves at seven in the morning. We need to be out of here by five."

Dexter hooked his backpack over his shoulder and slid his size thirteen feet into a pair of flip-flops. His new black Under Armour T-shirt was an XL and already strained at the shoulders.

"Thanks, Mom. For everything. I know I'm making it hard right now." His face was drawn and his eyes red and tired. The medication he'd been given seemed to have slowed him down.

"Shit happens, baby, to everybody. It's how we pick ourselves back up that counts. I have faith in you, son. This might be the hardest thing you'll have to deal with in your life, but you'll get through it and come out an even better man on the other side."

"What doesn't kill us makes us stronger, right?" He made a face.

"A lot of truth to that, sweet pea." She hugged him close before he could turn and walk out the door.

Minutes later a call came in from Pete Anthony.

"Hey, Pete," she said, still shaky from dealing with Dexter and having drunk too much and slept too little the night before. "Thanks again for all for your help getting my son released. I owe you, big time."

"Glad I could help. How're you doing?"

Turning her face to the morning sun streaming through the kitchen window, she closed her eyes and enjoyed the comforting warmth for a quick moment. "I got through the night and it's a new day, right? I'm about to leave for the office."

"Anytime you need help getting through the night, I'm as close as 9-1-1."

"Thanks, detective, I'll remember that."

Was he going to ask her out officially? What was she going to say?

"But listen," he said. His voice switched to business mode. "Got some news I wanted to share yesterday but figured you didn't need more to crap to deal with right then."

"Much appreciated." She braced herself against the kitchen island. "Okay, what's up?" Bea's journalistic antennae began to hum.

"As you know, Marlene and I've touched bases with the cops in OC and Santa Barbara about private plastic surgery clinics that could handle Mercer's injuries. We don't have a lead on much but we think he's in Santa Barbara County. The city cops found a male body washed up at a Hope Ranch beach last week."

"That's horrible. But what does it have to do with Mercer?" Bea took a long swig of coffee from her CNN commuter cup, then choked, seized by a torrent of possibilities. "Mercer killed the guy?" But Mercer was too disabled. "Or wait, he had him killed? Or—" Bea took a deep breath, her heart raced, "—was Mercer the victim? Is Mercer dead?" She prayed it was so.

"No, no," Pete said. "Whoa, Nellie, slow down. That brain of yours is pinging possibilities like pinballs at an arcade. This dude's mid-twenties and in great shape, no burns. All intact except for one thing that's a kick in the head, so to speak."

"What do you mean?"

Anthony cleared his throat. "His face was gone."

"Gone? Like ripped off? Or eaten off by fish?"

Anthony paused. "His face was surgically removed."

"What?"

"By an expert."

"My, God." Bea was stunned. She put her phone on

speaker then leaned her elbows onto the kitchen island, her head in her hands. The pixilated dance of a migraine began to sparkle in her peripheral vision once again. "What're y'all telling me? That Mercer —"

"Yep, we think Mercer may have had the face harvested and transplanted onto his own. From what I hear, the guy's a vain bastard. Wouldn't want to live with all that scar tissue for a mug."

"Sweet Jesus." Bea was thankful that he hadn't called her with this grisly information earlier. As a reporter, she should be all over any breaking news and never want a source to hold back information. As a human and a mother, the rules were never as clear cut.

She rooted around the bottom of her purse searching for the car key fob and thought again about the location of the corpse. "Isn't it strange that this body showed up on an exclusive beach? That's gonna get lots of attention. I mean, there are tons of other ways to disappear a dead body so no one ever sees it again."

"You got that one right," he said. "I think someone wanted us to find it. Kind of a 'fuck you.' Unfortunately, the fingertips have all been nibbled off by sea critters, so no prints. It will take us a while on the DNA results. We're also tracking down this dancer dude your daughter talked about. There's something messed up there. Not sure what it is yet, but we'll figure it out. You can take that to the bank."

"Thanks for keeping me in the loop, Pete. I'm running this story for the network focusing on the black tar heroin trade and how the Alvarez cartel plays in. But who the hell knows, maybe Mercer is the new *jefe*." She wanted to laugh at the absurd possibility but couldn't.

"I was thinking along the same lines, although how an

invalid could run that kind of a massive enterprise is beyond me. I think we need to meet and discuss it," he said, a little playfulness entering his voice.

"You mean the date?" Bea asked.

"Yep, the date. How about it? We'll take it slow, even put it in park. I swear I'll be good."

Bea paused. She was pretty damn sure he'd be good. "Okay, how about Friday night? My son leaves for Atlanta that morning and I have tons of stuff to do to get him ready between now and then." Switching her phone off speaker and grabbing it and her belongings, Bea headed for the garage. She was now running late for a staff meeting.

"He's a guy. Have him stuff some socks in a gym bag, hand him a charge card, and kiss him goodbye."

"That's not the way I roll, Detective," she said, doubting anew the wisdom of dating this man. Her vulnerability could get her into big trouble. But maybe this kind of trouble was what she needed.

# 19

Alyssa snuggled into a giant purple bean bag chair on the floor next to her bed and checked her texts. Dexter had left a message on his way to the airport saying he couldn't take her to "you know what," this week. Then he told her to "forget about this sketchy audition. There'd be plenty of opportunities in the future to try out for cool stuff." And blah, blah, blah. Sounded like another parent.

Deborah knocked on her door too loudly for eight in the morning on a day off from school. Today should be a day to chill. She had *Flashdance* queued up on Netflix.

"Come in," Alyssa said, impatient to start the movie she'd seen at least a hundred times. She'd memorized the song lyrics and knew every step Jennifer Beals danced throughout the whole film. One of her dreams was to someday star in *Flashdance: The Musical*, on Broadway. She hadn't shared that with anyone. Sounded pretty lame when she said it out loud.

Deb poked her head into the room. "You have *bat mitzvah* class this morning. If you want to do this you have to be responsible and take it seriously."

Alyssa's heart sank. "I want to do it but I need a break. I want to hang out today. Can't I miss just one session?" She burrowed into the bean bag and pulled a fleece throw up to her neck, trying to disappear.

"You can take a break tomorrow when it's the Sabbath. Come on, young lady, let's get moving." She closed the door. Alyssa heard her stepmother's footsteps recede down the squeaky wood stairs.

Sighing dramatically, Alyssa rolled off the bean bag and trudged into her closet where she fished out a pair of gray leggings and a Born to Dance T-shirt, both of which were only a day's worth of worn-in and had passed the sniff test. She grabbed a hot-pink hoodie. In the pocket was the bus schedule to North Hollywood where she'd audition soon.

She'd catch the Big Blue Bus in downtown Santa Monica and purchase the right transfers to get her to the North Hollywood orange line station in the valley. She folded the schedule carefully as if it were the map to a buried treasure site. The switching from bus to bus seemed pretty complicated. Her friend Avi, from New York City, always seemed so independent when he bragged about taking the train to school in Brooklyn when he was only ten.

Her BFFs, Rachel and Yael, were providing Wednesday's alibi. A day at the beach and lunch at The Surfer Taco in the food truck lot off Main Street sounded pretty darn good. Was she making a big mistake like Dexter had warned, heading off to this audition by herself?

She trusted Mr. Mark not to steer her wrong. He only wanted to help her jumpstart her career. Sweet. He got her, for sure. More than anybody, he seemed to understand. All Mom could think about was her new job and Dexter's problems right now. And Deborah, all she cared about was

Daddy, her job, and her baby Arielle, not the Hebrew-school-slacker stepdaughter who'd screwed up their perfect little family threesome. Alyssa was going to win a spot in this video and then they'd notice her, big time. She started humming the theme from *Flashdance*.

"Let's go, Alyssa," Deb called from somewhere near the front door.

Stepchild grabbed her backpack and tromped down the stairs, taking two at a time. Grabbing a Clif bar from the kitchen table, Alyssa called goodbye to the nanny, Tal, a twenty-year-old Israeli girl, and kissed her angelic baby sister before heading out to study Torah.

—

On Wednesday morning, Rachel and Yael met Alyssa near the pier to bid their friend good luck and verify the alibi plans. "Maybe we should come with you," Yael said as she hoisted her beach bag onto her shoulder. She was a pretty girl with fair hair and long legs, slim as broomsticks.

"I can't go, no way," Rachel said. Her curly dark hair sprang out of a loose ponytail and she smelled of sunscreen. "If my mom found out, I'd be grounded for life. And I think you should bail on this, Aly. You got no idea what this crispy critter dude is into. Maybe they're gonna abduct you and force you to be a sex slave or something. I read about that online all the time."

Alyssa laughed out loud, but the two friends didn't join in. "Come on, I'm not a clueless dork landing at the Greyhound terminal from, uh, some podunk town in, like, Nebraska, thinking I'm gonna be a star."

Yael and Rachel exchanged skeptical glances.

Beach-goers of all ages and ethnicities soon poured from the open doors of the bus and crashed like a human wave toward the sand.

"So, text us every half hour or we're gonna freak," Rachel said. "We'll meet you on the pier at the Ferris wheel at four and head home."

Passengers traveling into the valley from Santa Monica began pressing into the city's Big Blue Bus, jostling the last-minute commuters still trying to exit with strollers, coolers, and screaming toddlers in tow.

Alyssa gave her friends each a quick hug then moved into line behind a bad-smelling man with matted hair trying to board with a rusted bicycle.

"*Mazel tov*, Al," Yael called, her eyes clouded with concern. "Dance your brains out."

Alyssa grinned from the doorway and gave a fist pump to Rachel and Yael. Seconds later, the bus pulled from the station. Her heart pounded and she pushed down a tinge of regret as the girls turned and headed toward the beach, chatting, and lugging their towels and gear.

At Wilshire and Fourteenth Alyssa switched to the Metro line without much of a wait. She had to take four different buses to get where she was going. She clung to an overhead hand-hold as they crawled and lurched their way between changes, long waits, late buses, and disgruntled riders eating breakfast, doing their hair, changing their babies' diapers, and performing about every other form of morning prep. A whole new window on the world of Angelinos without cars opened in Alyssa's tween consciousness. She missed her mother's easy car rides but couldn't wait to get her own driver's license. So many of her friends could care less about driving.

Finally, she arrived in North Hollywood. She checked her watch. It was noon and her audition was at one in a warehouse area, kind of near the NoHo Arts District where Lucy had once taken Aly and Dexter to see a play. It was a mile and a half away, give or take, easy to make in thirty minutes. Then, another few blocks or so to the studio. She texted Yael and Rachel that she'd arrived in the valley. They sent back a selfie of the two of them frolicking at a lifeguard station.

The San Fernando Valley was hot and airless compared to the beach. Alyssa stopped at a drug store for a bottle of cold vitamin water, then headed up Lankershim Boulevard past Universal Studios. The area between the theme park and the back of Bob Hope Airport—now called the Hollywood Burbank Airport—was mostly what her sociology teacher would've called blue-collar Hispanic. There were gang tags everywhere. Alyssa shivered in the heat, feeling more intimidated than she'd anticipated. Cars whizzed by on their way to someplace else. A skinny pit bull mix emerged from between two buildings, pissed on a pile of discarded tires, drilled her with a wary look and disappeared back down an alley.

As she approached a side street, a shiny, deep purple pimpmobile bounced around the corner and cruised slowly past. The young driver wore reflective aviators and a black beret. He checked her out then made an obscene gesture with his tongue. Alyssa turned away, not wanting to give him the pleasure of a reaction. His sound system assaulted her with deep bass notes that made windowpanes rattle in a T-shirt store nearby. She prayed he'd keep moving and tried to look like she knew where she was going, marching toward Vanowen without making eye contact.

The driver sped up and headed toward Lankershim. Thank you, Jesus — the asshole wasn't all that much into further hassling her. She picked up her pace.

Nearing Tujunga, Alyssa wiped perspiration from her forehead with the sleeve of her hoodie. She took it off and tied it around her waist. The directions to the studio didn't seem quite right. When she stopped to check her phone's GPS near a boarded-up liquor store, two young Hispanic guys about Dexter's age, and covered with tats, emerged from an alley. They spoke to each other in rapid Spanish but switched to English as they advanced on her.

"You lost, baby girl?" The speaker was short, shaved bald, and built like a mountain gorilla she'd recently seen in a Jane Goodall documentary. His glassy-eyed partner was much taller with a faint, peach-fuzz wannabe mustache. From across the street, another man emerged from the shadows. Older, maybe mid-twenties, he wore a black Nike tracksuit, unzipped to show his shiny, waxed chest.

Alyssa gulped hard and started walking again, not too fast, not too slow. She tried to avoid panicking, but adrenaline pumped through her veins like an open fire hydrant.

"Need some help finding your way, *chica*?" gorilla asked. "You don't look like no local bitch."

The others watched from a short distance, moving on the periphery like a wolf pack tightening the noose on its prey.

"I don't need any help," she said, trying not to sound scared shitless. "I'm going to the Airport Studio, they're expecting me." She stood up straight and walked onward, eyes ahead.

"Ah, she's going to the studio," the tall, lanky one mocked. They all chuckled and began to close in on her from three angles.

Where the hell was she gonna run? Their raw scent shimmered in the hot air. She could barely breathe.

A taxi cab cruised slowly by and pulled to a stop beyond her. The window rolled down and a cabbie, dark-skinned and probably Middle Eastern, called out the window. "Come on, missy. Sorry I'm late."

"What? Oh, okay." She had no other choice. Alyssa ran to the

THE BURN PATIENT | 129

dusty green vehicle, yanked open the passenger door and hopped in, panting and praying that she hadn't stepped into another disaster. The taxi pulled away from the curb. Alyssa looked over her shoulder at the three scowling gangbangers standing on the sidewalk. The lanky one gave her the finger.

She turned back to the driver, hoping he wasn't some kind of pervert. "Thanks for that," Alyssa said. "Not sure if I have enough money for a cab. So, can you let me out at the next block?"

"Missy, what you doing here all by yourself? You crazy?"

Alyssa shrank in her seat and stammered, "I'm trying to find the Airport Studio, it's on Tujunga. I have an audition there." She checked her iPhone. "In fifteen minutes."

The cabbie shook his head. "I take you to this studio."

"But I'm not sure..." She rummaged in her purse. Where was that twenty?

"It's on the house." He pushed back his shiny, straight hair. His credentials hung from the rearview mirror. His name was Farouk Hassan. A picture of what looked like his family had been duct-taped to the console.

"Well, thanks a lot, sir. Those dudes were scary."

"I have a girl your age," he said, following her glance. "Big dreams, like you. Begging me to let her try out for The Voice. I said no way 'til she sixteen."

"That's kind of what my mom said, too," Alyssa admitted.

"You should listen to her," he said.

A few minutes later, he pulled up to a square, industrial-style stucco building with a small sign next to the glass front door that read Airport Studios.

A blue-and-orange jet thundered low overhead. Decomposing food wrappers, newspapers, and other detritus whirled in the downdraft.

"You're sure this is the place?" Mr. Hassan asked.

Alyssa nodded and pushed aside the urge to beg him to take her home. But there was no way she'd wuss-out on this audition. She'd come too far.

Hassan gave her a hard frown. "I hope you know what you're doing, young lady. This area's the center of the porn industry in LA. Did you know that?"

Alyssa's stomach clenched and she swallowed hard. She handed him a twenty-dollar bill she'd found, but he refused it. Instead, Hassan gave her his business card.

"Good luck with that music video." he said and smiled kindly. "Call me if you need another quick getaway."

# 20

Bea sat across from her new boss, Winfrey Chambers, a cable news veteran with a grouping of Emmys on a shelf in his floor-to-ceiling bookcase. She understood this meeting had something to do with a new information delivery format the network was exploring. He said he'd wanted to pick her brain. She was eager to find out what that would entail.

A light-skinned black man, he sported a gray goatee that fringed the chin of a face round as a beach ball. He appeared to Bea like a mix of Santa Claus and CNN's Fareed Zakaria — funny and nice, but tough and smart. They hit it off immediately.

Bea had heard from co-workers that Chamber's son was a twenty-something correspondent working for Vice, a newsgroup with an edgy, short-form documentary format that allowed coverage to run deeper than sound bites and talking heads. Kind of a nouveau 60 Minutes. Images of the kid on location hung on the wall behind his dad's desk. Vice was fast gaining a following in the younger demographics in which CNN, MSNBC, and FOX didn't seem to be able to gain a significant foothold.

Chambers glanced over his shoulder at a photo of his son wearing a Vice News T-shirt, holding a mic, and interviewing someone in what looked like Moscow.

Bea said, "You must be so proud of that young man of yours." Her thoughts went immediately to Dexter and his journalistic aspirations. If he still had any. The ground beneath his feet was so unsteady since Savannah.

"Proud, and scared shitless," Chambers said, fiddling with a pile of news clippings. "After graduating from Northwestern, Jamal had a great opportunity as a junior news writer at NPR in Chicago. Sounds terrific, right? I thought he'd accepted the job, but then I got a call from goddamned Ethiopia. He and a couple of friends from J-school signed on with this media start-up. 'Hey Mom and Dad, gonna be making short-form docs from hotspots all over the world. Awesome, huh?'" Chambers repeated. "His mother almost had a coronary, and I wasn't far behind her." He pressed his hand against his forehead. "Right now, oh Lord, he's in Yemen, we think."

Bea smiled. "I've got a son with similar aspirations. Kids. Who knew what an insane ride that'd be?"

"Quite the understatement, Miss Bea. Now I finally understand what my parents went through when they'd see me reporting from some war-torn faraway place." He shook his head and adjusted his tortoise-shell, professorish glasses. "Payback, right? But on to business — I have an idea I want to run by you."

Bea sat up straighter and moved to the edge of the too-deeply-padded leather chair. "I'm all ears." A niggle of anticipation hummed in her chest. Didn't sound like he wanted to fire her but she knew she'd been spending more time than she should on the black tar heroin story.

"I want try out something similar to Vice but focusing

on Southern California. I want you to stay with your current story and see if you can put something together for a trial run in a new format. I have several other people working on LA-based short-form stories. We'll do an opening with several two-minute pieces, then three longer segments, and end with a hot sheet of up-and-coming stuff. In addition to news content, the motion graphics will be amazing. We're going to title the program CNN-STAT after the medical term. Means immediate, urgent, of course."

Bea nodded, thrilled at the unexpected shift in her job assignment. "What does your son think about this? Are we going to be his competition?"

Chambers laughed. His eyes twinkled at the challenge. "I hope so. We've got backers lined up for a pilot, six episodes," he continued. The phone on his desk began to buzz, and he glanced at his Apple watch. "So, does this sound like something you'd be interested in taking on, at least in the short term?"

Bea grinned, struggling not to throw her arms around Chambers and kiss his chubby cheek. Maybe he really was Santa. She could barely contain her enthusiasm but didn't want to give away her hand. She needed a bit of bargaining power to make this a go. "Can I have a team, or will I be working alone?"

"You'll have a photog and access to a production assistant when you need one." He checked his watch again and Bea knew her time with the boss was over.

"I think this is exciting, Mr. Chambers." Insanely exciting.

"Please, you know we're on a first-name basis here, Bea. It's Win."

"Okay, Win, but I want my own photographer. She can function as an independent contractor, on call. We've worked together for years, and she'll bring a lot to the table. She has an awesome background."

"You mean Lucy?"

Bea couldn't hide her surprise. "You know her?"

Winfrey rested his chin on his hand and looked thoughtfully at his new employee. "I knew her uncle. Fine man and I heard she helped you cover the fire last week. And that she still hasn't filled out her paperwork." His eyes narrowed. "Not your ideal rule-follower type, perhaps?"

Bea smiled, almost laughed, but bit her lip. "I'll connect her to HR immediately, sir. She is normally conscientious." When she wants to be.

"Okay then, once she goes through the official hiring process for contractors, she's yours, but keep her in line. Oh, and anything more than fifteen freelance hours a week needs to be approved by me, directly."

"Absolutely." Bea was about to leap out of the chair with joy but she stood calmly as Chambers rose from his desk to end the meeting. "Thank you, Win. We'll nail this." They shook hands.

"I'm counting on it," he said and picked up his buzzing phone.

Bea trotted down to her office, shut the door, and leaned back against it. She gazed out across the murky Hollywood Hills horizon and finally laughed out loud. The dynamic duo, back together again on CNN-STAT.

—

Alyssa took a deep breath and tried not to freak out about the taxi driver's porn comment. She walked up to the studio building's front entrance, but the double glass doors were locked.

She wondered if Jennifer Beals started out at a creepy place like this before she landed *Flashdance*. Aly's hands shook. She pushed a doorbell and waited, hoping that more gangsters wouldn't show up and hit on her, or worse.

An anorexic-looking girl dressed like a 'ho in a silky white mini-dress and black jazz shoes appeared in the foyer. She pressed a speaker button. "Yes?"

Alyssa licked her dry lips. "Alyssa Strauss here to audition for O'Brody's music video. I have a one o'clock call time."

The girl sized her up with a critical once-over, then unlocked the doors. Alyssa's stomach twisted as she stepped inside the dim entry. It smelled of mold and sweat. Cheaply framed, faded pictures of hip hop dancers lined a yellowish, cinder-block wall. The girl locked the door behind them. Then double-locked it from the inside with a key she dropped into a small, leather cross-body purse.

Alyssa could feel sweat begin to dampen her neck and armpits. The dull, metallic sound of that deadbolt engaging was unnerving. This whole scene didn't feel right. In fact, it felt all wrong. She pushed her hands deep into the pockets of her hoodie and pulled out her cell phone along with the taxi driver's card. It was time to bail. Her fingers were slick on the buttons.

"Sorry, little Miss, Stein, is it? Melissa Stein?

"Alyssa Strauss." Her voice cracked.

"Sorry, shit reception here, Alyssa. Something about being directly under the flight path and FAA crap. But don't worry."

Alyssa looked desperately at her phone icons. No bars. Uh-oh. Rachel and Yael would be waiting to hear from her.

"Follow me. O'Brody's looking forward to seeing you." She turned with a swirl, revealing a winged-unicorn tattoo on her bony, thong-wearing ass. And what else? Bruises?

"You're the type he's looking for, sweetheart."

Alyssa gulped and followed the freaky receptionist.

Where was the music? Where was the sound of dancers shuffling feet and chatter?

Their footsteps echoed in the silent, empty hallway.

—

"They're tracking the fentanyl out of some lab in China," Marlene said as she and Anthony consumed burritos at a lunch truck near Spring Street downtown. She took a noisy slurp of Diet Coke. "Then on to Mexico where it gets cut with heroin and shipped up to our beautiful city. Chief says this shit's expected to hit the streets in about a week, week and a half."

"Fuckin' late-stage cancer drug. Thirty-to-fifty times stronger than H. Stock up on your naloxone kits, boys and girls. Bodies'll be dropping like goddamn flies. Makes me sick." He took a big bite, managing to contain most of the spicy dribble in the aluminum foil wrapper. "Damn, this is good."

When two customers finished up at a rickety picnic table, the detectives moved in and sat down beneath a faded sun umbrella.

"I was thinking this morning in the shower..." Marlene settled in and pushed up her eyeglasses.

"Sounds dangerous," Anthony said with a salsa-smeared smirk.

"Ah, stuff it, Peter Pan. I was thinking that this is the first big shipment since Luis Alvarez was killed. It may have real significance for the new leadership, whoever the hell that is."

"You mean, like proving they can deliver, that the Alvarez crew is still in business?"

Marlene nodded, tucked her remaining burrito debris in the foil and tossed it toward the trash can. Missed.

"Oh, crap." She began to stand and retrieve her over-shot, but Anthony beat her to it.

"Jeez, you really can be a gentleman once in a while. You practicing for your lunch with Bea? Tomorrow, huh?"

He shrugged and nodded. "None of your Bees-wax."

Marlene groaned. "*Oy vey*, really bad. This date thing is doing something nasty to your already limited brain function."

He sat back down, then threw her garbage at the can and hit it dead on. "But not my aim, baby. Seriously though, good thought on the cartel — I think you should shower more often."

Marlene rolled her eyes.

"What you're saying makes sense, Mar. Could definitely be a statement that they're still the main motherfuckers. A big ol' lethal pissing contest."

"Yep, back in charge, especially after the Ukrainian challenge. Bea and Lucy are thinking this could be the biggest, nastiest delivery, ever. If it breaks bad for the cartel, control may be up for grabs again."

"More hits, maybe more fires, a shit storm." Anthony finished his burrito and wiped his mouth with a mangled napkin. "Hey, partner," he said, "with all due respect to those two women, I think you gotta be more careful 'bout sharing intel with civvies, especially ones in the news biz."

Marlene finished her drink and pushed the empty cup toward the detective. "Pete, we're not going to get anywhere close to nailing these assholes without their help. They've been there. Lucy was captured by the cartel's people. She saw Alvarez go down. She has her auntie identifying the players from the Mexican boonies somewhere. We wouldn't have any of that without them."

Anthony sighed, hit another garbage can shot. "You're right, but it puts them in the crosshairs and that ain't good."

"We need to work harder to track this Mercer guy. I hate

to say it, but I think we should talk with Bea's daughter again, see if she can remember anything more that could give us a clue to where he's gone. Between pictures, conversations, an audition offer, she's had some significant contact with him."

Anthony nodded. "We gotta see who might be in Mercer's circle. The burn doctor seemed clueless but the nurse said our boy had some pretty rough-looking visitors. Maybe he should sit down with a sketch artist."

Marlene slid off the picnic bench and grabbed the handle of her rolling office. "I'll go back over to the Burn Center and talk with the staff some more, then make arrangements with Bea to meet with Alyssa."

"Okay, sounds good." Anthony followed her toward the car.

"Wanna go with me?" Marlene asked.

Anthony shook his head. "Got a previous appointment."

Marlene smiled. "A haircut? And a mani-pedi?"

Anthony refused to look at her. Stepped off the curb and beeped the key fob as he headed toward the driver's side of the dusty, city-issued Caprice.

"Bingo." She laughed out loud and hoisted her belongings into the back seat. "Beauty time, huh? Maybe your son'll loan you his Axe cologne. I hear they banned it in some junior highs — drove the teachers insane. It's always on special at Walgreens."

Anthony snarled. "I should strand you here with that sack of crapola you roll everywhere."

Marlene laughed so hard tears began to well in her eyes. She barely made it into the car before he sped away toward the station.

# 21

Brody Blackwell slumped against the wall in Mercer's posh room at the discrete Santa Barbara clinic. A dated, anonymous-looking stucco ranch house on the outside, on the inside the place made the Four Seasons look shabby. The filtered sun shone through expensive drapery, creating a golden glow. Frowning, Brody re-tied his cinnamon-colored dreads into a chunky ponytail. He folded his chiseled, dancer's arms across his broad chest; not being able to bring himself to join in the gathering.

The others crowded around the patient, like worker bees to the fucking queen. Oh, you look so good, Mercer, so handsome now. Resentment smoldered in Brody's heart like the burn of a terminally cramped muscle.

The bitch Toulusa was the worst. She sat quietly at the asshole's side, whispering in his ear as she sewed freaky animal hides together in little squares. Hovering near her was Valencia, The Accountant. Son of a former Medellin *primo*, he'd grown up in the trade. Altamont, the enforcer, was a stone-cold killer who loved his work. The firebug, Cardenas, was a small, mild-mannered hand grenade who people trusted before he burned their houses down. The inferno at the Ukrainian's place at the port was an epic example.

Other than the Mercer's bottomless access to funds, Brody was well aware of what drew them to the dude and engaged their loyalty. They'd all once made the homicidal mistake of crossing their former boss, Luis Alvarez. It was only because of Mercer's self-serving but critical intervention that each was alive today. He never let them forget that debt. He made sure it continued to grow in their minds like a cancer. They lived in a Stockholm syndrome mindset where Gary Mercer, formerly the Hand of the King, now the King himself, was their brutal captor and they kissed his melted ass.

Brody increasingly felt like an outsider. Who was he to Gary Mercer? The artist, dancer, procurer of girl whores, sampler of wares, show runner for the cartel's growing porn venture? Alvarez had appreciated his talents. To Mercer, he was becoming a replaceable pretty boy, a dime a dozen on the streets of Tinseltown.

His brother's face stared over at him, stretched across Mercer's skull like a rubber mask. Brody tried to hide his repulsion but his stomach churned with rage. His little brother had been a beautiful fool, but he was family. Mercer saw himself as having no boundaries, but this time he had gone too far.

The face-thief finally addressed him. "What do you think, Brody? Does it look better on me, or him?" The others followed Mercer's gaze and awaited Brody's reaction. The lightness in the room quickly grew suffocating with tension.

"This is, of course, your own fault." Mercer ran his fingers lightly across the stolen face. "What did I tell you about trafficking in underage girls?"

Brody stifled his anger, barely controlling his desire to strangle the man, to rip off the mask and tear out his brains.

"You said not to procure white silk girls, even though Alvarez required me to do it, and even though it's highly profitable. You said it puts our bigger plans in jeopardy."

"Very good. That's precisely what I said. And Alvarez is dead because of his shortsightedness in this regard, his inability to see the big picture. I'm still here." He licked his over-inflated Botox-filled lips. "Another failure to obey my directives and I've asked Toulusa to sew your face on my bathrobe. Do you understand me, Brody?"

Brody nodded, chilled to his marrow. He pushed away from the wall and took a step toward the group. "I understand."

The burn patient's dead, ball-bearing eyes stared out from behind his brother's lash-fringed lids.

"You have one chance to make this right. As you are well aware, the girl is coming to your studio this afternoon to, ostensibly, audition. I expect you to ruin her as I was ruined. Not her lovely face and body, but in here." Mercer gently tapped his skull. "Do her in every way possible, record everything. We'll send it to her mother, who'll undoubtedly share it with that cunt, Lucy Vega. They can carry the soul-crushing guilt for the rest of their short lives."

"Put it on the dark web and it'll go viral," Toulusa said in her sing-songy voice.

Mercer nodded. "Their actions made this happen. The poor girl will never recover from the trauma. Do I make myself clear?"

Restrained chuckles arose from the group.

Brody scowled. "Of course, perfectly clear." He glanced at his watch. He'd forgotten she was even coming today. "I have to run; the girl'll be waiting." She'd probably already been waiting at least a half-hour. It was two o'clock, and top speed and easy traffic, it would take him ninety minutes to get to North

Hollywood. He'd text his assistant instructions to give he girl something relaxing.

He bowed to the group and jogged from the room. His hands flexed, burning with the need to destroy Mercer. If not today, then soon.

———

Rachel sat cross-legged on a colorful beach towel next to the lifeguard station, gazing at her dreamboat. She'd recently confessed to crushing on the seasonal guard named Zach who was a grad student at USC and formerly on the water polo team. He stood on the platform with binoculars in one hand and his rescue buoy, or can, in the other. His lean torso was perfect, but even that wasn't holding her attention.

Yael sprawled on her stomach reading a romance novel on her Kindle. She'd untied her bikini top to avoid tan-lines.

Grabbing a handful of red grapes from a small cooler, Rachel checked her cell phone for the billionth time. "I can't believe Aly hasn't texted us. I'm getting worried. She should've been there a long time ago, and nothing, no text, no call. Swore she'd keep in touch the whole time."

"She's probably in the middle of the audition," Yael said, "dancing her buns off. Or signing a contract. You worry too much, Rachel." She reached back and tied her bikini top, then pulled out her own phone. It was a new Android that she kept in a baggie to avoid the sand. She checked the texts. "Nothing from her on mine, either." Yael turned over and rolled onto her knees, looked again at the small screen. "No, wait." A cry escaped from her throat. "Oh. My. God."

"What?" Rachel demanded.

"She texted — 'HELP ME.'"

Rachel grabbed her friend's phone to see the words for herself. "That was two hours ago."

"I swear to God it just came in. Maybe it got hung up in transmission somehow."

Rachel examined the text again then returned the phone to her friend, hand shaking. She gulped. "Alyssa could be dead by now."

Both girls looked at each other and seemed to go into a simultaneous panic. Their eyes popped and they whimpered, struggling not to scream. They hugged tight then let each other go.

Yael rapidly texted Alyssa SOS. *Nada*, no response. "Should we ask Zach for help?"

"He's gotta guard the beach. We need the police." Rachel squinted and looked back toward the boardwalk. Two officers on bicycles cruised toward the pier. "Let's go," she said. "We'll nab the bike cops."

Their grapes went flying and seagulls swooped in to claim the treats faster than both girls could stuff their gear into their beach bags and sprint toward the pier. The cops, a man and woman in navy shorts and white LAPD polos, had stopped and were approaching a pumped-up, buff dude with two big dogs running around off-leash. The woman officer pulled a pad of citations from her pocket.

"Help, we need help!" Yael made it to the police first, breathlessly interrupting the scolding of the dog owner.

Both cops turned toward her and the dog guy slithered away down an alley next to a row of sunglasses and tie-dye T-shirt vendors.

Rachel, panting, was steps behind Yael. Their words gushed out. "You gotta help us. Our friend's in trouble. She went to a dance audition at this weirdo place in Hollywood, uh, North Hollywood, and we haven't heard from her except for this."

Yael pushed the phone with the message HELP ME toward

the officers. She continued the story, talking even faster than Rachel. "This old dude, like thirty or forty, who was all burned from an accident, hooked her up with this choreographer who won an Emmy or something and she thought this would be her big break, and, and —" Tears began to form in Yael's watery blue eyes. Her shoulders trembled.

"And she's not calling us back." Rachel wiped sweat from her flushed forehead. "And she's by herself, and she's only in middle school, like us, and her mom said she couldn't go, but she went anyway and we were her, you know, her alibi, and —"

"Slow down girls, slow down," the tall, pony-tailed female cop said. She pushed the tablet of infraction forms back into her pocket.

Rachel grasped her hand. It was warm and strong. "You have to help us." She then broke down into full sob mode.

"Okay, girls, let's calm down," the male cop said. He was husky and shorter than the woman. "We can do something called a welfare check and send somebody over to this studio, make sure everything's okay. Sound like a plan?"

The girls looked at each other and nodded in agreement. Rachel struggled to stop crying. She began to hiccup in little squeaks and the woman cop patted her plump arm. "You have the address to this, uh, studio?" she asked.

Rachel pulled herself together and punched up the address for Airport Studio, deeply thankful that she'd taken the time to get the information from Alyssa. She'd almost blown it off but remembered her Girl Scout motto of "Be Prepared."

The man glanced at his partner, the expression on his face moved from skeptical to grim. "I know that place from when I worked Valley Division," he said.

The woman officer nodded and quickly pulled out her radio.

# 22

Alyssa sat alone in a short row of three canvas-backed director's chairs next to a mostly-empty craft services table on the edge of the sound stage. A piece of dried-out sushi on a tray, pretzel crumbs, plastic cups, and an empty box of gluten-free muffins were all that remained of the snacks. The stage was as big as her junior high school gym. Cool and dark, the place smelled of old socks and bleach.

She glanced at her phone. Still no bars. She'd been waiting almost two hours with assurances that Michael O'Brody would show up any minute. Alyssa'd never been on a real audition before and wondered if this was typical — creepy locations, even creepier people, and the star who may or may not actually show up. She wanted to leave, but the girl with the unicorn tattoo on her ass cheek had already ordered her to sit back down. She made it clear, in a loud pissed-off voice, that a young nobody should be grateful that O'Brody agreed to even see her at all. Few got the chance.

In a glassed-in, phone booth-sized office far across the stage, the unicorn-butt girl sat in the reflection of a monitor and typed. She eventually disappeared through an exit in the far corner behind a long, black curtain. Aly tried to tamp down her growing anxiety. This situation was all wrong. She stumbled along the stage's perimeter walls in the gloom, trying each of the three doors, but they were locked.

"Hey, where are you? I wanna leave! I'm going home!" She shook the door handle with all her might but it held as tight as a tomb. Screaming her brains would out be worthless because nobody could hear her. The place was supposedly soundproof.

Trying not to admit that she was scared shitless, Alyssa returned to her seat and chewed the nails on her right hand down to the quick. She was starting on the left when the unicorn-butt girl appeared with a drink in her hand. Alyssa jumped out of the chair, knocking it over, and bee-lined for the still-open exit.

"Miss, uh, Stein, wait." The girl moved like a ghost, hovering in front of the black drape.

Alyssa's face grew hot with anger. "It's Strauss. Like the musician. Ever hear of him?" She took a hard breath. "I tried to find you, but the doors were locked. I'm not your damn prisoner. I'm leaving. I don't know what's going on here but I don't see, like, any auditioning." She yanked the heavy, reinforced door, remembering that the girl had the key to the front entry in her pocket purse. "Come on, you need to let me out. Right now."

"Miss Strauss, Alyssa, I'm so sorry for the wait but this is an amazing opportunity for you. I'm Fiona, by the way, Brody's administrative assistant." She sighed. "Sorry, honey, if I was a rude bitch earlier but so many flakes come through this place. You seem like one of the nice ones."

Fiona approached Alyssa, round, puppy-eyes gleaming with, what? Maybe an apology? Was it real? Alyssa was reluctant to trust the fast change of tone. What caused the turnaround?

"I just now heard from O'Brody. He's twenty minutes out. His brother was found dead several days ago and he got hung up with the detectives. He's so stressed. His message came through. The reception here sucks the big one." She smiled and shrugged her slender shoulders.

The girl suddenly seemed much nicer. The nasty attitude was gone. Maybe talking to O'Brody shaped her up.

Alyssa's panic eased down a notch. "That's awful about his brother." She pressed her hand to her chest, remembering when her own brother, Dexter, had been kidnapped in Savannah, and how terrified she'd been. Should I stay or go? Her gut said, GO! "We can reschedule. I can come back another time."

"No, he really wants to see you dance today. Mr. Mark raved about you. There's only one spot left on the team and Brody'd love to have this all squared away before the funeral, so he can, you know, give his full attention to his, uh, grieving family." She wiped a tear. "Come on, stay. Persistence is everything in this business."

Alyssa felt herself waver. She appreciated that Fiona was being straight. And O'Brody, the poor guy, must be totally freaked. Deborah would want her to be compassionate and understanding.

"Hey, wanna split this energy drink?" She raised her pink plastic water bottle. "It's this amazing new stuff, all-natural. Totally sick. Everybody's obsessed with it. It'll give you a nice little boost, sweetie."

Alyssa shrugged, still tempted to leave.

"I got your music queued up in the dance studio. I would've put you in there to wait but the air conditioning's out. It's more comfy here." She glanced at her watch. "Hey, only fifteen minutes, now."

As Fiona grabbed a cup from the table and poured in half the brownish drink from her bottle, Alyssa gazed out across the dim sound stage. It all looked legit, from the director's chairs, cameras, and sound equipment, to the lighting, and the fancy set with a huge brass bed. Electrical cords ran everywhere, waiting to trip her up, like skinny black snakes.

She'd come this far. Fiona was right, never giving up was so important. "Okay, I'll wait. But if he's not here in fifteen minutes, I'm gone."

"He'll be so pleased." Fiona handed her the drink.

Alyssa hesitated and then accepted the glass. She hadn't had anything to eat for hours. Sitting back down, she sipped the liquid then scrunched up her nose. "Yuck, what is this?"

The girl chuckled. "It's kale from China and seaweed from Indonesia in a high-protein calcium broth. We're very into nutrition here. Hey, let's toast to your audition." They tapped cups.

Alyssa sipped a little more and stuck out her tongue.

Fiona bounced on her toes. Alyssa thought she looked happy and somehow relieved, maybe because Brody was on his way.

"O'Brody says this shit's more expensive than good champagne. Wonderful for your cute little body. Huge anti-oxidant properties. Drink it fast and you'll feel the pickup."

Taking a big breath, Alyssa downed the rest of the liquid and gritted her teeth at the bitter taste.

Fiona gave her a warm wink. "I'll be back in a few minutes, hon. And the stage doors'll be open, no worries." She disappeared into the darkness, her white silk micro-mini-dress swaying as she walked.

# 23

The electronic gate behind the studio slowly opened and Brody pulled his silver Porsche 911 Carrera convertible into the chain-link-fenced parking area. Several other vehicles were in the lot. Looked like cast and crew had arrived and were, hopefully, ready to go on the girl.

A jet came in low overhead, whining and spewing acrid exhaust fumes. He carded in through the back door and moved down the dark hall to the stage. As the heavy, sound-proofed door closed behind him, the outside noise became barely discernable. He relished the cool quiet — his head was killing him. He wanted Mercer's little project over with as quickly as possible. This wasn't just trafficking in runaway girls, this was the kidnapping and mega-rape of the daughter of some well-known LA journalist. If they ever got made for this, he'd fry and Mercer'd remain untouched. Brody's resentment and need for payback for his brother's snuff was growing like a tapeworm in his gut.

As he came into the huge room, Fiona appeared, gaunt and ghost-like. The girl's days on the mattress were coming to an end. She could take the heavy stuff like a trooper, though.

Few could.

"The kid's barely awake," Fiona said. "I helped her over to the bed. Dressed her in a school uniform and put her hair in pigtails like you wanted."

"You're the best, Fi."

She followed at her boss's heels like a puppy as he walked onto the set. The camera operators stood by, the sound guy adjusted a mic on a fish pole and the gaffer had the lighting nice and sexy. Something this raunchy would usually be done in a seedy basement somewhere but Mercer insisted on production value. So, Brody called in a highly professional group that could work on any major studio project and did. Couldn't beat the salaries in the pornies, though. And a bonus for this shoot. Quick and dirty, in and out. It always amazed and comforted him that so many had shit for scruples.

Brody hovered over the unconscious object of his assignment, tugging absently at the silver bullet threaded into one of his coppery dreadlocks. "Beautiful girl," he said, "kind of a black Brooke Shields in the old film, *Pretty Baby*. No, more like Lisa Bonet in *Angel Heart*. Remember that?"

Fiona nodded.

"Yeah, this'll go viral on Tor for sure." He smiled. Fiona caught his eye and winked.

Two men, a long-haired white dude dressed in a football uniform, and a skinny, nerdish black guy wearing a geeky shirt and tie, chatted with a severely augmented woman done up as a teacher. A craft services gal in her fifties poured Pringles into a bowl on the table behind them.

The actors sat on the directors' chairs, waiting. They turned toward Brody as he approached, Diet Coke in hand.

"Thanks for coming on short notice. This'll be fast, over the top, and worth your while," he said, voice curt. No time for small talk. "Here's what I have in mind but feel free to improvise."

———

When Fiona returned to her cramped desk, she gazed out across the sound stage. The crew was making last-minute adjustments to their equipment, and Brody was off in the corner, deep in conversation with the players. She felt a pang of sadness as she observed the girl moving fitfully on the big brass bed. She'd been in that place once herself, and life had never been the same. Now, between the good money and the free drugs, she knew she'd never leave until she was hauled out in a black plastic bag.

She put that unhappy thought away with a quick toot and some online shopping.

Tapping away on her computer checking out the latest apparel catalog from Tragic Beautiful, Fiona heard the doorbell buzz through the speaker on her desk. She switched screens to the surveillance cams and broke out in a cold sweat. The police were outside.

For a moment paralyzed, the administrative assistant watched a young, Hispanic officer talk into his radio, then she sprang out of the office and sprinted toward Brody and the actors.

"The cops." Her voice was shaky. "At the front door." They'd been raided twice previously and she still found it terrifying.

Brody froze at the news. The crew stopped what they were doing. He looked over at Fiona.

Feeling slightly dizzy, she couldn't stop hyperventilating and turned away.

"Fiona, get your shit together and answer the door," Brody ordered. "Be nice. You've done this before. Come on, girl."

She nodded her head and struggled to control her panicky breathing. She was the best damn assistant Brody'd ever had. She wouldn't let him down.

"Folks, relax. You know the drill," he said. "We're shooting a commercial. I'll get the girl and stash her. You all can split for now but be ready for a callback tonight."

Fiona stood rooted by his side.

"Go, Fi, what are you waiting for? Take care of the pigs."

She felt his critical glare and rushed toward the foyer.

As she exited the studio, pounding on the front doors became loud and insistent. The bell rang repeatedly. Fiona took a deep breath, then felt her mask of calm descend.

She pushed the intercom button. "Yes, can I help you?"

The two Hispanic cops, one slim in his early twenties and the other early forties and buff, gave her the nasty stare-down.

"May we come in, please?" the slim one asked. His veneer of courtesy felt as flimsy as toilet paper.

"Certainly officer. We were in the middle of shooting, couldn't come out until the director called Cut. You know how it goes." She smiled at the old guy, who seemed tougher to convince — the type who'd heard it all and believed nothing.

She unlocked the door and held it open like a gracious hostess. "How can I help you, gentlemen?"

They stepped into the foyer. Fiona watched their eyes scan, noses twitch, on the scent of their quarry.

The slim cop said, "We're looking for a twelve-year-old girl."

She's fucking twelve? Fiona took a deep breath. Brody always made a point to keep the babies out of the Airport Studio. This was their primo space, and he'd never risk it. What was going on?

He continued. "Light-skinned African-American, five-two, a hundred pounds, wearing a pink hoodie. Name's Alyssa Strauss. Came here for a dance audition."

Fiona's mind whirred as she struggled to figure out the safest response. With men, believability always involved sex. Vibes said they were straight. She put a hand on her hip and shook back her hair. "Oh, yes. The girl was here earlier but we sent her home. Our choreographer had to cancel at the last minute. I don't think she rescheduled."

The older cop studied his tablet. "The choreographer being a Michael O'Brody, also known as Brody Blackwell?"

Fiona nodded. "He's one of the most respected people in the field."

He sneered. "I'm sure."

She glanced over the officer's shoulder and spotted a black SUV and a new pick-up zoom down the street. The fuckers were bailing on her. Damnit, she was on her own. Resentment flared and she could feel her face flush. Then, Brody's Porsche flew past, taking off like one of the jets. Did he have the girl?

Slim followed her eyes and went for his radio. Called in the Porsche. Then he gave Fiona an assessing look. "Who was that? Came out of the parking lot, your studio lot."

Fiona shrugged, fear building in her chest. "Oh, that must belong to one of the crew. Probably wrapped shooting. Everybody wants to hit the road before crush hour."

He turned to his partner who stuck a toothpick in his teeth and said, "Give us the tour of this shit-hole, little lady."

Fiona knew the dance on this one. "I'm sorry, sir, but you'll need a warrant."

"We got probable cause," the seasoned cop growled.

Did he really or was he bluffing? Or did it matter?

A little muscle by his eye twitched, "Open up or we'll haul your ass to Van Nuys faster than you can say 'fuck off.'"

She saw slim guy grimace and flash his partner a look that told him to chill. Then he said, "It's a welfare check, ma'am. Let's not make this more complicated than it has to be."

The older cop stepped aside and called into his radio for back-up.

Fiona's face flushed again and her heart banged like a pornie woodsman going for the gold. She'd never been in jail, and she sure as hell wasn't going to take the fall for this. "Follow me, please," she said, spinning dramatically so they had the full show of swirling silk and near-naked ass.

# 24

When her daughter's friend Rachel phoned Bea at work to confess that Alyssa had disappeared on her way to a forbidden audition in North Hollywood, Momma Bear charged out of her office like a Super Bowl tackle after the quarterback — fast, focused, and furious. Commandeering a network SUV, she headed over the clogged Cahuenga Pass toward this off-limits studio. M-80s popped behind her eyeballs as she tried not to envision the possible scene.

She turned up the volume on the police scanner as an officer called in a speeding silver Porsche heading south. She took the 101 to the 134 and exited at Vineland. It seemed to be the most direct route.

As she approached the major intersection at Vanowen, she spotted a silver 911 convertible across the street near a stop sign on Kittridge raising its roof. Bea spotted a curly head slumped in the passenger seat as a man with long, gingery dreads talked fast into his Bluetooth. Had to be Brody.

Bea swerved across the two oncoming lanes, forcing the traffic to a screeching, dangerous halt. Horns honked; curses bludgeoned the air.

None of it registered. There was only Alyssa. She reached into the glove compartment and grabbed her Glock.

She cut in front of the Porsche, trapping it, and leaped out of her car, adrenaline a tsunami in her veins. The driver, clearly stunned, was a second late in trying to back up and escape this angry black woman drawing down on him like a panther intent on dinner.

The convertible top was still only partially-closed when Bea ripped Alyssa out of the car right through the window. She dragged her daughter's limp but breathing body away from the Porsche.

The dancer asshole rammed his ride into reverse and began to back over a steep curb. The bottom of his car scraped against the concrete.

Bea would not let him escape. She laid Alyssa on the grass behind the SUV and turned to Brody, ready for murder.

"You thinkin' what the fuck? THE MOTHER? Damn right. Mess with my child, you gonna pay."

His head swiveled. "I rescued her, you bitch. Found her wandering around Tujunga, all drugged up," he yelled as he wrenched the steering wheel.

"Sure you did, you piece of shit." She took aim.

He punched the gas. The side of a parking meter scraped across the car door's billion-dollar paint job as it lurched back onto the street.

Bea sneered. She took a shot.

Ping. It hit the license plate.

"Tell Mercer he's a dead man!" she screamed and shot again, this time hitting the rear window.

The Porsche disappeared down an alley as two cruisers pulled up behind her, lights flashing. The siren pealed with two short yelps.

Bea tossed the gun aside and held up her hands. Then, "Fuck it." She ran to her daughter.

# 25

Bea clung to Alyssa like a drowning woman as two police officers stepped from the cruiser. Hand on his holster, the driver, a tall, mustachioed man wearing aviator glasses, proceeded directly to her sidearm and picked it up with a rubber glove.

"The Porsche. Down that alley," Bea said. Words tumbled in gasps and tears. "Tried to kill my baby."

In her peripheral vision, she saw the male officer return to the cruiser, stash Bea's gun, and begin to talk on the radio.

"Beatrice Middleton?" A female African-American officer in her early thirties oozed calm and took several steps toward Bea. "Your daughter? Miss Alyssa Strauss?" She nodded toward the girl, who had her arms wrapped around her mother's neck. Mother and child were bonded with the superglue of what could have happened.

"Yes," Bea croaked. Tears dripped slowly down her face. "I'm Bea Middleton, this is my daughter."

"Ambo's on its way," the officer said. She approached slowly, then knelt next to them.

"You're letting that asshole get away!" Bea shouted.

"No, we're not," the female officer said, voice strong. She took a quick glance at the CNN logo on Bea's van. "Other units're in the area. We want to make sure you're both okay." She squeezed Alyssa's trembling shoulder. "How're you doing, young lady?"

Alyssa, mute, dug her head deeper into her mother's embrace.

The woman turned to Bea. "I'm Officer Drayton. I know this is a terrible time to bring on the questions, but we all want to catch this guy before he goes to ground. You have any idea who the driver is?"

Bea cleared her throat and loosened the death grip Alyssa had on her, a bit. "Yeah, I'm pretty sure his name is Michael O'Brody. He's a well-known choreographer in the business. My daughter was supposedly auditioning for one of his projects."

The officer tapped the information into a cell phone and pushed send. As she did, an ambulance pulled onto Kittridge and parked next to Bea's network van. Gear in hand, the EMTs bustled over to Alyssa.

Drayton stood and stepped away to give the medics room to work. Bea heard her say, "Girl needs to be tested for roofies, Ketamine, ASAP. And make damn sure they do a rape kit."

Bea wiped tears away again and tried not to be overwhelmed with horrific thoughts as to the damage that might have been done to her baby girl. Old recollections of damage that had been done to Bea herself when she was a naïve, clueless Savannah teenager not much older than Alyssa, threatened with evil whispers and pangs of terror.

A bright-eyed young medic whipped out his stethoscope. Alyssa struggled against his ministrations for only a moment, then went out again, mumbling and unconscious. After a thorough once-over, the emergency responders hoisted Alyssa onto a gurney and moved her to the ambulance, where they inserted a drip line.

"We're taking her to Valley Presbyterian," the medic with the stethoscope across his shoulders said. You want to follow us, or ride along?"

Bea jumped in next to her daughter. She stroked her cold, limp hand and prayed as the vehicle sped toward the hospital.

Between springing Dexter from the slammer and now Aly, drugged and on the way to the ER, Bea could barely keep her head from blowing up.

"She's going to be okay, ma'am. Heart rate's fast but her vitals are strong." The conscientious medic was doing his best to be encouraging but Bea shuddered.

If only it was the physical trauma to be concerned with, but it wasn't. It was the unseen wounds that had yet to be revealed. Bea looked down at her beautify baby, sweating and agitated. She'd make sure this Brody asshole danced his way to Hell.

—

When Lucy arrived at Valley Presbyterian Hospital, Alyssa appeared to be resting peacefully, but Bea looked like she'd gone through the car wash, strapped on top of a truck. Lucy didn't bother to ask Bea how she was doing or feeling. Her friend's face said it all. It was heartbreaking.

The two women embraced, then Lucy grabbed the rolling physician's stool at the end of the bed and sat down next to Alyssa. Bea had already pushed her recliner close to her daughter and held her hand.

Lucy studied the two beauties she loved so dearly. She didn't want to further upset Bea, but the elephant in the room sucked the air like a shop vac. Lucy took a deep breath. "Darlin,'" she hesitated, "was she — is she okay?"

Bea nodded. "Tests came back negative. Kid can't remember anything except that she accepted a vile-tasting energy drink from the receptionist. Some girl who had a unicorn on her ass. The stuff had been laced with enough Ketamine to put down a horse. Looks like the cops intervened, though, before the degenerates at the studio could do anything worse to her."

"Thank. God." Lucy glanced toward the heavens and prayerfully interlaced her fingers.

Bea sighed as if she'd been holding her breath for an hour. "Baby girl's lucky to be alive."

Lucy smirked. "I hear this Brody dude's lucky to be alive, too."

Bea's full, brown lips curled into a demonic smile. "His luck is about to run out."

Side by side, they quietly watched Alyssa sleep. The steady rise and fall of her chest was nothing short of a gift.

"Are Deborah and Eli on their way over?" Lucy asked.

"Should be here any minute." Bea chewed at her thumbnail. "I hope they don't push her for information. She woke up about an hour ago and the cops questioned her, but it's all a black hole."

Her cell phone rang. She pulled it from her pocket and checked the number. "It's Marlene." Bea locked eyes with Lucy for a moment, then took the call. "Hey, detective. I'm here in Aly's room with Lucy."

Lucy could hear some of Marlene's words through the receiver, faint and tinny as they discussed Alyssa's medical state.

"What?" Bea scoffed. "Don't tell me you got him."

"Yeah, Beebs, we got him."

"For real?" She pressed her hand to her chest as if she were trying to keep it from exploding. "No way."

Bea glanced at her sleeping child and then followed Lucy out into the hallway where she put the phone on speaker. "Say that again so Lucy can hear."

"Hi, Lucy. We got the piece of shit."

"That's what I thought I heard," Lucy said. She hugged Bea and they both swiped away tears.

Marlene continued. "Was heading up toward Palmdale when the CHP spotted him. Should've ditched that fancy ride. All ego, no brains."

"Is Michael O'Brody his real name?" Lucy asked.

"Brody Michael Blackwell's his legal name. Originally from Sacramento. Definitely a top choreographer, but with known tentacles into the porn industry, and he probably has links to your old pal, Gary Mercer. Supposedly worked for Luis Alvarez at one point as his part-time pool boy or something."

"Oh, my God." Bea choked out the words out. "But now this dancing asshole's in jail. Thank you, Lord, and CHP."

"Well, it's not gonna be that easy, hon."

"What do you mean? This the bad news part?" Bea asked.

"Yep, sorry to say," Marlene continued, "he made bail."

Lucy groaned, sickened.

"Lawyered up immediately. Swears he rescued her. Found her in North Hollywood collapsed on the sidewalk. She didn't look local, so he says he picked her up and was taking her to the hospital."

Bea began to pace. "No way in hell," she insisted. "Going a hundred-and-fifty-miles an hour, through back alleys? Hiding from the cops? Why didn't he call 9-1-1? He's a lying sonofabitch."

Marlene cleared her throat and responded briefly to a colleague in the office. Then, back to Bea and Lucy, "Listen, girlfriends, nobody believes him. We know the scam, but proving it is gonna be a challenge. These guys and their attorneys are the ultimate slimeballs and they know how to cover their tracks. We'll get him, Bea, I promise you that, but it may not be this time."

"Screw that. No way." Bea shuddered. "I'll go on the dark web, contract a hitman."

"I'm pretending like I didn't hear that, Miss Beatrice. This isn't the goddamn Wire."

Just then, Deborah and Eli bustled into the hall, faces ashen.

"Sorry, Mar, I'm losing it," Bea said. "The Strausses are here. I'll call you later. And, Marlene, thanks for keeping us updated." She ended the conversation and prepared to greet her co-parents.

Lucy grabbed Bea's hand and gave it a squeeze. They moved back into the hospital room ahead of Eli and Deb. The presence of Bea's ex-husband and his judgmental know-it-all wife would take an additional toll on her friend.

She moved aside to let Aly's other family near their child. For better or worse, Lucy knew Bea had to be with her daughter and kinfolk right now, so she would grab the baton and run the gun lap. The whole incident smacked of Mercer. Brody, a dancer and pool boy, wouldn't be the driving force behind the ruin of Alyssa Middleton Strauss. He might be the porn-meister, but this smelled like the burned man, like bitter, smoldering retribution.

Then, Lucy texted Marlene. "Meet me at Dunkin' @ Wilshire & Twelfth in an hour."

A minute later, Marlene responded, "Copy that, sister."

Two minutes after that, "Valley picked up the gal with the unicorn on her ass."

# 26

Lucy ordered an iced coffee and an apple cheese Danish. She'd made good time and was almost fifteen minutes early for her meeting with Marlene. Santa Ana winds from the desert tore at the patio umbrellas and pushed the mercury toward a hundred while lowering the humidity to dangerously near zero.

To avoid the oven, Lucy chose a spot inside the donut shop in front of the windows, so she could watch the neighborhood's comings and goings. Only a few customers patronized the nearby tables.

After a long gulp of caffeine and a munch of Danish, she pulled out her cell phone to check texts and emails. One message stood out.

Thrilled to see a note from her Aunt Catherine Lucia, Lucy smiled. She needed this blessed distraction. There was news of the weather, a child with pneumonia, and chickens with bumblefoot. She'd sent Lucy a link to subscribe to her blog on indigenous medicine. Her last posting about burn treatments had resulted in a surge of interest from a growing list of followers. So much so, that she'd been invited to a small conference in Santa Barbara this coming weekend. Although too busy to attend, and maybe not quite ready to leave her sheltered *clínica*, she was warmed and encouraged by the recognition.

Gears began to grind and take hold in Lucy's brain. A small conference in Santa Barbara? Hmmm. Maybe a lead was materializing. If Mercer went to a private clinic up there for further burn treatment, maybe those same folks would be interested in indigenous approaches to enhance their own toolbox. Combining traditional and modern approaches to healing was trendy again.

Lucy took another bite of Danish. Nothing focused her like caffeine and sugar.

She glanced outside — Marlene marched down the sidewalk past the empty patio. Her dark hair whipped around her face in the wind. Always looking more like an art teacher than a detective, she wore black pants and a gauzy, coat-like top with big pockets. The woman loved storage of any kind. She was trailing her rolling office behind her as usual.

A few minutes later, Marlene and her bag joined Lucy at the table with an iced tea and a bacon, egg, and cheese sandwich.

"How're Bea and Alyssa actually doing?" she asked before she took a seat. "You were with them — what's your take?"

Lucy took a swig of her iced coffee, rattled the melting cubes. "Aly doesn't remember much after she bit into the poisoned apple, so to speak. And Bea's consumed with horrible images of what could've happened. The Strauss crew arrived as I was about to leave. Eli will be kind and supportive. He's a decent guy but give Deborah five minutes in that room and she'll have Bea wallowing in guilt."

Marlene's eyes narrowed. "We're gonna catch these

assholes. I didn't mention it to Bea just now on the phone, because God knows the woman has enough on her plate, but I heard from SBPD. They've identified the body that washed up near Butterfly Beach in Santa Barb." She cleared her throat and took a sip of tea. "One finger on the guy's right hand still had enough skin to get a good print. Also, preliminary DNA came in."

Lucy pushed aside the remnants of her sweet roll and leaned toward the detective. "And? Is there a tie-in?"

"We think he's Brody Blackwell's brother."

Lucy almost fell off her chair.

"And, more." She cleared her throat again. "We think Mercer's wearing his face."

—

At six the next morning, Lucy left her Jeep in the empty parking lot at Malibu Yogurt and slid into the wing-woman seat of Marlene's freshly washed Crown Vic. A pine-scented cardboard deodorizer tree dangled from the rearview mirror. The windows were tinted as dark as eclipse-viewing glasses and there were enough electronics between the front seats to launch a small missile attack.

As Marlene pulled onto PCH, heading up the coast, dawn lit the sky with a violet haze. On a Saturday morning, traffic was light. She handed Lucy the agenda for the meeting: Indigenous Medical Practices and Modern Methodologies.

Marlene slowed slightly as a group of bare-bummed surfer dudes squirmed into their wetsuits along the road. "I'll never get tired of that sight," she said with a dreamy smile.

Lucy nodded, too distracted to join in her enthusiasm. Pushing back the fear that the Santa Barbara trip was going to be another exercise in disappointment, she found herself accidentally crumpling the program in her fist. They needed some kind of bead on Mercer. Now.

"So, Ms. Vega, what's our game plan?" Marlene asked, turning to business after one last glance in the rearview mirror.

They discussed strategy as they sped past Leo Carrillo State Beach where Lucy had spent many a Girl Scout camp-out, then continued on past Point Mugu and Port Hueneme, areas that had once been idyllic agricultural fields but were now wall-to-wall subdivisions. Lucy closed her eyes, recalling the scents of orange groves and onion fields the place once held. The old Joni Mitchell standard about paving paradise and putting up a parking lot played in her brain. She sighed at the loss.

They took Rice Avenue over to the 101 freeway and motored up the coast to Montecito, south of Santa Barbara, toward the Biltmore Hotel where the conference was based.

An hour later they pulled into guest parking at the magnificent Mediterranean-style lodge that routinely hosted presidents, sheiks, and movie stars. Since the Crown Vic screamed cops, Marlene found a discreet spot at the far edge under a palm tree behind a gardening shack. They crawled out of the vehicle and stretched, taking in the surroundings. Because it was still early for hotel guests to be checking in or out, the back lot was fairly full.

"So, I'm a freelance writer hoping to post my handiwork in an obscure medical e-zine, and you're my photographer." Marlene winked, looking how a quirky writer should look — black clothing, red-rimmed eyes behind big specs, and wild hair. She'd managed to pry herself away from her rolling office and carried a leather messenger bag instead.

"You got it, girlfriend," Lucy said. She took aim with her camera at an exquisite garden of shrimp-colored bougainvillea, creamy jasmine, and deep pink hibiscus flowers. "Wouldn't mind being a gardener here," she said, thinking for a moment about creating something similar at the ranch.

Alyssa loved to garden. Maybe she could hire her to help out in a part-time summer job. Nothing to get her in trouble but sweet ranch animals, flowers, and dirt. Or was there? Rattlers slithered beneath boulders, and tarantulas hid among the tomato plants. Lucy shivered.

They approached the main entrance, decorated with terra cotta pots overflowing with lush greenery. A kitchen staffer clipped oregano and lemongrass from an herb garden beneath a jacaranda tree. The fragrance was mouth-watering.

Marlene picked up the pace. "Once we're signed in, you're gonna nonchalantly take pics of the attendees and try to include name tags. We'll pass a photo release form around the room. Sound good? Everybody has an ID at this kind of event. Usually includes their company. We'll look for anything or anybody that smacks of secrecy."

"Not sure what that would be. Like maybe a tag without a company name?"

Marlene nodded. "Let's get moving or we'll miss the free breakfast spread."

Lucy glanced at her watch. "The opening speaker kicks off in twenty. I'll sit at the back and check things out, you circulate. If you can't find me, I'm on the beach."

Marlene chuckled. They modestly low-fived and mounted the brick steps into the airy, white-washed entry to the Four Seasons Biltmore. Underfoot, muted oriental rugs covered Saltillo tiles and heavy dark beams ran overhead. The artwork was museum-worthy and the furnishings expensively inviting.

A fresh-faced concierge immediately directed them to the registration table. While Lucy checked in, picking up their name tags on green lanyards, Marlene found the buffet as quickly as a homing pigeon to the roost. The array of fresh, luscious goodies was so overwhelming they almost missed the opening remarks.

A horseshoe of white-clothed tables was centered in a cozy green and white conference room. Floor-to-ceiling paned windows overlooked gardens and a burbling waterfall. A lovely notebook and pen etched with the Biltmore's logo, along with a bottle of mineral water, and a bowl of fresh grapes and strawberries awaited at each seat.

There was no back of the room, no place to slip from view — all one big happy family. Any surreptitious photography would be next to impossible. Lucy groaned. She'd ask for a group shot at lunch and would nab any recalcitrant posers with her cell phone camera.

The two women found spots next to each other at the end of the horseshoe farthest from the door. She hated being distant from the exit but at least her back wasn't to it. About half of the participants had fired up a digital device. Marlene broke out her laptop.

Each person introduced themselves, and then the Chair, a physician from a Florida medical school who specialized in tropical diseases, unexpectedly presented Lucy Vega as the niece of one of their newest and most interesting indigenous practitioners. Lucy cringed. So much for anonymity. She raised her hand in subdued acknowledgment.

A dark-haired man wearing a fashionable man bun and wire-rimmed glasses, dressed in perfectly pressed lilac scrubs, caught her eye. He smiled from the far side of the U. Lucy nodded and took a quick glance at what she could see of his name tag. The line indicating the company was hidden by his iPad.

The doc from Florida commenced his talk with a lame joke about skin rashes. During the speech, which was probably quite interesting if you were into African sleeping sickness, Lucy surreptitiously studied each nametag she could see. Her eyes blurred at the strain. Then, belatedly, she realized that all the names were listed at the back of the program, excluding hers and Marlene's — the last-minute add-ons. She was glad their presence was off the official record.

Except for three of the attendees, all were academics, specialized nurse practitioners, or physicians representing regional hospitals or med schools. The other conference-goers represented private facilities. One clinic, the well-known Santa Barbara Oceanview Plastic Surgery Center, was likely not a place Mercer would seek out. Paparazzi lurked in the bushes. The other two sounded like generic corporations — Acute Care Med-Spas International, and Pathway to Wellness, Inc. Participants from those private organizations included Richard Dillard, the lilac scrubs surgical nurse practitioner who earned his degree from Yale, and Juana Noriega, an M.D. from Texas.

At the first session break, Lucy headed toward Dillard but got waylaid by the Florida doctor who was the conference organizer. He and his minions greeted Lucy warmly and quizzed her about Sister Catherine Lucia. Marlene stayed in her seat, shoulders hunched over her computer.

"What can we do to convince her to join us next year?" he asked. His accent was Bahamian.

Lucy smiled. "She hasn't been away from her little corner of the planet for, probably, forty years or more. I'm sure the thought of leaving is terrifying. Maybe she'd be willing to Skype. She's not afraid of technology. Took to the computer like a duck to water."

"She's too much of a precious gem to keep hidden," he said with a little hitch in his voice. "I'd love to meet her." His nametag read, Dr. Bernie Peña. Probably in his late sixties, his hair was still black and his face was smooth and angular.

Lucy suspected he had a closet fascination with this elusive woman, not only with her medical practices. Catherine Lucia had mentioned their ongoing email conversations. "Not only is she brilliant, but she's also quite beautiful," Lucy said. "Long silver hair in a braid."

His eyes lit up. Yep, hot for the auntie.

Then someone pulled at his sleeve and he excused himself to start the meeting again. Lucy glanced over at Dillard chattering on his cell phone. She returned to her seat.

"Okay, Marlene whispered, "I got something. Pathway to Wellness is in Austin, Texas. It's a recovery center for folks who've had catastrophic accidents or illnesses. This other place, Acute Care Med-Spa, has clinics in Amsterdam, Vienna, Hong Kong, Brooklyn, and Santa Barbara. Beyond location and an info@ email address, there's *nada*." She turned the screen toward Lucy who took a good look.

The faces featured on the site were beautiful but vacuous. "Sounds like what our boy Mercer would've looked for," Lucy whispered back. Again, she glanced across at Dillard. Now he appeared to be checking text messages.

The meeting recommenced and talk turned to burn treatments. This topic seemed to be Dillard's area of interest. He told the story of a patient they'd received from the Hoffman Burn Center whose life had literally been saved by simple, yet sophisticated, methods he'd received from a folk practitioner.

Lucy's face flushed hot but forced herself to appear impassive. Here we go. Dillard is who they'd been hoping for. Marlene flashed her a thin smile.

It seemed like days passed until the lunch break. Before Lucy could stand up, Dillard disappeared out the door. In a panic, she pushed by conference-goers who wanted to meet her and pursued the nurse down the hall. His lilac scrubs vanished around a corner. "Richard," she yelled. "Wait."

She rounded the corner and slammed into him.

"Oh, my, Miss Vega." He grabbed her by the shoulders before she fell backward.

"I'm so sorry," she said, regaining her balance. Lucy bent to retrieve the notebook she'd knocked out of his hands and they smacked heads as he went for the item at the same time. Dillard started laughing. Lucy tried not to cry. The clunking of the noggins hurt, but the frustration at Mercer being in reach but still as ungraspable as mist, causing the real pain.

Marlene appeared at her side. The detective panted, out of breath. "We need to talk to you, Mr. Dillard. Immediately."

"And I to you," he said, still amused. "But I have to run to my office over lunch. I'll be back. Great conference. Drinks afterward?"

Ignoring the invitation, Marlene pulled her cellphone from her pocket and held the photo of Michael O'Brody toward the nurse practitioner. "Recognize this man, by any chance?"

He narrowed his eyes. Something tensed in his jaw.

Yep, he's seen the guy before.

He looked at Lucy, then at Marlene. "You're not a freelance writer, are you, Miss, uh, Simon?"

"That's Detective Simon." She snapped out her LAPD badge then held the phone closer to his face. "Have you seen him?"

Dillard blanched and hesitated. He pushed his hand through perfectly coiffed hair. An expensive watch caught the light. "I'm part of a private facility and you know I can't say anything about our patients — HIPPA laws. I'd lose my job in a heartbeat if I compromised confidentiality. I love my job. And they pay really, really well."

"The guy in the photo — he was a patient?" Lucy pressed.

Dillard swallowed hard. "No, not a patient, not him."

"Then you do recognize him and if he wasn't a patient you have no legal basis on which to avoid my question," Marlene said.

Dillard gulped. "He was uh, uh, a visitor."

"I think we'll accept your offer for those drinks right now, Nurse Dillard," Marlene said, taking his arm. "Call your office and tell them you won't be over for lunch."

# 27

Bea covered her head with her pillow but she couldn't block out the irritating sound of the doorbell. She opened one eye and looked at her bedside clock. It was 9:07 a.m. She'd been asleep for only three hours. Alyssa had been released earlier in the evening and was under lock and key with the Strauss family. Dexter was in Atlanta with Rio, so who the hell was waking her up? The doorbell rang more insistently. A bolt of adrenaline tased her chest. The FedEx guy would ring once and split. Had something else horrible happened? Please, God, no!

Stumbling out of bed in a faded T-shirt and disintegrating cotton gym shorts, Bea tripped down the steps to the front door. She squinted into the peephole. Something else had indeed happened. Pete Anthony. With breakfast.

Bea tore open the door. "Jesus, Pete, you scared the hell out of me. I just got to sleep. What're you doing here?"

"Nice to see you, too, Beatrice. You look like hell." He chuckled. "This is not how I pictured you on our first morning together. Maybe a long, white boyfriend shirt that just covers your ass, and bare legs."

She primped her matted tresses. "Fuck you, creep. Come on in. Welcome to real life."

"Whoa, harsh." Pete chuckled and stepped into the foyer. He placed the coffees and bag of goodies on the entry table next to a vase of wilted daisies.

"I'm so sorry to hear about your kid," he said.

She threw herself into his arms. Her body shook like she was standing naked in the Arctic, and she cried out. He drew her tightly against his chest.

"Let's get you back to bed. You need some serious rest before you're totally worthless."

"I'm never totally worthless," she whispered. Soft words like little darts. She took him by the hand and led him up the stairs. "Just hold me for a while until I can fall back asleep. Would you do that?"

"Okay, baby, but you do that for me, too. Eight gangbangers dead in a shoot-out and five ODs on my watch last night. Got to me this time."

"What a fucked-up world." Bea led him up the steps and into the bedroom where she slipped beneath creamy down-filled covers. Anthony undressed down to his shorts and T-shirt and placed his badge, phone, and firearm on the night table. The presence of this man and his gun was better than a shot of anti-anxiety meds.

He crawled in next to her and scooped her into his arms. Bea held on to him, and he to her, two people teetering on the edge, looking to each other for at least a moment of salvation.

—

It was conference lunch break at the Biltmore. Lucy and Marlene escorted the reluctant nurse, Richard Dillard, to a patio sitting area where a freckle-faced girl with sun-steaked hair took their bar orders.

"Northern European complexion," Dillard whispered as she walked away. "That one's a perfect candidate for melanoma."

Marlene nodded. "I'm sure you're a knowledgeable and conscientious practitioner, Mr. Dillard."

He smiled and adjusted his man bun. "I am indeed good at what I do, as you both appear to be. And Lucy, your aunt seems to be a singular talent — the brilliant, exotic medicine woman. Everybody wants to hear about her, including me."

"She's remarkable," Lucy said. Maybe they could use her aunt's cachet to encourage the nurse to talk. They had few other cards to play and time was ticking. If they couldn't nab Mercer before he'd recovered well enough to disappear into the wild blue, they'd never find him. Lucy refused to let that happen.

Moscow Mules arrived in pounded copper mugs, along with a ceramic bowl of nuts. The nurse raised his cup, took a deep gulp and smacked his lips. "So refreshing. Lovely choice."

Lucy slid her gaze to Marlene and smiled. The women sipped their own drinks, virgin Muscovites for them. While Dillard was in the restroom earlier, Lucy had enlisted the young server to help with their scheme — keep the witness liquored up and loquacious.

Marlene punched up the photo of Brody again and turned it toward Dillard. "I understand your commitment to HIPPA, but since this man was not the patient, you can tell us about him."

"I was barely in the room with him, but I must say, the guy was gorgeous, totally buff." Nurse Dillard's eyes blurred into middle distance for an instant. "And he was the first one to leave. Kind of stormed out and marched down the hall. I heard a door slam shortly after. I'd definitely say the hunk was pissed."

Another Moscow Mule arrived before he'd finished the first. As the nurse happily accepted the second mug, Marlene winked at the server.

"Any idea what he was angry about?" Lucy downed a few almonds.

"No, no idea. But there were some, I dunno, nasty vibes between him and the woman who was all lovey-dovey with the patient. Her name was something like Ta'loosa, or Toulouse, like Lautrec. You know, the artist? Did beautiful work, but famously a degenerate."

Lucy pictured the wizened alcoholic Frenchman wearing a big black top hat. She'd minored in art history.

"The chick was tall, dark-haired, and beautiful in a spooky, Gothic sort of way. She seemed fascinated by the doc's surgical stitchery. And, whoa, as she stood to leave, a flag pole came to attention beneath her black voile skirt."

"What do you mean?" Lucy knew exactly what he meant but wanted to hear Dillard extrapolate.

"Think Dr. Frank-N-Furter from *The Rocky Horror Picture Show*. When he walked out of the elevator in that corset and high heels. Well, I'll simply never recover."

"Me either." Marlene raised her glass and took a hefty gulp of her drink.

The plot thickened. "This Toulouse is transgender?" Lucy asked.

"I'd bet my closet full of purple scrubs on it, sweetheart. Or a transvestite—just digs the dress-up thing."

Marlene continued to push. "Anyone else there with the patient?"

Dillard pursed his lips in thought. "Kind of a buttoned-down accountant type with a heavy Spanish accent, a beard.

And a small, wiry guy, also a native Spanish speaker." He smiled and straightened his posture. "I'm fluent in six languages, by the way. So many international clients to care for. I tried to schmooze, but those two didn't talk much. Just scraped and bowed to the patient." He swirled his drink and then drained his cup.

"You remember what they were wearing?" Lucy asked.

"Hmmm." Dillard stroked his clean-shaven chin. "The accountant wore an expensive suit, I'd guess a Valentino. The short guy had on jeans and a USC sweatshirt. Both late thirties, early forties. I might be able to remember even more over dinner with your *curandera* auntie. Tit for tat, so to speak."

Lucy squinted. The game was clear. Access to Aunt Catherine Lucia for information on Mercer's pals.

The server immediately conjured a cheese plate, drink number three and an encouraging smile for the nurse. "So summery, aren't they?" she crooned as she rounded the table, ponytail swinging. Lucy'd make sure she got a helluva tip. Preferably on LAPD.

"I love these copper mugs," Dillard said as if they were all looking at a housewares catalog together. "Don't you? They're on sale at Pottery Barn."

Lucy clinked her cup to his. "They're really nice, Richard, but let's stay focused, then access to Sister Catherine Lucia might be a possibility."

His eyes lit up. "Of course, okay. These mules are kicking my butt. Just what you were hoping for, I'll bet." He giggled and swayed. "Oh, and the little dude smelled like Old Spice. My grandfather slathered on that stuff. Disgusting. That's about all I can think of."

"Any other visitors?" Lucy asked. "I'm sure my aunt would

be really grateful to anyone who helped put away the man that tried to murder her niece."

Dillard blanched. "Murder? Oh, Lord." He gulped hard and his eyes ping-ponged between Marlene and Lucy. "I didn't realize the gravity of the, uh, situation, here. Do I need a lawyer?"

"Not if you're only involved with patients as a legitimate medical provider," Marlene said. "Much better to deal with us now than have the FBI raid that private little clinic of yours. And most importantly, you'll help us save other lives. That's what your practice is all about, isn't it?"

"Yes, yes, of course." A thin film of perspiration dampened his forehead. He slugged down another gulp of Moscow Mule. "So, who else did I see? Well, there was a bodyguard with the patient the entire time. Tall, like six-foot-five or so, bald, a pro-wrestler type. Full-sleeve tats. One arm had Marine images, *Semper Fi*. I didn't really notice the rest. I had to be discreet because he wasn't somebody who wanted to be stared at."

Lucy nodded.

Marlene cleared her throat and tapped on her cellphone. "I'm going to email you some mugshots later, and I'd like you to look very, very carefully. See if you recognize anyone as a visitor to the burn patient. Then I'll make arrangements for you to meet with the Santa Barbara Police facial composite artist to see what you two can come up with. Okay, Mr. Dillard?"

He chewed at his lip and glared at Marlene. "Nuh-uh, no more cops. Just you."

"We need your help. We'll keep it completely confidential," she assured him.

Dillard finished his third drink and squinted at his watch. "I really must get back to the conference." He played his hand. "I'm dying to see your aunt whenever she comes to town, Lucy. Maybe a conversation with her could make me remember more."

Lucy glanced over at Marlene then back at the glassy-eyed nurse. "You do a good job for us here, Richard, and I guarantee you'll be invited to dinner with Sister Catherine Lucia. Deal?"

His cloudy face burst into a grin. "Deal. I'm in, girls. But my boss can't know about any of this."

"Agreed," Marlene said.

"Okay. I'll work on the facial recognition thing."

Lucy realized she'd been holding her breath. "And I'll make sure you have margaritas, I mean, wine and communion wafers with my aunt." Lucy wondered if Sister Catherine Lucia would ever agree to leave Guerrero.

"Oh, my God, she did such an amazing job with the burn patient," Dillard gushed.

"Glad to hear it," Lucy said. "Mercer, calls himself Garrett Mark, was in really bad shape. I think she saved his life."

"Without a doubt. Mark was a challenging case. We had a surgical team fly in from Vienna." He drained his drink. Then his eyes widened and he gritted his teeth. "Oh, shit. You're a crafty, crafty woman, Miss Vega." He patted her hand. "Mercer? Mark? I never mentioned these names."

Lucy smiled and motioned for the bill.

# 28

As Marlene navigated the Crown Vic south through congested traffic on the 101, Lucy tapped a summary of the day's new information into the detective's computer.

"Be sure to include that the youngish, dark-haired woman, possibly transgendered, showed an unusually acute interest in surgical procedures," Marlene said. "Not sure if that means anything."

"The unnamed patient referred to her as Toulusa Lautrec or something like that. Let's check and see if there's any variation of that name among the trans community." Lucy entered the intel on the digital LAPD form.

"Thanks to that promise about meeting your aunt, nursie boy'll sit down with the SBPD facial composite artist and see if he can come up with anything useful we can feed into recognition software. A long shot, but as Wayne Gretzky always said, you miss 100 percent of the shots you never take."

"I hope Dillard comes through for us. I can see him having second thoughts after the booze wears off."

"Send him some tantalizing photos of your aunt from when you were down in Mexico, something to keep his focus on the payoff. Clearly, he'd risk a lot to meet her."

Lucy closed her eyes and rubbed at her forehead. "Good idea." She winced as the detective pulled around a convoy of Wal-Mart semis, and gassed the road warrior. The vehicle moved like a high-mileage rice rocket. Cough, lurch, protest.

Marlene continued. "The way Dillard described the burn patient's Lautrec gal pal — she sounds dramatic-looking. Maybe a performer? I mean this is the entertainment capital of the world, right? Maybe she's a drag queen?" Marlene looked at Lucy as if her friend had a ready answer.

Lucy shrugged. "Sounds more like a transgender person. Male equipment but identifies as female."

"I seem to remember that you have a friend on the faculty at Valley College who's active in the LGBTQ community?"

Lucy nodded. "Andrew Nash, now Audrina, teaches Physics. We went to high school together. He, I mean she, was homecoming queen. And valedictorian. Finished her Ph.D. at UCLA last year and got a scary good offer from private industry, but loves the kids. Valley College is full of students of color, first-generation in higher ed. They're her passion."

"How about reaching out to her? If Toulusa is a performer, maybe she's got a following. Might be on Audrina's radar."

Lucy felt a tug of optimism. "Good idea. She's very much into the arts — I'll text her." She pulled out her phone and texted. "If Audrina has a break between classes, maybe I can swing over to the valley and meet her for coffee."

The radio gargled and spit out a request for Marlene's location and ETA downtown at the Police Administration Building. The detective responded as she pulled into the shopping center off PCH where Lucy'd left her ride.

Lucy's text alert dinged — she examined the fast response and smiled. "Audrina's got a few minutes in an hour so I'm on my way to the Val." The Vic slid into a parking space. She hugged Marlene *adios*, then leaped out and bee-lined for her car.

—

Two hours later, Lucy sipped a skinny vanilla latte with soy at a Starbucks on Burbank near Fulton Avenue, a block from campus. Students populated tables and overstuffed chairs, clicking on laptops, checking phones, and gossiping with one another.

A few minutes later, Audrina Nash elbowed her way through the gaggle crowding the counter, ordering up their java concoctions and pastries. Lucy couldn't help but stare. At six-one, she was slim bodied with loose, Renaissance curls any woman would die for, not to mention bone structure that made Scandinavian movie heartthrob, Viggo Mortensen, look baby-faced.

She wore black tights, a short black leather skirt, boots, and a baggy gray sweater that left one smooth shoulder fully exposed. Bra straps were hot pink.

Hey, Dr. Nash," a couple of kids called.

Audrina turned and gave them a nod. "Ramirez, Nguyen, I wanna see A's on the quiz tomorrow."

They mumbled promises.

Then, she spotted Lucy and hustled up to the table.

"Damn, girl," Lucy said. "So good to see you. Been too long. And you're looking fabulous."

"You, too, Lucia. If I had girl crush proclivities, I'd ask you out."

They embraced and gave each other air kisses.

"How do those students concentrate with a nerd-o-licious hottie like you parading 'round the classroom?"

Audrina rolled her green-tea-colored eyes and dropped

her leather briefcase onto the chair next to her. "If anybody starts going all gob-smacked on me, I hit 'em with rapid-fire questions on Newtonian mechanics. That cools their nasty little jets — although jets are all about lift and thrust."

"You're bad." Lucy laughed. She pushed a drink toward her friend. "Thanks for your time on such short notice. Figured you'd be on the run. I hope you still take your caramel macchiato with whip."

"My, my, aren't you sweet." She gathered up her long dark curls and secured them atop her head with a pair of chopsticks that seemed to magically materialize in her hands. She took a swig of her drink and gave a thumbs-up. "So, darling, fill me in on how I can help. It sounded urgent."

Lucy nodded. "I'm trying to track down a trans woman, a performance artist of sorts. Her name is Toulusa, and that's pretty much all I know. Thought you might have heard of her somehow. I know the LGBTQ community here is pretty tight."

"It's now LGBTQIA — added Intersexual and Asexual to our moniker."

"Whoa, the name is getting too long to handle," Lucy said.

"Nothing's too long for a girl to handle, sweet cheeks. And inclusivity is never an easy mouthful."

Lucy raised her cup and they toasted that thought.

"So, you're looking for Toulusa. She's been a hot item on the underground entertainment scene for several years."

Lucy felt her pulse quicken. She leaned forward.

"Likes to channel Edith Piaf and singers of that era. She's incredible — a world-class talent. Has a show in Palm Springs once every other month. Hard to get tickets — people reserve them a year in advance. And they're pricey as hell."

"A year? You're kidding."

"No, dearest. It's quite the scene. I've been twice. When

the spotlight hits Toulusa, that woman rules the world. Talk about charisma. If I remember right, she usually plays the first Saturday of the odd-numbered months."

Excitement kindled in Lucy's chest. "So, a performance must be coming up this weekend." She and Bea had to find a way to see the show. "Do you have any connections for admission?"

"Nope, I cut those ties. Bitch is too freaky for me."

"What do you mean?" Lucy plucked at the collar of her denim shirt.

Audrina continued. "The second time I saw her perform, maybe a year ago, I was invited backstage with a couple of acquaintances I knew from random trans events. We hung around for at least an hour while the diva removed her stage makeup, redid her face, tried on a bunch of outfits I could only dream of owning, before finally deciding she was ready to party at some mansion up in the hills above Palm Canyon Drive." Audrina fluttered her long, beringed fingers. Her French manicure was perfect.

"One of the women I was with kept calling her 'the seamstress.' When I asked what she was talking about, Toulusa had her stand up, ripped the woman's expensive silk blouse down the back, and showed us her handiwork." Audrina took a swig of coffee and grimaced.

"What was Toulusa's handiwork?"

"She likes to sew people's skin — like human patchwork quilts."

Lucy choked on her latte. She didn't like where her imagination was going. "What are you talking about?"

Audrina leaned in and lowered her voice. "She'd embroidered an intricate pattern across this woman's entire back with thick, colored threads. It might have been magnificent if it hadn't been on a bloody human back oozing infection. I wanted to hurl."

"Holy shit." Lucy wanted to hurl, too.

"Precisely. And it wasn't cool like a tattoo — the vibes were ultra-malign. There were little pieces of fur sewn into the skin. Looked feline to me. Or maybe worse."

Lucy pushed her coffee away.

"When the others headed to the party, I left. I could hear Toulusa cackle at the top of her lungs as I walked out. Bitch is evil, Lucy. I'd stay waaaaay away. The thought of her still gives me the heebie-jeebies."

Lucy let out a long, pensive breath. "What you're telling me is very helpful."

Audrina glanced at her watch. "Late for a faculty meeting. Gotta boogie, sweetie. How about lunch sometime soon? You can fill me in on all this fascinating intrigue."

"Sounds like a plan. And again, thanks for the spur-of-the-moment sit-down."

"My pleasure, and thanks for the coffee. In the meantime, if I hear anything about Toulusa, you'll be the first to know."

Audrina rose, grabbed her bag, and embraced Lucy.

She turned to hustle out, then paused and called over her shoulder. "If you're hot for those tickets — try the dark web. I think the site is Tix-to-Styx."

Tickets to Hell. Lucy nodded, waved goodbye, and dialed Bea.

—

As Lucy made her way up the long gravel drive to the ranch, dust rose like pale smoke behind her car. The bone-dry chaparral smelled of creosote and sage. She felt good about their progress. They were getting closer to Mercer, she could feel it. They'd find that sonofabitch with his pernicious stolen face. If Marlene was right, and the man who'd washed up on the beach turned out to be related to Brody, that could be their first opportunity to poke a chink in Mercer's tight group.

As she pulled up to the barn, Burleson's truck was parked askew in the driveway with the front doors open. His black hoodie and a flattened can of Coors lay in the dirt. Maddie whined from the top of the steps to the barn apartment. Alarm bells sounded in Lucy's head.

She paused for a second and did a quick visual scan for other signs of disruption in the ranch's usually calm atmosphere. Nothing else seemed awry, but everything seemed off.

Her shoes thudded like hammer blows as she dashed up the stairs. Something was wrong. "Michael!"

Lucy ran across the deck and pushed the apartment door half open. Through the glass panes, she could see Burleson's body sprawled naked, face-down on the bed.

For a terrifying moment, she stood paralyzed. The virgin Moscow Mules, nuts, and strong coffee congealed to a nauseating clot in her belly. She staggered to the porch railing, threw up into the shrubs below, then pulled herself together and cautiously entered the room.

The place stank of booze and sweat. How long had he been here? Elsa was in town for the day taking a UCLA Extension course. What had happened? More than a year sober, and now this. What in hell was the trigger? She was almost too terrified to check his breathing. Her father and mother, brother, uncle, all gone. Now, Michael?

No, no, no, not again.

Maddie whined and licked Burleson's face. A shaky hand reached out to touch the pup. Lucy almost fainted from relief. For a moment, pinpoint explosions of light clouded her vision. At least he was alive, for now. She knelt next to him and checked his pulse at the carotid. It seemed strong, but his breathing was shallow and his skin clammy.

He tried to wave her away, eyes opening to slits and then closing again. "Lucy, get out of here." His voice was raspy and weak. "I'm sick."

"Sick, my ass." Damn him. The hideous fear that he was dead turned to boiling anger. "You're shit-faced. What in the hell is going on?"

A drained bottle of Jim Beam and several empty six-packs were strewn on the floor. Maddie sniffed at the empties and went for a half-consumed carton of Chinese food instead.

Lucy wavered between fury and panic. He was pallid as snow, and his lips were bluish. "I'm gonna call an ambulance."

He sat up quickly and swung his legs over the side of the bed, head in hands. "Jesus, no. I'm fine. I mean I'm wrecked, but I've been worse."

Lucy wanted to take him in her arms and comfort him. She also wanted to slap the hell out of him. Either way, she wouldn't tell him it was all was going to be okay. She refused to be an enabler. Standing across from him, she folded her arms on her chest, seething.

With effort, she managed to keep her voice even. Sort of. "When you moved in here, I told you that no matter what my feelings for you, if you started drinking again, you were outta here."

He rubbed hard at his scalp. His hair looked like it had been chewed by a weed-whacker. "I know. I'm leaving. Tonight."

Lucy held out her hands in frustration, hot anger coursing through her veins like water through a high-pressure hose. "That's it? You're just walking out?" Struggling to hold back tears of fury, she picked up the Jim Beam bottle and hurled it against the wall, missing Burleson's head by inches. It shattered. Maddie tore out the door.

"I demand an explanation, you sonofabitch. If you don't want to be together anymore, be straight about it." She struggled to rein in her baser emotions. She wanted to do damage. This was a man she had trusted with her life. He had taken a bullet for her. The betrayal was devastating. "We always said we'd tell each other the truth."

His body shivered and a great sob sounded from the core of him. He was in pain. Good. Lucy grabbed his clothing and began hurling his belongings down the stairs into the dirt.

Hours, and a bucket of angry tears later, she slipped into the spot she'd shared with Burleson for many sweet and passionate hours. She had deeply believed that he was the one. Was what they had real? Or was it dissipating like cool mist on the skin of the early morning ocean? She twisted her hand into his pillowcase and held on tight.

—

Gazing out across the penthouse bedroom he'd moved into, Mercer was in the process of making the place his own, with the help of Toulusa's unique design sensibilities. Once the domain of Luis Alvarez, the space was the size of a small gymnasium with floor-to-ceiling windows that wrapped around one of the building's entire corners. Now covered in semi-transparent drapes to protect his damaged eyes from the sunlight, the room was cool and dim. Super-oxygenated air flowed from overhead vents. A command center had been set up next to his big, round, custom-made bed.

Mercer rested in a billowy cumulous cloud of creamy white silk sheets and pillows piled high. Toulusa, dressed in black leggings and a filmy, dark gray tunic, was a lurking thunderhead against the white environment.

Mercer linked his scarred fingers in Toulusa's. "You're perfect for me, my dearest girl. You're the sweet mother I always longed for and never had. But beneath the kilt, you're the man I always wanted." He smiled, knowing it remained a grotesque grimace despite the transplanted face. There would be more surgeries to come.

Toulusa squeezed his hand and chuckled. "This place is still too clinical, my love. I bought you an original vintage Rolling Stones poster with those Mick Jagger lips and cherry red tongue to hang over your oxygen tanks. Should be delivered this afternoon. You can think of me every time you take a breath."

Mercer was delighted, but laughter turned into a coughing spasm and the tight scar tissue on his face pulled painfully. A blue-uniformed nurse appeared from the darkness. Toulusa held up a hand and the nurse paused, then retreated.

"Poor, poor baby. But the doctor says the coughing is good, clears the *schmutz* from your lungs." Toulusa stroked Mercer's arm until the fit passed.

When the paroxysm was over, Mercer lay limp as a rag doll. Toulusa helped him raise his head for a drink of ice water through a straw.

As he sipped the liquid, he felt a profound change in mood wash through his veins — from light to dark, very dark.

"I can't rest, can't recover until the bitches are dead," he whispered.

"Ah, yes, the obsession. It must be sated." Toulusa pulled his chair closer to Mercer. "I completely understand, dear one." She examined her lover's new face.

Mercer winced. He envisioned what Toulusa saw. A tragic mask — uneven, puckered, strange, and covered with gelatinous, bitter-smelling salve.

"Brody failed miserably," Toulusa said.

"Indeed, he did." Mercer cleared his throat and wiped his lips with a tissue. "He suffered a sad overdose this morning. Too bad, he was so pretty."

A faint smile curled Toulusa's ruby-stained lips. "My darling, you're quite the man of action," she said. "And what is your plan for the two whores who want to bring my baby down?"

Mercer shut his eyes and burrowed into the soft covers. He tugged on Toulusa's sleeve. Slowly, she removed her clothes and crawled in next to the burn patient.

"Fire," Mercer said. "Fire for fire. The Santa Anas will be blowing this weekend. Cardenas will bring me the plans shortly. His contact in the county fire department will join us. It'll happen Sunday night."

"A brushfire?"

"Catastrophic. I like my statements, big, dramatic."

Toulusa plucked a cigarette lighter from her pocket and flicked it on and off. It flared in the oxygenated environment. "Many will die? Could be like Sonoma County."

The light glittered in Mercer's eyes. "Collateral damage. As long as Vega and Middleton are among the dead, that's all that matters. But if they somehow survive, at least they'll have been scared shitless."

Toulusa smirked. "I've never made anything out of burned flesh before." She kissed Mercer gently on his scabbed mouth. Then roughly turned him over.

# 29

Although a delicious bottle of Merlot winked at her from the counter across the kitchen, Lucy refused to pour herself a glass. She needed distance from any substance that could inflict harm. A benign cup of iced chamomile tea and Howard sitting on her lap purring like an outboard motor was what the doctor ordered.

She brushed stray tears from her eyes with the back of her hand. How could Michael leave her? Damn him. She was sure he still loved her. Lucy felt a tinge of guilt at her rage, but she'd been through this once before with a husband right out of college. He had been an anthropologist Ph.D. student at Stanford who fancied himself a reincarnated Indiana Jones. He was exciting, brilliant, and driven, but when he was drunk, which was often, he was another idiot who was scared shitless that behind the romantic *façade*, he was nothing more than another grad student who knew how to ace tests and impress the undergraduate girls. When one of said young women appeared at their door with a baby bump, it was over.

Lucy sighed. Life was one helluva ride.

Outside, as darkness dimmed the valley, Bugle and

Maddie barked, likely at a rabbit or squirrel. Then, the noise stopped. The two pups dashed through the dog door, tongues lolling, heading for the water bowl. In seconds the floor was a wet mess. They both stopped by with drooly kisses, then collapsed on a nearby rug beneath an air-conditioning vent. They knew the prime spot for comfort.

The Santa Anas, the devil winds, blowing into LA from the Mojave, had begun their hot suffocating whispers. In another few hours, the winds would be gusting hard, sucking away any remaining humidity from across the mountains. There wasn't enough moisturizing lotion on the shelves at Walgreens to keep your skin from itching, or enough conditioner to keep your hair from standing on end.

Lucy's cell phone chimed. Howard jumped off her lap and slinked toward the darkening living room. It was beneath him to compete with a phone call for attention.

"Hey, Bea," Lucy said. "You and yours doing okay?"

"All is good. No complaints from Alyssa about Deborah or Hebrew school since the event, so she's feeling appropriately contrite." Bea paused. "I'm not sure she really understands the seriousness of what could have happened, but I sure as hell hope so."

Lucy sighed. "Kids. They seem to have this dangerously clueless sense of their own invincibility."

"No kidding."

"Dexter okay?" she asked.

"Doing fine in Atlanta. They went to visit Emory today, Morehouse, and Howard tomorrow."

"Interesting that he's looking at some historically black colleges. That's cool."

"Since his week in Savannah with the family, he's re-examining his roots. It's all good. Looking forward to getting the scoop. If not from Dex, from Rio — God bless him. By the way," Bea hesitated, "I should mention FYI, I, uh, slept with Pete."

Lucy gulped. "Sweet Jesus. You said you weren't gonna get involved with anybody right now, especially a womanizer that you have to work with."

"Yeah, well, there's that little mistake, and, to add to the fun and games, my sewer system's backed up. I need to move out for a couple of days until they can get it fixed."

"Sounds like a pretty shitty situation."

Bea groaned.

"Come on up to the ranch and stay with me. Elsa's visiting her grandkids this weekend and Michael, well, things are not too fabulous there, either."

"What's going on?"

Lucy could hear the concern in Bea's voice. The woman didn't need any more anxiety to deal with, but she had to tell her friend the truth.

Bea sighed. "You know he loves you."

"But we both know that's not enough. He relapsed. I threw him out, and it's killing me."

"You had to keep your word and make him leave, for his own good, as well as yours. But the relapse's not surprising given what happened to his daughter."

Lucy felt an ominous catch in her chest. "What are you talking about?"

"I saw him in Santa Monica leaving Media House yesterday afternoon. He was heading to the ranch to tell you. I didn't want to call. Guess he stopped in for a few along the way."

"I found him drunk in the apartment. He didn't tell me anything."

"Oh, my God." Bea's voice dropped almost to a whisper. "You don't know."

"Know what?"

"His youngest daughter, Jaime, the one's that's a sophomore at UC-Santa Cruz. She OD'd last night."

Lucy's throat closed.

Bea continued. "Heroin. Thank the Lord above, she survived."

"Oh, my God." Lucy began to hyperventilate; a panic attack was on the way. "Michael thought Jaime was finding her footing. I threw him out when he needed me. He had to pick his favorite running shoes out of a cactus." Pressure constricted her diaphragm with harsh, painful pincers.

"He needs to deal with this relapse himself, Lucy." Bea's voice went steely. "He's got to stand up and be the father he never was. He wants to do that. You can't do it for him. And you can't control the choices he makes regarding sobriety."

Silence. Lucy slid down the wall and landed on her butt, panting. Bea was right, but the urge to try and rescue him was almost as strong as the knowledge that she couldn't.

"Breathe, Lucy. And take one of your anxiety pills. I'll throw some stuff in a bag and be there ASAP. Sounds like we need a girl's night, to say the least. I've got Point Dume Pizza on speed dial. I'll get the works. It's gonna be okay."

"Hurry. I feel like I'm dying." Lucy dropped her phone and crawled toward the bathroom on her hands and knees, too dizzy to stand.

Images of the car wreck and her mother's body lying on the road, of her dead brother with blue lips from the Slurpee he'd been drinking when the truck crossed the median. Of her dead uncle trapped in his car at the bottom of the canyon. The hell they'd experienced in Mexico, and now, Michael's daughter.

She shuddered. Anxiety had her in its cold grip. Time to see the therapist again. She'd thought those PTSD days were far in the rearview mirror. How foolish.

She found her meds and swallowed the tiny white pill dry, but couldn't get the cap back on the bottle. Her hands were going numb. It would be so easy to chug them all, easy as downing cookie sprinkles because this shit would never end. But then Mercer would get his way, and Bea would weep, and Michael would never hold her again. Michael — beautiful, good man. She'd phone him in the morning and send him love and support. It broke her heart, but she wouldn't apologize for making him leave.

Lucy wobbled across the kitchen and collapsed into Maddy's big dog bed, slowed her breathing, and shut her eyes.

—

Several hours later, Lucy slowly became aware of the smell of a Turbo Veggie Power Pizza, the poke of Maddie's foot in her ribs, and the popping sound of a wine bottle uncorking. When she opened her eyes and the brain-fog lifted, she found herself flat out on the pet bed, staring into Bugle's beady brown peepers. The dogs dislodged themselves from next to her as Bea sloshed a goblet full of red. Lucy crawled up onto one of the kitchen bar stools and rested her head in her hands.

"And I have marrow bones for your bedmates. Quite the three-way." They perked their ear at the sound of rustling butcher paper. "And one of those fake mice for Howard. He hissed and disappeared when I walked in."

The pups gratefully seized the bones. They ambled across the Spanish pavers and old braided rugs to the middle of an expensive, antique kilim carpet and began munching their greasy treats. How did they always manage to seek out the one place they were forbidden to go? Crunch, crunch, lick, slobber. What the hell. Lucy was too tired to shoo them off. They were happily taking advantage of her diminished state.

Bea rummaged in a Whole Foods bag and pulled out another indulgence. "We'll top it all off with a couple of pieces of cheesecake, or save them for breakfast — your choice."

Tears sprung to Lucy's eyes. "You know I love you, Bea. Thank you so much for being there for me, in so many ways." Tears began rolling hard.

"Okay, okay. Right back at 'cha, baby girl. And you're saving me from sewer system hell. We have each other's backs." She and Lucy embraced. Then Bea pushed the tissue box toward her friend. "Enough crying. You grab the pizza, I got the vino and paper plates. Let's hit the porch and watch the sun set."

"It already set." Lucy sniffled, took a handful of Kleenex, and blew her nose.

"Then we'll watch the stars come out. I can still see a few from out here in the semi-boonies. Will remind us of how tiny our problems are in the big universe."

Lucy followed Bea across the dark living room and opened the French doors to a high-ceilinged screened-in porch. A fan spun slowly overhead. They made themselves comfy on a couple of rocking chairs and each grabbed a slice.

"Except for no humidity, almost feels like Savannah, Georgia back here."

"I take that as a great compliment," Lucy said. She managed a little smile.

Bea took a long gulp of wine, then stopped and sniffed the air. "Smells a little smoky, or am I being paranoid?"

Lucy took a couple of deep breaths and coughed. "I don't smell anything, but my nose is totally stuffed-up." She heard the dog door open and close in the hall near the kitchen. "Can't believe they've bailed on those marrow bones already. Excuse me, gonna call 'em inside and shut their escape route. I lock them in at night — too many coyotes out there. And God forbid, a skunk."

Lucy went to call the dogs and returned a few minutes later with them at her heels. Howard the cat skulked to a far corner of the porch behind a footstool.

Sitting back down on the rocker, Lucy picked up her half-eaten slice of Turbo Veggie and took a big bite. She frowned.

"What's up with that look, Miss Lucy? You usually love that stuff, eat half a pie by yourself. Sure wish I had your metabolism."

"Ah, feeling a little nauseated. Must be the stress. I'll save it for breakfast with the cheesecake."

Bea chuckled and eased another wedge from the box.

"So," Lucy said, "spill."

"What are you talking about?" Bea slid Lucy a side-eye glance.

Lucy lifted a brow.

"Okay, okay, Pete Anthony." Bea sighed. "Was painfully sweet, so damn sweet. A big lug like that, all obnoxious and brash, it was like we were making love, true love. Who the hell is he?"

"Sounds amazing." Lucy pulled apart her half-eaten slice and gave it to the dogs. Chomp, gone, and back to the bones.

"It was awful. I didn't think he was gonna take me to a place so vulnerable that I wanted to cry. I actually did cry. Really, who needs that shit? I just wanted to get laid. It's over. He can find somebody else to ambush, not me."

"You're one hard woman, Beazy." Lucy blew her nose loudly. "So, when are you seeing him again?"

"Never."

"This weekend?"

"Yep. Shit."

As they laughed together, a big gust of warm wind filled the porch, blowing Point Dume Pizza napkins into the air. They swirled to the floor beneath the fan like little white ghostlings. Maddie whined and began to pace. Bugle remained oblivious, stretching out on his back, face next to his slimy bone.

"What time is it?" Lucy asked.

Bea punched her phone. "One-fifteen. Haven't been up this late to hang out for ages. Girlfriends gone wild." She laughed. "So, babka, as Marlene would say — I heard from her on my way over. Can you handle more news, Luce?"

"Sure, keep kickin' me in the head." Lucy picked a hefty parmesan-coated mushroom from the pizza, downed it. How could she be so hungry and ready to puke at the same moment?

"Okay, drop-kick: preliminary DNA from a soda can found at the Airport Studio, matches Brody to the faceless man. Brothers."

"Whoa," Lucy said, suddenly energized for the first time since her awful confrontation with Michael. "If Mercer had the brother murdered, then Brody might be incredibly pissed off. At least you'd think so. Maybe he'll work with us somehow. We hoped he might be a way into Mercer's organization. Revenge is one powerful motivator."

Bea finished off the wine. "Yeah, but here's the bad news. Brody was found dead in his home in Studio City two days ago."

Lucy let out a little gasp and tugged at her dark, wavy hair. The ponytail holder was long gone. "Damn. Sounds like Mercer's culling the herd. Now what?"

"Now what? is the big question. Better dealt with sober

and smart. I'm going to bed. Got nothing more in the tank."

Lucy nodded in the pale light of three battery-operated candles softly flickering on the coffee table. "Find your way to the guest room?"

"All settled in. And I like what you did to Henry's room. Airy and bright."

"Took the tour while I was out cold, did ya?"

"Yep."

"Good. I'll be up in a few. Gonna sit for a little while longer. Love you, Beebs."

"Love you, too, Luce." Bea rose from the rocker, pressed Lucy's shoulder, and headed for the stairs to the second floor. Bugle followed, but Maddie stayed curled on the porch floor while Lucy mentally sifted through the information they'd gathered.

From her Guerrero video, they knew that one of the major players was The Accountant, son of a former cartel boss. Cardenas was likely involved as a henchman. There was also a huge enforcer-type that Nurse Dillard was almost too intimidated to glance at, and a transgender entertainer with a voice like Edith Piaf — all seemed to be circling like moths to Mercer's awful flame. The forces that wanted to take them down had to move faster. The IDs from the artist at Santa Barbara PD were taking too long. Mercer was dumping poison into SoCal like a tsunami after a catastrophic temblor. And he was hell-bent on destroying Lucy and her loved ones at any cost. He'd almost succeeded with Alyssa. His next move could be the lethal one.

—

When awakened by Maddie's whining, Lucy was still cuddled in the rocking chair with a fleece blanket over her lap. The pale orange light of dawn tinged the far hillside. She rubbed her eyes, the smell of burn was now noticeable, despite her clogged nose. She squinted into the distance and rubbed her eyes harder. The distant glow, like a ribbon of bright paint behind the ragged purple hilltop, was coming from the direction of the sunrise.

The horses whinnied from the corral. An icy blast of dread shot through her body as a fierce gust of hot wind slapped her face. Tangled in the blanket, she struggled from her rocker.

A flare crested the summit.

Brushfire.

# 30

Lucy dialed 9-1-1 and held for too many unanswered minutes. Only a few miles away, an out-of-control fire could rage across the landscape and devour everything in its path in no time. Including the ranch.

It was 4:12 a.m. Perspiration dampened her face. She disconnected and dialed the number for the Malibu Fire Station directly. A local dispatcher picked up.

Lucy choked out the plea, "I need help. Brushfire, east of the Vega Ranch off Kanan. 9-1-1's not answering."

"Your name, ma'am?"

"Lucy Vega, the owner."

"Okay, Ms. Vega. We'll have a rig out immediately. In these wind conditions, I'd suggest you consider packing up and evacuating as soon as you can."

Lucy hung up and pressed speed dial for Cheyney Hitchcock. A retired stuntman, he lived across the road and helped Elsa on the ranch with the physical labor. He boarded his *Paso Fino* horse, Tripp, with Lucy's two paints in exchange for mucking out the stalls.

A tired voice answered. "Hello, Lucy. All okay?"

She hustled from the porch, across the living room to the library, packing her laptop and grabbing family photos as she spoke.

"We got a brushfire, coming fast. Need your help evacuating the animals."

She heard sheets rustle. "On my way, sweetheart. We'll get that soaker turned on to protect the house and barn, too. I'll bring the truck and we'll load out the horses first."

"Hurry."

Bea appeared in the doorway in pajamas and feet bare. "I saw it out the window. Looks like creeping hell. What do we do first?" she asked, fear in her voice.

"Throw on some shoes, get the dogs and Howard into your car and then help me catch the chickens. There are two big, wire animal crates out by the henhouse. We'll shoo them in with treats. Coconut flakes — in the plastic bin by the coop. Cheyney's on his way to load the horses, we'll put the two goats in with them."

Still in yesterday's clothes, Lucy checked her watch, eight minutes had elapsed. She ran toward the front door, pushed her feet into old black rubber Wellies and jogged toward the barn. She dropped the stuff from the ranch library on the front seat of her Jeep. The camera was already stowed. In the distance, she heard the wail of a fire engine.

When she passed the horse trailer, something looked off.

Bea rushed up behind her. "The tires are flat." She'd done a fast change into yoga leggings and a T-shirt.

"Damnit, I should've paid attention to the dogs last night. They were antsy, and I was too tired to check it out." Lucy immediately dialed Cheyney again. She swallowed down a pang of nausea.

He picked up. "Almost there, doll."

"Go back and get your horse trailer. It'll take four, right? Mine's been vandalized; tires slashed."

"Holy shit. Okay, but I've only got a double."

"It'll have to do." It was all about survival now.

"On it," he said and disconnected.

"I got the dogs in my car," Bea said, out of breath. "But I can't find Howard."

"Damn critter. When he wants to hide, he knows how to do it." Lucy looked to the hills where gnarly fingers of flame scrabbled over the rim. The winds gusted hard. She saw a neighbor's barn, a mile away, blow up in flames. Her heart hammered. "Let's corral the chickens, fast." She would not let her animals die.

Bea shook the plastic container of coconut flakes and sunflower seeds she'd retrieved.

"Toss 'em into the cages then get ready to scramble. It's like herding goldfish," Lucy said.

By 4:30 a.m., the coconut-sated chickens were in the cages and parked in the back of Lucy's Jeep. Feathers stuck in Bea's hair. Cheyney pulled up to the barn with his two-horse trailer in tow and his sixteen-year-old nephew, Cody, riding shotgun. Bomber, his German Shepherd rescue hung his big head out the back window, nervously whimpering and licking his chops.

Tall and slim, Cheyney moved sloth-like. Painful arthritis, due to countless daredevil injuries, had collected its toll. Cody, a stuntman in training, had the same rangy build. Excitement flashed in his big green eyes.

"We'll get your two paints in the trailer and Cody'll ride Tripp on down the hill behind us. Don't know how else to do it."

"What about the pygmy goats?" Lucy asked. "My car's full

of chickens, Bea has the canines and, hopefully, Howard. Still can't find him. You got the horses."

"I can fit those two little stinkers in my cab with Bomber."

"They'll trash your cab. Got two more big ol' dog crates in the barn we can stick them in." She turned to Bea who trotted up, shaking her head.

"No Howard."

"Damn." Lucy struggled to stay calm but pulsing red cinders dancing in the air were terrifying harbingers of the escalating danger. "See if you can find the carriers for the goats, behind the haystack next to the workbench. I'll help you grab the kids in a sec."

"I'm no goat herder." Bea hustled toward the barn. "I think I come more from West African rice farmer stock."

"Ready, Uncle Cheyney?" Cody called from the paddock. He cinched Tripp's saddle.

The air grew thick with ash, collecting like an infestation of gray moths on every surface and crevasse.

Let's get the horses." Cheyney slid into his truck and backed the trailer toward the paddock. He and Cody wrangled Lucy's two reluctant equines into the transpo. The horses nickered nervously, eyes wide, spooked. Cody pulled hoods over their brown and white heads to help them settle.

In the distance, helicopters materialized over the blaze. Smoke billowed hundreds of feet high, obliterating a shy pink dawn. Surging down the hillside, the fiery gates of Hades opened wide, hell-bent on obliterating the Vega Ranch and everything in between. Two mule deer bounded down the driveway toward Kanan Road and a flock of blackbirds flew noisily overhead.

Cheyney hop-limped toward Lucy. "You didn't get the sprinklers going, doll. We need to soak the area. Wanna give these buildings every chance of survival." He took off his stained, putty-colored Stetson and scratched his bald pate.

"I tried but the turn-on handle was jammed tight," she said.

"Lemme take a quick look, then we better haul ass outta here. Still don't see any fire department planes."

Lucy's eyes scanned the horizon. "Flames are probably moving faster than the tankers can muster."

Cheyney grabbed a wrench out of a toolbox in the back of his truck and proceeded to the site of the main turn-on valve beside the garage. He came back with a piece of pipe in his hand. "Damn, sweetheart, your sprinkler system's been screwed with. Looks like you're on somebody's shit list."

Lucy gritted her teeth and tried to control her rage. She looked up to see Bea pulling the dog cages over to the goat pen and rushed to help.

"It's Mercer, all this is Mercer." Lucy snarled. "The fire, slashed tires, jammed sprinkler system. And who the hell knows what else is waiting?"

"Focus on getting out of here, Luce. I'll help you nail his ass later," Cheyney promised.

Bea turned out to be pretty good at luring the kids into the cages. "Maybe we were goat herders back in Sierra Leone after all," she said.

When all the animals were packed and ready to go, extra food and water stashed, Lucy dashed back into the house one more time to the library where their important papers were stored. As she grabbed the metal file box, she was overwhelmed by a great wave of loss. This house had been her solace, her safe place. No longer.

She heard the sound of an explosion nearby. A firebrand blasting out from some resinous plant? Cheyney yelled her name. Lucy ran for the front door.

# 31

Forty-two minutes had passed since the 9-1-1 call. Lucy slid into the driver's seat and grabbed the camera from its case. Her eyes and lungs burned as she snapped quick images of the nightmare raging down on them. She put the Jeep in gear. Red cinders that could ignite blazes miles away pulsed in the wind with the biting scent of smoldering scrub.

Their caravan—a Beemer, a Jeep, a beat-up truck with trailer, and a teenager on a horse, slowly descended the steep gravel drive toward Kanan Road. With Lucy in the lead, they approached the bridge over a seasonal stream. But all she saw was the steep embankment, with no way across.

The bridge was gone. Not possible. The ancient sycamores clustered along the wash had seen it happen but stood mute.

Damn Mercer to deepest Hell.

Lucy pressed the brake and jumped from the Jeep. Her heart hammered. Shards of wood and concrete were scattered like shrapnel across the ground around them. The Vega Ranch bridge, now jagged wreckage, had taken a deadly hit.

Were they trapped? She struggled to tamp down her rising terror.

Cody rode up beside Lucy. Tripp, nickered and stomped. Lucy stroked his muzzle.

"We came over it a half-hour ago," Cody said. "What the hell?"

Lucy caught a faint odor of gunpowder. *That sonofabitch. He's somewhere smirking while we struggle for our lives.*

Cheyney limped over to join them. Bea was in her car on the cellphone.

"Okay, change in plans." He wiped sweat from his forehead. Cinders scorched dark prick marks into his felt hat. The air temperature could bake a pizza and was rising.

The siren-sound of fire rigs speeding up Kanan split a momentary calm in the howling winds. Lucy rubbed her neck muscles. A vice-like headache was looming but she had to stay focused.

They scanned the streambank. It dropped about eight feet to a silty, damp creek bed.

"No way can we get our vehicles across this sucker," Lucy said, coughing. The window of opportunity for escape narrowed by the minute.

"You're right, doll," Cheyney said. "We'll load out the animals and get 'em all across. Abandon the cars." He scratched at his whiskered chin. "Dammit, just had the truck detailed."

Bea ran up to the group. "Got through to the fire department. They're sending a trailer up from an animal rescue group on standby near the station. ETA ten minutes, hopefully." She didn't look too sure.

"Okay, let's move," Lucy said. "We'll get the critters across to meet them. Cheyn, you and Cody get the horses. Bea and I'll handle the rest."

Bea followed her to the back of the Jeep where they

pulled out the chicken coops and together, stumbled down the bank and across the muddy streambed. The hens clucked and protested. Bea tossed more treats to the girls, and they calmed. Cody helped lug the pygmy goat carriers while the old stuntman finished wrangling the equine.

A loud crackle sounded from the hillcrest behind. Lucy looked up at the barn. A whiff of smoke from the roof, benign against a blue patch of sky, suddenly took a dervish-like spin and became a cyclone of fire. Lucy gasped and tears sprang to her eyes. The barn would burn to the ground.

As they struggled to transport the menagerie across the arroyo, a dusty silver Dodge Ram pulling a six-stall horse trailer bumped up the road on the far side of the blown-out bridge. Lucy's heart took a little leap. Maybe they'd finally caught a break.

A slim, blonde woman in her mid-fifties jumped out of the truck and yelled across the creek where Cheyney, Lucy, and Cody still struggled with an unwilling horse. "Cheyney, load 'em puppies up and let's get the hell outta here!"

"You're a sight for sore eyes, April," he called back.

The explosive sound of falling timbers rocked the barn. Odin, Lucy's young gelding, reared, whinnying, terrified by the noise. With a panicked shake of the head, he broke away from Cheyney's grip and galloped in confusion toward the flames.

"Odin, no! Come here!" Blood thundered in Lucy's temples. She struggled to calm her voice. "Over here, baby boy. Come on." She rushed after him.

The horse danced across the burning grass. His nostrils flared and white foam hung in lathery strings from his mouth. Cody, still mounted, charged off in pursuit of the runaway. He desperately coaxed his sturdy trail horse, Tripp, up the hill toward the burning barn. Only a couple hundred yards away a wall of flame bore down on them.

With his hood on, Odin was blind. Lucy called to him again, trying to soothe him and bring him around toward her, but he was in full freak-out mode.

Cody galloped up alongside the terrified animal. Odin circled and bolted again, this time toward the crumbling barn.

"Odin!" Lucy shrieked.

Cody, crazy stunt-kid with zero fear managed to maneuver Tripp next to Odin, squat atop his saddle, and leap.

He landed on Odin's bare back and struggled wildly for balance. If he fell he'd be trampled. The horse reared. Cody grabbed the horse's mane and righted himself. He fumbled for the bridle and was finally able to reach it.

He turned Odin back toward the streambed, slowing the terrified animal, murmuring soft words, patting his neck, and taking control. Lucy rushed up with a blanket and slapped out the fire flaring in the horse's tail. She narrowly avoided being kicked.

Tripp trotted close behind them, panting, and nickering. Lucy took his bridle and kissed his muzzle. Her whole body shook from the adrenaline rush.

Cody slid down from Odin and glanced up the hillside, coughing hard. His Dodgers World Series cap had blown off his head. In the distance, it rose into the air, flared, and shriveled.

—

The horses, goats, and chicken cages were soon secured in April's six-stall trailer. Lucy insisted that Cheyney, looking pale and more hobbled by the minute, ride in the truck's cab. The dogs clambered into the backseat where they had no opportunity to jump out and cause further havoc.

Lucy, Bea, and Cody pitched their belongings into the back of the pick-up, then scrambled in and settled on top of a pile of horse blankets, clutching each other.

They fled down the long, rutted quarter-mile drive from the ranch where the fire now raged, blocking the road. Plunging through the inferno, they careened onto Kanan and accelerated toward PCH. Smoke was now thick as fog and the taste of ash on Lucy's lips was acrid and sharp. Her lungs burned as the fire sucked up oxygen and spit out poison. On the slope behind, a red-orange storm moved like fast-flowing lava, incinerating everything it touched. Odin whinnied and thrashed inside the trailer.

Lucy recorded video of the scene. The work of capturing meaning though a camera lens usually centered her, this was too close, too personal. She could barely control her unsteady hands.

The muffled sound of an approaching plane echoed through the canyon from the direction of Agoura Hills and the 101 — an air tanker carrying fire retardant. Too late for the barn. Probably too late for the ranch house and everything else — even Howard.

Lucy wiped away tears. "If Maddie hadn't woken me up, we could all be dead."

Bea whispered, "But we're still alive."

Lucy gritted her teeth and added, "Mercer, you bastard. Your days are numbered."

# 32

They drove south toward the Malibu Fire Station staging area. In the distance, Lucy watched several tankers and a chopper drop their hot-pink fire retardant in the vicinity of the ranch.

The winds shifted, and the blaze seemed to be taking a northerly turn, at least temporarily.

"I think your uncle's spread might get lucky this time," Lucy said to Cody.

He nodded but didn't look convinced. Long dark trails of soot streaked his handsome young face. The bright, shiny eyes of adventure had been dimmed by grim reality.

He snapped a few pictures of the inferno and texted them off. "Think it was arson?" he asked.

Lucy and Bea exchanged glances.

"I'll bet the investigators are already at work on that," Bea said. "They'll get the story, and I'll be on it. In fact, I'm texting the county fire chief right now."

"She's a reporter," Lucy said. "Bea Middleton—used to be Jackson."

Cody cocked his head and took a closer look at Bea. Any

remnant of TV glamour had long been shed. She was an exhausted, pretty black woman with chicken feathers in her rumpled hair and gray ash smudging her clothes and skin.

"Pleased to meet you, ma'am." Cody pulled himself up a bit straighter. "I'm not one of those kids who gets all their news from social media."

Bea nodded. "Smart man."

He went back to texting.

Bea was texting, too. "Letting everybody know we're okay." She turned to Lucy. "Can you send that stuff you shot to my editor? Gonna make something of this fiasco."

Cody gazed back toward his Uncle Cheyney's place, his eyes narrowed. New clouds of smoke roiled from the surrounding hills. He bit hard at his lower lip.

"Thanks for your help with this evacuation, Cody," Lucy said. "Especially with Odin. That was epic. We might've lost him without you."

Cody nodded. "Pleasure, Miss Lucy. Neighbors take care of each other."

She pressed his hand. "They do, for sure."

—

When they finally arrived at Fire Station 71, cops were everywhere, directing traffic toward the big field across from the public library. Going about their normal lives, surfers still bobbed in the water and hipster customers still walked out of Starbucks with their lattes, while only a few miles away, all hell was loose on the land.

April and Cheyney crawled out of the cab and shut the doors. The three dogs bounded into the front seats, noses stuck out the windows as if they'd been completely deprived of oxygen.

"Bea, Lucy, Cody, I'm April Cordelli." She walked up

to the three still hunkered in the back and offered a strong handshake. "Didn't get a chance to say hey in all the rush."

Lucy sprung up and gave her a grateful hug. "You saved our butts, April. Thank you doesn't begin to cover it."

"Glad I could help." She glanced at the billowing smoke in the distance and shook her head. "I live over in Lobo Canyon, Lucy. The fire's in front of us there, blowing toward the ocean, so we're not at risk. This time. I've got room for your animals, so I thought rather than camp here in this mess, we could take your tribe over to my place."

"That would be amazing," Lucy said, feeling immense relief. Then it hit her again — there was no relief. Not as long as he was still alive. "Thank you, April, your offer is generous." Lucy gulped hard. "But I can't accept it."

Cheyney adjusted his cinder-scorched hat, "What are you talking about, sweetheart?"

"Slashed tires, blown-out bridge. You said I'm on somebody's shit list, and you're right. Bea and I are pretty sure we know who started this fire. And the grudge is personal. April, you won't be safe with my animals."

Bea rubbed at the scar from Mercer's bullet that pock-marked the smooth brown skin of her shoulder. Her fingers often went there.

Lucy shuddered. "We'll have to come up with another solution."

April lifted a brow, a flinty shine in her eyes. "We have an incredible neighborhood watch in Lobo Canyon. We've burned before and there's only one paved road out, so we work with the police and fire department to keep our families secure. We're a tough bunch. Your animals'll be safe."

Lucy shook her head. "I couldn't handle it if you were collateral damage. This asshole has immense resources."

April bristled. "If you know who started this hell storm, then I want to be part of catching the piece of shit. If keeping your animals helps make that happen, then let me do it."

Cheyney stretched his bowed back and grimaced and turned to Lucy. "It's not like you have a ton of options, doll."

"Then it's settled," April said. "Agreed?"

Lucy realized this was probably the only choice. But it scared the hell out of her. She rubbed her aching head. Bea gave her a reassuring hug.

"Agreed," she finally said, with a prayer for everyone in Mercer's deadly crosshairs.

# 33

April checked a traffic app on her phone. "We'll take Topanga across while it's still open, hit the 101 and get into my ranch from the Agoura side. There's an Enterprise car rental place nearby in Thousand Oaks, so you can pick up transportation."

"Sounds good. Can't believe my Beemer's toast," Bea said, antsy. Her foot tapped against the wheel well. "Got to get mobile and back to work. I'll call the rental place and reserve a car. Need one, Lucy? Cheyney?"

"I have an old Honda SUV Cheyney can use," April said. "Cheyney and I go way back."

Did a Mona Lisa smile flicker on her lips? Lucy made googly eyes at the stuntman. He shot her an I'll explain later look.

April passed Clif bars and water to everyone then hopped back into the truck. The dogs whined and whimpered as they were herded into the rear seat. Lucy felt a faint glimmer of optimism begin to ease her tattered nerves.

———

Topanga Canyon Road was clogged up like the 101 on a mid-summer Friday afternoon. They were not the only ones with this exit strategy. In the open back of the pick-up, wind thrashed

Lucy's dark, wavy hair into her eyes and mouth. Shielding her phone screen from the bright sunlight, she squinted to more closely view the image of a shadowy figure creeping from the barn. In the chaos of the evacuation, she'd overlooked the ranch's new security system.

"Bea, check this out." She pulled her friend close.

"I forgot that our new cameras record and archive the footage for a week. Sends it to my phone and laptop."

Bea examined the recording. "Let's forward the files to Marlene over at Police Administration. Maybe their experts can enhance the scene. Send it to me and I'll pass it to the fire chief, too."

"Okay. Done."

"Luce, our point-person from County F.D. is a Captain Chuck Stewart. We're meeting him at Edison Road and Kanan-Dume tomorrow around noon. He'll call to confirm, based on the fire and the weather. So far, seven structures have burned."

Cody looked at his phone screen. "Weather Channel says the winds are supposed to quiet later this afternoon. Could give firefighters the chance they need. Or, not."

Lucy nodded and took a long, shaky breath. Bea squeezed her shoulder. No sign of the winds dying yet. The gusting Santa Anas rattled the trailer. It fish-tailed into loose gravel along the road. Tires spun. Odin banged in protest.

The young wrangler put in his earbuds and settled back to listen to music. He appeared to reach for his ballcap but it wasn't there. He glanced over at Lucy and shrugged.

# 34

Bea and Lucy stood at the flashpoint with fire captain and chief arson investigator, Chuck Stewart. A grizzle-bearded man in his late fifties, his sharp blue eyes never stopped scanning the terrain. A ragged black carpet of burned chaparral rolled toward the ocean and disappeared into the thick fog.

With the land still smoldering, the air remained harsh with toxic particles. Although the major blaze was out, firefighters in full turnout gear still roamed, looking for festering hotspots that could re-erupt and wreak further havoc. Lucy spotted an overhead drone that provided additional eyes on the aftermath. Stewart glanced at its live-streaming view on his digital tablet.

Several miles off, what remained of the Vega Ranch hid behind a charred hillside. Now Kanan Road was open but Lucy hadn't been able to bring herself to visit the wreckage.

"So, this is where it started?" Bea asked.

Stewart adjusted his yellow helmet. "Yup, point of origin. Not much attempt to hide the crime. Looks like he wanted us to know exactly what he'd done, or they'd done. Perfect spot, too. This narrow gully acted as a chimney and radiated fire out across that meadow and the hillsides." He pointed toward the mist-shrouded horizon.

Lucy recorded the landscape with her camera then drew back to three ignition spots that looked like burned-out campfires.

"Any indication of who, or how many arsonists were involved?" Bea glanced toward a cordoned-off area about fifty yards from where they stood.

Stewart rubbed at his ginger-stubbled chin. "We isolated two sets of footprints in that sandy area over there. A man's running shoe, been told it's a size nine, Nike. I'm sure they thought the wind would take care of any trace, but God knows the Santa Anas are tricky as hell."

Bea nodded. "And the other one?"

The captain puffed his cheeks and blew out a long sigh. His eyes were red and irritated-looking, likely from the nasty air and lack of sleep. "This has to be off the record for now. I need your guarantee. I hear you're two of the reporters with some integrity left, Ms. Middleton, Ms. Vega."

Lucy wanted to speak up for their smart, hard-working, honest colleagues but kept her mouth shut. This was not the time for a debate on the media's trustworthiness.

Bea stashed the mic in her jacket pocket and nodded to Lucy to switch off the camera. Lucy knew they'd have to honor his request or lose the cooperation of the county firefighters during this investigation, and maybe forever.

"You have my word, Captain. Off the record. We've told you who we think might be responsible, the Cardenas asshole, so now it's your turn. What can you tell us?"

Stewart adjusted his helmet again. "We think he got help from one of our own."

"Whoa." Lucy cut a glance at Bea.

"The second print was made from a boot like mine." He kicked at the dirt. "Our investigators are on it. I'll keep you posted. This has become personal. Gotta stay on the down-low for now. Don't want to spook him."

Bea gulped hard. "I need to share this among the detectives we're working with — Pete Anthony, major narcotics, and Marlene Simon, homicide. I trust in their confidentiality completely. May I have your permission?"

He hesitated for an instant, then nodded. "I know Anthony. He's solid."

"So's Simon," Bea assured him. "Thanks, Captain. We'll coordinate with you."

There was shouting from the field. They turned to watch a trio of firefighters jog toward a flare, prepared to put it down.

"Why in the hell do people set these fires?" Lucy muttered out of frustration, even though she knew the answer.

"Starts with anger," Stewart replied. "Often a history of family abuse and neglect. Later on, the motive's profit. Your guy has probably moved from point A to B. He's skilled, has been at this a while. And as for our guy, firefighting's the perfect career for somebody obsessed with this shit." He checked his watch.

"Okay, let's grab a quick sound bite and we'll get you on your way. I know you're extremely busy," Bea said. "Appreciate you meeting us here."

The captain nodded. "No problem, and let's hope the lead you gave us pans out."

"It will." Lucy tightened her camera onto the tripod. "I'd stake what's left of my ranch on it."

—

As the two women hauled their equipment down the road to

their cars, Bea gave a wave to a Ventura County fire truck as it headed toward Stewart's vehicle. They responded with a quick siren trill. Lucy gave them a thumbs-up. Then, her phone chimed. She pulled it from her pocket, took a quick look at the caller ID and stopped short.

"What is it?" Bea asked. A flicker of fear lit her eyes.

Lucy took a deep breath and cleared her throat. "It's Michael. I left a message for him last night."

"Ah, yes." Bea gave her friend an encouraging smile. "Don't just stand there staring at your phone, take it. You want me here with you?"

"No, I'm fine." Lucy opened her car door and slid in. "I'll see you downtown at the PAB — three o'clock meeting with the team, right?"

"That's a big 10-4. In the meantime, I'm gonna go check in at my office." Bea blew Lucy an encouraging air kiss then turned toward her car. Finally pulling out past the various fire department vehicles and a growing collection of looky-loos, she turned east toward Agoura Hills and the 101.

—

The phone stopped chirping. Lucy hit Call Back.

Two rings, then he picked up. The moment of silence between them felt endless.

"Lucy," he finally said.

Her throat tightened with pain. "Why didn't you tell me about your daughter?"

His hesitation was palpable. "Because then you'd have let me stay."

Lucy knew he was right.

"You'd have said you were sorry for throwing me out and would have been all supportive." Anger edged his voice. "I'm the only one who should be sorry. I fucked up everything. No excuses. My daughter almost died from an OD and I handle it by going on a bender. So sick. Another backslide is not an option."

"Will you be coming back to LA soon?" Lucy asked.

"I need to stay up here in Santa Cruz for a while. Gotta figure things out with my children, or I can't be good for anybody, even you, Lucia, my love."

The man she'd dreamed was her soulmate was drifting away like an untethered boat. Dream — maybe that was the operative word. But they had once literally and figuratively saved each other's lives. It couldn't get any more real than that.

Lucy gulped back tears. "Reconcile with your family, or that aching hole in your heart will never mend."

"Exactly. I'm tired of being damaged, of always feeling half alive, not whole."

Lucy was choked to a whisper. "And Michael, it's all or nothing for me."

"You deserve better than half. We both do."

Impressions from their relationship scrolled through her mind like a movie trailer. Warm skin, cool sheets, shared laughter, trust.

He continued after a long pause. "Those days in your apartment above the barn were the most blissful of my life. They reminded me that real happiness is possible."

"They did for me, too. But the barn's gone. And the ranch house. All of it. Burned to the ground yesterday."

"What?" Shock and disbelief rocked his response.

"Doubtlessly Mercer-inspired. We saved the animals, except for the cat."

"Our little man, Howard?"

"Yep. Poor buddy. Can't believe he's gone. Had him since

high school." She sighed. "I'm going over to check out the full damage tomorrow."

"Oh my God. I'll come down to be with you."

Lucy yearned to feel his strong, protective arms around her again, but it would be deadly for them both. They'd get back together, it would be great for a while, then they'd come to this same awful place again. "No, huh-uh. Take care of your business in Santa Cruz. I can deal with things here. I'm meeting the insurance adjuster. We'll rebuild. No worries."

"But, Lucy..."

"We'll talk soon." She hoped. "I've gotta run — meeting Bea and the detectives all the way downtown." She had to disconnect before she broke apart. "And Michael, you know I love you."

"I love you, too, Lucia. Wish me well."

"Always."

# 35

The Police Administration Building, or PAB, down on First Street had replaced the historic Parker Center a decade ago but was still the "new" LAPD headquarters, maybe always would be. The edifice looked like a huge gray panel had been lifted from an ultra-max prison wall and sliced through a glass cube of offices overlooking the entire metro. The biggest slab of glass reflected City Hall, a block to the south. The overall effect was sharp and dangerous, despite a nice center greenspace and the proud Leadership in Energy and Environmental Design insignia.

Lucy passed through security without incident and was met by Marlene at the elevators. Together they headed up to a conference room in the Robbery-Homicide Division where they'd join Bea and Anthony to review the case and figure out a strategy for moving forward. Marlene was generous with the supportive hugs, words of condolence on the ranch, and an offer of the free use of her second bedroom.

Lucy was touched, close to tears again. "Thanks, my friend. Finding Mercer is all the help I need."

"Then let's do it, sister."

They entered the airy, blue-walled conference room. The not-too-secret lovers, Bea and Pete, sat on opposite sides of the wood-grained Formica table trying to look professional and unconnected. Each clutched a McDonald's coffee cup.

An empty apple pie wrapper was crumpled in front of the detective.

Lucy grabbed diet colas from an icy bowl on a nearby counter for herself and Marlene. The two women slid into their seats and pulled out their notebooks. Lucy's was electronic, Marlene's a worn, yellow-lined jotter with an Office Depot logo on the front.

"Okay, people," Anthony began. "Let's move right into it. What I've got in Major Narcotics is a wave of newly imported heroin laced with fentanyl at fifty times the potency of the usual shit. It's moving up the coast like the wildfire that took Lucy's ranch." He looked her way, his eyes wide and mournful. "And I'm truly sorry for your terrible loss. Bea told me the story."

Lucy nodded. "Thanks, Pete." She cleared her throat. "Why do you think they're making the stuff so much more potent this time?"

"With dope being legal, the cartels are losing market share. Make heroin cheap, available, and concentrated, or laced with hardcore shit like fentanyl, and you cultivate more users. If they don't die first. It's Econ 101."

Lucy nodded and thought of Michael's daughter, of all the sons and daughters. So many lives devastated.

"We netted quite a few low-level runners," he continued, "but we'd stalled out on the leadership until yesterday. A middle manager was caught selling to an undercover vice cop. We think he'll turn to protect his junkie girlfriend who'd just won a spot on America's Top Spokes Model contest."

"What's that? A new reality show?" Lucy asked.

He snorted. "Yup. Sounds as exciting as West Bumfuck's Top Hamster Trainer. Supposed to start shooting in two weeks. The girl wants this break more than life, so her sugar-daddy will likely blab to save her ass."

Anthony finished his coffee and grimaced. His face softened as he caught Bea's gaze. "We're clawing our fucking way into Mercer's inner circle, but it's not looking good. Does anybody have something more, uh, positive to add here? What's up with the arsonist?"

Bea leaned in toward the group. "Lucy and I met with Captain Stewart this morning, and for this room only, he thinks one of their own guys is in cahoots with Cardenas."

"*Oy, vey.*" Marlene scribbled a note.

"I know Cap Stewart," Anthony said. "If they can keep the scumbag from rabbiting, he'll nail the cocksucker to the wall. You don't betray your brothers and sisters in the county F.D."

"He definitely had that 'take no prisoners' attitude about him," Lucy said. She turned to Marlene. "What's the news from Santa Barbara on Nurse Dillard's IDs of Mercer's visitors?"

"Okay, kids. Ritchie turned out to be quite the *mentsh*." Marlene said. "He cooperated fully." She passed around detailed drawings of the clinic visitors. "I sent them to you digitally as well."

"These are really nice," Bea said. "Not cartoony, realistic."

Marlene nodded and readjusted her glasses. "We think his inner circle includes the firebug, Jorge Cardenas, and Brody Blackwell, the pornie producer and dance choreographer. As you know, Brody's dead. Allegedly OD'd more likely murdered. The drawings also include an enforcer named Alan Montez, called Altamont." She referred them to the picture of a bull-necked, empty-eyed giant with a shaved head.

"Former Special Ops, mostly in Afghanistan, dishonorably discharged for a suspected homicide involving an MP. Then he became a contractor for a defense group out of Somalia. Total psychopath."

Lucy cringed at the description. A man who could do anything to anyone and feel nothing.

Marlene rustled through her papers and held up the next image — a photo of a man lounging on a yacht. "The accountant is definitely Estevan Valencia, son of the Medellin cartel boss we talked about earlier. Stanford grad. Brilliant financial and business mind. Then there's the woman, actually a male, probably transgender but supposedly still has his family jewels intact. Dillard popped in unannounced one afternoon and noticed some action beneath her gypsy skirt. Name's Toulouse or Toulusa. Got a good likeness, but nothing much on her except that she seems ghoulishly interested in surgical procedures. Nurse Dillard says she's Mercer's lover. Ran her through facial recognition yesterday but came up empty."

"Toulusa's a performer," Lucy said. "A friend of mine who's tight with the LGBTQ community filled me in on her. Has a show in Palm Springs once every other month — I'm gonna be at this next one."

"All yours," Marlene said. "She may be the closest person to Mercer right now."

"And then there's our boy Mercer," Bea said. *The Phantom of the Opera*. Pulling strings behind the scenes."

"And Toulusa's his Christina?" Marlene conjectured.

"No." Bea looked hard across the table. "It's you, Lucy."

Lucy's head snapped up. She felt her face flush. "What are you talking about?"

"He could have taken you out so many times, but you just manage to escape. He terrorizes you, almost succeeds in killing you, then he backs off. That's how I'm starting to see it."

Lucy glared at her friend. "You're so wrong."

"Hear me out," Bea insisted.

"No, I can't believe you'd make that comparison. I have no sympathy for him, I'll kill him if I get the chance. And if you have any doubt about that —"

"It's not about your feelings for him, Lucy, it's about his toward you."

"Come on, Bea, he hates me. And you, too."

"Just listen for a minute, okay?" She glanced at Pete and Marlene for support.

Lucy crossed her arms over her chest and huffed.

"Almost two years ago, you literally talked him in from a ledge over Hollywood Boulevard. He was high and suicidal and told you things he hadn't confided to anyone."

"Yeah, that he murdered his own mother. Then he tried to strangle me and pounded my head against the wall 'til I blacked out. I thought my number was up." Lucy shuddered at the memory of that awful night.

Bea persisted. "He knew the cops were about to break down the door and that you weren't going to die. Since then he's tried to push you out of a helicopter, let you escape from a hideous cartel prison that he supposedly controlled, and burned your ranch to the ground."

"Sweet fella," Pete said. "You're welcome to use the department grenade launcher to smoke his ass."

"I'm on board with that." Lucy uncrossed her arms and took a deep breath. She'd try to listen. Bea was seldom off base, dammit.

"What I'm trying to point out," Bea continued, "is that maybe we can use this vulnerability to our advantage."

Lucy winced, unwilling to concede that Bea was on the right track. Her friend hadn't seen the look in his eyes as he crushed her head against the wall the night of his attempted suicide. Hadn't breathed in Mercer's hatred when he slapped her to the floor of the cartel prison in Mexico, snarling like an animal. She half-listened as they wrapped up the meeting, then left, determined to find Toulusa.

# 36

Back at her Santa Monica condo, Lucy settled into her desk chair and fired up her laptop. Perusing her record of recent searches, she groaned. How to start a brushfire; how to process a falsely registered .357 Magnum; female impersonator reviews in Southern California. Any day the FBI would be at her doorstep demanding her hard drive.

Then, she found something out of Palm Springs which seemed more esoteric and closer to what Audrina described as Toulusa's French chanteuse style. In the passing decades, the desert had morphed from a playground for Hollywood luminaries to an LGBTQ vacation mecca. Periodically, *Carnaval de la Belle Époque* was presented at a pricey, intimate venue on South Palm Canyon Drive called *Le Chat Noir*, the black cat. Toulouse Lautrec was a *Belle Époque* artist with a penchant for painting black cats. Toulusa had taken a version of his name as her own.

The main marketing image for the show, along with the cat, was a portrait of a *Parisienne* prostitute at the *Moulin Rouge* holding a glass of champagne while displaying lots of black-stockinged leg and rosy bosom. The performance was

Saturday night and had been sold out for weeks. Beyond that, details were sketchy.

Lucy hesitated, still annoyed from the conversation at the PAB. She was not, as Bea inferred, Mercer's "secret weakness." Nevertheless, she called her friend to let her know she was heading to Palm Springs in the morning.

Jeez, what a schlep," Bea said. "The traffic through Riverside's gotten impossible. Could be a total waste of time. Why don't you email the picture to the owner or the artistic director?"

"Because they'd probably blow me off or tell Toulusa that we're onto her. I need to be there in person and be innocently persuasive."

"The show's tomorrow night?"

"Yep, happens only once every other month. Wildly popular, sold out everywhere."

"Okay, you're right, you need to be there, but no way are you going alone. We'll not only have to be persuasive and persistent, but devious. That's why I gotta ride as your wing-woman. I'll bring you something glittery for the evening."

"Already got my shiny .357," Lucy said.

"Not exactly what I had in mind, girlfriend. But no worries, my closet's full of fun little frocks."

Lucy cringed.

"And stop being pissed off about what I said about you and Mercer."

Lucy rubbed her head and tried to conjure calm thoughts. "There is no 'me and Mercer.' "

"Maybe not in your mind, but I'm pretty sure his obsession with you might be more complicated than you realize."

Lucy shrugged. "Okay, I may not agree with you, but you make a point. I'll try to keep an open mind." After I blow the bastard's head off.

"Good, 'cause we need to come at him with eyes wide open from every angle. Now, let me go get my glitter thang on. You'll love what I'm bringing for you."

"I'm not wearing it." Lucy could feel her heels dig into the carpet below the desk. She'd seen Bea's "something fun" before.

—

She wore it. And was grudgingly glad she had. Gold, low cut, high-hemmed and beaded, Lucy felt like a product model at the LA Auto Show. The crowd at *Le Chat Noir* was dressed to the nines — men in top hats, cravats, and silk vintage suits, women in designer gowns as stunning as those worn by pop stars at the Emmys. Women, men, who could tell who was who, and who cared? Definitely a trans vibe.

As patrons prepared to file into the theater, the big question on Lucy's mind was how the hell were they going to score tickets? They'd gone online to all the usual sites, from Craigslist to StubHub, and nothing. Bijan had helped them navigate the dark web ticket site Audrina had suggested — *nada*. They'd even tried the old ploy of wheedling through the backdoor as cast members, but that hadn't worked.

Lucy had a handbag full of cash with which they attempted to bribe the burly red-haired bouncer, but the price he wanted was way too high — a blow job, from each of them.

Bea's eyes shot sparks. "Uh, no way in Hades is that going to happen. What? Are you the Harvey Weinstein of bouncers? You perv."

He paled, then reapplied a smirk. When Bea bared her teeth at him and made nasty biting gestures, he growled at them to "Get the fuck out."

While the two women loitered on the sidewalk assessing

their options, a scream sounded from behind them, a few steps down the block. They whirled toward the source. A Sonny Bono look-alike was bashing his Cher counterpart with a fringed leather courier bag. Still strapped cross-body, he practically strangled himself with each attempted swat.

"You bitch. You've been cheating on me with that sleaze for months. I wouldn't go to this cab-a-fucking-ray tonight with you for all the money in the world, you feckless bastard!"

Cher ripped the bag from Sonny's neck and threw it into the street, along with a pair of what appeared to be theater tickets. "I was only with him because you've been cold and distant ever since that little incident with my chiropractor."

Bea ran for the curb and snatched up the tickets. Bingo. "Uh, we'd be happy to take these off your hands. Sounds like you two are having some issues tonight."

They paused their squabble and gawked in shock at the ballsy black woman in the red-sequined mini-dress.

"Lucy, give him the money." Bea's eyes widened as she checked the ticket price. "Uh, two-fifty each?"

Cher straightened and took a step toward the women. "Three. Each. These are premium seats."

Lucy'd never paid more than fifty bucks for a ticket to anything in her life except a Tina Turner anniversary concert at the Staples Center. Those were a steal at seventy-five dollars. "I'll give you four hundred for both," she said.

"Three each, or nothing," Sonny returned, backing up his gal pal. They sniffed away tears and residual anger from their lover's quarrel, then joined hands in solidarity.

He turned toward Cher, "I got you, babe."

She made juicy kissing noises and tossed her long dark hair.

Bea rolled her eyes.

"We could get two off-season tickets to Maui for this much," Lucy complained.

"Then go to Maui," Cher sneered.

Lucy shrugged. This Cher clearly knew she had the advantage.

Bea and Lucy rummaged through their purses and scraped together the money with nine bucks to spare. Lucy pushed the dough into Cher's slender, beringed fingers and then dashed toward the theater before they could change their minds.

"I hope things work out for you two," Bea called over her shoulder. They were already locked in a deep make-up grope and didn't reply.

Breezing past the red-haired blow job guy, they waved their tickets, which were collected by a waifish middle-aged woman in a French maid's costume. Festive, rowdy theater-goers partied while waiting to be seated. Champagne and hors d'oeuvres circulated. The escargot, caviar on herb-crusted croutons, and filet-mignon-stuffed mushrooms were fantastic. Two men dressed in black berets sang French drinking songs to rev up a crowd already on overdrive.

"This is one of the best shows I've ever been to, and it hasn't even started yet." Lucy bit into what the server had described as baked brie with raspberry compote in a filo crust. "Orgaz-a-matazzmic."

"Uh-huh, whatever you said, I agree." Bea snagged another glass of bubbly. "I wonder if they sell season passes. To hell with my philharmonic tickets."

"Absinthe, *mademoiselle*? A black attired server asked Lucy. He was armed with a carafe of pale-green liquid ready to pour into a small wine glass.

"Is that stuff even legal in this country?" Bea asked.

Lucy knew it wasn't, at least not the traditional recipe.

"*Oui*," he said, then shrugged, "*...et non*. "But tonight, *oui*."

Lucy smiled, tempted, then declined the beverage. She turned to Bea, "Once the show begins, let's pray we spot Toulusa. If he's not part of this deal, we've busted the bank for nothing and we're back at square one."

The doors to the theater opened and the crowd thronged into the gilt-wallpapered foyer, singing and laughing. A silk top hat landed on Lucy's head. A beautiful woman — or person — with long blonde hair said, "So sorry, *ma petite chère*," and kissed her enthusiastically on the lips, *avec* tongue, before retrieving the *chapeau*.

"Woo-hoo," Bea said. "Hang onto your undies, girlfriend."

Lucy nabbed Bea with a stern look. "Enough booze for you. We're working."

"Oops, you're right. *Excusez-moi*." She drained her glass and plunked it down on a passing tray.

As the revelers filed into the theater, Lucy noted framed headshots of the cast mounted to the right of the doorway. She grabbed Bea's hand and pulled her over to the photo wall.

"There she is." Lucy pulled the cell phone from her purse and snapped a photo of the headshot and the name beneath it: Toulusa Lautrec played by Charmaine Modigliani.

Bea squinted through glassy eyes. "Also, an artist's name, Modigliani. Another *nom de plume*?"

"No doubt. We should talk to the owner and say we're casting directors. We need her real name and her agent's name. The agent might be more forthcoming if he or she thinks there's lucrative work for the client."

"They'll spot us as imposters," Bea said. "It's a small business, everybody knows everybody, and nobody has heard of us."

"I can ask my friend Michael Lee over at CAA to make the call. We've been buds since undergrad. Toulusa's peeps would be over the moon to talk with him."

"Good idea."

The two women hustled in from the foyer as the lights began to dim. They were seated at a round café table in the second row, stage left with Ron and Betty, a loquacious couple visiting from Cedar Rapids, Iowa. It was their fortieth wedding anniversary.

Lucy had picked up a playbill but hadn't gotten a chance to check it out before the stage went black and the music increased in volume. Edith Piaf trilled about not regretting anything. Most of the audience knew the lyrics and enthusiastically sang along. Lucy felt as if she'd slipped into a European time warp from an earlier century with a darkly haunting "Hotel California" backdrop.

A spotlight cut the darkness.

Toulusa was the black leather-clad, whip-wielding cabaret ring mistress—*Le Chat Noir*. Furry feline ears reminiscent of devil horns and a swishy tail at her perfect derriere rounded out the look. Tall, with legs to die for and a face that was half horror show, half Elizabeth Taylor in her glory days — the femme was spectacular. No one could take their eyes off her.

"What a presence," Bea whispered, following her every preening, hip-swiveling move. She snapped the whip with a mere flick of her wrist.

Lucy glanced at Ron and Betty. Their mouths hung open, eyes like saucers behind their trifocals. You're not in Iowa anymore, Lucy thought and strapped herself in for the ride.

—

The show was Broadway-caliber, maybe even better because of its intimacy and interaction with the adoring crowd. Two naughty action-packed hours later that concluded with a rousing audience-participation can-can, Bea and Lucy said goodbye to their table-mates and slipped into the alley where their ride was parked in a municipal lot. Dodging drunk, singing revelers, the two whispered plans to pull the SUV rental behind the theater and wait for Toulusa. Then they'd follow and see where *Le Chat Noir* slinked off to. A desert hotel? Or back to LA? In the meantime, Lucy sent the photo of the headshot and the alternative name to Marlene. Maybe she could discover something further with this new information.

Once in the car, they changed from sparkle to innocuous stake-out clothes. At 1:37 a.m. the crowd finally dispersed, migrating toward an all-night bar down the block. A hundred yards from the theater's rear door, Lucy and Bea pulled their dark gray SUV behind a tourist souvenir shop dumpster. It overflowed with cardboard boxes that hadn't been broken down and flattened. Surreptitiously, they watched performers, techs, and other hangers-on slowly exit the dimly lit theater in twos and threes.

From her purse, Lucy took the playbill she hadn't had a chance to read. A classic Toulouse Lautrec black cat graphic decorated the cover. Seconds later, she couldn't help but let out a low whistle.

"Not sure I like the sound of that," Bea said. "Fill me in."

"Charmaine Modigliani is both Le Chat's owner and the artistic director. Glad we didn't try to contact her before the show. Would have blown our cover, tout suite. She's Canadian, from Quebec City, thus the French." Lucy shielded her phone's bright screen and took a shot of the bio, then immediately forwarded it to Marlene.

Bea zipped her sweatshirt and pulled up the hood. A half-hour had passed, and the cold was seriously uncomfortable.

The chilly nighttime temperatures in the desert were a shocking contrast to the hot spring days. Lucy was about to turn on the ignition and coax some warmth from the heater when Toulusa stepped into the alley, garment bag in one hand and rolling suitcase following her in the other.

Bea and Lucy slid down in their seats.

Dressed in a long, patchwork fur coat, Toulusa paused and glanced across the alley toward the over-stuffed dumpster.

A silver Porsche sped by them and stopped in front of the actor. Lucy steadied her camera's telephoto on the steering wheel and streamed images.

Click, click — Lucy captured the license plate. Only three of the numbers were legible on the screen, but better than rien, or nothing. Partials could be traced.

The valet, a short man in his early twenties, hopped out and helped Toulusa in behind the wheel of the gorgeous, sleek vehicle. He placed the luggage in the trunk, shut the door, and *Le Chat Noir*'s namesake immediately took off.

Lucy waited until Toulusa's car exited the alley and turned left toward Palm Canyon Drive before she pulled out after her. Traffic was Sunday-morning light. Looked like Toulusa was heading back toward LA.

They followed at a quarter-mile until they cleared the city lights, the moonlit desert road opened like a black vein before them. Toulusa accelerated. Her silver Porsche disappeared into the night like the Batmobile, leaving Bea and Lucy's rented SUV in the proverbial dust.

"Think she made us?" Bea pressed her hands against the dashboard vent that dribbled tepid warmth into the van.

"Doubt it. She'd have no reason to think she was being followed, and we hardly have the vehicle to keep up."

Lucy slowed from eighty miles an hour, where the poorly

aligned SUV shook like a tin rattle, down to sixty. She pulled onto the 10 West behind a caravan of semis heading through the night to Vons and Wal-Mart and Home Depot. Now almost three in the morning, the women settled in for the several hours' ride back to Santa Monica.

# 37

After a long, tension-filled night, Bea and Lucy were too wired to immediately return home and fade into any kind of restful sleep. They sat at one of Bagel Nosh's outdoor tables off Wilshire Boulevard. The air was cool but the rising sun warmed Lucy's tired shoulders like a towel straight out of the dryer. The first customers of the morning, they scarfed eggs and raisin bagels with *schmear*. Then, Marlene's text came through to both their phones, simultaneously.

She had some news: Girl Scouts, we got us some cookies.

Bea and Lucy smiled at each other.

Lucy dialed the detective and put the phone on speaker — they were the only ones outside at the restaurant.

Marlene picked up immediately and jumped right in. "We nailed your entertainer with the license plate. Our techs were able to enhance it enough to get all the numbers. I'll be sending you my summary shortly."

"Awesome," Bea said. She pushed her plate aside and pulled out her tablet. "So, bring it on, detective."

"Name's Charles Laurent Benoit, twenty-nine years old. Born in Montreal, raised in Quebec City by a musician mother who was also a seamstress for *Le Cirque de Lumiere*. His father was a performer — killed in a trapeze accident under sketchy circumstances. Parents never married. 'Toulusa' came here as a seventeen-year-old student and studied pre-med at UCLA. Was supposedly quite brilliant."

"When did she graduate?" Lucy was an alumna.

"Never. Was expelled in his, her first year for something that happened in a biology lab. The file's sealed, but I've put in a petition to release it. Finally finished her degree at the Fashion Institute five years ago."

"Is she legal?" Bea asked.

"Can't get her on immigration stuff. Benoit's had a green card for a decade. Legally changed her name to Toulusa Benoit Modigliani at about the same time."

Lucy suspiciously eyed a sixtyish couple walking toward them, but they passed by and took a table at the far end of the terrace out of hearing range. "Anything on where she lives?"

"Address is a warehouse she owns. Five blocks from where the fire happened down in Long Beach and the place is worth a lot of money. Up for redevelopment. 'Curiouser and curiouser, cried Alice,' right?"

Marlene loved that book. "We're not stuck down the rabbit hole yet," Lucy said, fighting feelings of discouragement. Toulusa was a property-owner in an up-and-coming neighborhood. That would involve access to some serious *dinero*. They were getting closer with every new bit of information. "What're the chances of getting a search warrant for the place?"

Marlene sighed. "We have nothing to tie her to any suspected crime."

"Other than being the lover and confidante of a murdering drug lord." Lucy couldn't keep her voice from raising loud and angry. "Gotta be something in that relationship to implicate him in collusion of some kind."

Bea patted her arm. "Chill, girlfriend. This is all good news but shouldn't be shouted across the city."

"Sorry," Lucy said. She finished her glass of iced tea and buried her face in her hands, suddenly exhausted.

"Thanks, Mar," Bea said. "We're gonna catch some shut-eye and check in with you later today."

"Sounds good. I'll be working to get my hands on the UCLA student file and see if there's any way we can wrangle a search warrant for her residence. It will be tough on a Sunday, so don't get your hopes up. Got a car watching the place in Long Beach, as we speak. More soon, ladies. Nighty-night."

Lucy clicked off the phone. "I've felt so stalled-out, but this info could blow things open."

"Sure as hell hope so. We need a break." Bea checked her watch. Lucy did the same. It was now six-thirty.

"Elsa's coming home tomorrow," Lucy said. "She'll stay with me in Santa Monica until we figure out what's happening with the ranch."

"Glad you'll be together. And Dexter's coming back on Tuesday." Bea took a long breath. "Alyssa and I are making a little 'Welcome Home' dinner for him. Chicken parm."

"Nervous about seeing him?"

"Heck, no. I'm his mama, he's my son."

Lucy drilled her with a skeptical look.

"Okay, well, it's been a week, and all I got is a couple of innocuous texts shinin' me on. And Rio didn't share much either, except that my son's a great kid, and I have to trust him. I do trust him, but still, he's a kid. Needs his Mama's guidance."

Lucy finished off the last of her bagel. The eatery was

beginning to fill up. Harried young women in power suits slid into the table next to then.

"Bea, he's not a kid anymore. He lost that when he was kidnapped in Savannah last year. He's a young man, still needs his mom, but on his own terms now." She cleared her throat. "If he feels like you're trying to control him, it won't be good, for either of you."

Bea wiped a tear and put on her sunglasses. "What makes you so smart?" The two rose from their table and moved toward the service area to throw their rubbish into the various recycling bins.

Lucy smiled. "I have momentary flashes of insight then it all goes back to fuzzy, gray static again."

"My whole life feels like gray static."

They collected their belongings and trudged down the block toward their ride.

—

It was a picture-perfect postcard day in Southern California. Lucy's eyes scanned the coastline toward Point Dume. The gray plumes of smoke had dissipated into a relatively benign haze. The five-hundred-acre blaze, labeled the Vega Ranch Fire, was officially relegated to the record books. Small potatoes by California brushfire standards, it had still wreaked its own devastation.

Lucy pulled into the short-term lot at LAX, locked the car and made her way across the pedestrian walkway. The Southwest baggage claim area thronged with travelers where the big conveyors spit bags onto the carousel. Lucy immediately spotted Elsa standing nearby with her battered red roller-bag in tow. Then Elsa saw Lucy. They ran to each other's arms and hugged each other tightly. So much to say, and no words to describe the sense of sadness and loss they both shared. At least Elsa hadn't been there to experience the horrific escape firsthand.

Lucy paid the exorbitant parking fee then drove toward Lincoln Boulevard, then Marina del Rey, Venice, and finally, Santa Monica. Along the way, she filled Elsa in the best she could on the fire and the current state of the ranch.

"So, the adjustor is coming to meet you after lunch, like in about two hours?" Elsa's eyes darted to the clock set in the middle of the dashboard display.

"Yeah, it'll be my first real look at the place since it burned."

"Will be a tough sight to see."

The rest of the trip passed in relative silence.

Twenty minutes later, Lucy pulled into her condo driveway and hit the garage remote. The door rattled and slowly rose. "You can rest here while I go up the coast and I'll bring us something home for dinner."

Elsa pushed her silver-framed glasses into place and narrowed her eyes. Her pale gray hair was a bright, cottony aura about her head. Lucy could feel the intensity of her gaze.

"Young lady," Elsa said, "if you think I'm going to stay here and 'rest' while you're up there facing what happened to our ranch, then you're sorely mistaken. I'm with you. You may own the place now, but this is our house. So, don't get all 'protecting the old woman from reality' on me, hear?"

Chastened, Lucy nodded and her eyes teared up again. She felt a strong pang of guilt about relegating Elsa, the heart and soul of the Vega Ranch, to the role of the waiting oldster. "I'm sorry." She took Elsa's hand and gave it a squeeze. "Of course, we'll both go. We'll always both go."

"Then back this jalopy out of here and let's head up PCH. We'll have lunch along the way and then meet these insurance people together."

Lucy nodded and ground the gear into reverse.

# 38

They left the SUV off Kanan Road at the foot of the long driveway that led to the ranch compound. They switched out their shoes for rubber boots and tromped up the hill. Lucy helped Elsa scale the arroyo where the remnants of the exploded bridge lay in heaps of rubble. Past the three burned-out cars — Lucy's Jeep, Bea's BMW, and Cheyney's beloved truck — the ruins became visible. One arm planted in the ground, the other reaching heavenward, all that remained of the ranch house was the main joist, slashed with a charred crossbeam, suspending it on its side. Like a broken mast on a ship or a fallen crucifix, the damage was near complete. The artifacts of their history, gone.

Lucy shuddered and swallowed a pang of nausea. She pulled Elsa close, deeply thankful that they were facing this together.

The barn was a rectangular black footprint, scarred at the far end by a hulking, blistered carcass of the tractor. The caustic stink of devastation would likely remain for months. Lucy would never forget the stench.

"The old bunkhouse looks like it survived," Elsa said, a

sparkle in her Nordic-blue eyes.

Little puffs of black ash rose with each footstep as they trudged toward the only thing still standing — a twenty-by-twenty-four-foot cabin, unpainted, slightly dilapidated, with shuttered windows. A shred of stained plastic covering a collapsed dog door flapped in the breeze. The cabin stood a hundred yards beyond the main compound on a gentle rise overlooking a dry, cactus-filled gulch.

"The metal roof helped save it." Elsa squinted at the tarnished tin surface caught in the sun's glare. "And look, the fire stopped over there and took a one-eighty toward the barn."

Lucy examined the scorch pattern. "Santa Anas are so damn shifty. One ranch burns to the ground and the next place over survives completely."

Elsa nodded, attention still drawn to the cabin. "Never really was a bunkhouse. We didn't have any workers to bunk. I seem to remember catching you and a couple of your underage friends drinking in there a few times, yes?"

"You must be thinking of someone else." Lucy failed to suppress a grin.

"Uh-huh. Guess I'm remembering someone else's empty bottles of Wild Turkey. Disgusting stuff." Elsa stepped onto the wooden porch. The boards groaned. "Became the storage shed — everything from old tires to dog food in here. Our first cat, Cleo, had kittens inside before we could get her spayed. Such a tramp. Howard was the only male of the litter, remember? Cute as a button, he was."

Lucy nodded. "Howard. I sure miss that little dude of ours."

"Me, too." Elsa stepped back and perused the bunkhouse like it was the first time she was really seeing its potential.

"Maybe we can clear this place out for me to live in. It has a bathroom and electrical. We can build another storage shed and transfer over all the junk. Home Depot has some good-sized models displayed in their parking lot. Cheyney can help us. And I can be here to oversee the rebuilding when you're gone."

"Well, maybe that could work, at least temporarily." Lucy tried to animate her voice and keep her gaze away from the horrible skeleton of the ranch house.

Elsa's excitement was unexpected and took Lucy by pleasant surprise. God, she sure could use some optimism. Raking up enthusiasm for rebuilding was like pushing a car stuck in a sinkhole, but she'd make it back onto the road.

A weird thought suddenly struck. Lucy looked at Elsa and chuckled. "You know what? This could be an opportunity to try something different."

"What do you mean?"

"I've always wanted to live in a yurt. Even the word is cool."

Elsa laughed out loud and clapped her hands. "A yurt! My grandfather had one in Norway. We used it as a hunting cabin and cross-country skied to it in the winter." Her eyes went all dreamy. "Always had hot chocolate and snacks ready for cold children — including your dad and all the cousins."

"Sounds wonderful. We're a yurt family. We'll put it across from your bunkhouse. And get the corrals and chicken coops up next. All the critters are with April Cordelli in Lobo Canyon. You know her?"

"Ah, April, of course. Cheyney was sweet on her. It was a decade ago, maybe more, but she left him for somebody else. I always thought April and Cheyney had just met too soon after she divorced that lousy tomcat husband of hers."

"Well, something may be rekindling." Lucy smiled at the thought, then it was pushed down by a wave of sadness. She wondered if the relationship she and Michael shared would find a spark again someday.

"One can only hope," Elsa said. "I've always liked her. Not surprised she rode to your rescue."

A thump and a yelp sounded from inside the bunkhouse. Lucy and Elsa looked at each other, startled.

"Rats?" Elsa climbed back onto the porch.

Lucy gazed at the wreckage around her. "Wonder where the key is." They'd be lucky if they found anything at all, let alone a key.

"Probably thirty years ago, Henry put it down on the porch railing and a crow swooped in and flew away with it. They love their shiny stuff. We had such a laugh over that. Hasn't been locked since." Elsa tugged hard at the warped wooden door but couldn't get it to budge.

"First I heard of that story." Lucy stepped up beside her and gave the door a hard yank. Then another one. A rotting piece of the door jamb groaned, splintered, and the door popped open.

A moment of astonished silence, then, "Oh, my God." Lucy rubbed her eyes. "Look at that!"

Elsa peered into the dim interior. "Lordy, be."

Howard sat atop an open bag of dog food. He stretched with a bit of attitude. What took you two so long to show up? Then he hopped down and rubbed himself against Lucy's legs, purring deep in his chest.

Tears sprang to her eyes as she picked him up and forced him to endure a shower of kisses, then handed him to Elsa for more love. A whimper sounded from behind a broken chair covered with a tarp. Two dark brown eyes peeped out.

"What is that? A squired?" Elsa asked, eyes squinting dubiously. "A raccoon? They carry rabies."

Howard squirmed down from her arms and padded over to the critter, meowing proudly.

"I think it's a puppy," Lucy said.

"Probably both got in through that half-boarded-up dog door."

A gangly little mutt, maybe eight weeks old, skittered toward Howard. He looked nervous and shy but followed the cat toward Lucy and Elsa. He even accepted an ear scratch, although his knees were bent, ready to spring away.

Lucy grinned. "Elsa, I think Howard's new toy is a coyote pup."

"Oh, no. What in the world are we going to do with a baby coyote?"

After an enthusiastic licking of the puppy's singed whiskers, Howard purred loudly and turned to Lucy and Elsa. His big yellow eyes asked — Can we keep him, Mom?

—

Lucy and Elsa walked the entire ranch several times with the friendly, bald insurance adjustor from Woodland Hills. Photos were taken, reports written, and promises of action were forthcoming. By the time all the forms were filled out and the animals were squared away in the bunkhouse with water and food for another few nights, it was dusk. The two women hiked back out to the SUV, edged it onto a busy Kanan Road, then turned left and took PCH back to Santa Monica. The bay shimmered before them as lights came on, defining the graceful shoreline against the darkening haze.

Forty minutes later they cruised down Main Street with its hipster eateries, boutiques, and tacky tourist shops on the way to Lucy's condo. After Bugle and Maddie's frenzied greeting, then a little supper for them all, Elsa and the two canines sacked out. Lucy left them snoring softly in the guest room. It had been another long, trying day.

Before taking a sorely needed hot shower, Lucy plunked down on the couch to check emails. She'd been so consumed with the ranch, she'd barely glanced at her phone.

All appeared unremarkable except for a voicemail from Marlene. Lucy's stomach knotted as she listened. "Found a sympathetic judge. Member of my congregation. Serving the warrant at five tomorrow morning. Address following. See you there," Marlene's recording said.

Lucy hugged the phone to her chest, her breathing ragged. Yes!

# 39

It was still dark when Bea and Lucy pulled across from Toulusa's four-story cement-block warehouse in Long Beach. In an aging industrial area, the street was deserted and graffiti metastasized across the building as high as a hand holding a can of spray paint could reach.

Marlene and two uniformed officers stood in front, unhappy looks on their faces. The metal door appeared to have been ripped off its hinges then boarded up. Crime scene tape flapped in the cold wind off the bay.

Bea hopped out of the car and after locking up, Lucy followed. Beep went the sensor. It was the kind of neighborhood where a chop shop could dismember your vehicle in minutes and have it on a container ship bound for anywhere in hours.

"What's happening, Mar?" Bea pulled up the collar of her dark gray blazer. The misty dampness of the pre-dawn raised goosebumps.

Marlene frowned. "Pete Anthony and major narcotics hit here at three-thirty this morning. The first two floors are a drug lab, processing heroin and mixing it with fentanyl. Arrested seventeen people."

"That's fantastic," Lucy said. "Anybody spot Toulusa?"

"Nope, no sign." Marlene sniffed and pushed up her big glasses.

"Her apartment on the upper floors?" Bea scanned the roofline.

"Top floor is the living area. Pete said the third looks to be Toulusa's art studio where she cuts shit up and stuffs animals."

"Taxidermy." Lucy shuddered.

"Okay, let's get a move on." Bea stepped up onto the curb toward the front door. She pursed her lips acknowledging the two uniforms bookending her. Both young men in their twenties, their assignment seemed to be door duty. Their faces were serious as stone.

Marlene showed her ID and demanded access.

The taller of the two shuffled his feet and placed his hand on the butt of his gun. "I'm sorry, ma'am, we can't let you inside in. Been locked down until Detective Anthony's people can process everything."

"I'm not, 'ma'am,' I'm Homicide Detective Marlene Simon and I have a warrant to search this place. Now."

The two cops looked at each other, unsure. They had to be total rookies.

Bea raised her chin in the way she does when something smells rotten. "Anthony needs to process this dump for narcotics; we need to see the place on a murder charge. We have the paperwork. Since when does narcotics trump a homicide investigation?"

Marlene stepped away from the officers and moved in close to Lucy and Bea, lowering her voice. "Listen, I have to play nice, I work with these people. Need to keep them on my side."

"We gotta get in there, Mar." Lucy pressed her forehead

in painful frustration. "We might find something to implicate Mercer and nail his ass once and for all. This is the best lead we've had."

The detective glanced up and down the empty street. "Come on, wonder women, let's go for a walk. There's a back way."

Marlene called over her shoulder to the two uniforms, "Checking out the food truck. Can I bring you back a coffee?"

"No thanks," they grumbled.

The trio took off down the block. Turning left onto Seventeenth, it was only a few steps to the service alley running behind the buildings. Marlene lugged her rolling office bag behind her. It looked heavier than usual.

"There's one of those pull-down fire escapes at the back," she said. "It's padlocked but I brought my bolt cutters and a few other handy tools. There's a dumpster we can move underneath so we can reach it."

"Oh, my God," Lucy said with a fist pump. "Brilliant."

Bea hugged Marlene then helped her drag the heavy piece of luggage down the alley. "I won't even ask what y'all have in there."

"Good, 'cause I have to keep the Detective Marlene Simon bag of tricks mysterious."

When they arrived at the rusted green trash container, they pushed it directly beneath the fire escape ladder. Fortunately, the bin was empty. Full, they might not have been able to budge it. Bea, the tallest of the group at around five-ten, crawled up top. Her balance was solid.

"She played Division I basketball at USC," Lucy said with a proud smile directed at Bea.

"Glad at least one of us is athletic." Marlene unzipped the bag and pulled out an industrial-size bolt cutter and handed it up.

It took Bea about five minutes of grunting and teeth-gritting, but the bolt finally broke. By the time she finished, her arms shook from the effort. "Thought I had a pretty good set of biceps, but that was tough."

"Good job." Lucy took the tool and jammed it back into Marlene's bag, as a harsh-looking man on a silver Japanese-made motorcycle turned into the alley. He cruised slowly past the women. His eyes flitted to the fourth floor. He slowed to a halt at the trash bin. His hair was tied in a grayish braid that hung to the middle of his back beneath a matte black helmet.

He scratched the soul patch on his chin. "You cops?"

"Huh-uh. Friends of Toulusa's." Marlene crossed her arms on her chest and narrowed her eyes. "Who the hell are you?"

He looked them over, lips curled in disdain. Nicotine-stained teeth flashed. "You bitches're either working girls or cops." He made eye contact with Bea's breasts. "I vote cops." He spit a wet loogie at their feet then accelerated, peeling out in a cloud of fumes and gravel.

"Asshole. Got his picture," Lucy said. "Sending it on."

Marlene faux jogged a couple of steps. "Okay, *bubalas*, we better get up there before our meager cover's blown. The uniforms make a round every fifteen minutes, and Pete's gonna circle back with his crime scene techs, so let's move it."

She pushed her bag behind the dumpster and used it as a step stool. After they managed to help each other clamber onto the fire escape, which was no easy feat, Lucy pulled up the ladder.

At each level, the metal stairs passed a big window equipped as an egress port for an emergency. On the fourth floor, Marlene pulled out a cloth-wrapped hammer and broke the glass at the latch. They opened the window and all tumbled inside onto Toulusa's gray leather couch. The throw pillows, a half-dozen fat rectangles in various shades of mystery fur, slid across the shiny, hardwood floor.

Bea winced and avoided touching them. "Must be part of Toulusa's Road Kill Design line."

Lucy brushed aside the glass on the sill and closed the window. They could only hope that the officers didn't notice that a pane was out.

Now, time to get to work.

The big open living-dining-room-kitchen was stunning in a quirky, Boho sort of way. Lots of paisley against gray, and a Toulouse Lautrec poster of the *Folies Bergère* that could be an original, hung next to a sports-bar-worthy TV. Huge abstract oil paintings and a collection of medical etchings from early twentieth-century Britain decorated surrounding walls.

"Bizarre shit," Bea said, perusing the vintage images. "If we had any question about her proclivities, I think these have answered it. The chick's a freak with a capital F."

"Look at these costumes." Marlene walked out of the bedroom with two dazzling couture gowns on velvet hangers. "They look handmade. The sewing is exquisite. I wonder if her mother made them when she worked for *Le Cirque.*"

Lucy inspected the stitchery and beadwork. "Or maybe she made them himself. The nurse, Dillard, said she seemed fascinated with surgical needlework."

At that moment, from a nearby room, they heard Bea let out a strangled cry. Then another one. Lucy and Marlene hustled up behind her.

Toulusa's place was weird but still extreme HGTV until they entered what appeared to be the studio.

Before they could react, a loud pounding rattled the front

door to the flat.

"Marlene, open up, dammit," Pete Anthony yelled.

"Shit, I didn't expect him so soon." She hurried to let him in before he broke the door down. When he began to angrily bitch her out, Lucy heard Marlene tell him to shut up and follow her. In seconds they'd joined Bea and Lucy, who both now stood in the center of a large, windowless room.

There was a moment of shared silence as they took in the view.

"Well fuckin-A," Pete whispered, eyes wide.

Leering down at them were huge poster blow-ups of Mercer's injuries, from the first visit to the Burn Center to his current condition with a morbidly mask-like new face. There were also photos of the dead donor and of Toulusa and Mercer in graphic sexual situations. Smaller close-ups of wounds and stitches were posted to a corkboard wall.

On a worktable, a many-textured patchwork quilt was in process of completion. Lucy skimmed her fingers over a shiny, dark square. Then she froze and slowly withdrew her hand as if trying to avoid being bitten by a rattlesnake.

"Oh. My. God. This isn't just roadkill." She peered closer and gagged. "That's a human face."

There were several more interspersed with animal hides and what appeared to be human scalps and rectangles, of what? Pubic hair?

"Holy shit." Pete fired up his radio and directed his crime scene team to stand by.

Bea rushed from the room. The sound of vomiting and a flushing toilet echoed down the hall.

"Looks like this bastard isn't just an ancillary player. She's Mercer's fangirl." Pete's eyes narrowed and he took a deep slow breath. "She's key. Cozy with the kingpin, the labs, murder, mutilation. Shit."

In a few moments Bea returned and stood outside the studio, tissues pressed to her lips. Lucy joined her. She'd had more than enough of Toulusa's sickness. Her skin was beginning to itch just being in proximity to the depraved artwork. She couldn't wait to get her hands on some soap or sanitizer to purge the contamination from where her fingers had grazed the obscene quilt.

Marlene and Pete followed them into the living area. He gave Bea a tender squeeze, then seemed embarrassed and reverted to hard cop mode.

Lucy looked intensely at each of her colleagues. "What's our next move?"

Pete spoke first. "Marlene and I can handle it from here. We'll rally all our resources."

Marlene frowned. "And you can thank us women for the break. Your people would've taken days to get this far, worked their way up one a floor at a time, right?" She was clearly still pissed off at his attempts at stonewalling her investigation.

"I was following protocol, and you know it," he said, equally pissed.

"Since when do you give a rat's ass about protocol, except when it serves you?"

Pete began to flush. "Listen, Detective Simon, you're not exactly the Mother Teresa of open communication."

"Stop it," Bea said. Her face had regained most of its natural color and she'd stuffed the tissues into her pocket. "We have to be on the same page and stop trying to out-maneuver each other or we'll blow this whole thing. Listen up. Now."

She had their attention. "We can safely assume that Toulusa knows this location's compromised by now. I think we met one of her scouts in the alley."

Lucy nodded. "The asshole on the Kawasaki."

Marlene stepped toward the door. "They're gonna scatter. Go back under their rocks. We gotta work fast."

"We know that the former cartel *capo*, Alvarez, had a penthouse condo on Wilshire somewhere in Westwood," Bea reminded them. "I think that's the first place we should look. Mercer isn't going to leave the metro area with all the medical challenges he still has to deal with."

"With the resources that asshole has at his beck and call, we can't assume he'll stay in place either. Marlene and I will get our people organized for a Westwood surveillance." Pete followed them to the elevator. The door slid open revealing one of the uniforms who'd been guarding the front door. He said, "Sir, we need you downstairs. We found a box of C-4."

# 40

Bea and Lucy sat in the car together, still stunned by the revelations in Toulusa's loft. Besides the drugs, the C-4 plastic explosive that had been used to start the fire in the warehouse down the street had probably been taken from the cache they'd just found in the lab downstairs. It all connected.

They stared off into middle space for several quiet minutes, then Lucy reeled herself back in. "Okay, let's try to refocus."

Bea nodded but Lucy could tell she was someplace else. Lucy checked a chiming text then squeezed her friend's hand. "Eye contact, Beatrice, look at me." She made the two-fingered sign pointing to her own eyes then to Bea's, indicating she needed her attention.

Bea pressed back against the headrest and blinked into the present. She turned toward Lucy. "So, what's happening with the Westwood search?"

Lucy put her cellphone in the cupholder then pulled the SUV onto the street. "Marlene said LAPD's running a check on luxury condo ownership and rentals along the Wilshire corridor, targeting between Fairfax and Highland. Seems like the kind of real estate where a rich Hollywood-obsessed criminal like Luis Alvarez would want to plant himself. When Alvarez died, Mercer moved in."

Bea nodded and glanced at the dashboard clock. Lucy followed her gaze. It was now seven-thirty in the morning, and rush hour on the freeways would be in full swing.

"When's Dexter coming in?" Lucy could sense her friend's anxiety over the return of her son.

"He should be down in a couple of hours. The plane left Atlanta on time. I'm gonna go home, change, and head out to LAX."

"It will be so interesting to hear how the visit went and find out what he's thinking."

"If he'll tell me anything." Bea pressed her fingers to her temples and shut her eyes. "Alyssa will be with us this weekend, so at least he'll probably talk to her, and she still tells me everything. Or maybe those days are over, too." Bea winced. "Now that I think about it, they are over. This kids-growing-up stuff really sucks."

Lucy sighed. "Call me if you need an emergency bottle of Merlot."

"Plan on a case." Bea's phone buzzed. She pulled it from her purse and eyed the caller ID. "It's Pete."

"I'd ask how you two lovers are doing, but I know you'd tell me you're just friends."

"Friends with bennies," Bea said, a mischievous gleam in her big brown eyes easing the look of sadness, at least for a passing moment. Then she tapped on the call. "What's up narc, honey?"

As she listened, Bea appeared to shift uncomfortably in her seat, pulling at her seatbelt, face grim. "Pete, hold on, can I put this on speaker? Lucy's right here with me."

"I'll link you to the car's Bluetooth so you don't have to hassle with the phone." After Lucy touched several icons on the car's console screen, the call filled the cabin.

"So, he was released today." Pete's voice was deep against office background noise.

"Who are we talking about?" Lucy edged onto the 405 from the 710. It was slow going.

"Luis Alvarez's little bro, Carlos. Released from the federal pen at Lompoc on a technicality an hour ago."

"Shit, I thought he was in for the next decade." Lucy stepped on the accelerator for a fast few hundred yards, then the artery clogged again like grease in a fast food restaurant drain pipe.

"We all thought he was in for the dime. But he's out, and word on the street is he wants the cartel back in the family. Since Mercer's big hurt, Carlos is a shark in the water smelling blood."

A big semi idled noisily in the next lane. Bea turned up the volume on the speaker a couple of notches. "The perfect time to make a move is when the competition's down on the mat."

Pete's voice boomed. "Precisely. We've got cars following him down the 101 from Lompoc and under-covers staked out at the best high-rises in the Wilshire-Highland area."

Bea checked her watch again. "Well, this is sure a kick in the head."

"Mercer probably knew before we did that Carlos is out and gunning for him. The masked man's gonna have to ride out of Dodge real fast and secure his hold in Guerrero."

"Won't be easy to leave LA." Bea continued to fiddle with the volume which seemed to either blast or whisper. "Probably still needs his sterile environment and lots of medical equipment. Not like putting extra panties in a purse.

I mean the dude's seriously handicapped."

"Looked pretty spry in some of Toulusa's photos." Lucy's stomach clenched at the graphic recollection.

Bea groaned. "Never refer to those pictures again."

"If only we could un-see them."

With traffic now at full-stop, Lucy switched her attention to the gnat-like news-and-weather choppers buzzing overhead while Bea and Pete continued to strategize. When the helicopters swarmed, as they were doing now, it usually indicated an accident, a SIG-alert, or some other random drama that could trap drivers on the road for hours.

Then a real idea began to percolate in her brain. "Hey guys, we should see which residential buildings have heliports. That would be the only quick way out of town. Mercer wouldn't risk getting stuck in this infernal traffic."

Pete cleared his throat. "You're on to something there, Lucia. Marlene and I were thinking along the same lines. Gonna work that angle ASAP. I'll be in touch. Later, lovelies."

Bea disconnected then squinted at her phone screen. "Got a voicemail from Atlanta. Looks like Rio."

"Calling to tell you Dexter got off fine, and they had a terrific week together."

Bea barely nodded and pressed Call Back after popping her migraine meds.

Rio picked up on the second ring. "Hey, Bea."

His voice came through on Bluetooth. "Hey, sweet brother."

"Wanted to touch base with you. Just got a call from Dexter at the airport," he said.

"Oh, no, he's here already?" Bea gulped hard. Her words poured out in a nervous gush. "He didn't leave a message. I'll call him. I'm stuck on the freeway. He can Uber home — I should be there within the hour."

Lucy knew Bea could talk faster than a jackhammer when she was stressed.

"Alyssa and I are making chicken parm for him tonight. And deep-fried pickles. His fave. And his dad'll be over tomorrow to spend some time with him. Maybe go golfing. Kevin hasn't been the most responsible father but he loves his son. And —" The words dried up in Bea's throat.

The air went silent.

"Rio? What is it?" Bea's hand pressed against her heart.

"Dexter called me — not from LAX — from Jackson-Hartsfield. He didn't get on the plane."

"What?" Bea's face paled to gray.

"He's okay, doing fine, not sick or anything. Just not ready to go home yet."

"What are you talking about? He has to come home, ready or not. School starts Monday. He's in his last months of his junior year. Has scholarship offers."

Lucy winced at the sheer panic in her friend's voice.

"Bea, it's going to be all right. He'll call you this evening and explain everything. I didn't want you to be blindsided. I know this is hard. But he's okay, really."

"Why doesn't he want to come home?" She choked out the words. "What have I done wrong?"

"Baby, you've done everything right. He went to a PTSD survivors' group with me, a lotta young cats in their twenties, mostly military, but not all. Something clicked for him. Thinks this is what he needs right now. I encouraged him to trust his gut. And he can stay with us as long as he wants."

Quiet tears streamed down Bea's cheeks. Lucy could sense her trying to hold it together.

"He'd live with you? You'd do that?"

"Hey, I lived with your family from middle school on, saved my life. I'd do anything for you and yours, you know that, sweetheart."

"He'd lose a semester." Bea swiped at her drippy nose. Lucy handed her a tissue.

"No, he'll go to school here at University High for the term and attend therapeutic group meetings. It's out-patient. Focuses on the positive, on looking forward, doesn't wallow in the past. Lots of community service, you know, helping others helps ourselves. He'll thrive, Bea."

She paused to steady her breathing. "Oh, God, this is so hard. Okay, I trust you with my son, with my life. Tell that little shit I love the hell out of him and he'd better call me, tonight."

"Will do. I'll take good care of him. Never doubt that."

Bea let out a long exhalation. "Love you, Rio. I don't have words to tell you what this means."

"No words needed. Love you, too, little sister." The line disconnected.

# 41

Immediately, Bea's phone sounded again but she looked too dazed to respond.

"Let me get it." Lucy grabbed the phone from Bea's limp fingers and accepted the call still on Bluetooth. "Pete, it's Lucy. Your girlfriend's indisposed right now. We're almost to Ocean Park. What's up?" She exited the freeway.

"Carlos Alvarez isn't going to Westwood; he's heading for the desert."

"Whoa. You think he's planning to ambush Mercer there rather than in Westwood?"

Pete cleared his throat and continued. "My guess is, Mercer takes a chopper out of LA and hauls ass straight to that airstrip near the Salton Sea. It's remote as hell and one his group has used before when coming in and out of Guerrero. There'll be a plane waiting to take him over the border where his organization can protect him. But Carlos Alvarez and his goons will be ready. Before Mercer figures out what's going down, Carlos'll murder them all at the airstrip, then disappear."

"Makes a lot of sense." Bea blew her nose and perked up.

"We have people watching for copter landings on Westwood rooftops. I got one waiting to run Marlene, me, and three of our folks out to Coachella. We'll meet up with the Fibbies. If Carlos and Mercer's crews converge at the airstrip, could be the gunfight at the O.K. Corral, but worse."

"Sounds like a decent plan. You leaving from Santa Monica Airport? We're ten minutes away." Lucy glanced over at Bea.

"This is police work, Luce. We'll handle it."

"What kind of chopper, Pete? A Bell 206A?"

"Uh, yeah. I think so, why?"

"Holds eight."

"Holds five. Sorry, Lucy. I couldn't transport civilians even if I had the space. I think the best thing you and that other extremely stubborn woman you hang with can do is go home and wait to hear from me."

Lucy huffed. "Oh, okay, detective. Sure thing."

"Why does, 'oh, okay,' sound a lot like 'fuck you'?"

Bea's slumping posture straightened. She scowled. "Because, narcolicious, that's exactly what it means."

Lucy smirked and pressed Disconnect.

They pulled onto Ocean Park Boulevard near Bundy and parked at a curb. Two scruffy teens bombed past them on skateboards. A dog-walker with five doxies and a hyper-active labradoodle struggled after them.

"What's next?" Lucy drummed on the steering wheel, thinking of her own pups, and missing them.

Bea's focus turned dark and unreadable. She seemed deep in thought and then turned to her friend. "The cops have eyes out for choppers landing in Westwood, and Pete and Marlene are covering the desert. What if the helicopter is a ruse and Mercer's sneaking out the back door after all?"

Lucy shrugged. "If he did hit the street, we'd never catch him. No information on residential ownership or rental records that link his way. Probably all under a shell corporation. He could be holed up in any of a hundred different places. Impossible to cover."

Bea pressed her temples again like she was trying to conjure a vision. "If I had to pick one place in Westwood a cartel boss rolling in cha-ching would want to live, it would be the Watertower Regency. The Times did a feature on them a few months ago. Sand-bottomed swimming pool for every individual condo unit and legendary security."

"Where is it?"

"Wilshire near Manning. It's beyond LAPD's target area. They're monitoring buildings closer to Westwood Village."

"Picking a random pricey residence because you saw it in the newspaper is like a like a huge stretch," Lucy said. "Chances of Mercer being there are about zip."

Bea shook her head. "Yeah, except I'm remembering something Alyssa told me about one of her little conversations with Mercer at the Burn Center."

Lucy stopped drumming on the steering wheel. "What are you talking about?"

"I think Mercer told her he lived in a fancy high-rise building near Century City where he could see the ocean and where there was a swimming pool in every unit. Called her a 'neighbor' and it creeped her out. Come on, Luce, let's check it, nothing to lose."

"Okay *Top Gun*, what the hell, let's give it a shot. Anything's better than sitting here bitching at each other. Fire up the GPS and find us a way into this place." Lucy hauled out from the curb and made a quick, illegal U-turn toward Westwood and Century City. Horns honked. "Bite me," Lucy muttered.

"You tell 'em, girl." As they sped down Ocean Park, Bea studied her phone. She smiled, then brought the Earth view up on Lucy's console map. "Lookie there, it has a heliport."

—

It took them twenty-five minutes, including a quick drive-thru at an In-N-Out Burger on Gayley, before entering the service alley behind the residence. Lucy drove slowly then edged in behind a Southern California Edison truck that marked its space with orange traffic cones. Lined up across the way were vehicles from a florist, a catering outfit called SkyMeals, and a Watertower Regency maintenance truck.

Lucy took a long swig of diet cola then bit into her cheeseburger. She chattered with her mouth full. "You know I hardly ever eat red meat except when you drag me out for Georgia barbecue, but having one of these on occasion is like, like..."

"A religious experience?" Bea chomped down a hefty bunch of french fries.

"Yeah, something like that. Mmm, exactly like that." Lucy scanned the wide alley. A bicycle delivery woman with a load of pizza boxes strapped onboard pedaled by.

"You carrying?" Bea asked between chews.

"Got the .357 I took from Mercer's Land Rover in Mexico in my backpack. You?"

"The Glock my brother bought me for my birthday, nylon shoulder holster. In my bag." She grimaced and patted her large, brown leather purse. "How long do you think we should stay here surveilling?"

"If Mercer's gonna beat Carlos to the Salton Sea airstrip and then disappear into Mexico, they gotta leave within the hour."

"I was thinking the same thing." Bea took another bite of

burger.

With low expectations, the two glanced up now and then to check the alley. Then Lucy heard the distant whomp-whomp of chopper blades reverberating. They both stopped chewing in unison.

Lucy looked at Bea. "You hear that? They're coming to pick him up."

"Probably a traffic copter." Bea slowly began to chew again.

Lucy opened the sunroof. The shadow of whirling blades cut across the alley before the bird materialized above, then disappeared to hover noisily atop the building. She grabbed the camera from the floor behind her seat and sidled into a position that would allow her to take full advantage of the scene. "Bea, this is it. Your hunch was brilliant."

"I have my moments. Hope this is one of them."

Seven-and-a-half minutes later, the helicopter lifted up from the heliport, whirred above them, banked hard, then vanished. The sound was quickly swallowed by the din of the city.

Bea reached for her cellphone. "Could you see how many passengers were inside?"

Lucy sank down from her spot against the edge of the sunroof. "Windows were tinted, couldn't tell. Caught part of the tail number. N23-something. Let's call Pete so he can alert his people. Tell him I'm texting the video."

Bea dropped her unfinished meal into the paper bag and rang Pete on speed dial.

"Yes, dear," he said with an exaggerated simper in his voice.

"Listen up — Lucy's sending you the video of the chopper that landed and took off from the Watertower Regency. I think this may have been the pick-up."

While Bea filled Pete in, Lucy noticed the door to the loading dock rise. A tall, scrubs-clad woman in a fancy chignon hairdo and dangly earrings stepped out. "Oh my God," Lucy choked.

"What is it?" Bea tried to follow Lucy's line of vision.

"I think that's Toulusa."

Bea said to Pete, "I'll call you back in a minute." She disconnected and craned her neck across the dashboard to try and see what Lucy observed.

A quick intake of air. "Lordy, be," Bea said. "I think you're right."

The SkyMeals truck ahead of them immediately backed up to the dock. The driver hopped out and swung open the rear doors.

Bea squinted "The driver looks like that firebug-piece-of-crap, Cardenas. I wish I had a long-range flamethrower in my pocket. Fry his skinny ass."

Lucy snapped images, then switched to video mode. A patient dressed in white, face completely covered by bandages, emerged from the dark loading bay in a wheelchair. He was pushed by a male orderly in the lilac version of Toulusa's scrubs. The patient was transferred to a gurney and carefully loaded into the truck.

Bea's eyes went as round as a couple of chocolate truffles. "Lucy, is that Nurse Dillard with Mercer?"

"No freakin' way." Goosebumps pocked her arms.

Bea nodded vigorously. "Sure as hell is."

Mercer disappeared inside the truck with his henchmen. Lucy's heart was ready to pop out of her chest like in *Alien*. Cardenas slammed the rear door and returned to the cab. A clean-cut blond guy in his mid-thirties rode shotgun. Lucy wondered if he was the rogue Ventura County firefighter who helped start the Vega Ranch Fire. She'd send Captain Stewart his picture.

The SkyMeals truck pulled down the alley. Lucy handed Bea the camera and took off discretely behind them. "Call Pete back. He can send people to grab these creeps right now."

Bea hit redial and endured a half-dozen fruitless rings. "Damn, went to voicemail." She texted him with the SOS, texted Marlene with the same.

Turning onto Wilshire toward the 10 Freeway, Lucy accelerated up the entry ramp. She followed the SkyMeals truck south onto the 405, staying about three cars behind and a lane over on the inside. Perspiration dampened her neck. "Good chance they're heading toward an airport. They can get inside under the guise of a catering truck. Looks legit, maybe it is."

"Definitely won't be going to LAX. Too risky. Maybe they're making for Hawthorn-Northrop Field or Compton." Bea punched up Compton Airport on the GPS. "We've got to get them before they leave the ground. Come on Pete, pick up. Marlene? Where in Hades are you?"

"Probably so noisy in the helicopter they can't hear anything."

Bea shrugged and snapped several shots of the SkyMeals wing-man which she forwarded to LACFD Cap Stewart.

Lucy edged in front of a lumbering RV that threatened to block her view. She ignored the driver's lewd protest. The SkyMeals truck skirted LAX and turned onto the 105 heading South. The freeway was clipping along at a steady fifty-five mile-an-hour pace when the truck made a fast, no-blinker exit at Crenshaw Boulevard. Lucy gripped the steering wheel — her knuckles turned white from the effort. She made a two-wheel exit behind the caterers and about rolled the SUV.

"Sweet Jesus, girl," Bea gasped. "I wanna live to see Mercer die."

The SkyMeals truck accelerated and turned into a gated airport service entrance. Cardenas swiped a card key. The barrier gate arm lifted, then immediately lowered.

Lucy pulled onto the shoulder fifty yards from the entrance. "I think they made us. Turning so fast — a classic way to try and lose a tail."

Bea nodded. Her phone finally buzzed.

"What took you so long?" She was pissed. "We followed them here to Hawthorne Airport. They're in a SkyMeals catering truck. You can bet they're gonna be airborne and out of here within the hour, or within the next ten minutes for all we know."

"Slow down," Lucy heard Pete shout through the receiver.

"We got Mercer, Toulusa, Cardenas, a blonde surfer dude who could be the arsonist firefighter. and Richard Dillard, the nurse practitioner from Santa Barbara who helped with Mercer's face plant."

"You sure about all this, Bea?"

"Send in the stormtroopers, Pete. I'd guess we have about a twenty-minute window and then, *adios*."

—

Lucy and Bea sat in the stuffy SUV on the shoulder of the airport road for an hour and a half, miserably inhaling jet fumes and finishing their cold In-N-Out meals. Planes and helicopters came and went. When a MedEvac with a red cross on its side zoomed down the runway and ascended, Lucy slapped the steering wheel and threw open the car door in frustration.

"That's probably Mercer. Off he goes. What a cluster fuck."

Bea dialed both Marlene and Pete again, to no response. The MedEvac plane became a dot then vanished.

At least I got the tail number. Lucy texted it to Pete and Marlene. "For all the good it'll do at this point."

"Let's get out of here." Bea pressed the bridge of her nose. "Our window of opportunity's history."

As the clock ticked toward two hours and they prepared to leave, an armored black LAPD SWAT van careened in front of Lucy's vehicle and stopped hard in a cloud of dust. A team of shooters exploded from the back doors and danced their infrared dots recklessly across the bodies of the two women.

# 42

"Don't move!" The SWAT team leader, whose features were sharply cut and dark as obsidian, crackled with intensity.

Lucy swallowed her terror, slowly stepped from the car, and leaned against the SUV's door frame with a nonchalance she didn't remotely feel. Her eyes met the man's hard glare. Anger bubbled in her chest. "A little late to the dance, guys. The prom queen is gone."

The red laser dots still boogied. What the hell was going on? Lucy beat back the panic that squeezed her throat. This boys club wouldn't blast two innocent women. Would they?

"Have your stormtroopers stand the fuck down," Bea commanded with an attitude that would give a drill sergeant pause.

He raised his hand and the team eased their weapons. "Damn. We thought one of you might be this Toulusa person."

Bea cocked a hip. "Either one of us look like a six-foot-two transgender female in surgical scrubs?"

"Sorry, ma'am. The description was sketchy. You Vega and Middleton?"

"That's us," Bea said. "I'm Middleton. And you are?"

"Captain Joe Packer." He nodded but didn't offer his hand.

"Where the hell have you been?" Bea rounded the front of the SUV and stood next to Lucy by the driver-side door.

"We were sent to Compton/Woodley." His eyes never ceased scanning the environment.

Bea's fists clench and unclench. "I specifically told Detective Anthony, Hawthorne Airport." Lucy thought she looked ready to take a swing.

"We got the directive from the top floor at PAB, ma'am. They said Anthony fell off the radar."

Bea and Lucy exchanged concerned glances.

"We'll follow up here, ladies, find out everything we can." He turned toward the terminal. "Thanks for your work on the case, and again, sorry for the, uh, little glitch. Just doing our due diligence."

"Little glitch? Punk ass." Bea muttered.

The team loaded back into the vehicle as quickly as they'd stampeded out and headed for the service entrance. An airport security van was there to escort them in.

Bea scuffed at the dusty road shoulder. "Where was security when we were trying to get in?"

The SWAT encounter seemed surreal to Lucy like she'd watched it on a bad TV cop show. The bloody-hole-like infrared dots would pock her dreams. She shuddered adrenaline draining, leaving her shaken.

"That was pretty messed up." Bea folded her arms across her chest. "I can't believe they drew down on us. And what the hell did they mean that Pete was off the radar?"

"I don't know, but it can't be good. I think it's all coming to a nasty blow-out in the desert. Have you tried to text our detectives again?"

"Five minutes ago. *Nada.*"

"Damn." Lucy slid back into the SUV while Bea still paced, kicking up dirt and gravel in a show of vexation. She eventually plunked down onto the passenger seat, the door still open. "We've got to get out there, girl. Like, now."

Lucy shrugged. "It'll take us three or four hours, maybe more. We've wasted too much time here waiting, and for nothing. Whatever was going to happen in the desert — it's probably over and done."

"Maybe so, but we gotta see it for ourselves. We gotta be sure they got him. You know we do."

Lucy wiped perspiration from her forehead. There was a long silence. Stuck gears began to loosen and turn in her brain. Squinting her eyes against the sun's glare, she scrutinized the airfield. An array of private planes and copters were parked and tied down. Her attention was drawn to a sleek helicopter. "That red and white one looks very cool."

Bea followed Lucy's gaze. "And fast, like a Maserati with rotors."

"You're right, Bea, we need to know what's going down."

Bea nodded and redialed the detectives. Again, no answer. "Pete and Marlene disappearing from coms is pretty weird. He'd never make the mistake of sending troops to the wrong airport. What happened?"

"Let's find out." Lucy slurped the last drop of warm cola and stuffed the crumpled paper cup into a Von's plastic grocery bag she used for litter. "Hell, I'm rich now. Let's rent that chopper and scramble."

Bea smiled. "Deep pockets look good on you, sister."

—

Ten minutes later they parked at the modest cement-block

FBO terminal. A small VIP lounge was freshly painted pale gray with matching couches and the information desk was clean and organized. A tall, slim man in his sixties appeared to be the coordinator of aeronautical services. A big sign behind him described all the services offered: fueling, hangaring, tie-down, parking, aircraft rental, maintenance, plus flight instruction. And, Lucy hoped, he could hook them up with the slick chopper and a *Top Gun* pilot who didn't need a lot of details.

"How can I help you gals?" He had a straight-up military bearing and one of those jar-head haircuts.

Lucy leaned on the counter. "We need that red-and-white helicopter, the one tied down out there, and an experienced pilot to get us out to, uh, kind of an off-the-grid airstrip near the Salton Sea." She tried to look cool but between the unsettling SWAT team experience and the notion that Mercer could be escaping for good, she knew she wasn't fooling anyone.

He paused before answering and took their measure. "What's your business out there? You cops?" Icy blue eyes came to life in his weather-worn face.

Bea raised her chin. "No, not cops. I'm Beatrice Middleton, a reporter for CNN and my friend here, Lucy Vega, is a photographer. There's a story we have to nail. Right now. It's breaking news, as they say every five seconds on my network." She showed ID.

He chuckled, then picked up the phone on the counter and hit a call button. Waited a few seconds. "Natalie, honey, can you take the desk for a spell? Got us a couple of customers that need some special help."

A plump woman in her late thirties with hair in a messy ponytail trundled out from a back office. Her great smile turned an ordinary face to something special. "I overheard you talking to Dad about hiring a chopper pilot. He's the best. Chief Warrant Officer 5, Nam. Can fly or fix anything that spins."

The Chief Warrant Officer rolled his eyes and gave his daughter a peck on the cheek. Lucy decided she liked them both.

"I'm Ren Gelber." He flipped up the hinged countertop, came through, then dropped it carefully behind him. He joined Lucy and Bea. "My daughter gets a little carried away. But it's nice to have a cheering section." They all shook hands.

"Now, about that chopper you were referring to, it's not for lease. Guy owns a wind turbine farm out in the San Gorgonio Pass and likes his transpo available day and night. Flies it himself. I got something that moves almost as fast, but she ain't cheap."

"I'm good for it," Lucy said. "Check or Visa? Bitcoin?"

He chuckled. "Well, okay, then, Ms. Vega. Natalie will take your card and I'll go get Rosie ready." He turned back toward his daughter who typed on a laptop. "We're flying Sister Rose out to the desert, Nat."

"Sister Rose?" Bea looked confused.

"She's a Sikorsky Jayhawk. Named her after my sister, Rose. She died of breast cancer ten years ago."

Bea and Lucy conveyed sincere condolences.

A faint smile curled Bea's lips. "Rose is my mom's name, too."

"A tough old girl with a heart of gold?" he asked.

"Ah, you must know her." Bea followed Ren out a side door while Lucy took care of the finances. She gulped at the number on the bottom line but signed anyway.

—

Lucy expected something like the stripped-down Huey she'd

last ridden in. The Sikorsky's interior, however, was luxurious with buttery tan leather seats, cup holders, tray tables, and a TV. A vining rose had been etched into the pilot's corner of the windshield.

Ren seemed to have noticed her admiration of the posh digs. "We really tricked-out our old Rosie. Sis liked to go first class. I've hauled everyone from law enforcement brass, to rock stars and even the Vice-President in this ol' gal."

"Stories to tell, I'll bet." Lucy rummaged in her purse for an anti-anxiety med. Her pillbox contained a single battered Ativan and a couple of lint-flecked antacids which she immediately swallowed. "I hate to fly," she confessed.

Ren smiled. She saw where his daughter got her grin. "I promise I'll get y'all out there safe and sound." He flashed a Boy Scout salute. "Now, put on your headgear so we can gab to each other. Maybe you can fill me in a little on what we're up to."

With that final instruction, the turbines whomped to max drive and lifted them into the air. Lucy squeezed Bea's hand as they circled the airport and then made a hard bank to the South toward Coachella. Her stomach threatened to empty. But the spectacular coastline to the west pulled her attention. Turning her mental focus to visual distractions was always a lifesaver.

Orange County passed below, then San Bernardino sprawled like terra cotta dominoes thrown into a wide valley contained by rugged mountain ranges. On the horizon, parched velvety browns, taupes, and chalky whites painted the desert landscape.

Bea adjusted her Ray-Bans. "Is that San Jacinto Peak?"

Ren nodded. "Yes, ma'am, almost 11,000 feet. Lots of nice snow."

Lucy eased her death grip on Bea's hand. The Sikorsky was making good time and the Ativan was kicking in. She swallowed hard and licked her dry lips. Bea handed Lucy a bottle of water — she took a sip then began an explanation. "Ren, thanks for jumping in on this. I'm sure you've sensed our little excursion isn't your usual fly-and-deliver passengers to some golf club." Bumpety-bump went the helicopter. Lucy gulped more water and grabbed the armrest. "You deserve to know the basics of what's going down." God willing, not us.

"Appreciate that," he said. "Maybe I can be helpful."

As they headed through the pass, turbulence bounced them around like hamsters on a trampoline. Ren was oblivious. Lucy felt perspiration dampen her neck and her pulse tapped faster than a line of Celtic dancers. She was grateful when Bea took over the explanation.

"Here's the skinny," Bea said. "We think three groups are converging at a small random airstrip on the west side of the Salton Sea. Group one — the extremely ill *capo* of the Guerrero black tar heroin cartel. Group two — the little brother of the former cartel chief, just out of Lompoc, who wants the cartel back in the family, and group three is law enforcement. LAPD Homicide and Major Narcotics, plus the Feds. Group one murdered Lucy here's uncle and almost killed both of us." Bea adjusted her T-shirt to expose the bullet scar on her shoulder.

Ren's brows furrowed. "Got it. We're group number four." He cranked up the airspeed.

Lucy found her voice again. "We need to get to that airstrip and see what's going on. We lost communication with the LAPD Major Narcotics detective and his crew, so we're damn worried."

"You're talking about the old Salty Dog. Used to be where crop dusters landed and took off. In the last decade, word is it's been commandeered by drug runners. The landing surface sucks."

"You know the place." Lucy nudged Bea.

"I know all the places." He winked. "Been flying the desert probably since before you two were born."

Lucy's felt her anxiety soften a tad. The knowledge that Ren seemed familiar with the area was comforting.

He continued. "Salty Dog's getting too damn popular for the narcos. There's an even more remote landing field on a mesa at the eastern the edge of the Chocolate Mountains where they spill into the Salton Trough. Maybe sixty miles due south of the Navy's aerial gunnery range. It's totally off the grid, no coms — was abandoned by the military after the Vietnam War. If you lost your LAPD folks, could be their mission led them out there." He adjusted the bill of his faded LA Dodgers ball cap. "How about we fly over the Dog. If it looks like there's no action, we'll head east."

"Sounds like a plan to me. You cool with it, Lucia?" Bea asked.

A rough patch of air rocked the little ship again. "I'm cool." Lucy gasped. If only.

# 43

Lucy snapped topographical photos of the wide desert sprawl from the helicopter window. A green stamp collection of irrigated golf courses, commercial enterprises, date palm groves, and residential enclaves came to a hard stop at the northern edge of the Salton Sea. At almost two-hundred-fifty feet below sea level, the area's highly salinized soil and lack of rainfall had proved too daunting a challenge for either agricultural interests or real estate developers. All who'd tried had largely gone bust. The lake's briny concentration, increasing pollution, and the distinctive smell were not big tourist draws. Lucy swore the aroma made a pig farm seem like an aromatherapy cure. She wrinkled her nose. From the air, however, it appeared to be a desert paradise.

She continued to record landscape images from their elevation of about eight thousand feet. "Sits right on the San Andreas fault, doesn't it?" Then through the lens, she spotted a faint, gray vine of smoke undulating upwards from a point to the east, exactly the direction they were headed. Lucy's pulse accelerated.

She lowered her camera. "Ren, smoke at our ten o'clock."

"I see it." He handed her a pair of high-powered field glasses.

"A rangeland brush fire?" Lucy asked. Images of the Vega Ranch inferno crackled in her bones.

"Don't think so. That's the Salty Dog. I'd say we're about ten clicks out."

Lucy blew out a long, shaky breath then adjusted the binoculars. She scanned the horizon for several minutes before handing them to Bea.

Bea pushed her sunglasses up on her head and peered toward the dark thread. "Please, God, let Pete, Mar, and their crew be safe."

Ren said nothing and pumped up the airspeed. Rotors whined at a higher pitch. "We'll circle from a distance and see what we have. If it's an aircraft, I'll radio regional FAA and law enforcement folks to send out the troops."

Lucy switched her camera to video mode as they came in fast over the Dog. At the north end, several hundred yards before the runway, flames, and smoke engulfed a what appeared to be a wrecked MedEvac plane. Remnants of a red cross bloodied what was left of the door frame. The tail lay another hundred yards behind the mangled body of the craft. Other than the wreckage, the locale appeared abandoned.

"Looks like a C-130 turboprop," Ren said. The Sikorsky circled closer to the wreckage. "Likely the MedEvac that took off from Hawthorne before you two gals showed up. Shit."

"Oh, my God. Mercer and his people were in it. We saw it leave. LAPD SWAT showed up too late to intercept." Lucy struggled to steady her trembling hands and continued to record the scene below.

Ren glanced away for a moment, then cleared his throat and looked again at the smoldering mess. "If it's the plane

I think it is, the pilot's a friend of mine." His knuckles went white on the throttle.

Bea's mouth dropped open; the binoculars fell onto her lap. "Oh, no." She turned to Lucy, eyes wide with dread.

"I gotta report this right away." Ren dialed into the radio frequency for the local FAA and the Imperial County Sheriff's Department in El Centro. Lucy heard him say he intended to land and do a quick scene assessment. Whoever was on the other end of the communication knew Ren Gelber and gave him the go-ahead.

He maneuvered the chopper over the airfield and assessed the situation with the same military-mode intensity Lucy'd seen in the LAPD SWAT team leader. They observed the crash site at several hundred feet, then he set the bird down at the far end of the rutted runway. As the rotors slowed and finally stopped, they hopped out and jogged toward the plane, Ren in the lead.

Old tire tracks, empty booze bottles, and bleached-out remnants of generic trash lined both sides of the strip. The stench of aircraft fuel was strong. A gut-punch of nausea threatened to drop Lucy to her knees. Bea grabbed her arm.

"The burn was hot and fast," Ren said as they approached the plane. He had a good-sized fire extinguisher in hand, but the craft was well past saving. He put it down on the decomposed tarmac and turned away forlornly. "Definitely the MedEvac. Ah, hell."

Lucy shivered in the desert heat. If his friend was dead, there was nothing she could say to ease the tragedy.

Somehow a half-empty bag of saline with a disconnected IV catheter tube had survived, still mounted on a hanger. It flapped like a pennant in the hot wind. But that was the only thing that had survived. Human parts mixed with shards of shrapnel that had been the plane.

Lucy could barely cough out the words from her tightening throat. "Bea, look for signs of Mercer's snake tattoos. And Toulusa was wearing blue scrubs, Dillard purple."

They examined the ruins with frantic energy, careful not to contaminate any possible evidence. The smell of burning fuel and flesh drew its own toxic line around how close they could move into the scene. Still, within ten minutes, they were able to identify what appeared to be the remains of three passengers, plus the pilot. Tears smudged Lucy's face.

Ren stood at a distance, taking in the big picture, and perhaps fighting his own demons.

Bea tried to call Pete and Marlene again and received the same frightening result. Nothing.

Lucy felt a sudden drain of energy, little bombs of light popped in her vision. Soot dusted her skin. "No evidence of Mercer, Dillard, or Toulusa. Looks like a two-person medical staff and a female patient. More innocents lost." She choked back a sob. "The MedEvac plane was a decoy. Carlos's people thought Mercer was in it like we did."

In the crushed cockpit, the pilot smoldered, still strapped into his seatbelt. Ren squatted a few feet from the body. Despite the dead man's charred visage, he recognized his friend. The worst-case scenario was true. Removing his sunglasses, Ren rubbed his eyes hard, as if trying to wipe out too many other horrors tripped off by this latest abomination.

"It's Benny." His voice broke. He put his sunglasses back on. "Idealistic old sonofabitch. Left the military still thinking he could save people. I loved the goddamn guy."

"I'm so, so sorry, Ren." Bea rested her hand on his shoulder and he gave it a quick press of acknowledgment.

After a few seconds, he stood, stepped back,

compartmentalized, and slowly began to examine the plane. Lucy watched him scrutinize the gnarled surfaces. Beneath the craft's skin, the flayed interior disgorged a chaos of medical debris. A box of bandages rested like an island in a pool of blood and sand. Lucy captured the image. It's what she did to keep from drowning in misery.

Ren stopped pacing and took in the distant surroundings again as if searching for some kind of a sign. "What the hell?" He looked at the aircraft then back across the desert. "I think it was hit by a goddamn rocket launcher, at close range. Likely, an FIM-92, a Stinger. Hit the plane right, could definitely take it down."

Lucy almost dropped her camera.

Bea clarified. "One of those shoulder-fired deals that can blow a jetliner out of the sky?"

"Nasty sumbitches." Seemingly re-energized, Ren trotted off in the direction he'd been observing from afar, Bea and Lucy at his heels.

Ren halted and pointed to a rocky rise the distance of a football field from the crash. "I'll bet my bottom dollar the shooter launched from somewhere over there. The trajectory would fit. Seen this same shit too damn many times in Nam."

Lucy took a photo with her long lens. "A heads-up for boot prints, dirt bike, or ATV tracks. Terrain's too rough for anything else."

And then they found it. Coming down a parallel wash that had probably been dry since the dinosaurs, dirt bike tracks bit into the sand.

"Must've been carrying something heavy," Bea said. "Those imprints are deep."

Ren nodded and moved on. The desert heat beat down on them with pugilistic intensity. Lucy snapped images of the prints from various angles then ran to catch up. She'd be sure to get Pete and Marlene every picture they needed before things became tainted. Mopping perspiration from her face, her head spun with questions about where Mercer and Toulusa could be. At that outpost of an airstrip in the mountains? Shooting it out with Pete's crew? Were her friends okay? Had they been brought down by the same rocker launcher? She had to get out there.

The threesome followed the dirt-bike trail to the edge of a rocky outcropping. Amid a patch of cholla cacti and creosote bush, boot prints scuffed a sandy bald spot about six feet across.

Bea squinted at the marks. "My kid hit a size thirteen, and this dude has even bigger feet."

"Check this out." Ren pointed to a pile of tumbleweed accumulated at the edge of the circle, bunched up against the rocks. A scorpion the size of a chipmunk dashed across a ledge. "The Stinger's back-blast fried those bushes. When the weapon shoots, an explosion exits the rear of the firing tube, like when a rocket takes off from a launchpad. He was too close to the growth behind him. And looky here, right in the middle of all that stickery shit, excuse my French, ladies."

Bea leaned in to examine the find. "Sort of like the inside core of a roll of paper towels. What is it?"

"Probably part of the launch tube. The asshole blasted the MedEvac out of the sky as it was landing. The people on that C-130 were clearly murdered. I don't know what the hell my man Benny was doing out here, but ladies, this is now personal. I'm in it with you."

Lucy felt a fleeting twinge of relief at hearing those words, but also an added burden of responsibility. Mercer couldn't be allowed to take another life. But Ren was an experienced soldier. He knew what could happen.

Carefully skirting the prints to avoid disrupting the scene, she snapped close-ups, then paused to wipe her face with the corner of her sweaty T-shirt. "There's some kind of serial number on that tube. Maybe it can help with a trace. A history of the weapon might point us to who pulled the trigger."

Ren nodded. Overhead, a chopper displaying an Imperial County Sheriff logo began its descent.

Lucy took a few more photos, then she and Bea joined Ren for the slog back to the Sikorsky to meet with the county officials. Lucy's skin crawled with urgency. They had to get to the landing strip in the mountains. Pete and Mar could be in grave danger, or worse.

Ren waved at the incoming helicopter, then turned to Bea and Lucy. "They're gonna try and tell us to stay the hell out of the airspace anywhere near *la Cama del Diablo*. That's what they call the old landing strip."

Bea's gaze met Lucy's. "Devil's bed, how fitting."

"Sweet dreams, Mercer," Lucy whispered. "They'll be your last."

# 44

Two deputies landed in the shiny single-engine sheriff's chopper next to the Sikorsky. It looked brand new. After the mini-sandstorm from the rotor downwash subsided, the men climbed out and intros were made all around. The pilot, Sergeant Lopez, was a small, compact man with a meticulously clipped mustache. The co-pilot, Officer Nielsen, looked fresh from middle school, with skin so white he'd be a billboard for melanoma by the time he was thirty. He patted the H-125 like it was a new puppy.

"Just got this baby, an Airbus," Lopez said. "First chopper ever for Imperial County. We've had to rely on our citizen Aero Squadron. They're great, but Imperial's so high-traffic for narcos, been hard for us to keep leaning on volunteers for support."

It quickly became apparent to Lucy that the officers were more in the mood to show off their new machine than receive information on what had happened with the crashed MedEvac. Lucy sucked in several deep breaths and tried to keep herself from screaming. Time was ticking and the risk escalating. Sure, they needed to alert the locals as to what happened in their backyard, but how long did that have to take?

Ren pointed down the runway to the ruined C-130, then quickly turned away. "Be careful of your new toy, gentlemen, there's an asshole out there blowing planes out of the sky with a rocket launcher."

Nielsen's pale beady eyes widened. Lopez blanched and gazed protectively at their gleaming machine.

"An RPG? Really?" He raised a bushy brow, thick as his mustache. "You sure that's how it went down?" He hacked and spit into the sand.

Lucy suppressed a groan. Did they really need a macho pissing contest?

Ren tipped his chin toward their prized piece of equipment. "I've had thirty years in the military fixing and flying these babies, and ten as a forensic crash investigator."

Bea planted her hands on her hips in one of her signature "take no shit" stances. "Now that's a damn, impressive resume. I suggest you listen to what Mr. Gelber has to say."

Lucy saw Lopez and his co-pilot exchange glances then grudgingly, agree.

"We'll be sure to investigate thoroughly," Lopez said.

Sick of stupid delays, Lucy jumped in to explain about the dangerous situation. When she mentioned Carlos Alvarez and the Guerrero black tar heroin cartel, plus the LAPD, Lopez straightened and fingered his gun. She'd finally gotten their full attention.

"Thanks for the heads-up." Nielsen reached into the helicopter and pulled out what looked like a tool kit. A streamer from a roll of yellow crime scene tape flapped from the closed case. "We're here to preserve the evidence. I hope you people didn't contaminate our scene."

Lucy wanted to slap the pretentious little worm. "This

ain't our first rodeo. And I hope you don't miss part of the launch tube in the cholla." Asshole.

Lopez stepped in front of Nielsen. "Settle down, folks, SIU's on their way. They'll do the complete crime scene analysis. I'll fill headquarters in on the details and we'll try to get this coordinated with the DEA."

Lucy practically jogged in place. "Great. We gotta move on, Bea, Ren."

"We'll be in touch," Lopez said. "Thank you for the intel. And be sure not to wander into *la Cama del Diablo* airspace on your way back to LA."

Ren winked at Lucy and Bea with an "I told you so" expression. "We'll be really careful," he said.

"You've been warned." Lopez pulled out the satellite radio clipped to his belt.

Ren offered an informal salute. "Roger that, Sergeant. Message received."

—

Lucy glanced at her watch. It had been two and a half hours since they'd left Hawthorne. An eternity when lives hung in the balance. She gripped the armrests as Ren hit the throttle and the Sikorsky rose into the shimmery dry air. Her stomach threatened to empty its contents.

"I got you, girl." Bea squeezed Lucy's hand.

Lucy nodded in appreciation and held her breath until the spasm of nausea passed. Below, the two Imperial County officers ambled toward the crumbled MedEvac.

"Heading south-southeast." Ren jacked up the airspeed. His eyes roved across the Sikorsky's dials and gauges, then out to the dusky horizon. "Only a few more hours of light. The night'll be like a black bag over your head. You gals packing any firepower?"

They both nodded.

Ren smiled. "Thought so."

"You?" Bea asked.

"Yup. Winchester 70-300 with a Leopold scope, and some night-vision stuff."

Lucy looked out toward the barren moonscape terrain of the Chocolate Mountains darkening with long, toothy shadows. The contrast between such bitter country and its sweet name seemed a cruel taunt.

—

Nurse Richard Dillard watched Toulusa file her black-painted fingernails.

"The medical plane was supposed to touch down at the Salty Dog, pick up Altamont then fly over here to get us. We should be in the Juarez clinic, safe and sound by now," Mercer whined.

Toulusa's metal file slipped and pierced her palm. "Shit."

Dillard felt a pang of glee.

Mercer rested atop a white sheet on the floor of the crumbling gold miner's cabin. A squashed tarantula lay kicked to the corner. "We shouldn't have let the helicopter go before the plane was here. Something's obviously wrong."

Toulusa licked her bleeding hand then dabbed it with a tissue. "It'll be here soon. We have a half-dozen good people up in the hills behind us, taking care of us like angles until our transport arrives. You worry too much, sweet pea."

Mercer, twitchy and pallid, turned his head toward the nurse. "I need more pain meds."

Nurse Dillard's lilac scrubs, usually crisp and pressed, were now crumpled and soaked under the arms with sweat. His man bun was in serious disarray. He despised looking disheveled. Standing morosely at the shack's window, he stared west across the darkening landscape. The sun was dropping into the Salton trough beyond the mountains on its way to China. "Getting fucking cold in here." The days could be in the hundreds but the desert nights could turn bitter cold. He winced and crushed another dish-sized tarantula that skulked from a hole in the floor.

"Pain meds, dammit," Mercer croaked.

If Toulusa didn't have that big ol' machine gun on her lap and an ammo belt strapped across her big-tittied chest, Dillard swore he'd force a handful of Oxy down Mercer's throat and watch him OD. The Florence Nightingale nurse's pledge to care for the sick at all costs was moot when you'd been kidnapped at gunpoint from your cozy little Santa Barbara condo in the middle of the night.

The nurse went to his medical bag and broke out the morphine and fentanyl.

Toulusa licked her puffy, enhanced lips. "Fuck up that dosage, Nurse Dildo, and you'll be exceedingly sorry."

Dillard gritted his teeth. With that threat in mind, he administered the perfect happy-dance prescription and returned to the window.

Far above, a jet headed south toward Puerto Vallarta, Cabo, or Cancun. A small helicopter flitted over the mountains, probably ten miles away. A bird coming to his rescue? Fat chance — without communications, no one knew he was a hostage here, or that the psychopath, Toulusa, had mowed down the LAPD detectives with a barrage of gunfire right out of a Rambo movie.

Toulusa flashed her heavily made-up eyes at the nurse. "What do you see out there?"

Dillard sighed. "Tourists heading to the Mexican Riviera. I wish I was with them." He didn't mention the helicopter.

Toulusa snickered and slowly, meticulously, applied antibiotic ointment to her minor stab injury as if rubbing sacred ointment into the wounded hand of Christ.

In minutes, Mercer's meds kicked in and he began humming "Livin' La Vida Loca." The tune ground at Dillard's already insanely frayed nerves. Toulusa's attention shifted to the singing patient. She loosened the strings on her pants and slid from the chair, gun still in close proximity. They began to get it on. Again.

"I can't watch this." Dillard's stomach lurched and he headed for the door. "I'm going out to sit on the rock pile."

"You move from those rocks and I'll hunt you down and eat your intestines for dinner," Toulusa warned.

"Duly noted." Dillard hustled out the door and scrambled up the mound of mining scree to a flat-topped stone the size of an air mattress. It overlooked a desolate plateau less than a quarter-mile away that had once been a landing strip for a military live-fire zone. Three mule deer wandered across the ancient runway. It seemed like a perfect place to be beamed up by aliens, which would be a welcome alternative to Toulusa and Mercer.

Inside, the bizarre duo sang Queen's "Crazy Little Thing Called Love" together. The sound of a cat in heat would have been more appealing. Dillard thought he would snap any second and go insane. "Eat my guts and choke to death," he muttered.

Then he spotted the helicopter again, skimming behind a nearby ridge. The lovers grunted and squealed so loudly, Dillard was pretty sure they wouldn't hear the dull pounding of the rotors. Enough of their own pounding — maybe the shack would collapse and crush them.

The air went silent as a tomb and the chopper disappeared.

Dillard wiped tears from his eyes. He curled up atop his perch where the stone was still warm in the fading light and popped a couple sleeping tabs. A brief moment of oblivion was on its way.

# 45

A cold lick of metal pressed against Dillard's temple. His sleeping heartbeat leaped from zero to panic in a nanosecond.

He opened his eyes but could make out little in the darkness. "I didn't leave the rock. I'm here, I didn't do anything. Don't shoot me!" His voice was strangled and his body quivered as he tried to rise.

"Shut the fuck up or you'll get us both killed."

The hushed male voice didn't belong to either Mercer or Toulusa. The steel pressed harder. Thunder rumbled to the west and lightning tumbled from the clouds like burning pick-up sticks.

"Gotta get you outta here or it'll be too late. Marlene needs help, and Alvarez's goons are on their way."

Nurse Dillard recognized the voice. "Detective Anthony? Oh, my God. I thought you were dead."

"Not yet. Follow me on the next round of thunder. Hand on my shoulder, we'll move together. Storm's moving this way fast. That mine shaft a couple of hundred yards above us was boarded up but we can crawl in." Lightning flashed. "Ready?"

Then the boom. "Now!"

The detective winced as Dillard grabbed his shoulder. It was sticky and smelled of blood. The nurse said nothing but a prayer as he trailed Anthony into the black night.

—

Lucy, Bea, and Ren situated themselves on a ledge high above the old mining camp. Lucy was happy to accept the dark hoodie and sweats Ren had supplied them from his cache of emergency search and rescue gear. Intermittent raindrops began to spatter. A thunderstorm roiled across the Imperial Valley, headed in their direction.

Ren removed his night-vision goggles and handed them to Lucy. "Looks like maybe a half-dozen men in the hills above the camp," he said. "At two o'clock, somebody's got a fire going. Stupid for them, great for us. Tells us they probably aren't night-vision equipped. Looking at the fire up close would burn their eyeballs out."

Lucy pulled the contraption onto her head and the scene lit up like a green flare. "They probably didn't gear up for night duty — figured they'd be across the border drinking tequila by the pool eight or ten hours ago."

She hunkered against a boulder and studied the camp. A crumbling old cabin and a pile of rubble dimly took form. It was beyond the goggle's best range. Her shoulders tensed. "Jesus, I think there's a body on top of those tailings. Check it out."

Lucy passed the specs to Bea, who adjusted the headgear and turned her attention to the area near the shack. "Definitely a body. Whoa, wait a minute. Somebody's coming down from the mine entrance, real slow-like."

Lucy and Ren sat in silence, anticipating Bea's next observation.

"Okay, he's with the body. Both look like men. The dead guy, no wait — he's sitting up. Not dead."

Lucy let out an uneasy breath. "Recognize anybody?"

For a long minute, Bea remained still as the rock on which she perched. Then she said, "Now they're moving. The guy who came down from the mine looks like Pete." She removed the goggles from her head and handed them back to Lucy. "See if I'm crazy."

Lucy watched two figures struggle up the steep hill to the mine. "Maybe. I can't tell for sure, but something feels like him. The other guy's dressed in a light color."

"Light color? Definitely, not Pete." Bea stood and rubbed the small of her back. "We need to move in closer."

"Let's go." Lucy took the lead, using the goggles to determine their path.

Ren whispered as Bea slipped on loose scree. "Steady, girl. Slow down."

Inching along the ledge, Lucy led them into a narrow gully that would shield them from view and bring them nearer to the mine entrance and the hill where the man in the light clothes had been lying. After several hundred yards, the trio halted at a notch in the rock overlooking the camp.

Lucy studied the two figures as they scrabbled toward the mine entrance. The man in the dark clothing staggered and fell. He appeared wounded, shaky on his feet. Light clothing guy helped him up.

Lucy's pulse accelerated. "It's Pete," she said, "for sure. And, you won't believe this — he's with Richard Dillard."

Bea stifled a gasp, then turned to Ren and filled him in on the players.

Lucy looked back over her shoulder at the mountains and valleys shrouded by the storm. A flash of lightning lit the landscape for an instant. Distant headlights bumped along a road. "Jesus, somebody's on their way to join the party from hell. A caravan, five vehicles. Could be law enforcement, if Nielsen and Lopez did their jobs."

"Could be Carlos Alvarez and his asshole crew, if they didn't." Bea pulled up the hood of her sweatshirt and tied the strings beneath her chin.

Ren's broad shoulders filled the width of the notch. "Must be on the old Bradshaw Trail. A real tough ride will take them a while, especially in these conditions." He stepped back onto the rock-strewn path, which was barely a foot wider than he was.

Lucy followed him back onto the path and squeezed into her spot at the head of the line. Adjusted her headgear. "We should try to get up to the mine and join forces. Pete said earlier he had Detective Simon and three officers from the LAPD with him. Could be they're all holed up in there, or maybe, God forbid, the rest are dead." She gulped hard and pushed away thoughts of that terrible possibility.

The rain came faster now. A rivulet trickled through the pinched gully. "We gotta move it, ladies," Ren said. "A flash flood could be hankering to swallow us whole."

Lucy plunged ahead. Next came Bea, with Ren covering their backs. In half a minute, the rivulet splashed against their calves. Rocks and gravel slid from high above and tumbled into the slot canyon, barely missing them. A minute later, the quick-flowing trickle, now a growing stream, rose to their knees.

Except for the holds they gleaned from pushing their hands against the narrow walls of the slot, they'd have been washed away. The rough stone scraped the skin off Lucy's fingers and palms. She gritted her teeth and grappled for purchase. Sharp stones and a bucket load of gravel rained down, knocking her off balance. Her heart lurched in terror. Falling against the slippery canyon wall, she was sucked forward into the full-on flash flood.

Bea and Ren went down behind her like bowling pins.

Bone-chilling water gushed from everywhere. Lucy gagged on a mouthful of silt and tried to right her body to a feet-first, down-river position. Easier said than done. She finally had to roll and bump helplessly over jagged, hard surfaces and pray. Her lungs felt ready to explode and the brutal panic of imminent drowning set in. In seconds she'd be breathing in water.

Finally, the trio spewed out the end of the crevasse and was dumped onto a small alluvial plain at the edge of the camp. They scuttled to higher ground on their hands and knees, coughing and gagging. The floodwater roiled and snapped behind them like a living creature.

Lucy gasped, hair dripping, clothes soaked. "Everybody okay?"

Both Bea and Ren choked out an affirmative.

Lucy felt a wave of relief as strong as the flash flood. They'd survived.

The rain was now torrential. The sentries in the hills had likely taken cover. Lucy couldn't believe the night goggles were still on her head. She, Bea, and Ren continued up toward the mine entrance, stumbling and falling with every other step. Sand and sediment liquified below their feet, threatening to engulf them. They pressed on, one exhausting tread after another.

At last, the cave's entrance appeared. Beneath a low overhang, wet, bleeding, and breathless, they slumped against the crumbling wooden mine closure. A Private Property sign hung on a nail was like a rusted-out cheese grater, full of jagged bullet holes. Several boards meant to seal the access were askew. It looked to be the only way inside.

A bolt of lightning illuminated the mining camp, the flash practically blinding Lucy. She ripped off the goggles. Knees weak, the orange and purple after-effects stippled her vision.

Ren grabbed Lucy's arm to steady her, then whispered, "I'll go in first."

She moved toward the entry. "No, they don't know you. Might start shooting. I'm going in." She turned to see Bea disappear into the mine ahead of them all.

# 46

"Pete?" Bea tumbled through the opening onto the gritty floor inside the mine. There was zero light, nothing ambient, only a black void. From overhead came a noise like crunching paper, and then tiny squeaks sounded from what had to be bats. A rush of wings swished near her head. Bea shuddered. The smell of the shaft bloomed cool and metallic.

"Pete, it's me," she called out. "I'm here with Lucy and our chopper pilot, Ren. Pete?" She could hear Lucy struggling through the mine opening behind her.

A beam popped on from a down the tunnel, then immediately extinguished. The light was perhaps twenty yards ahead. "Halluh-fuckin'-looyah. Please join us, Miss Bea." It was Dillard. "Walk carefully. Last one in, secure those boards behind you and then we'll turn on the flashlight."

She took a tentative step forward. "Pete? Is Pete okay? And Marlene?"

"I'm okay, Bea." Pete's voice was weak and sounded far away. "Marlene, not so good. Two others dead, one missing. We were ambushed when we landed."

Bea uttered a cry, then felt Lucy's hand take hers.

"I'm in," Ren said. "Entrance sealed."

The flashlight switched on, guiding them through the rock and guano-strewn cavern. Hundreds of agitated bats hung upside down from high above. "Follow me." Lucy tugged Bea's hand. "Watch out. Looks like bat shit everywhere."

"How appropriate," Bea whispered.

When they arrived at the bend in the mineshaft before it took a vertical nosedive toward the center of the Earth, Dillard and Pete sat leaning against a blackened wood piling, their faces drawn with exhaustion.

Bea's breath caught in her throat at the sight of the detective. "Peter, what happened?" She rushed over and tenderly laced her fingers in his. Shirt soaked in blood, his breath was shallow, panting. Not like him, he was a man in top shape. He played the tough guy well, but Bea knew his condition was grave. Her eyes met Dillard's and she found no reassurance.

Pete winced despite Bea's gentle touch. "Got shot through-and-through, at the shoulder."

His voice was barely discernable above a sonorous roaring, like the sound of the ocean in a seashell, emanating from deep in the mine. Or was it just in Bea's brain? Then, she spotted Marlene laying beneath a silver emergency blanket, behind Pete. "Oh, God!" She ran to her friend and knelt by her side. Unconscious, Marlene's face was ghostly pale and splattered with blood.

Lucy crouched next to Bea and placed her hand on Marlene's forehead. "Clammy, cold — not good signs."

"I'm concerned for Detective Simon," Dillard said. "Took two shots. Pulse weak and thready. She's lost way too much blood. Even if I had my medical bag, all I could provide would be pain management, and she's already out cold."

Lucy carefully pushed damp hair from Marlene's face.

Ren stood, casting a long shadow up the wall. "We have to get her to a hospital, but first, we need to assess our status, fast." His voice switched to military mode. "Imminent threats we're not aware of? And what resources do we have?"

Dillard spoke first. "Toulusa's down in that shack with Mercer. They've got a machine gun. I don't know anything about that stuff so I can't tell you what kind. They also have a couple of handguns. Probably a half-dozen of their creeps are up in the hills with all sorts of weapons."

"Yeah, we saw them." Lucy continued to hover at Marlene's side.

Ren stood over Marlene, then turned to Dillard, his face hard. "You know anything about the MedEvac that was shot down?"

"Shot down?" The nurse gulped and cleared his throat. "Holy shit. The plane was supposed to grab that huge freak, Altamont, at a landing strip somewhere near the Salton Sea, then pick us up and get us to a clinic in Juarez, hours ago."

"We think it may have been Altamont who took out the MedEvac, with a shoulder-firing rocket launcher," Bea said.

Pete pressed his hand against his injury and grimaced. "Shit, if he took out the plane, then the bastard's changed sides — working for Carlos Alvarez now, not Mercer."

"Holy shit," Lucy murmured.

Dillard continued. "Right after they kidnapped me, I heard Toulusa talking to his flunkies about how much the big thug hated Mercer because he took Toulusa away from him. Supposedly, Altamont and Toulusa are common-law married." Dillard's eyebrows raise to copious heights at a sudden realization. "All this shit could've been started by a goddamn love triangle?"

"Wars have been fought over less," Bea said.

Ren stayed on-task and filled Pete and the nurse in on the caravan they'd spotted from the notch. "Probably a half-hour out by now. No idea who they are. We hope it's the good guys. We had a chance to talk to the Imperial County Sheriff before we came up here. Said they were going to coordinate with the DEA."

Pete moaned and struggled to get his shoulder into a comfortable position. There was no comfort to be had. His pallor rivaled Marlene's. Bea glanced at Dillard for reassurance, but he could only shrug.

"As to resources, we're plum out of ammo," Pete said. "*Nada.*"

"I've got a fully loaded Winchester." Ren chambered a round. "And a Sikorsky, less than a mile from here."

"Nice," Pete said. He sat up straighter and tried to position his back against a fallen boulder. Then, he gave up and slowly stood.

"I got a Glock," Bea said.

Lucy removed a gun from the zipped pocket of her hoodie. "I have this .357. Used to belong to Mercer. I'm hoping to return it to him, personally."

"Anything else?" Ren asked.

Pete responded. "A flashlight with good batteries, a little water, and a hunting knife."

Dillard rustled something in his pocket. "I got some sleeping pills and some Oxy. And gum. Anybody want a piece?" No one responded. "What are we doing, a MacGyver episode here?"

"Never know when something random could come in handy," Ren responded.

Bea glowered at the nurse. "This is not a goddamn reality

show, Dillard." She fished a soggy tissue out of her pocket and blew her nose. The damp began to snake cold fingers throughout her body. She beat down thoughts of hypothermia.

"I know, of course not. Sorry. I get stupid when I'm scared shitless."

"So, what's the plan?" Lucy asked. "Blow this joint before the storm's over and we're totally vulnerable."

"That's it," Ren said. "Any other ideas? Thoughts?"

Lucy moved next to Ren. "Why don't you take the lead with the night vision and the firepower. Bea and Dillard can start out carrying Marlene in that thermal blanket. Pete can take the Glock and follow Bea. I'll bring up the rear."

"I'll bring up the rear," Pete insisted.

Lucy crossed her arms over her chest. "No way, I'm going to keep an eye on you. You're a little shaky, big guy."

"Listen to Lucy," Bea said. "Hear me?"

"Guess I have no chance of winning this one." Pete's face darkened and he stumbled. His left arm hung uselessly at his side.

"Can you manage with that injury, detective?" Ren asked

"Yeah, my gun hand is fine."

Ren nodded. "We have what we have. Everybody clear on what we're doing?"

"Clear as mud." Bea handed the Glock to Pete.

"Sometimes that's as good as it gets. Leap of faith time, folks." Ren pulled on the night-vision goggles. "Let's roll."

# 47

Wet and tired, Lucy crawled from the shelter of the mine entrance and wrapped her arms around herself for a bit of warmth — it didn't help. The epicenter of lighting and thunder had moved to the east, but the rain still fell in hard, blustery sheets beyond the overhang. Ren, wearing the night-vision goggles, stepped into the downpour first, followed by Dillard and Bea carrying Marlene in a hammock they'd fashioned from the solar blanket. Pete trudged behind them. The footing was tenuous and the going slow. Lucy, taking up the rear, winced as Pete stumbled repeatedly but drove himself forward. His condition scared her. She continued to scan their perimeter, but she couldn't see a damn thing. Trusting Ren to lead them in the right direction was all they could do. That, and pray.

For reassurance, she slipped her hand into the pouch of her hoodie and touched the .357 — Mercer's .357. Would the bastard get away again? Would he ever pay for murdering her uncle — for so many other hideous sins? Old feelings of grief and rage began to suck at her bones. She couldn't go there; it was too much.

Lucy slipped and fell onto her hands and knees. She cursed to herself — she'd let her mind lose focus. Escaping this nightmare and getting help for Pete and Marlene was everything. She scrambled to get up.

Just as she found her footing, a gloved hand covered her mouth, pressing so tightly she thought her teeth would snap. Lucy grappled and strained to escape. She couldn't breathe, let alone scream. Her head was wrenched back, viciously. She felt something pinch her neck. A knife? Oh, Jesus, a needle.

Then came the terrifying rush.

Then, nothing.

—

Bea glanced at her digital watch. They'd been walking for twenty hard minutes, felt more like hours. Ren led the group past the slot canyon where they'd almost drowned. Water still spilled from the opening, but not with the fury of that first blast. He guided their rag-tag procession to a narrow clearing behind an outcropping where a muddy wash disguised the path leading to the Sikorsky. The footprints they'd left as they came into the valley had long been washed away.

Finally, beyond the area where they were likely to be spotted by Mercer's goons, Bea let herself breathe a small, tentative sigh of relief. They might actually make it out of here. If only the detectives could hang in until Ren got them to the hospital.

The biggest danger was now the caravan, drawing closer by the minute. Bea knew they couldn't wait around to see if they were friends or foes. She hoped the convoy hadn't gotten close enough to discover Ren's helicopter. Without the chopper to get them out of the mountains, they were doomed.

Ren turned to the group and held up a hand. "Stop here for a minute, folks."

Bea and Dillard rested the hammock carrying Detective Simon on the ground between them. They each took a knee and gave a break to screaming muscles.

"It's not far now," Ren said. "Everybody hanging in?"

The question was acknowledged with grunts and labored breathing.

Bea glanced down the line, Pete was barely discernible in the darkness. A stab of cold fear twisted her stomach. Her throat tightened. "Where's Lucy?"

Silence. All peered back into the rainy darkness.

Bea stood, her body feeling tight as a wire. Her moment of relief turned to strangling fear. "What the hell? She wouldn't take off after Mercer by herself."

"She's done stuff like that before." Pete's voice was a phlegmy whisper.

"Come on, she has an impulsive streak, but she's not insane. Maybe she fell. Maybe she's hurt. We have to go back, right now."

No one moved.

"People, listen up." Ren's voice, low and no-nonsense, cut through Bea's panic. "Whatever happened to Lucy, we have to get these gunshot victims to the med center immediately. Five lives are at risk here, Bea, two critically."

Bea cried out, then covered her face with her hands. "We can't leave her behind. We can't."

"Bea, Marlene's in rough shape. We have to hurry." Dillard gently pressed her shoulder.

She also saw Pete's uncontrollable shaking. He was in rough shape, too. Rougher than he'd ever let on.

"I promise you, we'll come back as fast as humanly possible." Ren turned toward the path to the Sikorsky. "With the posse."

Rain and tears streaming down her face, Bea picked up her end of Marlene's makeshift gurney and followed. All she could do for Lucy now was pray.

—

The first thing Lucy became aware of was the cold, and that her feet and fingers felt cast in cement. Sprawled on her back, she rolled to her side and folded into a fetal position. Nausea burned in her stomach. Slowly, she opened her eyes. In the low, shadowy light, the dead carcass of a large brown tarantula was splayed inches from her face on a filthy wood floor. She vomited. Body protesting, Lucy edged away from the intimidating arachnid. Where the hell was she? How long had she been out?

Her eyes began to acclimate. Her head pounded like a chopper rotor but her senses slowly focused. The rain had stopped. The silence was deep, like after a snowfall up in the Sierra. She realized she wasn't bound, but where could she go? And she was too weak to be a threat.

She heard scuffling, tittering.

"Lucille."

Lucy gagged and almost threw up again. Mercer. Shit. "That's not my name, you asshole."

He laughed. Never calling her by her right name was his ongoing joke with her. Their sick dance.

Lucy struggled to sit, pushed herself against the splintery wall of a small cabin. She kicked the dead tarantula away. Others littered the floor. Mercer, with his mask-like new face slathered in shiny ointment, sat on a bench cloaked in a white sheet. The .357 Magnum lay in his lap. Toulusa and Altamont stood sentry behind him in flickering shadows from an oil lantern. Toulusa was tall, but the other guard was the Hulk.

Lucy took slow, deep breaths to keep herself from quaking.

Perspiration dampened her forehead. She was going to die. Nothing but a Hail Mary had a chance here. Maybe she could buy a few more moments by lobbing out Bea's conjecture about who shot down the plane at Salty Dog. Had Altamont actually switched sides?

She gritted her teeth and willed herself into a semblance of control. Bile rose in her throat. "Not sure why the big guy's still here with you, Gary." Her voice quavered. "Him shooting down your rescue plane with that shoulder-firing Stinger really put you in a bad situation, with Alvarez on his way here and all." It felt like she was talking through a mouth stuffed with a gym sock.

Altamont twitched; his eyes were boreholes. "Lying bitch."

Toulusa touched his arm.

Lucy felt nausea rise again. Something was off. Did the arm touch mean anything? Was she over-thinking it? Or was Toulusa in on Mercer's betrayal?

Mercer's neck swiveled toward Altamont, the .357 in his hand. A shot exploded and the giant began to list, then fell with a crash. No warning, no last words.

Toulusa cried out.

The cabin shook and debris showered down. Lucy struggled for breath. The remains of Altamont's head, sticky with blood and brain matter, splattered across her legs and clothing. She licked her dry lips and tasted him. She wiped her mouth with the back of her hand and hyperventilated until blackness threatened to close in again. She'd die fighting, face-to-stolen-face with Gary Mercer.

Mercer stood, wrapped in bandages and wearing white silk pajamas. The white sheet fell to the floor. Altamont's blood wicked along the edges. "The tarantulas are all dead, but now I have two black widows right here — Toulusa and

Lucille. Much more dangerous creatures."

Anger dented the fear that had been roiling in Lucy's veins with more force than the flash flood. "Don't you dare call me a black widow, you shit. You know damn well I've never been anything but honest with you. And honestly, you deserve to die."

Mercer smirked.

She struggled to stand. He would not look down on her. Slivers of wood ripped at her back as she pushed herself up the wall. The room swooned and spun but she managed to stand.

Toulusa stood in the shadows, her face dark with uncertainty. She held a high-powered semi-automatic rifle in her hands. "How can you doubt that I love you, Gary? That I'd ever betray you?" Her voice was smoky, *Le Chat Noir*.

"You must have used my funds to buy the Stinger." Mercer's face remained implacable. It looked like it was beginning to harden into a leather helmet.

"That's not true. How insulting. I had nothing to do with his stupid launcher."

Mercer stood dead still, then began to stroke the .357 like it was a cat. "You and Altamont have been plotting against me from the beginning." Tears collected in his eyes but didn't fall.

"You're insane." In the darkness, Toulusa's fingers slid toward the trigger. "He obviously thought you and I both were in that plane. If I was colluding with him, why would he try to kill me, too? Jesus, Gary, get real."

Lucy's heart hammered. Mercer's brain would be jumping with conspiracy fantasies.

"The big asshole turned. He's working for Alvarez," she said like she knew what she was talking about. True or not, it would stoke his anxiety and divert his attention from her.

Mercer still seemed unsure about Toulusa.

Both continued to clutch their weapons in a standoff. Who'd shoot first? If Toulusa let loose with a barrage, Lucy'd be directly in the line of fire. But Mercer could pull the trigger before his lover could raise her bulkier weapon. Mercer'd take Toulusa out then he'd turn on Lucy.

Pop-pop-pop. The sound of automatic gunfire rang from the hills above.

"Get back," Mercer ordered, gun raised toward Lucy's head again. "Don't move."

She complied, pulse racing. Would the Imperial County Sheriffs come through, or were they still waxing their new helicopter? Or was it Alvarez — hell-bent on reclaiming the cartel leadership he thought was his legacy?

Again, pop-pop-pop.

"Shit." Toulusa lowered her rifle and fished a small radio from the pocket of her scrubs. She held it to her mouth and thumbed the button.

"What the fuck is going on?"

A scratchy voice responded. "Incoming, maybe a dozen. No ID. Could be Alvarez."

Toulusa glanced at her watch. "Less than a half-hour 'til dawn when transpo can see enough to land. Shit. Whoever's out there, hold them the fuck off. Copy?"

"Copy that."

Toulusa jammed the radio back into her pocket. Her voice became sweet and fawning as she addressed Mercer. The barrel of his heavy .357 Magnum listed Toulusa's way. "Watch where you're pointing that damned cannon, sweetheart. We're in this together, forever. Just like I've always said." She appraised Lucy with a deadly gaze then caressed Mercer's arm. "Let's do the cunt right now, get rid of one last loose end."

Mercer turned again toward Lucy. His eyes smoldered from ugly pits in his mask face. He aimed the gun.

Lucy gulped hard. She had to keep them talking. "If it's law enforcement, you need me as a hostage, or you won't leave here alive."

Silence. Then Toulusa pressed closer to Mercer and gently pushed down the hand holding the gun. "She's right, doll-face. Soon as we identify our harassers, we'll either keep her as a bargaining chip or shoot the bitch dead." She leered at Lucy. "In the meantime, we could play a few quick games with her."

Lucy held her breath and struggled to tamp down a stab of pure terror. She'd seen Toulusa's idea of playtime in photographs on the walls of his loft. Sex, cutting, sewing, blood.

Gunfire echoed again from above in the foothills. This time it lasted for minutes rather than seconds. Things were heating up. A barrage of bullets strafed the walls of the cabin, a mere foot above their heads.

They hunched low.

Toulusa reached back into her pocket for the radio. "Cardenas, what the fuck?" No response.

"Cardenas."

Empty air.

She threw the radio across the room, shattering it against the wall.

Another barrage hit the cabin, waist-high this time. Lucy dropped onto her stomach, heart hammering. Dillard's medical bag took a slug, knocking it to the floor and spilling its contents.

Toulusa hissed and leaped onto the supplies like a panther after prey. She grabbed a roll of surgical tape, then sprang toward Lucy. "Gotta tie this bitch up." They wrestled across the floor for possession. Lucy's reactions were still drugged. She hit Toulusa in the face with all she had, but it wasn't enough.

Toulusa grabbed Lucy's arm and wrenched it hard. She shrieked in pain — her shoulder almost dislocated. With at least a fifty-pound advantage, Toulusa subdued Lucy and secured her hands behind her with the tape.

Mercer crouched on his haunches and smiled his horrible, lipless grin. "I love a girl fight," he said in his raspy voice.

Lucy clenched her teeth in fear and frustration. The binding cut into her wrists. Tears sprang to her eyes.

Toulusa leaped to secure Lucy's ankles but a kick to the head connected and stunned her. Then, another. Lucy would not be further restrained. — it could mean death. One more kick. The roll of tape flew away.

Toulusa groaned, her mouth bloodied, the imprint of Lucy's boot stamped on her face. Lucy scuttled on her butt across the floor toward the door. Toulusa struggled to grab her, but when another spray of gunfire assaulted the shack, *Le Chat Noir* had risen about six inches too high. Her body convulsed.

Mercer let out a high keening wail. Toulusa crumpled on top of Lucy like a hefty sex doll with the air plug ripped out.

# 48

Another barrage in the hills. Tense shouting. Then only the thrashing sound of Lucy's heart and Mercer's labored breathing. A bleeding watercolor of red soaked his white silk pajamas as he crawled to Toulusa's side and collapsed over her.

Lucy twisted and flailed her legs, fighting to extricate herself from beneath the two and crawl to the cabin door. Her only chance at survival was if the shooters were cops. God willing, the leaden dawn would offer enough light to identify her as a friendly.

If they weren't the good guys, her options had run out.

In the distance, the reverb of an incoming helicopter pulsed. Mercer struggled to rise and then grabbed Lucy by the hair, yanking her to her feet. He clutched the back of her shirt and wrapped a scarred arm around her chest, the .357 leveled at her temple. His body taut against hers, he pushed through the cabin door and stumbled outside onto the decomposing porch. The smell of his ointment and something like hand sanitizer mixed with blood was sickening.

The rotor noise drew closer. "That's my ride," he whispered

in her ear. "And you're coming with me, Lucille."

Lucy shuddered.

A deep voice commanded from a loudspeaker in the hills just above the camp. "Imperial County DEA. Gary Mercer put the gun down and your hands up. It's over."

Lucy felt a rush of relief — the shooters were cops, not Alvarez.

Her nanosecond of hope was immediately crushed.

"Fuck you," Mercer screamed. "I'm getting on that copter. I'll kill her if you try to stop me."

Lucy saw his chopper fly in low and begin to hover, ready to land. Painted dark camo and unmarked, Mercer's cartel Gestapo had arrived for the rescue. Where was Altamont's rocket launcher when you needed it?

Mercer dragged her off the porch and they sidestepped toward the helicopter, about a hundred yards away on the edge of the plateau runway. Would a sharpshooter be close enough to take the kill shot? Or would they get her by mistake? If she and Mercer made it to the helicopter, would he throw her out as they crossed the border into Mexico?

She was not getting into that chopper. No way in hell.

Blood and sweat from his body dampened her clothing and slicked her arms. She tried to shake him off as they struggled up a slope of loose stone, but the gun muzzle drilled into her jaw, and he twisted her arms painfully. She gasped and spoke through gritted teeth. "Talking you off that Hollywood hotel ledge two years ago — biggest mistake I ever made."

He wrenched her arms sadistically and dragged her up the rise. Lucy bit her lip to avoid screaming. Despite his handicap, he was stronger than he looked.

"You adore me, Lucille." His ruined fingers gouged her ribs. His loose pajama pants flapped in the wind like a bloody flag. "You think of me every day and wonder where I am. Where you'll see me. Which of your loved ones I'll fuck up next." His breath was hot against her neck.

The only thing he'd gotten wrong was the love part. Lucy felt nothing but hatred for Gary Mercer, and maybe a dark pang of pity. He'd detest that the most.

A watery morning sun inched over the dark mountainside. Lucy discerned shapes of a dozen or more Imperial County police and DEA officers. She spotted Bea wearing a DEA Kevlar vest and her yellow visor. She prayed that Pete and Marlene were alive and safe.

Lucy and Mercer were now only about twenty-five yards from the hovering aircraft. Vibration from the pounding rotors was a dentist's drill in her brain. Her hands and arms had gone numb. The surgical tape had twisted into a rope — if only she could get it around Mercer's neck.

He moved faster as they closed in on the transport. Ten more yards. She could feel its powerful downwash. Bea started to move in their direction, but Ren pulled her back.

A gunner in a black flak suit climbed from the chopper and darted toward Mercer, who struggled to haul Lucy up onto the old runway. Loose gravel slid beneath her feet. She screamed and fell backward. Mercer lost his balance, twisted, and tumbled hard on top of her. Breath whooshed from her lungs. Then the world became an incandescent tsunami of pain. Yelling and screaming came from deep underwater, and bloody teeth pressed against her face.

—

Mercer's helicopter exploded. A white-hot fireball blasted into the atmosphere. The ground trembled.

Bea gasped, stunned, immobilized. "What the hell?"

Ren squinted, face contorted with disbelief. "Holy, shit.

Altamont's Stinger?"

Lopez, the Imperial County cop, dropped the launcher from his beefy shoulder. He glanced toward Ren and nodded.

Bea threw Ren's hand off her arm and sprinted toward Lucy, tripping and falling across the rugged terrain. She felt no pain, no sense of danger, only blinding terror that her friend was dead.

Torched fuel blackened the low gray sky. The stench of fumes stung Bea's nostrils. She could sense law enforcement personnel rushing behind her — several yelled for her to stop. There'd be no stopping.

Mercer sprawled atop Lucy, his blood drowning her. His head was wrenched at an odd angle and his mouth had been ripped so his teeth protruded as if grinning from a bony skull, preparing to tear into Lucy's neck.

Bea paused for an instant to see the whole scene. The soldier who'd jumped from the chopper had vaporized. There was nothing left of him. The helicopter was an unrecognizable jumble of smoldering scrap.

Ren and several DEA agents made it to Lucy and Mercer just behind Bea. Shaking, she and Ren dragged Mercer's dead body off her friend. Bandages unraveled from his body like a mummy losing its wrappings. An Imperial County Fire Department paramedic rushed up and dropped her kit next to Lucy, fingers moving directly to the jugular. Bea held her breath.

A dark-skinned woman in her late twenties, the paramedic nodded, face grim. "She's alive."

# 49

Bea turned off Kanan Road onto the newly named *Calzada de la Vega*, a dirt road to Lucy's ranch site barely a quarter-mile long. Lucy came up with the name and Cheyney made the sign with his router. Bea smiled at their handiwork. She parked the rental Nissan van next to several other vehicles, including a dark green Wildlife Rescue and Reunion pick-up truck near where the new bridge across the arroyo was under construction.

After the bridge had blown up, and the request to rebuild was made, county inspectors descended with a fist full of new regulations. Gone was the rustic wooden bridge forever. Concrete and steel would replace it.

"There's our cars." Bea cringed at the burned-out skeletons of her BMW sedan and Cheyney's beloved truck on the far side of the creek. She'd never forget the insane dash to escape the firestorm. The air still smelled vaguely of ash, but tiny green shoots already threaded upwards through the charred grass. Life was all about resiliency.

In cut-off jean shorts and a hot-pink sleeveless T-shirt, Alyssa slid from the passenger seat and slammed the door behind her. Mouth agape, her eyes scanned up the drive to the spot where the barn and ranch house had stood.

She turned to her mom, a stunned look on her face. "I had no idea."

Arm in arm, mother and daughter walked the hill together. The bright hard edge of a perfect Southern California day was beginning to soften into dusk. Strings of white lights strung on poles sparkled above the old barn floor which now held picnic tables covered with red-and-white checked cloths. Cheyney hovered at the grill. April pulled suds from a beer keg. In a wheelchair, Marlene was parked next to April, brew in hand, with Howard the cat puddled on her lap. She chatted with two animal rescue workers, young women in dark green polo shirts and jeans. From an old-timey speaker sitting on a hay bale, the Beachboys sang "California Girls."

Maddie and Bugle dashed up to welcome Bea and Alyssa as the two made their way toward the party. Pete, arm in a sling, chatted with Elsa in front of the new storage shed, which was also home to the chicken coop. Ren's Sikorsky sat on a flat rise behind a new deck with what looked to be a yurt-raising in progress.

"Got the yurt from a family in Ojai who moved back to New York. Just had it delivered two days ago," Lucy said, limping up to Bea and Ally. "Isn't it awesome?"

Alyssa threw herself into Lucy's arms. Lucy winced but returned the love with equal enthusiasm. "How's my beautiful goddaughter?" she asked.

"I'm fine. How are your lungs? Mom said they were both punctured in that explosion. I've been so worried about you. You haven't returned my texts."

"Sorry cutie, been off all social media, including texts and email. Just needed a break."

Ally nodded. "Can I see the baby coyote?"

Bea fingered the bullet scar on her shoulder. They were the walking wounded here tonight, even the coyote pup, but they'd all survived. She squeezed Alyssa's hand.

"You're just in time, Al," Lucy said. "The folks from a wildlife rescue group are gonna try and reunite him with his family tonight. I want to hear that little guy singing in the valley with his pack real soon. Cross your fingers."

"Oh, my God, I'm crossing everything!"

Bea followed Alyssa's gaze to a good-looking teen-aged boy ambling their way.

"Cody," Bea called out, arms open. The two hugged.

"Good to see you, Miss Bea," he said with a shy smile. "The story you turned in on the fire was awesome. I even got a stunt gig on a pilot for a TV series out of it. Kind of a remake of the old Bonanza — my gramps's favorite show of all time. Made me sit through every episode on DVDs."

"Congratulations, hotshot." Bea beamed at the kid, recalling him wrangling the horses to safety as the inferno closed in. "Cody Hitchcock, meet my daughter, Alyssa. Aly, Cody helped save our lives when the ranch burned down."

He shrugged like it was no big deal.

Lucy took Bea's arm. "Cody, would you mind showing Alyssa the baby coyote while I talk to Bea a sec?" she asked.

"No problem." His eyes lit up. "Little dude's up at Elsa's place." He began to fill Alyssa in on the story behind the foundling.

"Oh, Lordy." Bea watched the two youngsters stroll toward the cabin, side-by-side. "Uh-oh."

Alyssa glanced back over her shoulder at her mom and smiled.

Lucy chuckled. "They're both good kids."

"I can feel the pheromones percolating. Don't talk to me about kids. I hate kids," Bea said.

"Well, sorry to hear that, because I have something —"

Pete rushed up to the women, beers in hand. "Here you go — brewskis for our wonder women." He passed each a red plastic cup, then gave Bea a sweet kiss on the cheek. She snuggled against his shoulder.

He pulled her close then cleared his throat. "By the way, got some news from HQ."

"No business, you promised," Lucy raised the beer to her lips, then hesitated and lowered the glass.

"Yeah, yeah, but you'll wanna hear this." He glanced at his phone.

Marlene rolled up in her wheelchair with hugs for all. "The brats are ready but the turkey burgers are a little singed. The veggie shish kabobs look awesome. Let's eat, *mishpocha!*"

"I was just about to tell Bea and Lucy the latest from the DEA."

Marlene raised her glass in approval. "Go for it. Spread the joy, detective."

He checked his phone one more time and jammed it in his pocket. "Little brother Alvarez left the country before we could nab him. Now Guerrero's a hot mess with that big vacuum left by Mercer's death, so once again, gangs are offing each other for control."

"It never ends," Bea said. "Just the faces change. Mercer knew that, literally."

Marlene picked up the story. "Carlos Alvarez was killed early this morning, nailed by the dude that Mercer's people called The Accountant. Estevan Valencia, son of the former Medellin *primo*. Looks like he's the new *jefe*, at this hour anyway."

Lucy sighed. "At least Mercer's burning in Hell with his sidekick, Toulusa. They won't be destroying anybody else — murdering, raping, stealing faces, or cutting up body parts for skin coats." She shuddered. "Rest in peace, Uncle Henry." She wiped tears from her eyes. "We finally got some justice."

Bea gave her a hug.

Marlene and Pete exchanged quick glances.

"What?" Lucy demanded.

"Mercer's worm food, but the guy-chick, Toulusa. She's in the wind."

Lucy's face paled. "What do you mean?" She clutched her stomach.

Pete continued. "She survived the Chocolate Mountain fiasco. Disappeared from the hospital in San Diego yesterday. Was supposedly handcuffed to her bed."

Bea winced.

"Grub's on!" Cheyney yelled from the grill. "Let's go, people. *Vamos, vamos!*"

Pete finished his beer and motioned for all to gather around the picnic tables. "My guess is she'll scram to Canada as soon as her perv ass is back in action. Nothing for her here but solitary in a supermax for life. No fun access to roadkill there."

Richard Dillard sprinted up to the group. It was the first time Bea had seen him in anything other than lilac scrubs. He looked handsome in jeans and a lilac golf shirt. "So sorry to be late. Extra fussy patient today. You all know how that is. No new faces on the docket, just a few derriere enhancements." He smiled. "What a world."

"Hey, Nurse Dillard. Dilly-dilly!" Marlene grabbed his hand and he pushed her chair toward the picnic. The sky was turning a hazy purple and the tiny white lights where the barn once stood, twinkled like fireflies. From somewhere across the valley, a sweet hint of night-blooming jasmine perfumed the air.

Bea and Lucy lingered behind. "So, what do you have to show me?" Bea asked, feeling so sick about Toulusa's escape she thought she'd vomit into her beer.

Lucy pulled out a white plastic wand the size of a pencil and held it up for Bea to examine. There was a pink plus sign in the middle.

Bea gasped. "Huh? No way. The doctors said you couldn't get pregnant. And those things give tons of false positives."

"This is the fourth stick I've peed on in two days."

"Oh, my God. Burleson?" Bea's eyes went back to the pink verdict.

Lucy nodded.

"You two were a formidable force."

Lucy nodded again and pressed her still-flat belly.

"No more alcohol for you." Bea took Lucy's red plastic cup and downed her friend's brew, swallowed hard. "I'm not sure whether to be happy or completely panicked. What are you going to do?"

"Doc says my chances of taking it to term are about nil. No stretch in all that scar tissue. It will be high risk."

Bea's shoulders sagged, then she sighed, searching for something profound from the bottom of a beer glass. "Then I guess you're gonna —"

"I'm gonna go for it."

"Oh, Lordy. Always flying so close to the flame." Bea gave her friend a long, tender hug. "I got your back, girl."

"And the most incredible thing is that Aunt Catherine Lucia said she'd come up to help me through this." Lucy wiped more tears. "Hasn't left her little community in fifty years, but she's coming. Wouldn't take no for an answer."

"I heard that," Dillard called. "The nun-herbalist is coming and I get my promised dinner with her. 'Yahoo,' as that cute little Cody cowboy would say. Come on now, girls. April's potato salad is to die for."

—

On a private rooftop bar overlooking *Bahia de Manzanilla* in Acapulco, The Accountant and his entourage clapped wildly at *Le Chat Noir*'s brilliant cabaret performance. That this gorgeous gem of a thespian could also be a superb political strategist and a keen business advisor, all wrapped into one extraordinary human being, made his heart race. Despite Toulusa's close call in the Chocolate Mountains, the scars on her neck added to her magnetism and her stunning voice had become a raspy purr. All else had gone as planned. The Guerrero black tar heroin cartel, now *el Gato Negro de la Montana*, was back in business.

Have a brief peak at the next installment of the Vega and Middleton Novels:

## The Mermaid Brokers

### 1

Isabelle "Izzy" Abbott slowly swam to the surface of dark unconsciousness. Pale light flickered from above. She moved toward it. Feet kicked and fingers stretched. She followed the rise of silvery bubbles only to discover that she was not underwater but lying on a bed. When Izzy tried to move her body, she felt restraints and pulled against them but there was no give. Zip ties? Handcuffs.

Oh shit, where was she? What had happened? A car accident? Was she in a hospital? A jail? Eyes forced open. Her lids were made of concrete—heavy and gritty. The room spun.

What the hell? Her heart hammered in her chest. She could hear faint, distant strains of music--discordant wind chimes accompanied by the moaning, agitated sounds of whales. As a marine biologist, she recognized the vocalizations immediately as those of animals under grave duress. What sicko would want to weave animal misery into a song? She gulped hard.

Cool, damp air moved across Izzy's skin and smelled of salt. She widened her eyes, blinking, trying to acclimate. The small, square space around her appeared to have tiled walls like an operating room or a lab. It was illuminated only by a large window into a deep blue aquarium of some sort. Suddenly, a huge school of small, pinkish fish glided by and disappeared. Piranhas?

She still couldn't completely focus. Her head ached as if she'd been clubbed by a two-by-four. Maybe she had been. What was going on?

A body lay on a cot across from her. A girl, a teen—about the same age as her Biology students at Santa Monica High School. Pale, lank hair, face smeared with gold paint or make-up. Sleeping? Dead? Was she wrapped in a straight-jacket? Yes.

Izzy tried not to panic. Was she in a mental institution? This couldn't be a dream, it seemed vividly real.

Izzy tried to call out to her roommate, but her throat was so dry, all that came out was a whisper. She licked her parched lips and tried again.

"Hey! Hey, over there! You awake?"

The girl's eyes, sunken and terrified, fluttered open. Izzy suppressed a gasp. This was not any kind of hospital, this was something else, something not in the realm of her experience.

The girl struggled against her bindings and banged her head against the bedframe. "Help me, please help me. I can't breathe," the young woman pleaded. "I'm claustrophobic, can't handle tight spaces--this thing is destroying me."

Isabelle winced at the aching sound of desperation in her voice. "I can't reach you. I'm cuffed to this bed." Again, she pulled hard against her restraints, but no give. "Where the are we?"

The girl started to cry with big, deep sobs, then she stopped herself, slowed herself down, clearly struggling for control. "We're in hell," she gasped.

Izzy sensed the girl was right. "How did you get here?"

"A dive trip off Catalina. They drugged me." She paused and shut her eyes. They were ringed with dark circles and bruises shadowed her cheekbone. "I remember the stink of something weird over my face, in my mask."

The memory of something foul began to crawl into Izzy's consciousness, too. The koi, the empty pet store. 'We're moving to a larger space,' the kindly man who'd met her at the door explained. He invited her in to see the rare specimen she was seeking.

He poured lemonade. A bit more, sweetheart?

Had she been roofied? It was all a jumble.

The girl began to sob again then struggled once more to settle. "Breathe in, breathe out, slower, slower," she murmured.

Izzy knew if they wrapped her in one of those straight-jacket contraptions she'd go off the rails, too. Her head began to pound. "Why did they take us? What do they want from us?" She tried to position her body more comfortably on the rubber mattress, but it was impossible.

"Rape, female bodies to mutilate, murder." The girl began to shake uncontrollably. "I never believed this could happen. Only on TV, not to real people."

Izzy's stomach tightened and she felt ready to vomit. Chill, girl. They both had to calm down and think clearly if they wanted to survive. "What's your name?" she asked gently.

There was a sustained, almost fearful hesitation, but finally an answer. "I'm Celeste."

"I'm Isabelle. How long have you been here?"

Another pause. "Maybe a week or ten days, near as I can tell." Slow tears tracked down her cheeks.

"So, how does this all go down?"

Celeste now lay still as a board, breath shallow. Only her mouth moved. "They're on a world sex adventure tour. Ventura is the "Mermaid Fantasy" experience. They make us wear exotic mermaid costumes like players from *Cirque de Soleil* then they put us in a huge tank, big as a gym, bigger." Her eyes flitted to the aquarium window, then closed tight. "We swim around, and they turn off our air if we don't perform." Her voice dropped an octave. "Assholes pick a mermaid to fuck. Afterwards, they can choose to let us live, or watch us die."

"Die?" A gush of hot adrenaline coursed through Izzy's veins. She wretched and tried not to throw up.

"Yeah, beyond sick. Then, they're off to Japan and Thailand."

"How do you know this?"

"One of the clients filled me in. A Saudi guy." She attempted to turn toward Izzy. "I think he might have been gay but had to play the macho role for his friends. He was kind of sweet, didn't do anything to me, just wanted to talk. I was lucky, this time."

"They actually kill people? Like a snuff thing?" Her brain wanted to reject the information, but here she was, handcuffed in the darkness in a room that smelled of dead fish.

Celeste gulped and swallowed a cry. "One woman was murdered yesterday. They threw her into the aquarium filled with piranhas, the kind that can clean a cow down to the bones in minutes."

Isabelle shook her head. "That's urban legend."

"It's not! They went crazy and took huge chunks out of her. Maybe they starve the fish to make them hungry. Maybe they're a weird breed. There are sharks, too. Big ones." Celeste trembled. "I freaked out. That's why I'm in here. They tased the hell out of me. The next tour group comes in five days. I'll be eaten alive." She began to hyperventilate.

"No, no, we'll get out of here." Isabelle's eyes wildly scanned the room for opportunity. Nothing. "We're not going out this way, Celeste.

The young woman laughed, then screamed in fury.

A fast tap-tap-tap of footsteps came toward their room.

"Oh, shit," she said. "I'm so sorry."

There was a dinging sound before the door flew open. Blue light filled the room. An orderly, a thick-set man with a bulbous nose and low-hanging ape-like arms, whipped a taser from a tool belt around his waist and hit the lithe blonde in the neck. Her body convulsed, and she passed out. Small mercies.

He turned to Isabelle. "You wan' summa dis?" His voice was deep with an Eastern European accent. The taser whined as it powered back up. "Or you be good girl?" He stroked her damp hair then ripped at it, brutally, with his rubber-gloved hand.

Izzy choked, quaking. "I'll be good." Until I can get that taser and make you pay, you sadistic asshole.

He licked his wormy lips and turned toward his victim. Checking Celeste's jugular with his fingers, he nodded his head. Foamy saliva leaked from the corners of her mouth. With a last dim smirk at Izzy, ape-man shuffled from the room.

The lock clicked hard, like an empty chamber in a game of Russian Roulette. She shuddered--if they didn't find a way out fast, and if Celeste was right on what the kidnappers were up to, they could be dead with the next spin of the revolver.

# Acknowledgements

Deep appreciation to the Rocky Mountain Fiction Writers (RMFW) and my amazing critique group at Tattered Cover in Littleton, especially Mindy McIntyre, Michael Hope aka Michael Arches, Mary Ann Kersten, Michele Winkler, Susan Schooleman, Kathy Reynolds, Rick Duffy, and others. All amazing writers, teachers, and colleagues.

Sincere gratitude to Susie Brooks, publisher at Literary Wanderlust. It's a privilege to be part of this great indie team.

Props to my husband, Alan Klein, who's been patiently watching me disappear into reading and writing for years, and to my amazing beta readers Lacey Klein, Marlene Simon, and Carolyn Olson. Thanks to friends in the LGBTQIA community for their guidance, and to Michael Paré for his advice on weapons and helicopters.

# About the Author

Sue Hinkin is a former college administrator, television news photographer, and NBC-TV art department staffer. With a B.A. from St. Olaf College, she completed graduate work at the University of Michigan and was a Cinematography Fellow at the American Film Institute. A long-time Los Angeles resident, she now lives with her family in Littleton, Colorado.

Her Vega & Middleton mystery series includes *Deadly Focus*, *Low Country Blood* and *The Burn Patient*. Her fourth novel, *The Mermaid Brokers*, is forthcoming in 2021.

9 781942 856450